FIRST CONTACT

"I understand Hoffer informed you that the signal stopped altogether last night."

"Yes. That's why I came in."

"It was down for precisely four hours, seventeen minutes, forty-three seconds."

"Is that significant?"

Gambini smiled. "Multiply it by sixteen, and you get Beta's orbital period." He watched Harry expectantly and was clearly disappointed at his lack of response. "Harry," he said, "that's no coincidence. The shutdown was designed to attract attention. *Designed,* Harry. And the duration of the shutdown was intended to demonstrate *intelligent* control." Gambini's eyes glittered. His lips rolled back to reveal his teeth. "Harry," he said, "it's the LGM signal! It's happened!"

Harry shifted his weight uncomfortably. *LGM* meant *little green man . . .*

Ace Science Fiction Specials edited by Terry Carr

THE
HERCULES TEXT

JACK McDEVITT

ACE SCIENCE FICTION BOOKS
NEW YORK

This book is an Ace Science
Fiction original edition, and
has never been previously
published.

THE HERCULES TEXT

An Ace Science Fiction Book/published by arrangement with
the author

PRINTING HISTORY
Ace Science Fiction edition/November 1986

ISBN: 0-441-37367-4

Ace Science Fiction Books are published by The Berkley Publishing Group,
200 Madison Avenue, New York, New York 10016.
PRINTED IN THE UNITED STATES OF AMERICA

ACKNOWLEDGMENTS

I am indebted for the technical assistance of Bob Neustadt, who knows about computers; and Mark Giampapa, of the National Optical Observatory, who knows about stars. Miscarriages of their ideas should be laid at my door.

For John and Elizabeth McDevitt
with love

INTRODUCTION

by Terry Carr

Every publishing venture is a gamble for a lot of people. Writers decide on plots, themes, and characters in hope that their resulting novels will be appealing enough to keep food on their families' tables for a while; editors buy books hoping that sales will be high enough to keep them from being fired the next time their companies are forced into the game of editorial musical chairs; publishers print, package, and offer books for sale, gambling that enough people will buy them to net the profit to keep them in business; and readers buy books hoping they'll be entertained.

The original Ace Science Fiction Specials series was published from 1968 till 1971, when I left New York City and moved to California. The thirty-seven Specials in that original series sold well and won two Nebula Awards, the Hugo Award, and the John W. Campbell Memorial Award; but when Ace hired me to edit a new series of Specials in 1984, more than a dozen years had passed and the science fiction readership had changed considerably. Could this new series of science-fiction-novels-for-adult-readers be successful enough to justify its costs? After all, we'd be publishing books by first novelists and paying those writers more money than anyone else did; though the authors had established their literary and imaginative credentials with excellent short stories and novelettes, most buyers of science fiction novels didn't read the sf magazines and wouldn't be familiar with their by-lines.

So the New Ace Science Fiction Specials series was a larger-than-usual gamble for everybody in 1984 — especially for the folks at Ace. I take this opportunity to thank them for their faith in the enterprise, which included a belief that many science fiction readers would be looking for new ideas and new approaches in the books they bought and that such readers would choose books for purchase because of their honest merits. That's the way publishing ideally works, after all, but in truth it doesn't always.

The Ace Science Fiction Specials, both in their original late-sixties version and their early-eighties revival, have been devoted to novels that in most cases went beyond anything published before. Such innovation—even in the science fiction field, which prides itself on new ideas—has always been unusual and has ordinarily gone unrewarded, either by substantial sales or by awards. The New Ace SF Specials published in 1984 and 1985 managed to break this pattern, for they created quite a stir in the genre. Not only did those novels sell very well but they also received glowing reviews, and most of them were nominated for awards. William Gibson's *Neuromancer*, a first novel by an author who had published fewer than a dozen short stories, swept most of the major ones, including the Nebula, the Hugo, and the Philip K. Dick Memorial Awards.

Now, with *The Hercules Text* by Jack McDevitt, we continue the New Ace SF Specials series, and you can expect to see further Specials every few months in the future. The bases for the books' selection remain the same: each is a first novel that impressed me as outstanding; and often, probably because they *are* first novels, they bring to the sf genre new ideas and new approaches in writing them. (This doesn't mean these books are "experimental" science fiction. As a reader of sf for nearly forty years, I welcome literary experimentation, but I'm aware that most experiments in writing or any other endeavor prove to be failures; when experiments succeed, they're hailed as innovations. It's the latter for which I look in choosing these books.)

The Hercules Text certainly isn't experimental in its basic plot, which involves a project to search for messages from alien intelligences in the far reaches of space, and the detection of such messages from a very strange world in the Hercules constellation. In its basics, this novel is similar to many that have gone before, including most recently Carl Sagan's bestseller *Contact* (though McDevitt wrote his book before *Contact* was published). But McDevitt adds quite a lot to what has gone before: he's an excellent fiction writer (one of his first short stories, "Cryptic," was nominated for the Nebula Award a couple of years ago) who brings to this book a smooth, matter-of-fact style and the depth of characterization essential to a first-rate novel; in addition, though he's done his homework and gives us fascinating details about how scientists work and interact, his novel is concerned not merely with science but rather with the moral implications of the scientific discoveries he describes.

Call this book a thoughtful extrapolation of our future and its meaning for humanity, if you must label it. But in truth the story McDevitt tells here transcends such categorizations: yes, this is a serious novel and yes, it has excellent characterizations and a strong theme; but at heart *The Hercules Text* is a novel written to be enjoyed. I'm convinced that you'll enjoy it very much, and I'm delighted to present it to you.

_1_

HARRY CARMICHAEL SNEEZED. His eyes were red, his nose was running, and his head ached. It was mid-September, and the air was full of pollen from ragweed, goosefoot, and thistle. He'd already taken his medication for the day, which seemed to accomplish little other than to make him drowsy.

Through the beveled stained-glass windows of the William Tell, he watched the Daiomoto Comet. It was now little more than a bright smudge, wedged in the bare hard branches of a cluster of elms lining the parking lot. Its cool unfocused light was not unlike that reflected in Julie's green eyes, which seemed preoccupied, on that night, with the long, graceful stem of a wineglass. She'd abandoned all attempts to keep the conversation going, and now sat frozen in a desperate solicitude. She felt sorry for Harry. Years from now, Harry understood, he would look back on this evening, remember this moment, recall the eyes and the comet and the packed shelves of old textbooks that, in the gloomily illuminated interior, were intended to create atmosphere. He would recall his anger and the terrible sense of impending loss and the numbing knowledge of helplessness. But most of all, it would be her sympathy that would sear his soul.

Comets and bad luck: it was an appropriate sky. Daiomoto would be back in twenty-two hundred years, but it was coming apart. The analysts were predicting that, on its next visit, or the one after that, it would be only a shower of rock and ice. Like Harry.

"I'm sorry," she said, shrugging her shoulders. "It's not anything you've done, Harry."

Of course not. What accusation could she bring against faithful old Harry, who'd taken his vows seriously, who could always be counted on to do the decent thing, and who'd been a reliable provider? Other than perhaps that he'd loved her too deeply.

He'd known it was coming. The change in her attitude toward him had been gradual but constant. The things they'd

1

once laughed over became minor irritants, and the irritants scraped at their lives until she came to resent even his presence.

And so it had come to this: two strangers carefully keeping a small round table between them while she inserted shining utensils like surgeon's tools into beef that was a little too raw and assured him it wasn't his fault.

"I just need some time to myself, Harry. To think things over a bit. I'm tired of doing the same things, in the same way, every day." I'm tired of *you,* she was saying, finally, with the oblique words and the compassion that peeled away his protective anger like a thin slice of meat. She put the glass down and looked at him, for the first time, it might have been, during the entire evening. And she smiled: it was the puckish goodnatured grin that she traditionally used when she'd run the car into a ditch or bounced a few checks. My God, he wondered, how could he ever manage without her?

"The play wasn't so good either, was it?" he asked dryly.

"No," she said unsteadily, "I didn't really care much for it."

"Maybe we've seen too many shows by local playwrights." They'd spent the evening watching a dreary mystery-comedy performed by a repertory company in an old church in Bellwether, although Harry could hardly be accused of having made an effort to follow the proceedings. Fearful of what was coming later, he'd spent the time rehearsing his own lines, trying to foresee and prepare for all eventualities. He'd have done better to watch the show.

The final irony was that there were season tickets in his pocket.

She surprised him by reaching across the table to take his hand.

His passion for her was unique in his life, unlike in kind any other addiction he had known before or, he suspected, would know again. The passing years had not dimmed it; had, in fact, seeded it with the shared experiences of almost a decade, had so entwined their lives that, Harry believed, no emotional separation was possible.

He took off his glasses, folded them deliberately, and pushed them down into their case. His vision was poor without them. It was an act she could not misinterpret.

Bits and pieces of talk drifted from the next table: two people slightly drunk, their voices rising, quarreled over money and relatives. A handsome young waiter, a college kid probably, hovered in the background, his red sash insolently snug round a trim waist. His name was Frank: odd that Harry should remember that, as though the detail were important. He hurried forward every few minutes, refilling their coffee cups. Near the end, he inquired whether the meal had been satisfactory.

It was hard now to remember when things had been different, before the laughter had ended and the silent invitations, which once had passed so easily between them, stopped. "I just don't think we're a good match anymore. We always seem to be angry with each other. We don't talk. . . ." She looked squarely at him. Harry was staring past her shoulder into the dark upper tier of the room, with an expression that he hoped suggested his sense of dignified outrage. "Did you know Tommy wrote an essay about you and that goddam comet last week? No?

"Harry," she continued, "I don't exactly know how to say this. But do you think, do you really believe, that if anything happened to Tommy, or to me, that you'd miss us? Or that you'd even know we were gone?" Her voice caught, and she pushed the plate away and stared down into her lap. "Please pay the bill and let's get out of here."

"It isn't true," he said, looking for Frank the waiter, who was gone. He fumbled for a fifty, dropped it on the table, and stood up. Julie slowly pulled her sweater around her shoulders and, Harry trailing, walked between the tables and out the door.

Tommy's comet hung over the parking lot, splotchy in the September sky, its long tail splayed across a dozen constellations. Last time through, it might have been seen by Socrates. The data banks at Goddard were loaded with the details of its composition, the ratios of methane to cyanogen and mass to velocity, of orbital inclination and eccentricity. Nothing exciting that he had been able to see, but Harry was only a layman, not easily aroused by frozen gas. Donner and the others, however, had greeted the incoming telemetry with near ecstasy.

There was a premature chill in the air, not immediately evident perhaps because no wind blew. She stood on the gravel, waiting for him to unlock her door. "Julie," he said, "ten years is a long time to just throw away."

"I know," she said.

Harry took the Farragut Road home. Usually, he would have used Route 214, and they'd have stopped at Muncie's for a drink, or possibly even gone over to the Red Limit in Greenbelt.

But not tonight. Painfully, groping for words that would not come, he guided the Chrysler down the two-lane blacktop, through forests of elm and little leaf linden. The road curved and dipped past shadowy barns and ancient farmhouses. It was the kind of highway Harry liked. Julie preferred expressways, and maybe therein lay the difference between them.

A tractor-trailer moved up behind, watched its chance, and hammered by in a spasm of dust and leaves. When it had gone, its red lights faded to dim stars blinking between distant trees, Harry hunched forward, almost resting his chin on the steering wheel. Moon and comet rode high over the trees to his left. They would set at about the same time. (Last night, at Goddard, the Daiomoto team had celebrated, Donner buying, but Harry, his thoughts locked on Julie, had gone home early.)

"What did Tommy say about the comet?" he asked.

"That you'd sent a rocket out there and were bringing a piece of it back. And he promised to take the piece in to show everybody." She smiled. He guessed that it took an effort.

"It wasn't our responsibility," he said. "Houston ran the rendezvous program."

He felt the sudden stillness, and sneezed into it. "Do you think," she asked, "he cares about the administrative details?"

The old Kindlebride farm lay cold and abandoned in the moonlight. Three or four pickups and a battered Ford were scattered across its overgrown front yard. "So where do we go from here?"

There was a long silence that neither of them knew quite how to handle. "Probably," she said, "it would be a good idea if I went to live with Ellen for a while."

"What about Tommy?"

She was looking in her bag for something, a Kleenex. She snapped the bag shut and dabbed at her eyes. "Do you think you could find time for him, Harry?"

The highway went into a long S-curve, bounced across two sets of railroad tracks, and dipped into a tangled forest. "What's that supposed to mean?" he asked.

She started to speak, but her voice betrayed her, and she only shook her head, and stared stonily through the windshield.

They passed through Hopkinsville, barely more than a few houses and a hardware store. "Is there somebody else? Someone I don't know about?"

Her eyelids squeezed shut. "No, it's nothing like that. I just don't want to be married anymore." Her purse slid off her lap onto the floor, and when she retrieved it, Harry saw that her knuckles were white.

Bolingbrook Road was thick with leaves. He rolled over them with a vague sense of satisfaction. McGorman's garage, third in from the corner, was brightly lit, and the loud rasp of his power saw split the night air. It was a ritual for McGorman, the Saturday night woodworking. And for Harry it was an energetic island of familiarity in a world grown slippery.

He pulled into his driveway. Julie opened her door, climbed easily out, but hesitated. She was tall, a six-footer, maybe two inches more in heels. They made a hell of a couple, people had said: a mating of giants. But Harry was painfully aware of the contrast between his wife's well-oiled coordination and his own general clumsiness.

"Harry," she said, with a hint of steel in her voice, "I've never cheated on you."

"Good." He walked by her and rammed his key into the lock. "Glad to hear it."

The baby-sitter was Julie's cousin, Ellen Crossway. She was propped comfortably in front of a flickering TV, a novel open on her lap, a cup of coffee near her right hand. "How was the show?" she asked, with the same smile Julie had shown him at the William Tell.

"A disaster," said Harry. He did not trust his voice to say more.

Julie hung her cardigan in the closet. "They did all the obvious gags. And the mystery wasn't exactly a puzzle."

Harry liked Ellen. She might have been a second attempt to create a Julie: not quite so tall, not quite so lovely, not nearly so intense. The result was by no means unsatisfactory. Harry occasionally wondered how things might have gone had he met Ellen first; but he had no doubt that he would, in time, have betrayed her for her spectacular cousin.

"Well," she said, "it was a shaky night on the tube, too." She laid aside the novel. Then the pained silence settled in on her. She looked from one to the other and sighed. "Gotta go, guys. Tommy's fine. We spent most of the evening with Sherlock Holmes." That was a reference to a role-playing game that Harry had discovered the previous summer. His son played it constantly, prowling with Watson through the tobacco shops and taverns of 1895 London.

Harry could see that Ellen knew about their problem. It

figured that Julie would have confided in her. Or maybe their situation was more apparent that he thought. Who else knew?

Ellen kissed him and held him a degree tighter than usual. Then she was out the door, talking on the walkway with Julie. Harry shut off the television, went upstairs, and looked into his son's room.

Tommy was asleep, one arm thrown over the side of the bed, the other lost beneath a swirl of pillows. As usual, he'd kicked off the spread, which Harry adjusted. A collection of hardbound *Peanuts* comic strips lay on the floor. And his basketball uniform hung proudly on the back of the closet door.

He looked like a normal kid. But the upper right-hand drawer of the bureau contained a syringe and a vial of insulin. Tommy was a diabetic.

The wind had picked up somewhat: it whispered through the trees and the curtains. Light notched by a venetian blind fell across the photo of the Arecibo dish his son had bought a few weeks before on a visit to Goddard. Harry stood a long time without moving.

He'd read extensively over the last year about juvenile-onset diabetes, which is the most virulent form of the disease. Tommy faced a high probability of blindness, an army of other debilities, and a drastically shortened life expectancy. No one knew how it had happened: there was no sign of the disease in either of their families. But there it was. Sometimes, the doctors had said, it just happens.

Son of a bitch.

He would *not* give up the child.

But before he got to his bedroom, he knew he would have no choice.

It began to rain about 2:00 A.M. Lightning quivered outside the windows, and the wind beat against the side of the house. Harry lay on his back staring straight up, listening to the rhythmic breathing of his wife. After a while, when he could stand it no more, he pulled on a robe and went downstairs and out onto the porch. Water rattled out of a partially blocked drainpipe. The sound had a frivolous quality, counterpointing the deep-throated storm. He sat down on one of the rockers and watched the big drops splash into the street. A brace had fallen off, or blown off, the corner streetlight. Now the lamp danced fitfully in gusts of wind and water.

Headlights turned off Maple. He recognized Hal Esterhazy's

Plymouth. It bounced into the driveway across the street, paused while the garage door rolled open, and vanished inside. Lights blinked on in Hal's house.

Sue Esterhazy was Hal's third wife. There were two more wandering around out there somewhere, and five or six kids. Hal had explained to Harry that he remained on good terms with his former wives and visited them when he could, though he admitted it wasn't very often. He paid alimony to both. Despite all that, he seemed perfectly content with life. And he owned a new van and a vacation home in Vermont.

Harry wondered how he did it.

Inside, the telephone was ringing.

Julie had picked it up on the extension before he got to it. He climbed the stairs and found her waiting at the bedroom door. "It's Goddard," she said.

Harry nodded and took the phone. "Carmichael."

"Harry, this is Charlie Hoffer. The Hercules signal changed tonight. I just got off the line with Gambini. He's pretty excited."

"So are you," said Harry.

"I thought you'd want to know," he said awkwardly.

Hoffer was the duty officer at the Research Projects Lab. "Why?" asked Harry. "What's going on?"

"Have you been following the operation?"

"A little." That was an exaggeration. Harry was assistant director for administration, a personnel specialist in a world of theoretical physicists, astronomers, and mathematicians. He tried hard to stay on top of Goddard's various initiatives in an effort to retain some credibility, but the effort was pointless. Cosmologists tended to sneer at particle physicists, and both groups found it hard to take astronomers, perceived as restricted to confirming the notions of the theorists, seriously. Harry's M.B.A. was, at best, an embarrassment.

His job was to ensure that NASA hired the right people, or contracted out to the right people, to see that everyone got paid, and to keep track of vacation time and insurance programs. He negotiated with unions, tried to prevent NASA's technically oriented managers from alienating too many subordinates, and handled public relations. He'd stayed close to Donner and the comet, but had paid little attention to any of Goddard's other activities over the past few weeks. "What sort of change?"

At the other end, Hoffer was speaking to someone in the background. Then he got back on the line. "Harry, it stopped."

Julie watched him curiously.

Harry's physics wasn't very good. Gambini and his people had been observing an X-ray pulsar in Hercules, a binary system composed of a red giant and a suspected neutron star. The last few months had been a difficult period for them, because most of Goddard's facilities had been directed toward the comet. "Charlie, that's not all that unusual, is it? I mean, the goddam thing rotates behind the other star every few days, right? Is that what happened?"

"It's not due to eclipse again until Tuesday, Harry. And even when it does, we don't really lose the signal. There's an envelope of some sort out there that reflects it, so the pulse just gets weaker. This is a complete shutdown. Gambini insists something must be wrong with the equipment."

"I assume you can't find a problem?"

"The Net's fine. NASCOM has run every check it can think of. Harry, Gambini's in New York and won't get back for a few hours. He doesn't want to fly into National. We thought it might be simplest if we just sent the chopper."

"Do it. Who's in the operations center?"

"Majeski."

Harry squeezed the phone. "I'm on my way, Charlie," he said.

"What is it?" asked Julie. Usually she was impatient with late calls from Goddard; but tonight her voice was subdued.

Harry explained about Hercules while he dressed. "It's an X-ray pulsar," he said. "Ed Gambini's group has been listening to it on and off for the last eight months or so." He grinned at his own joke. "Charlie says they aren't picking it up anymore."

"Why is that important?"

"Because there's no easy explanation for it." He strolled into his bedroom and grabbed an armful of clothes.

"Maybe it's just some dust between the source and the Net." She shrugged the nightshirt off and slipped into bed in a single fluid gesture.

"SKYNET isn't affected by dust. At least not the X-ray telescopes. No, whatever it is, it's enough to bring Gambini back from New York in the middle of the night."

She watched him dress. "You know," she said, striving for a casual tone, but unable to keep the emotion entirely out of her voice, "this is what we've been talking about all evening. The Hercules Project is Gambini's responsibility. Why do *you* have to go running down there? I bet he doesn't head for your shop when some labor relations crisis breaks out."

Harry sighed. He hadn't got where he was by staying home in bed when major events were happening. It was true he didn't have direct responsibility for Hercules, but one never knew where these things might lead, and a rising bureaucrat needed nothing so much as visibility. He resisted the impulse to suggest that she was no longer entitled to an opinion anyway, and asked instead that she lock the door after him.

The X-ray pulsar in Hercules is unique: it's a free-floater, the only known stellar configuration not attached to a major system of some sort. More than a million and a half light-years from Goddard, it is adrift in the immense void between the galaxies.

It is also unusual in that neither of the components is a blue giant. Alpha Altheis, the visible star, is brick red, considerably cooler than Sol, but approximately eighty times larger. If it were placed at the center of our solar system, it would engulf Mercury.

Altheis is well along in its helium-burning cycle. Left to itself, it would continue to expand for another ten million years or so before erupting into a supernova.

But the star will not survive that long. The other object in the system is a dead sun, a thing more massive than its huge companion, yet so crushed by its own weight that its diameter probably measures less than thirty kilometers: the distance between the Holland Tunnel and Long Island Sound. Two minutes by jet, maybe a day on foot. But the object is a malignancy in a tight orbit, barely fifteen million miles from the giant's edge, so close that it literally rolls through its companion's upper atmosphere, spinning violently, dragging an enormous wave of superheated gas, dragging perhaps the giant's vitals. It is called Beta Altheis, a peculiarly mundane name, Harry thought, for so exotic a body.

It is the engine that drives the pulsar. There is a constant flow of supercharged particles from the normal star to the companion, hurtling downward at relativistic velocities.

But the collision points are not distributed randomly across Beta: rather, they are concentrated at the magnetic poles, which are quite small, a kilometer or so in diameter and, like Earth's, not aligned with the axis. Consequently, they also are spinning, at approximately thirty times per second. Incoming high-energy particles striking this impossibly dense and slippery surface tend to carom off as X-rays. The result is a lighthouse whose beams sweep the nearby cosmos.

Harry wondered, as his Chrysler plowed through a sudden burst of rain, what kind of power would be needed to shut down such an engine.

The gate guards waved him through. He made an immediate left, and headed for Building 2, the Research Projects Laboratory. Eight or nine cars were parked under the security lights, unusual for this time of night. Harry pulled in alongside Cord Majeski's sleek gray Honda (the Chrysler looked boxlike and dull in contrast with the turbocharged two-seater) and hurried under dripping trees into the rear entrance of the long, utilitarian structure.

The Hercules Project had originally been assigned a communication center with an adjoining ADP area. But Gambini was politically astute, and his responsibilities, and staff, tended to grow. He'd acquired two workrooms, additional computer space, and three or four offices. The project itself had begun as a general-purpose investigation of several dozen pulsars. But it had quickly narrowed in on the anomaly in the group, which was located five degrees northeast of the globular cluster NGC6341.

Harry strolled into the operations center. Several technicians sat in the green glow of monitors; two or three, headphones pushed off their ears, drank Cokes and whispered over newspapers. Cord Majeski leaned frowning against a worktable, scribbling on a clipboard. He was more linebacker than mathematician, all sinew and shoulder, with piercing blue eyes and a dark beard intended to add maturity to his distressingly boyish features. He was a grim and taciturn young man who nevertheless, to Harry's bewilderment, seemed inordinately successful with women. "Hello, Harry," he said. "What brings you in at this hour?"

"I hear the pulsar's doing strange things. What's going on?"

"Damned if I know."

"Maybe," said Harry, "it ran out of gas. That happens, doesn't it?"

"Sometimes. But not like this. If the pulsar were losing its power source, we'd have detected a gradual decline. This thing just stopped. I don't know what to think. Maybe Alpha went nova." Majeski, who seldom showed emotion, flipped the clipboard across the table. "Harry," he said, "we need access to Optical. Can't you pry Donner loose for a few hours? He's been looking at that goddam comet for three months."

"Submit the paper, Cord," said Harry.

Majeski tugged at his beard and favored Harry with an expression that suggested his patience was in short supply. "We're supposed to be able to observe a target of opportunity."

"Observe it tomorrow night," said Harry. "It won't be going anyplace." He turned on his heel and walked off.

Harry had no serious interest in pulsars. In fact, on this night, nothing short of a black hole bearing down on Maryland could have roused him. But he had no inclination to go home.

The rain had slackened to a cold drizzle. He drove north on Road 3 and eased into the parking lot outside Building 18, the Business Operations Section. His office was on the second floor. It was a relatively Spartan place, with battered chairs and bilious green walls and government wall hangings, mostly cheap art deco that GSA had picked up at a cutrate price from one of its bargain basement suppliers. Photos of Julie and Tommy stood atop his desk, between a Cardex and a small framed reproduction of a lobby card from *The Maltese Falcon*. Tommy was in a Little League uniform; Julie stood in profile, thoughtful against a gray New England sky.

He lit the desk lamp, turned off the overhead lights, and fell heavily into a plastic sofa that was a little too short for him. Maybe it *was* time to quit. Find a deserted lighthouse somewhere along the coast of Maine (he'd seen one advertised in Providence once for a buck, but you had to move it), maybe get a job in the local general store, change his name, and drop out of sight altogether.

His years with Julie were over. And in the terrible unfairness of things, he knew he'd lost not only his wife but Tommy as well. And a sizable portion of his income. He felt a sudden twinge of sympathy for Alpha, burdened with the neutron star it couldn't get rid of. He was forty-seven, his marriage was a wreck, and, he suddenly realized, he hated his job. People who didn't know what it was like envied him: he was, after all, part of the Great Adventure, directing the assault on the planets, working closely with all those big-shot physicists and astronomers. But the investigators, though few were as blunt, or as young, as Majeski, did not recognize him as one of them.

He was a compiler of schedules, the guy who answered questions about hospitalization and retirement benefits and other subjects so unutterably boring that Gambini and his associates could barely bring themselves to discuss them. He was, in the official terminology, a layman. Worse, he was a layman with a substantial amount of control over operational procedures at Goddard.

He slept fitfully. The wind died, and the rain stopped. The only sound in the building was the occasional hum of the blowers in the basement.

At about eight, the phone rang, "Harry." It was Hoffer's voice again. "The pulsar's kicked back in."

"Okay," said Harry, trying to focus on his watch. "Sounds like equipment. Make sure you haven't overlooked anything, okay? I'll get Maintenance to run some checks later. Gambini get here yet?"

"We expect him any time."

"Tell him where I am," said Harry. He hung up, convinced that the night's events would, indeed, eventually be traced to a defective circuit board.

The Center was peaceful on Sunday mornings; and the truth was that, although he tried not to examine his motives too closely, he was always happy for sufficient reason to sleep in his office. Odd: despite his passion for Julie, there was something in the surrounding hills, in the mists that rose with the sun, in the solitude of this place and its direct connection, perhaps, with the night sky, that drew him. Even now. Maybe especially now.

IRA DENIES BOMB HIDDEN IN POPULATED AREA
British Say Troop Withdrawal from Ulster Not Connected
Civil Strife Continues; 600 Hurt in Rioting

SENATE SINKS ABM BILL
(Washington Post News Service)—A coalition of northern Democrats and farm belt Republicans today voted down the Sentinel ABM System, handing the President another setback....

TAIMANOV PROPOSES JOINT MEASURES
AGAINST NUCLEAR TERROR
Polish Dissidents Reported to Have Bomb

SOLAR SYSTEM AGE REVISED TO 5 BILLION YEARS
Samples recovered from Daiomoto Comet last month are at least a billion years older than expected....

SOVIET SUBMARINE BASE
REPORTED AT CAMRANH BAY

U.S. DISASTER AID TO ARGENTINA GOES ASTRAY
Food, Medical Supplies Show Up on Black Market;
More Quakes Expected; Typhus Raging

COCAINE HAUL IN DADE COUNTY BIGGEST EVER

DIVORCE RATE UP AGAIN
(New York)—Nearly two-thirds of all marriages now end in the courts, according to a recent study completed by the National Council of Churches....

NEW TV SEASON HERALDS RETURN TO WESTERN

__ 2 _____

If Edward Gambini had been awake all night, it didn't show. He scurried around the operations center, driven by restless energy, a thin birdlike man with a sparrow's quick eyes. He possessed a kind of avian dignity, a strong sense of his position in life, and the quality that politicians call charisma, and actors, presence. It was this characteristic, combined with a superb sense of timing in political matters, that had resulted in his appointment the previous summer, over more seasoned candidates, to manage the pulsar project. Although Harry was considerably the taller of the two men, persons familiar with both might not have been aware of it.

Unlike most of his colleagues, who reluctantly recognized the advantage of befriending administrators, Gambini genuinely enjoyed Harry Carmichael. When Carmichael occasionally lamented his lack of formal training (he'd begun life as a physics major at Ohio State), Gambini assured him that he was better off. Although of course he never explained why, Harry understood his meaning: only a mind of the first water (like Gambini's own) could survive extensive work in the disciplines without losing its intellectual edge. Harry's dry sense of humor and occasional outrageous perspectives would never have emerged intact from detailed study of the Schmidt-Hilbert Method or the Bernoulli Theorem.

Gambini cheerfully conceded that persons in Harry's line of work had a valid place in the world. And, God knew, rational administrators were hard enough to come by.

It was just after nine when Harry arrived, carrying a cinnamon role for Gambini who, he knew, would not have eaten.

Cord Majeski sat in front of a monitor, his jaw pushed into one palm, while lines of characters moved down the screen. His eyes did not move with them. The others, computer operators, systems analysts, communications experts, seemed more absorbed in their jobs than usual. Even Angela Dellasandro, the project heartthrob—tall, lean, dark-eyed—stared intently at a console. Gambini picked out a spot well away from everybody and took a substantial bite out of the cinnamon role. "Harry, can you get full optical for us tonight?"

Harry nodded. "I've already made arrangements. All I need is a written request from you or Majeski."

"Good." Gambini rubbed his hands. "You'll want to be here."

"Why?"

"Harry, that is a *very* strange object out there. In fact, I'm not sure it should exist at all." He leaned against a worktable piled high with printouts. Behind him, centered on a wall covered with photos of satellites, shuttles, and star clusters, was an Amtrak calendar depicting a switcher in a crowded freight yard. "In any case, it certainly shouldn't be where it is—way the hell out in the middle of nowhere. Harry, stars don't form between the galaxies. And they also don't wander out there. At least we've never seen one before."

"Why not?" asked Harry. "I'd expect a galaxy to throw one loose once in a while."

"The escape velocities are too high."

"How about an explosion? Maybe it was blown free."

"That's a possibility. But that sort of catastrophe would also have scattered the system. This thing's a binary.

"There's another mystery: it appears to have come from the general direction of the Virgo Cluster."

"And—?"

"The Virgo Cluster is sixty-five million light-years away from where Beta—that's the pulsar—is now. The system is moving away from it at about thirty-five kilometers per second. That's slow, but the point is that the vectors don't converge. We're sure it didn't originate in Virgo, but the stars aren't old enough to have got where they are from anywhere else. And I say that despite the fact that Alpha, the red giant in the system, is extremely old." Gambini leaned toward Harry, and his voice took on a conspiratorial tone. "There's something else you should know."

Harry waited, but Gambini slid off the table. "My office," he said.

It was paneled in red cedar, decorated with awards the physicist had received over the years: the 1989 Nobel for his work in high energy plasmas; the Man of the Year in 1991 from Georgetown; Beloit College's appreciation of his contributions to the development of the Faint Object Spectrograph; and so on. Before transferring to NASA from his former position with

the Treasury Department, Harry had indulged in the bureaucratic tradition of hanging plaques and certificates of recognition on his walls, but his stuff had looked pathetic by contrast:
the Treasury Department's Exceptional Achievement Award, a
diploma from a three-day executive development program, that
sort of thing. So Harry's eyewash now rested in a box in his
garage.

The office was located behind a broad glass panel that overlooked the forward compartment of the L-shaped operating
spaces. The floor was covered with a thick woven carpet. His
desk was awash in paper and books, and several yards of
printout had been draped over a chair back. Gambini snapped
on a Panasonic stereo set in a bookcase; the room filled immediately with Bach.

He waved Harry to a seat, but seemed unable to settle into
one himself. "Beta," he said, crossing the room to close the
door, "has been transmitting bursts of X-rays in an exceedingly
regular pattern during the two years we've been observing it.
The details don't matter, but the intervals between peaks have
been remarkably constant. At least that was the situation until
this morning. I understand Hoffer informed you that the signal
stopped altogether last night."

"Yes. That's why I came in."

"It was down for precisely four hours, seventeen minutes,
forty-three seconds."

"Is that significant?"

Gambini smiled. "Multiply it by sixteen, and you get Beta's
orbital period." He watched Harry expectantly and was clearly
disappointed at his lack of response. "Harry," he said, "that's
no coincidence. The shutdown was designed to attract attention.
Designed, Harry. And the duration of the shutdown was intended to demonstrate intelligent control." Gambini's eyes glittered. His lips rolled back to reveal sharp white teeth. "Harry,"
he said, "it's the LGM signal! It's happened!"

Harry shifted his weight uncomfortably. LGM meant little
green man: it was shorthand for the long-sought communication
from another world. And it was a subject on which Ed Gambini
had long since lost all objectivity. The negative results of the
first SKYNET survey of extrasolar planetary atmospheres two
years before had broken the physicist. And Harry suspected he
had never entirely recovered. "Ed," he said carefully, "I don't
think we should jump to conclusions."

"Goddammit, Harry, I'm not jumping to conclusions!" He

started to say something else, caught himself, and sat down. "There *is* no other explanation for what we've seen. Listen," he said, suddenly calm, "I know you're thinking I'm a loony old bastard. But it doesn't matter what *anybody* thinks. There's no question about it!" He looked defiantly at Harry, daring him to object.

"That's the evidence?" asked Harry. "That's all there is?"

"It's all we'll ever need." Gambini smiled tolerantly. "But yes, there's more." His jaws worked, and an expression that was a mixture of smugness and anger worked its way into his features. "Nobody's going to pack me off to a shrink *this* time."

"What else is there?"

"The consistency of the pattern is on the record. With minor variations, in intensity and pulse width and so on, the basic sequence of events never changed during the several months we've been observing Beta. There were almost always fifty-six pulses in a series, and the series repeats every three and a half seconds. Slightly less, actually." He churned energetically around the room while he talked, waving his arms and jabbing fingers in Harry's direction. "Son of a bitch, I can't believe it yet. Anyhow, after we recovered the signal this morning, we could still recognize the pattern. But there was an odd difference. Some of the pulses were missing, but only from alternate series. And always the same pulses. It was as if you took, say, the Third Concerto and played it straight through, and then played it again, with some notes removed, but substituting rests rather than shortening the composition. And you continued to do this, complete, and truncated, with the truncated version always the same." He took a notepad out of the top drawer and wrote 56 at the top. "The number of pulses in the normal series," he said. "But in the abbreviated series, there are only forty-eight."

Harry shook his head. "I'm sorry, Ed. I'm lost."

"All right, forget all that. It's only a method for creating a recurring pattern. Now, what is particularly interesting is the arrangement of the missing pulses." He printed the series: 3, 6, 11, 15, 19, 29, 34, 39, 56. His gray eyes rose to meet Harry's. "When it's finished, we get fifty-six pulses without the deletions, and then the series runs again."

Harry stared back. "Say it in English, Ed."

Gambini looked like a man who'd won a lottery. "It's a code," he said.

Two years before, when SKYNET had gone operational,

Gambini had expected to solve the basic riddles of the universe. Life in other places, the creation, the ultimate fate of the galaxies. But it hadn't happened that way, of course. Those questions still remained open. He had been particularly interested, for philosophical reasons, in the role of life in the cosmos. And SKYNET had revealed, for the first time, terrestrial worlds circling distant stars. Gambini and Majeski, Wheeler at Princeton, Rimford at Cal Tech, and a thousand others had looked at the photos and congratulated one another. Planets floated everywhere! Few stars seemed so poor, so sterile, as to be destitute of orbiting bodies. Even multiple star systems had somehow produced, and held on to, clusters of worlds. Often they fluttered in eccentric orbits, but they were there. And Gambini had offered Harry his opinion one Sunday afternoon in late April that he no longer had any doubts: the universe was rich with life.

That optimism had all changed in the long shadow thrown by the Faint Object Spectrograph. Light analysis showed that planets of terrestrial mass located within the biozone of a star (at a distance from their primary that would allow liquid water to exist) tended to be like Venus rather than Earth. The data had, in fact, revealed the nearby universe as an unremittingly hostile place, and the Saganesque vision of a Milky Way populated with hundreds of thousands of life-bearing planets had given way to the dark suspicion that humans were, after all, alone. Gambini's dream dissipated, and, ironically, it was his own work with the Faint Object Spectrograph that had made the knowledge possible.

It was a grim time, traumatic for the Agency and for its investigators. If, after all, there was nothing out there but rock and gas, why were the taxpayers pumping money into long-range projects? Harry had no inclination to go through it again. "I think we need better evidence," he said, as gently as he could.

"Do you?" Gambini's tongue flicked across his lips. "Harry, I don't think you've looked closely at the transmissions." He pushed the pad on which he'd scrawled the numbers closer to Harry, picked up the phone, and punched in a number. "We'd better tell Quint," he said.

"What about the series?" asked Harry. "And by the way, I wouldn't be in a hurry to get the Director out here." Quinton Rosenbloom was NASA's operations chief, now also wearing the hat of Director at Goddard. An automobile accident a few weeks before had left the position suddenly empty. The change in leadership at this time was unfortunate: the old Director had known Gambini well and would have been tolerant of this latest aberration. But Rosenbloom was an old-line conservative, utterly dedicated to rock-bound good sense.

Harry examined the numbers, but saw nothing out of the ordinary.

Rosenbloom was not available. Harry's experience had taught him that Rosenbloom was seldom available on Sunday mornings. Gambini's correct course would have been to leave some indication of the nature of the emergency. That would have resulted in a response within half an hour or so. But he disliked Rosenbloom and consequently failed to exercise his usual tact. He directed the person at the other end to have Rosenbloom call "when he gets in."

"I assume there's some sort of sequence," Harry said.

The physicist nodded. "Of the most basic sort. At the start of the series, there are two pulses, set off by the pulse that does not appear. Then two more, and then four. An exponential group. Followed by the three that appears between sites eleven and fifteen, another three between fifteen and nineteen, and a nine between nineteen and twenty-nine. Two-two-four. Three-three-nine. Four-four-sixteen. Could anything be clearer?"

Quint Rosenbloom was overweight, rumpled, and ugly. He needed his glasses adjusted and could have used a competent tailor. Nevertheless, he was an administrator of considerable ability. He'd come to NASA from COSMIC, the Computer Software Management and Information Center at the University of Georgia. His initial assignments had encompassed systems integration for the Ground Spaceflight Tracking and Data Network. But the application of bureaucratic pressure appealed to his mathematical instincts: he enjoyed wielding power.

He did not generally approve of theorists. They tended to get lost easily, and their hold on everyday reality, slippery in the best of times, inevitably made them unreliable. He recognized their value (much, perhaps, as the theorists recognized the value of the signature on their paychecks); but he preferred to stay at least one level of management above them.

Ed Gambini was a classic example of the type. Gambini was addicted to asking the sort of ultimate questions about which one could speculate endlessly with no fear of ever arriving at a solution. That was not really a problem in itself, of course, but it biased one's judgment sufficiently to render it, in Rosenbloom's view, unreliable.

He had vigorously opposed Gambini's appointment, but his own superiors, whose scientific backgrounds were limited, were unduly impressed by the physicist's Nobel Prize. Moreover, in an action that Rosenbloom could not bring himself to forgive, Gambini had gone over his head. "The little bastard knew I wouldn't have given him the job," he once told Harry. There'd been a fight, and in the end Rosenbloom had been overruled.

If Rosenbloom doubted Gambini's results that Sunday morning, it was not because he felt that such a thing wasn't possible, but rather that it simply did not happen in well-run government agencies. He also sensed that, if events were permitted to take their course, he would shortly face one of those fortunately rare situations in which there would be considerable career risk, with little corresponding opportunity for advantage.

His irritation was obvious from the moment he arrived at the operations center. "He doesn't like being called out on a Sunday," Gambini remarked, while both men watched him stride stiffly through the whitewashed door. But Harry suspected it went deeper than that. Rosenbloom had a long memory and no inclination to go another round with Gambini's demons.

It was warm: he had a worn blazer slung over one shoulder, and his knit shirt was stuffed into his pants in a manner that suggested he'd come directly from the golf course. He passed through operations like a shabbily dressed missile and exploded quietly in Gambini's office. "I don't have a better explanation for your dots and dashes, Ed. But I'm sure someone else will. What's Majeski's opinion?"

"He can't offer any alternative."

"How about you, Harry?"

"It's not his field," observed Gambini, nettled.

"I asked Harry."

"I have no idea," said Harry, his own irritation rising.

Rosenbloom extracted a cigar from an inside pocket of his coat. He inserted it unlit into his mouth. "The Agency," he said reasonably, "has a few problems just now. The rest of the moon operation's going to hell. The Administration is unhappy with our foot-dragging over the military's pet projects. The Bible-thumpers are still suspicious of us, and I don't need to remind you that there's a presidential election next year."

That had been another embarrassment for the Agency. The year before, NASA investigators, using SKYNET, had got on the track of a quasar they'd suspected of being the Big Bang and had begun issuing periodic reports that the press promptly labeled Creation bulletins. The Agency's position had become untenable when Baines Rimford, at Cal Tech, had said he no longer believed a Big Bang had occurred. "The Administration's in trouble with the taxpayers, the Congress, and most of the fringe groups in the country," Rosenbloom went on. "I suspect the only solid support the White House has left comes from the NRA. Now, it strikes me, gentlemen, that the President would just love to have a cord wherewith to strangle this organization. To take us by our collective throats and hang us out to dry. If we start talking about little green men and we're wrong, we're going to be handing him the rope." He was sitting on a reversed wooden chair, which he tilted forward. "Maybe," he added, "even if we're right."

"We don't have to make any statement at all," objected Gambini. "Just release the transmissions. They'll speak for themselves."

"They sure as hell will." Rosenbloom was the only person in the organization who would have taken that tone to Gambini. There was much about the Director's methods for handling subordinates that reminded Harry of a tractor-trailer with a loose housing. "Ed, people are already jittery. There's a lot of war talk again, the economy's a mess, and we've recently had a nuclear demonstration by the IRA. The President is not going to want to hear about Martians."

Harry's eyes were beginning to water. Pollen was getting down into his throat, and he sneezed. He felt slightly feverish and began to wish he could get home to bed. It was, after all, a Sunday.

"Quinton." Gambini twisted the name slightly, drawing out the second consonant but he kept a straight face. "Whoever is on the other end of that transmission is far away. *Far* away. There were cavemen here when that signal left Altheis."

"It is my earnest desire," Rosenbloom continued, as if no one else had spoken, "that this entire issue should just go away."

"That's not going to happen," said Gambini.

"No, I don't suppose so." Rosenbloom's chair creaked. "Harry, you didn't answer my question. Would *you* be willing to stand up there and tell two hundred million Americans that you've been talking to Martians?"

Harry drew a deep breath. He didn't like to be perceived as opposing Gambini on his own grounds. Still, it was hard to believe the entire thing wouldn't turn out to be a defective flywheel somewhere. "It's like UFO's," he said, trying to be diplomatically noncommittal, but realizing too late that he was saying the wrong thing. "You can't really take them seriously until somebody parks one in your back yard."

Rosenbloom closed his eyes and allowed a picture of contentment to settle across his features. "Carmichael," he said resonably, "has been here longer than any of us. He has an instinct for survival that I admire, and he has the best interests of the Agency at heart. Ed, I suggest you listen to him."

Gambini, stationed behind his polished desk, ignored Harry. "What Admin thinks is irrelevant. The fact is that nothing in nature creates exponential sequences."

Rosenbloom chewed the unlit cigar, removed it, turned it between his thumb and forefinger, and flipped it into a wastebasket. (Gambini's disapproval of smoking was public knowledge, and Harry could not miss the implied derision in the Director's actions.) "You're wrong, Ed," he said. "You spend too much time in observatories. But Harry understands the realities here. How badly do you want to see SKYNET finished? How important are the Mare Ingenii telescopes?"

Gambini's cheeks were reddening, and a nerve quivered in his throat. He said nothing.

"Okay," continued Rosenbloom, "you push this business with the pulsar, create another stir, and I guarantee you it'll be the end. All you've got is a goddam series of beeps."

"No, Quint. What we have is hard evidence of intelligent control of a pulsar."

"All right, I'll buy that. You've got *evidence.*" He rose ponderously and pushed the chair away with his foot. "And that's it. Evidence is a long way from proof. Harry's right: if you're going to talk about little green men, you better be prepared to march them into a press conference. This stuff is *your* specialty, not mine. But I looked up pulsars before I came down here this morning. If I understand my sources, they're what's left after a supernova blows a star apart. Isn't that correct?"

Gambini nodded. "More or less."

"Just so you can reassure me," he continued, "what's your answer going to be when someone asks how an alien world would have survived the explosion?"

"There's no way we could know that," objected Gambini.

"Well, you'll want to have a plausible story ready for Cass

Woodbury. She's a cobra, Ed. She'll probably also want to know how anyone could control the kind of energy a pulsar puts out." He drew a piece of paper from his pocket, unfolded it with deliberate ease, and adjusted his glasses. "It says here that the power of your basic X-ray pulsar could generate about ten thousand times the luminosity of the sun. Could that be right? How could anyone control that? *How*, Ed? How could it be possible?"

Gambini rolled his eyes toward the ceiling. "We may be talking about a technology a million years beyond ours," he said. "Who knows what they might be capable of?"

"Yeah, I've heard all that before. And you'll bear with me if I suggest to you that that's a hell of a poor answer. We'd better be ready with something a little more convincing."

Harry sneezed his way into the conversation. "Look," he said, wiping his nose, "I probably shouldn't be in this at all. But I can tell you how I'd try to use the pulsar if I wanted to signal with it."

Rosenbloom rubbed his flat nose with fat short fingers. "How?" he asked.

"I wouldn't try to do *anything* with the pulsar itself." Harry got up, crossed the room, and looked down, not at the Director, but at Gambini. "I'd set up a blinker. Just put something in front of it."

A beatific smile lit up Rosenbloom's languid features. "Good, Harry," he said, his manner heavy with mockery. "It must come as something of a surprise to your associate to discover that there's some imagination outside the operations group."

"Okay, Ed, I'm willing to concede the possibility. It *might* be artificial, or it might be something else entirely. I suggest we keep our minds open. And our mouths shut. At least until we know what we're dealing with. In the meantime, no public statements. If the signal changes again, you notify *me* first. Clear?"

Gambini nodded.

Rosenbloom looked at his watch. "It's, what, about ten and a half hours now since it started. I take it you're assuming this is an acquisition signal of some sort."

"Yes," said Gambini. "They'd want to attract our attention first. Somewhere down the line, when they think we've had enough time, they'll substitute a textual transmission."

"You may have a long wait." The Director's eyes fell on Harry. "Carmichael, you get in touch with everybody who was in here last night. Tell them not a word of this to anybody. Any of this gets out, I'll have someone's head. Ed, if there's anybody special you want to bring in, clear it with my office."

Gambini frowned. "Quint, aren't we losing sight of our charter here a little? Goddard isn't a defense installation."

"It also isn't an installation that's going to have people laughing at it for the next twenty years because you can't wait a few days—"

"I have no problem with keeping it out of the newspapers," Gambini said, his temper visibly rising. "But a lot of people have worked on different aspects of this problem for a long time. They deserve to know what happened last night."

"Not yet." Rosenbloom appeared maddeningly unconcerned. "I'll tell you when."

The Director's aura hung oppressively in the office. Gambini's good humor had evaporated, and even Harry, who had long since learned the advantage of maintaining a clinical attitude in these squabbles, felt unnerved.

"Damn fool," Gambini said. "He means well, he wants to protect the Agency, but he's a walking roadblock." He flipped through the Cardex, found the number he wanted, and punched it into his phone. "Last night, Harry," he said quietly, "you and I lived through the most significant moment in the history of the species. I suggest you record everything you can remember. You'll be able to write a book on the subject soon, and people will read it a thousand years from now." He turned to the phone. Then: "Is Father Wheeler there? This is Ed Gambini at Goddard."

Harry shook his head. He disapproved of turf struggles; they caused rancor and inefficiency, and he habitually regarded people who engaged in them with contempt. (Although he'd caught himself indulging on occasion.) And this one was particularly annoying, since he'd already been drawn in.

The walls were lined with books, not the reassuring personnel manuals and federal regulations in black binders that filled Harry's shelves, but arcane volumes with abstruse titles: Stephen Hawking's *Cosmological Perspectives*, Rimford's *Molecular Foundations of Temporal Asymmetry*, Smith's *Galactic Transformations*. Well-thumbed copies of *Physics Today, Physics Review*, and other magazines had been dropped on every available surface. It vaguely upset Harry's sense of propriety: the first requisite of a government office is order. He was surprised that Rosenbloom had not commented, had not even seemed to notice. Probably it suggested that there was not, after all, much difference between the two men.

"I'd appreciate it if you could reach him and ask him to call me right away. It's important." Gambini hung up. "Wheeler's in D.C., Harry. Lecturing at Georgetown. With luck, we can have him here this afternoon."

Harry got up uneasily and walked to the window. "Ed, you're playing games with our careers. I thought Rosenbloom made himself reasonably clear. He wants approval before anyone is called in."

"He can't do anything to me," said Gambini. "I could walk out of here tomorrow, and he knows it. And he can't touch you either. Hell, nobody else knows how to run the place. Anyway, if it'll make you feel better, I'll see that his office gets informed. But if we have to wait for Quin-ton's okay, we might as well close up shop."

Harry demurred. "Why create a problem? He'd have no objection to your bringing Pete Wheeler in." Wheeler was a Norbertine cosmologist who shared Gambini's intense interest in the possibilities of extraterrestrial life. He'd written extensively on the subject and had predicted long before SKYNET that living worlds would be exceedingly rare. He also had a direct connection with Rosenbloom, who had been his partner in a number of area bridge tournaments. "Who else do you want?"

"Let's go outside," suggested Gambini. Reluctantly, because the pollen would be worse, Harry went along. "When things begin to happen, we're going to need Rimford. And I'd like to have Leslie Davies on hand. Eventually, if we *do* make contact, we should also get Cyrus Hakluyt. If you could get the paperwork started, I'd appreciate it."

Rimford was probably the world's best-known cosmologist. He'd become a public figure in recent years, appearing on television specials and writing books on the architecture of the universe that were always described as "lucid accounts for the general reader," but which Harry could never understand. In the latter years of the twentieth century, Gambini maintained, Rimford's only peer was Stephen Hawking. His name was attached to assorted topological theorems, temporal deviations, and cosmological models. Yet he, too, found time to play bridge (he was a ranking expert), and he had something of a reputation as an amateur actor. Harry had once watched him play, with remarkable energy, Liza Doolittle's amoral father.

But who were Davies and Hakluyt?

They came out through the front doors into a bright sunlit afternoon, cool with the smell of mid-September. Gambini's enthusiasm was returning. "Cyrus is a microbiologist from Johns Hopkins. He's a Renaissance man, of sorts, whose specialties include evolutionary mechanics, genetics, several branches of morphology, and assorted other subdisciplines. He also writes essays."

"What sort of essays?" asked Harry, assuming that Gambini meant technical papers.

"They're more or less philosophical commentaries on natural history. He's been published by both *The Atlantic* and *Harper's;* and a volume of his work came out just last year. I think it was called *The Place without Roads*. There's a copy of it down in my office somewhere. He got a favorable review in the *Times*."

"And Davies?"

"A theoretical psychologist. Maybe she can do something for Rosenbloom." It was going to be a lovely day. And Harry, noting the solid reality of a passing pickup, of the homely Personnel offices across Road 3, of lumber and sheeting stacked against one wall of the building from which they'd just come (the residue of a remodeling project that had been abandoned), wondered whether the Director wasn't right about Gambini.

"I understand why you want Wheeler," he said. "And Rimford. But why these other people?"

"Just between us, Harry, we already have all the astronomers we need. Wheeler's in because he's an old friend and deserves to be here. Rimford has been part of every major discovery in his field for thirty years, so we couldn't slight him. Besides, he's the best mathematician on the planet. If contact occurs, Harry, *if it actually happens,* the astronomers are going to be close to useless. We'll need the mathematicians to read the transmission. And we'll need Hakluyt and Davies to understand it."

At around seven, Harry drove home. When he got there, Julie's car was gone. The air was filled with the smell of burning leaves, and the temperature was dropping rapidly. The trees already stood stiff and stark in the gathering dusk. The yard needed raking, and the neighborhood kids had knocked his wooden gate flat again. The damned thing had never worked right since the day he'd brought it home: you had to be careful how you opened it or it came off its hinges. He'd repaired it a couple times, but it didn't seem to matter.

The house was empty. He found a note propped up on a loaf of bread:

Harry,

We are at Ellen's. There's lunch meat in the fridge.

Julie

Momentarily, his heart froze. But she wouldn't have done that, left so soon, with no warning. Still, it brought everything back with painful clarity.

He cracked a beer and carried it into the living room. Several rolls of Julie's blueprints—she was a part-time architectural assistant for a small firm in D.C.—were tucked behind the dictionary stand. They were reassuring: she would not have left them behind. Him, maybe, but not the blueprints.

Several of Tommy's plastic dragonmen were gathered into a shoebox fort on the hassock. They were absurd creatures with long snouts and alligator tails and clearly inadequate batwings. Yet they were nevertheless comforting, old friends from a better time, like the antique secretarial cabinet he and Julie had bought in the first year of their marriage and the birch paneling they'd struggled to put up three or four summers back.

The beer was cold and good.

He shook off his shoes, turned on the TV, but reduced the sound to a murmur.

The room was pleasantly cool. He finished the beer, closed his eyes, and sank into the sofa. The house was always quiet when Tommy was out of it.

The telephone was ringing.

It was dark, and someone had placed a quilt over him. He groped uncertainly for the instrument. "Hello?"

"Harry, did you get Optical for us?" It was Gambini. "Control isn't aware of any change."

"Wait a minute, Ed." The television was off, but he could hear someone moving around upstairs. He tried to get a look at his watch, but he couldn't find his glasses. "What time is it?"

"Almost eleven."

"Okay. I notified Donner that he was being preempted, and I sent a memo over to Control. I'll call them to make sure they haven't forgotten. You're scheduled to pick up the system at midnight. But they tell me that Champollion won't line up until after two."

"Are you coming in?"

"Is anything going to happen?"

"Hard to say; this'll be our first look with the full system. Up until now, it's been mostly radio and X-ray. The only optical photos were taken with the orbiting units." Harry heard Julie coming down the stairs. "But, no, we'll probably just collect some technical information. Nothing likely to be worth your making a special trip. Unless, of course," he added mischievously, "the bastards are sending a visual signal as well."

"Is that possible?"

Gambini thought a moment. "No, it wouldn't really be very rational."

Harry stayed on the line, talking about nothing in particular, waiting perhaps for Julie. She paused at the bottom of the staircase, between Harry and the dining room window, silhouetted against the soft glow of the starlight in the garden. "Hello," she said.

Harry waved. "Ed," he said, "I'll be over in about an hour." And the pleasure he got from the act, from letting Julie know that he was walking off again, surprised him. After he'd hung up, he returned her greeting, not wanting to be cold, but somehow unable to avoid it, and asked if Tommy was in bed.

"Yes," she said. "An hour ago. Are you all right?"

"Fine." She looked disappointed. Had she expected that he would put up more of a fight to keep her? His responses to her now were ruled by his instincts, which dictated that any show of weakness, any direct effort to retain her, would only earn her contempt and reduce any remaining possibility that he might still manage to hold on to her. "I've got to get a shower and some fresh clothes," he said. "Things are pretty busy. I'll probably sleep at the office again tonight."

"Harry," she said, turning on a small table lamp, "you don't have to do that."

"It has nothing to do with us," Harry said, as gently as he could. But it was difficult to control his voice: everything seemed to come out either gruff or strained.

He detected a fleeting reflection of uncertainty in her features. "I talked with Ellen," she said. "She can make room for us, for Tommy and me, for a while."

"Okay," said Harry. "Do what you think best."

He showered quickly and drove back to Greenbelt. It was a long ride.

The Reverend Peter E. Wheeler, O. Praem., lifted his lime daiquiri. "Gentlemen," he said, "I give you that excellent scientific organization, the federal government, which has, I believe, manufactured an historic moment for us." Gambini and Harry joined the toast; Majeski also raised his glass, but he was clearly more interested in surveying the women among the clientele, many of whom were young and possessed of striking geometrical attributes. It was midnight at the Red Limit.

Overhead, in high orbit, an array of mirrors, filters, and lenses rotated toward Hercules.

Sandwiches arrived: a steak for Gambini, roast beef for Harry and Majeski. Wheeler contented himself by picking at a dish of peanuts. "Pete, you sure you don't want something to eat?" asked the project manager. "It might be a long night."

Wheeler shook his head. His round dark eyes, receding black hair, and sharp features combined to create a distinctly Mephistophelian impression. It was a resemblance to which he was sensitive, as Harry had learned in an unfortunate moment years before when he'd thoughtlessly mentioned it and seen Pete's defensive reaction. "I ate before I came over," he said, with a smile that dispelled the momentary infernal image. "Nothing worse than a fat priest." Wheeler was relatively young, barely forty, although the last time he'd been at Greenbelt he had solemnly informed Harry that he was over the hill. "If a cosmologist hasn't made a major contribution by the time he gets to be my age," he'd said, "it isn't going to happen." Later, Harry'd asked Gambini about it, and he had agreed. Wheeler sipped his drink. "You're not," he asked, "expecting the textual signal in the X-ray ranges, are you?"

"No," said Majeski. He was gazing past the priest at a pair of young women seated near the bar. "They wouldn't be able to get enough definition for it to be practical. Too much quantum noise, for one thing. We're assuming they'll switch to a wide band signal of some sort. Something they'd figure we couldn't miss."

"But we're taking no chances," added Gambini. "Everything we have is locked on them now. Including the Multi-Channel.

If they transmit anywhere at all in the EM range, we should pick it up."

"Good," said Wheeler.

"Let's hope," added Majeski, "they're on the same sort of temporal dynamic we are. It would be nice to find, during our lifetimes, what they have to say for themselves." One of the two women in his line of sight looked his way. He excused himself, took his rum and Coke, left the roast beef, and sauntered over to her table.

"Pity you can't deal with your aliens in so direct a manner," Wheeler said.

Gambini sighed. "I wonder how the twentieth century would have gone if we'd had a lascivious Einstein?"

The priest grinned. "Possibly there'd be no atom bomb," he said.

They toasted those sentiments, and the three fell into good-natured banter. When the laughter subsided momentarily, several minutes later, Harry asked why Optical had suddenly become so important.

Gambini explained between mouthfuls of steak. "We don't know what to expect," he said. "It's logical to assume that there'll be a second phase to the transmission, since the acquisition signal does nothing more than alert us to their presence. A civilization able to manhandle that pulsar may be capable of damned near anything. And by the way, Harry, there's good reason to suspect that they *are* able to manipulate the pulsar, whether they use a screen or not. Anyhow, we'd like to try to get a look at their neighborhood."

Wheeler finished his drink. "Ed, I take it we're sitting on this little bombshell."

"Rosenbloom wants to wait awhile before we announce anything."

"Exactly the right course," Wheeler said, looking hard at Gambini, who did not respond.

Later, while the project manager was in the washroom, Harry asked the priest what he thought about the Hercules signal. "Are there people on the other end?"

Wheeler tried to attract the attention of their waiter. "It's hard to argue with the evidence. I don't know what's out there, any more than anyone else does. But, Harry, we're talking about something we all want very much to find. And that automatically makes Ed's conclusions suspect. Let's wait awhile and see what happens."

Harry pushed the food around on his plate. "What could cause a signal of that type? Naturally, I mean."

The waiter arrived, and Wheeler ordered coffee for everyone. "I haven't the slightest idea. But I can tell you what it isn't: it isn't what Gambini thinks it is."

"How do you know that?"

"Harry, do you know what a pulsar is?"

"It's a collapsed star that blinks."

The priest peered closely into Harry's eyes. "It's the corpse of a supernova. A supernova, Harry. Gambini himself tells me they're estimating it happened less than six million years ago." He caught up a few peanuts, dropped one, and swallowed the others. "A blast of that magnitude would either incinerate or scatter any planetary group that existed. If anybody's out there with a radio transmitter, he doesn't have a world to sit on."

"Rosenbloom raised that point," Harry said.

"It's a valid objection."

Two twenty-four-meter telescopes overlook the west wall of the Champollion Crater at thirty-seven degrees north latitude, on the far side of the moon; two more are under construction near the Mare Ingenii in the southern hemisphere. The Champollion reflectors are the heart of SKYNET. Functioning in tandem with an Earth-orbiting array of eight 2.4-meter Space Telescopes, they are fully capable of reaching to the edge of the observable universe.

The system, which was barely two years old, had been completed only after a long struggle over financing. There'd been internal bickering, delays, cost overruns, and, in the end, political problems. The flap over the creation event had heavily damaged efforts to fund the second pair of telescopes; the discovery that planetary systems out to more than a hundred light-years were as desolate and devoid of life as the moons of Jupiter had guaranteed that the imagination of the taxpayer, and consequently the interest of the politician, would not be engaged.

SKYNET also included a system of radio and X-ray telescopes and, for enhancement, a bank of computers whose capabilities were believed to be second only to those of the National Security Agency. When operating as a fully coordinated optical unit—in other words, when all ten reflectors were locked onto the same target—the system could magnify remote objects more than four hundred thousand times. During SKYNET's early months of operation, Harry had stood under the monitors with Gambini and Majeski and Wheeler, silently absorbing the blue-white curve of majestic Rigel, the vast trailing filaments of the Whirlpool Galaxy, and the fog-shrouded surface of the terrestrial world Alpha Eridani. They'd been rousing days, filled with promise and excitement. The investigators, the news media, and the general public had all got caught up in a near frenzy of expectation. Harry had been forced to put on four extra people in the public relations office to answer telephones and quash rumors. But he, like everyone else, had been carried along by the rising tide.

But the big news never came: the long bleak winter was filled with the increasingly familiar patterns of carbon dioxide spectrograms. And in April, with the coming of spring, Ed Gambini had broken down.

Linda Barrister, who manned the comm link, was talking softly to NASCOM when Harry followed Gambini and the others into the operations center. She smiled prettily, spoke again into the phone, and looked up at the project manager. "They're still a few minutes from calibration, Doctor."

Gambini nodded and took a position near the communications monitor, where he quickly tired of waiting and began to wander through the spaces, holding brief whispered conversations with the technicians.

Majeski went back into ADP.

Wheeler fell comfortably into a chair.

"You don't expect much out of this, do you, Pete?" asked Harry.

"Out of Optical? No, not really. But who knows? Listen: last year I'd have denied the possibility of a free-floating binary. There are a few questions to be answered here."

Two technical assistants, both bearded, fortyish, and overweight, pulled their earphones down on their necks and bent forward over their consoles.

Somewhere, probably in one of the workrooms, a radio was playing Glenn Miller. Harry leaned against a supply cabinet. Directly overhead, an auxiliary monitor was flashing sequences of numbers more quickly than the eye could follow. "It's the satellite," Barrister explained. "TDRSS." That would be the Tracking and Data Relay Satellite System. "It's the X-ray signal from Hercules."

She touched a slim finger to her right earphone. "Champollion's locked in," she said.

Gambini, who was trying to retain his customary dignity, trembled. Despite the air conditioning, damp crescents stained his shirt. He moved closer to Linda's monitor.

"We're getting a signal," she said.

The lights dimmed.

Majeski came back into the room.

Wheeler pulled off his plaid sweater and tossed it into the supply cabinet.

"Recording," said one of the bearded technicians.

The monitor darkened, and a red point of light appeared at its center, framed in a starfield. Someone exhaled, and there was a general rustling throughout the several rooms of the operations center.

"They're foreground stars, most of them," Pete whispered. "Probably a couple of galaxies in there, too."

"Mag is two-point-oh," said Barrister. That was a magnification of two hundred thousand.

"Take it in," said Gambini.

The peripheral objects rotated forward off the screen; the red star, Alpha Altheis, brightened.

"It wouldn't be a good place to live," said Wheeler.

Harry did not take his eyes from the monitor. "Why not?"

"If there *were* a world, there'd be no stars in its sky. The moon would be red; the sun's being eaten."

"Three-oh," said Barrister.

"A culture that developed under those conditions—"

"—would," observed Majeski, "sure as hell be God-fearing."

Harry couldn't see Wheeler's reaction, but there was no softness in Majeski's voice.

The red light that was Alpha Altheis grew brighter. Then someone across the room grunted. "What the hell's that?" Gambini, trying to get closer, stumbled over something in the dark, but popped back up without missing a beat.

A yellow pinprick had appeared west of the giant star.

"Spectrograph," snapped Gambini.

Barrister checked her instruments. "Three-six," she said.

Wheeler was out of his chair. He laid a hand on Harry's shoulder. "There's a third star in the system."

"Class G," said the analyst. "No readings yet on mass.

Absolute magnitude six-point-three."

"Not very bright," said Gambini. "No wonder we missed it."

Harry grinned at Wheeler. "There goes your supernova problem," he said. "Now we know where the planets are."

"No, I don't think so. If that class G *is* part of the system—which, out there, it damned well would have to be—the explosion would have taken out *its* worlds, too. Still—" Wheeler looked perplexed. He turned toward Gambini. "Ed—?"

"I see it, Pete," said the project manager. "It doesn't make much sense, does it?"

Harry could make out nothing but the two stars, a bright sharp ruby and a dull yellow point of light. "What is it?" he asked. "What's wrong?"

"There should be a shell of gas around the system," said Wheeler. "Some remnant of the supernova. Ed, I don't understand this at all."

Gambini was slowly shaking his head. "There's been no supernova here."

Wheeler's voice was barely audible. "That's not possible, Ed."

"I know," Gambini said.

. . . The sites at Champollion and Mare Ingenii for the fixed 24-meter telescopes were chosen to provide an optimum number of objects both within and outside the Milky Way which could be simultaneously targeted by both units. This capability will permit a degree of image enhancement approximately 30 percent beyond that of either unit acting alone. (The percentage declines somewhat when the fixed telescopes are employed as part of the overall system of fixed and orbiting units; but even under these circumstances, the improvement would be considerable.)

A fully operational SKYNET will open the entire observable universe to direct examination. It will constitute a stride of incalculable value, of far more benefit to the species than any other imaginable project now technologically within our reach. Even a mission to Alpha Centauri pales in contrast.

In light of the funds that have already been expended on SKYNET and the relatively modest sum that would be required to complete the system, we urge—

—From NASA's Annual Report to the President

. . . Let us look at the facts:

We know that, beyond this Earth, the Universe is unremittingly hostile, a place brutally hot or brutally frigid, a place that is mostly void, with a few rocks and some hot gas adrift. It is the sort of place that some Northerners might want to visit, but it holds little interest for Tennesseans.

We know also that even NASA can no longer provide a shadow of any tangible benefit to be derived from examining boulders so far away that light from them cannot reach us during a man's lifetime.

And we also face the stark fact that the Government would like to spend an additional $600 million to complete the telescopes based at Mare Ingenii. Their argument for doing so seems to be that, having already wasted so much on the project, it would be unconscionable not to waste some more.

The time has come to call a halt.

—Editorial, *Memphis Herald* (September 12)

. . . The reality of it all may be that our concepts have so thoroughly outstripped our technology that the latter can no longer keep up. Case in point: SKYNET.

Theoretically, it should be possible to use the techniques I have described in this paper to create a magnetic lens whose diameter would be equal to the diameter of Earth's orbit. This lens could be manipulated to create a focal point in the same manner that a glass lens does. One hesitates to speculate on the sort of magnification such an achievement would permit. And while we cannot yet construct such a device, there is, in principle, no reason why it should not work.

—Baines Rimford, *Science* (September 2)

__3__

BAINES RIMFORD STOOD on a wooded hill out near the rim of the Milky Way, looking toward galactic center. He could sense the majestic rotation of the great wheel and the balance of gravity and angular momentum that held it together. Relatively few stars were visible over the lights of Pasadena, hurtling down their lonely courses.

The sun completes an orbit every 225 million years. During this latest swing around the galaxy, pterodactyls had flown and vanished; the ice had advanced and retreated, and near the end of the long circuit, men had appeared. Against that sort of measure, what is a man's life? It had occurred to Rimford, at about the time he approached fifty, that the chief drawback in contemplating the enormous gulfs of time and space that constitute the bricks and mortar of the cosmologist is that one acquires a dismaying perception of the handful of years allotted a human being.

To what microscopic extent had the sun depleted its store of hydrogen since he'd sat reading about Achilles and Prometheus on the front porch of his grandfather's row home in South Philadelphia? How much deeper was the Grand Canyon?

He was suddenly aware of his heartbeat: tiny engine of mortality whispering in his chest. It was one with the spinning galaxies and the quantum dance, as he was one with anything that had ever raised its eyes to the stars.

It was in good condition, his heart, as much as could be expected for a mechanism designed to self-destruct after a few dozen winters.

Somewhere below, lost in the lights of Lake Avenue, a dog barked. It was a cool evening: the air conditioners were off, and people had their windows open. He could hear fragments of the Dodgers game. Pasadena was, if more prosaic, at least more sensible than the universe. One knew why traffic lights worked, and where it had all come from. And, taken from the perspective of Altadena and Lake, the Big Bang seemed rather unlikely.

Curious: in the days when he had been constructing the

37

cosmic model that bore his name, many of his creative insights had come while he stood atop a hill like this one on the edge of Phoenix. But what he remembered most clearly from those solitary excursions was not the concepts, but the dogs. While he juggled matter and hyperbolic space, the night had seemed full of barking dogs.

It was getting late. The comet and the moon were both low in the west. Rimford wasn't much interested in comets, and he couldn't understand people who were. There was, he felt, little to be learned from such an object, other than the trivia of its composition.

He started slowly down the hill, enjoying the cool night air and the solitude. Near a cluster of palms, about a hundred yards from the top, there was a spot from which he could see his house. Like a child, he always stopped to savor its warm light and familiar lines. All in all, he had little of which to complain. If life was desperately short, it had been nevertheless good.

There was a story in Herodotus of a Greek philosopher who'd visited an Asian kingdom, where the ruler inquired of him who was happiest among men? The philosopher understood that the king himself wished to be thought of as occupying that enviable position. But the visitor had other ideas. "Perhaps," he replied, "it might be a farmer of my acquaintance, who lived near Athens. He had fine children, a wife who loved him, and he died on the field of battle defending his country." Rimford didn't expect to see any armed combat, but he had nevertheless waged the good fight, not for a particular flag, but for humanity.

In the dark, his lips curved into a smile. He was feeling satisfied with himself. The probability was that the Rimford universe would one day join Euclidean geometry and Newtonian physics as a system with much to recommend it, but in the end inadequate. It didn't matter. When the great strides of the twentieth century were being counted, they would know that Rimford had been there. And if he and Hawking and Penrose had got some of it wrong, or even much of it wrong, they'd made the effort.

He was content.

His colleagues expected him to retire shortly. And possibly he would. He had sensed the decline of his conceptual abilities recently: equations that had once been visions were reduced to mathematics. His creative work was over, and it was time to step aside.

Agnes was on the phone when he walked in. "He's here

now," she said into the instrument. She held it out to him with a wink. "Ed Gambini," she said. "I think he needs help."

Leslie Davies drove in Monday evening from Philadelphia, spent the night with friends in Glen Burnie, and proceeded next morning down the Baltimore-Washington Expressway to Goddard.

The Space Flight Center is nestled among the close-cropped hills and sober middle-class homes of Greenbelt, Maryland. The complex consists of seven office buildings, eleven laboratories, and several support structures, spread across a rolling tract of almost twelve hundred acres. There are a few dish antennas, mounted on concrete aprons and on rooftops; a water tower; and a visitors' center. The overall impression is less of a high-tech space-age facility than of a small military base.

She identified herself at the front gate. They gave her a temporary plate, logged her in, and provided directions to the Research Projects Laboratory.

Leslie had no idea why she'd been asked to come to Goddard. Gambini had been secretive over the phone, and she suspected that they were having some serious problems with their personnel. She'd read the research and was aware that people in technological professions, and particularly in the space sciences, scored quite high in stress analysis surveys. Worse, there was evidence in a wide variety of studies that the types of personalities drawn into these occupations tend to be unstable to begin with.

But even if people were coming apart here, why they should choose to come to *her* was a mystery. God knows, there were plenty of experienced shrinks in D.C., and undoubtedly a few with the right specialty.

Whatever it was, though, she was glad for the change of pace. She'd been doing cross-discipline research on the nature of consciousness for a Penn study group, and having a difficult time. Moreover, her practice, which was limited to two mornings a week, wasn't going well. She'd begun to suspect that she wasn't really helping her patients, and she was too good a psychologist to hide that fact from herself.

A well-tailored young woman met her at the entrance to the lab and inquired whether she'd had any trouble finding the Space Center. She got a visitor's badge and was led down one floor. "They're waiting for you now," her guide said. Leslie repressed an urge to ask who was waiting for her, and why.

They turned left into a short corridor. Voices spilled out of an open door ahead, and she recognized Ed Gambini's studied diction.

Gambini and two men she did not know sat around a conference table in intense conversation, which her entrance did nothing to hinder. The young woman who'd accompanied her smiled politely and withdrew. Leslie stood just inside the door, trying to make out the direction of things: she caught references to red giants, vectors, radial velocity curves, and sling effects. The youngest of the three was doing most of the talking. He was bearded, blown-dry handsome, energetic. He spoke with the cool confidence of a man who has never known disappointment. At one point, while holding forth on something called Fisher's Distribution, he took her in at a glance, and dismissed her.

Leslie bristled, but observed that the young giant had a similar effect on others. Ed Gambini sat with his back toward her, his eyes closed, and his head slightly inclined. But his own hostility was visible: he'd pressed his fingertips together in an unconscious steepling gesture, signaling his awareness of the speaker's inferior position and, probably, a repressed desire to inflict punishment.

The man opposite Gambini was lean, with black hair and quick perceptive eyes. He, too, was showing signs of impatience. A visitor's badge was pinned haphazardly to the pocket of a plaid shirt.

Gambini had somehow become aware of her presence. He swiveled around, rose, and shook her hand. "Leslie," he said. "Good to see you, again. Have you had breakfast yet?"

She nodded. Once, years before, during more enlightened times, she and Gambini had sat on a commission to advise the White House on funding for various science projects. She remembered him from those days as a man with a wide range of interests, unusual in the narrow disciplines of the scientific community. It had made him an ideal choice for the commission.

What she recalled most vividly, though, was an evening after they'd listened to a presentation for funds to expand the SETI program. It had been a night full of numbers. An astronomer whose name she'd forgotten had delivered an impassioned plea, illustrated with flip charts, slides, and massive collections of statistics purporting to imply the existence of thousands, and possibly millions, of advanced civilizations in this galaxy alone. It was a subject in which Gambini was intensely interested, and yet he'd voted against the proposal. When Leslie had asked why, he'd replied that he could not take mythical projections seriously. "All the numbers are predicated on the terrestrial experience," he'd complained. "As far as we know, Jehovah assembled us bag and baggage. No, if they're serious about the money, they'll have to give us a rational reason why." And later, while they'd sat in a small restaurant on Massachusetts Avenue, he'd added that, next time, if they asked him, he'd be glad to do the presentation for them.

"Yes," she replied. "I've eaten."

"This is Pete Wheeler," he said, indicating the man in the plaid shirt. Wheeler stood; she offered her hand. "And Cord Majeski."

The bearded young man nodded peripherally.

"I assume," Gambini said to her, "you'd like to know what this is about?"

Julie packed Monday night.

In the morning, Harry stayed home and ate breakfast with his son. Tommy was pleased to see him, and said so. But the boy, who knew only that he was going to visit his cousin for a while, slid rapidly into the sports section while Julie paced nervously through the house, trying to keep occupied. When it was time to leave for school, she pulled his jacket over his shoulders and handed him his plastic lunch pail.

"Tommy," she said, "I'm going to pick you up this afternoon. We'll be going to Ellen's for a while. Okay?"

"How about Daddy?" He looked around at Harry, and Julie paled.

"He's going to stay here," she said uncertainly.

They'd agreed on this approach last night; but somehow it sounded different now. "Tom," Harry broke in, determined to get it over, "your mother and I aren't going to be living together anymore."

"Damned fool," snapped Julie.

Tommy's eyes grew very round, and he looked from Harry to his mother. His cheeks reddened. "No!" he said.

Julie knelt beside him. "It'll be all right."

"No, it won't. You know it won't!" Harry felt proud of the boy. He hurled the plastic lunch box across the room. It bounced off the sofa, popped open, and the sandwich and Coke and cake spilled out. "No!" he screamed, tears welling out of his eyes. "Daddy, you wouldn't leave us!"

Harry wrapped the child in his arms. "It isn't exactly my choice, Tom," he said.

"Good," hissed Julie. "Blame it on me."

"Who the hell do you want me to blame?" Harry's voice was thick with rage.

Julie's eyes flared. But she looked toward Tommy and simmered quietly. The boy had buried his face in Harry's shirt and was sobbing uncontrollably. "So much for school," she said. "I think things would be easier if you went to work."

"By all means," he rasped, "let's not have any difficulties about this."

She tried to disengage Tommy, assuring him that he would still see his father frequently. But the child struggled hysterically to get back to Harry. She looked up at him, pleading silently for him to leave.

Harry glared at her, said good-bye to his son, an act that provoked a fresh scream, and walked out.

It was a little after nine-thirty when he arrived in the Hercules conference room and met Leslie Davies. She was slender and efficient in a gray business suit, with a classically chiseled jaw and brooding, distant eyes. "Leslie thinks," said Gambini after the introductions were complete, "that the aliens operate along logical parameters similar to our own."

"It never occurred to me," said Harry, "that there could be any doubt. What other logical parameters are there?"

"There are other possiblities," said the psychologist. "Logic will depend heavily on things like the range and quality of perceptions, the initial value system, and so on. But we need to wait a little: we don't have much yet to speculate with."

"Maybe wait a lot," offered Harry. "Majeski mentioned that the Altheans might be on a time scale different from ours."

"I don't think we need worry about that," she said. She was a slim, almost diminutive woman. Yet she commanded attention, and Harry eventually decided, since she was not particularly striking, that the attraction must lie in her seawater eyes, which seemed extraordinarily reflective of both mood and color. They were set wide apart and were enhanced to some degree by an expressive mouth and (when she chose to show them) strong white teeth. Her reddish brown hair was cut short, and her manner of speaking was pointed. She was, on the whole, an economical woman who seemed disinclined to waste either movement or words. "Their temporal sense can't be too much different from ours; I doubt that we'll have to wait the ten thousand years or so for additional events that some of you were concerned about—"

"How do we know that?" asked Harry.

"It's obvious," she said. "The signal itself demonstrates a capability to modulate extraordinary amounts of power in fractions of a second. There's other evidence as well: for example, that they switched off and on in a single morning. No, I think we're safe in concluding that, if there is to be a text transmission, we'll have it within a reasonably short time. Incidentally, I'd be willing to bet that the very nature of physical processes would prevent a being with a frame of reference appreciably slower than our own from ever achieving any sort of technological capacity."

"Would we be different in any major way," asked Harry, "if our skies were blank? If we had no stars, I mean. And a badly distorted sun?"

Her eyes settled on Harry; they were bright and good-humored now, as she warmed to her subject. "This project is going to produce a lot of unanswerable questions, and that's one of them, in this sense: we're finely attuned to our environment. Circadian rhythms, menstrual cycles, all sorts of physiological characteristics are tied in to lunar cycles, solar cycles, you name it. Furthermore, the visible tableau in the skies has always affected the way we think about ourselves, although, since everyone sees more or less the same astronomical show, we can't be sure about the details. We ally ourselves with sun-gods, and think of death as a retreat into the underworld.

"Look at the difference between Norse and classical mythology. In the Mediterranean, where the sun's warm and people can go for a dip whenever the mood hits them, the gods were, on the whole, a playful lot, mostly concerned with war-gaming and seductions. But Odin lived in a place like Montana, where a man went to work when it was dark and came home when it was dark. The result: not only a far more conservative pantheon in northern Europe, but one that is ultimately doomed. In the end, they face Ragnarok, the ultimate dissolution. Germany, where the winters are also bleak, had a similar fatalistic system.

"I'd never thought of it before in quite these terms, but I can't help wondering whether the Germans would have unleashed the two world wars had they been located along the Mediterranean."

Wheeler looked up. "The Arabs," he said, "live along the Mediterranean. And they've certainly shown no reluctance to spill blood."

"Their lands are hot, Pete," she replied. "And I think there's a special situation in the Middle East, too. Well, no matter. To answer Harry's question in a word: yes, certainly your aliens would be influenced by their peculiar environment, and I'd be willing to hazard a guess that the influence would not, from our point of view, be in a positive direction. But I don't think I'd care to go further than that."

"Incidentally, does anyone care to theorize why they are transmitting in the first place? Whoever sent the signal is a million years dead. Why did they do it? Presumably, it required an engineering feat of considerable magnitude, and there was no chance of a reply, and certainly no assurance of success. One wonders why they'd bother."

"Aren't you assuming the existence of organic life forms?" asked Majeski. "We could be listening to a computer of some sort. Something for which the passage of long gaps of time means nothing."

"I don't deal in computers," she said, smiling sweetly.

"Nevertheless," observed Gambini, "it's a possibility we'll have to consider. But let's get back to the question of motive."

"They're throwing a bottle into the ocean," said Harry. "The same way we did with the plaques we put on the early Pioneers and Voyagers."

"I agree," said Leslie. "In fact, unless we're dealing with something that is, in some way, not really subject to time—a computer, a race of immortals, whatever—I can imagine no other motive. They wanted us to know they were there. They would have been a species isolated beyond our imagination, with no hope of intercourse of any kind outside their own world. So they assembled a vast engineering project. And sent us a letter. What activity could be more uniquely human?"

In the long silence that followed, Pete Wheeler got the coffee pot and refilled the cups. "We don't have the letter yet," he said. "Cord, you dated the class G. What sort of result did you get?"

"I don't know," said Majeski. There was a strange expression on his face.

"You don't know? Was the lithium exhausted?"

"No, that wasn't the problem."

"I think I can explain," said Gambini. He opened a Manila envelope that lay on the table in front of him. "A class G star," he explained to Harry and Leslie, "uses up its supply of lithium as it gets older. So we can get a fairly decent idea of its age by looking at how much lithium remains." He extracted from the envelope several pages of trace paper with color bars and passed them around to Wheeler. "This is Gamma's spectrogram. We've run it several times, and it keeps coming up the same way."

Wheeler must have been surprised by what he saw: he leaned forward, straightened a crease in the sheets, and then spoke in subdued tones. "How long have you known about this?"

"We got the readouts the first night. Saturday. Sunday morning. Whatever. Then we checked the equipment and ran it again. We've relayed the test data to Kitt Peak." He raised his eyes significantly. "They came up with the same result."

"What is it?" asked Leslie.

"One of the problems we've had all along," said Gambini, "is to find a source for this system. The thing had to coalesce before being expelled from its parent galaxy; Altheis could not have formed by itself, in the void. And here we were, looking at three stars, which appear to have been out there for a longer time than the stars have been burning. So it was very difficult to account for their presence at all."

"And now," said Leslie, "you feel you have a solution?"

Wheeler was still staring at the spectrogram.

Gambini nodded. "We have an intriguing possibility."

Harry cleared his throat. "Could somebody explain to the rest of us what we're talking about?"

"This is an extremely atypical spectrogram for a class G," said Wheeler. "There are no metallic lines, not even H and K lines. No calcium, no iron, no titanium. No metals of any kind. Gamma appears to be pure helium and hydrogen. Which is why you couldn't date it, Cord. No lithium."

Majeski inclined his head, but said nothing.

Harry listened to the silence all around him. "I still don't think I know what it means," he said.

Gambini tapped a pen restlessly on the tabletop. "Class G's are Population I stars. They're metal-rich. Even Population II stars, which are not, have some metals boiling in the pot somewhere. But this one"—he held up a second set of spectrograms—"has none."

Harry noticed that all the color had gone out of Wheeler's face. "What's the point?" he asked.

The priest turned puzzled eyes toward him. "There's no such thing as a metal-free star," he said. "Ed, what about Alpha?"

"Same thing. Somehow, the original spectrogram was made and filed, and apparently no one ever looked at it. We got it out after *this* turned up. Neither one of those stars seems to have any metal at all."

MONITOR

CUBA DEMANDS RETURN OF GUANTANAMO
Claim Storage of Nukes Violates Lease

GUERRILLAS INCREASE PRESSURE ON THAIS
Bangkok Accuses Hanoi of Arming Insurgents

INDIAN MOB RIFLES SOVIET EMBASSY
Shipment of Russian Arms to Bangladesh Sparks Riot
Ambassador Gets Out Back Door;
Kremlin Demands Apology

BILL WOULD REQUIRE POLITICAL CANDIDATES
TO REVEAL RELIGIOUS VIEWS
"What Have You Got to Hide?" Asks Freeman

SOVIETS MAY HAVE A-BOMBS IN SPACE
London *Times* Report Denied by Kremlin

DOCTORS IN MEDICARE SCAM
Physicians in Seattle, Takoma Caught in FBI Sting

TULSA BRIDGE COLLAPSES DURING RUSH HOUR
Hundreds Feared Dead; Passed Inspection Last Month

GUNMAN KILLS SIX IN BAR
Goes Home for Shotgun after Ejection
Blames Spree on Full Moon

RIOTS IN BRAZZAVILLE

NRC RECOMMENDS BEEFING UP SECURITY
(Minneapolis Tribune)—In the wake of the near seizure of the
Plainfield nuclear power plant by a lone gunman last week,

the Nuclear Regulatory Commission has issued a new set of guidelines. . . .

KANSAS COED WINS MISS AMERICA
Aviation Major Hopes to be Commercial Pilot

__4__

RIMFORD WAS SCHEDULED to come into National on an afternoon flight.

Ed Gambini insisted on driving out to pick him up. Harry, who'd briefly met the celebrated cosmologist on several occasions but who'd never really had an opportunity to talk with him, went along. Despite his excitement, Gambini seemed reluctant to discuss the Althean transmission. Harry wondered whether he wasn't psyching himself to play the hard-nosed skeptic for his incoming guest. They engaged, instead, in some desultory conversation about the weather, their mutual dislike for Quint Rosenbloom, and the probability of a long season for the Redskins. But on the whole the two men rode south on the parkway locked in their own thoughts.

Harry was trying to come to grips with the fact that Julie was gone, and beside that hard piece of reality, the eccentric behavior of a trio of stars unimaginably far away seemed of little consequence. But it was a pleasant sort of early autumn afternoon when he could bring himself to look at it and absorb its texture, filled with hordes of kids in their big-shouldered armor on high school fields, and people standing over smoldering piles of leaves, and lovely women in short-sleeved jackets. It was the sort of afternoon to be out with a woman, strolling through tree-lined parks.

"Tell me about Gamma," he said. "Is it really possible that someone has altered it?"

The sun was bright on the surface of the Anacostia. They threaded their way between clean white government buildings, riding with the windows open. For a time, Harry thought Gambini had not heard. The physicist guided the black government car onto the Southeast Expressway. To their right, and ahead, the Capitol dome glittered. "Harry," he said over the rush of wind, "there's damned little that's impossible if you have the technology. I don't think you can travel faster than light, and I'm damned sure you can't go backward in time. At least not on the macroscopic level. But a little engineering with a star? Why not?

"The real question is not whether it *can* be done, but whether we're looking at a bona fide example of that kind of engineering. Stars always show metal lines in their spectrograms. *Always*. Maybe a lot, maybe a little, but a star without metal just doesn't happen in nature."

"As far as you know."

"As far as we know. But we know how stars form. This one's a Population I star, which is to say it's second generation. All class G's are. They're made up of the remnants of Population II stars, which manufactured a lot of iron and other metals. In fact, they manufactured most of the metal in the universe. When they explode, we get the makings of stars like the sun." He hesitated. "I can't imagine any natural process that would produce a Population I star without metal lines."

A battered green pickup roared past, doing about seventy-five.

"So someone removed the metals? Why?"

"That's the wrong question. Listen, Harry, nobody's going to go to the trouble of draining metal from a star. There'd be no point. I mean, my God, it doesn't improve the star, it's not as if it works better. And surely they weren't mining." His face twisted slightly, as though the sun were in his eyes, but it was off behind his shoulder. Harry decided that a decision was being made as to whether he could be trusted. "I'm not entirely sure how this will sound, but I'll tell you what I believe, the only thing I can think of that *does* make sense.

"Gamma is probably not a natural sun. I think it was built. Assembled."

"My God," gasped Harry.

"The metal serves no purpose, so they left it out."

"Ed, how the hell could anybody make a sun?"

"There's no physical law that precludes it. Obviously, or nature wouldn't be able to do it. All that's required is energy, and a lot of gas. Out where they are, there's a hell of a lot of free hydrogen and helium. All they'd have to do is get it together somewhere, and gravity would take care of the rest."

They crossed South Capitol Street. A long freight train was moving east on the Penn Central tracks, boxes and hoppers mostly, with a few empty flats. "And that," he continued, "raises another interesting possibility.

"X-ray pulsars are notoriously short-lived. They are the

mayflies of the cosmos: they blink on, last perhaps thirty thousand years or so, and blink off. The odds against finding one in the only free-floating system we've yet seen are extremely long." He winked at Harry. "Unless it's always there."

Harry watched the car's shadow racing along the guard rail. "You're suggesting," he said, "that they built the pulsar, too."

"Yes." Gambini's face was radiant. "I think they did."

The flight was almost an hour late. Normally, the delay would have angered Ed Gambini, but on that morning, no mundane frustration could reach him. He was meeting a giant, and because of the nature of the discovery at Goddard, Gambini realized that he, too, was on the threshold of joining the immortals. It was an exhilarating feeling.

Harry sensed all this. And he recognized the importance of the meeting with Rimford. The California cosmologist might well see other possibilities, suggest alternative explanations. If, however, he could not, Gambini's hand, and probably his confidence, would be greatly strengthened.

They waited at the cocktail lounge in the main terminal. Gambini sat nervously, toying with a drink, totally absorbed in his thoughts. Harry recalled the obsession of a year and a half earlier. He wondered whether Gambini might be another Percival Lowell, seeing canals that were visible to no one else.

They met Rimford, finally, in the security area. He was a man of ordinary appearance: his hair was whiter than it appeared on TV, and he dressed like a mildly successful midwestern businessman. Harry almost expected him to produce a card. But, like Leslie, he had eyes of compelling quality. They were subdued during those early moments of that first meeting; but Harry would later see them come to life. At such times, there was no confusing Baines Rimford with a hardware salesman. When Gambini solemnly introduced him, Harry caught the amused flicker of a smile in those eyes. Rimford's handshake was warm. "Nice of you to invite me, Ed," he said. "If you've really got something, I wouldn't want to miss it."

They walked down to the baggage pickup, while Gambini outlined the evidence to date.

"Marvelous," said Rimford when he'd finished, and, turning to Harry, he remarked that it was a wonderful time to be alive. "If you're right about this, Ed," he said, "nothing is ever again going to be the same." Despite the words, however, he looked perplexed.

"What's wrong?" asked Gambini, whose nerves were close to the surface.

"I was just thinking how unfortunate it is: they're so very far away. I think we all assumed that, when it came, *if* it came, there'd be at least some possibility of a two-way conversation." He threw his bags into the trunk and climbed into the front seat beside Gambini. Harry rode in back.

The visitor had a lot of questions. He asked about the various orbital periods of the Althean system's components, the characteristics of the pulsar, and the quality and nature of the incoming signal. Harry could not follow much of it, but his interest soared when they settled on the physical peculiarities of Alpha and Gamma. Gambini very carefully did not advance his thesis, but Rimford blinked at the spectrogram. From that moment, though he continued his questioning, he did not appear to be listening to the answers. For the most part, he sat staring pensively through the windshield, his eyes hooded.

By the time they reached Kenilworth Avenue, everyone had lapsed into silence.

Harry had never before paid much attention to the men and women who habitually ate alone at the Red Limit, Carioca's, or the William Tell. But now, installed in a dimly lit booth trying to read a newspaper, he was painfully aware of the blank expressions and drawn countenances that marked so many of them. Solitude is seldom voluntary, at least among the young. Yet here they were, the same people night after night, well-heeled derelicts, alone with their flickering candles and pressed linen napkins.

Harry was glad to see Pete Wheeler come in. He'd decided to eat at the Red Limit on the probability that somebody from the office, or from Operations, would appear. (He'd avoided coming right out and asking someone to join him for dinner, since that would have entailed explanations, and he did not feel capable of admitting to those who knew him that he'd lost his wife. Harry had been giving serious thought to how he would break the news around the office. They'd agreed it wasn't working anymore, that would be the approach to take. After all, there was some truth to it. Somewhere.) Wheeler saw him right away and came over.

"Well," he said, "I think we've impressed the Great Man."

"He came in impressed," said Harry.

"Gambini's making plans to take him out to his condo for the weekend. I'm not sure he isn't more excited at having Rimford call him by his first name than by all the rest of this business." He smiled. "You ever been there, Harry?"

"Once." Gambini had a place just off the Atlantic near Snow Hill, Maryland. He retired to it most weekends, and even occasionally for extended periods when the mood struck him and he felt his physical presence at Goddard was not necessary. The condo was tied in with the Space Center's communications and computer network, though his access to various systems was necessarily restricted. "Anything new with Hercules?"

"No," said Wheeler. "The signal just keeps repeating."

"What's so funny?"

"I'm not sure. Leslie, probably. Gambini's notion that we can bring in a psychologist to put the aliens on a couch. And he always derided the attempts of Drake and Sagan and the SETI people to create a statistical basis for estimating the possibilities of advanced civilizations in the galaxy, on the grounds that we were working from a single sample. He's not very consistent."

They ordered drinks and steaks, and Harry settled back comfortably, his fingers entwined behind his head. "Are they out there, Pete? Aliens, I mean. You looked convinced the other day."

"By the spectrograms? Actually, Harry, if it had been anybody but Gambini, I think I'd have been persuaded right from the beginning. The evidence is hard to argue against. It's the concept that's difficult to buy. Especially when you consider that Gambini wanted so badly to find something like this. That alone makes everything suspicious. He makes himself extremely difficult to agree with."

"But despite all that, you think we *do* have some sort of civilization in the Althean system?"

"Yes. I think we do. And I suspect Rimford is telling Gambini that right about now. We're all headed for the history books, Harry."

"All of us?" Harry laughed. "Who was Columbus's first mate?" He felt a sudden surge of elation and noticed that some nearby people were watching him curiously. It didn't matter, though. He refilled his wineglass and poured the rest of the wine into Wheeler's empty goblet.

Wheeler drank up and leaned toward Harry, still smiling.

"I can't help thinking," he said, "that we're bound to get some surprises out of this. Gambini thinks he has everything under control, but there are too many unknowns here."

"How do you mean?"

"We keep assuming they're like us. For example, everybody's waiting for the follow-up message. But the Altheans have announced their presence. They may not see any reason to go further. After all, what have *they* to gain?"

"Jesus," said Harry. "I never thought about that."

Pete's eyes were bright with mischief. "It could happen. It's really a pretty funny picture, in which our people get old waiting for the rest of a transmission that's already complete. Can you imagine what that would do to Ed and Majeski?"

"You're vindictive, Pete," Harry said in a light tone, though he was nevertheless uncomfortable at Wheeler's reaction. "It would kill Gambini."

"Yes, I suppose it would. And I think that says a great deal about what Ed's done to himself." He looked at the glass. "The wine's good," he observed. "There are other possibilities. We tend to assume that any transmission will contain a lot of technological material. They're going to tell us how to capture one hundred percent of the sun's energy. Stuff like that. I was listening to a conversation between Ed and Rimford this afternoon. They're talking in terms of Grand Unified Theories. But this is a species that has had technology of a high order for a long time. They may take it pretty much for granted that everybody already knows the technical stuff; or they may think it's too trivial to bother with. If we *do* get a textual transmission, a second message, I'd be surprised if they don't send us something entirely different from what we expect. Something they're proud of, but which might not amuse Gambini."

"For example?"

Wheeler's dark eyes glittered in the candlelight. More than the others, for whom cosmology and astronomy were primarily mathematical disciplines, he had the appearance of a man who understood what a light-year really was. "How about a novel?" he suggested. "A clash on a cosmic stage between creatures of advanced philosophies and alien emotions. Perhaps they would consider it their ultimate achievement and wish to share it with the universe at large. Can you imagine NASA's reaction to that?

"Or maybe it will be a symphony."

Harry emptied his glass. "As long as it doesn't sound like

'Chopsticks.' But you don't really believe anything like that's going to happen?"

"Hell, Harry. Anything's possible in this kind of situation. We have no previous experience; and the senders can expect nothing in return save the satisfaction of having put out a signal. You mentioned the plaques on the Pioneers and Voyagers. We didn't, of course, have room to say much, but even if we had, I'm sure it would never have occurred to anyone to put in the instructions for, say, splitting the atom, in case some fossil-powered civilization happened on it. No. It may well be that we've already received the only significant message that will be coming: that they're there. If there's more, I hope we have the sense to recognize it for what it is, and extract whatever profit is to be had, without reviling the sender."

The steaks were good, and the plates were heaped with wedge fries and toasted rolls. "There's too much," Harry said over his coffee.

"Are you working late tonight?" asked Wheeler, probably wondering why Harry wasn't eating at home.

"No." The word trailed off uncomfortably. Harry had known Pete Wheeler longer than he'd known Gambini, but the relationship had always been at long range. Now he looked across the table, tempted again to take advantage of the opening and say something to someone about Julie. But how many pathetic stories had Wheeler been forced to digest over the years simply because he was a priest? "I gave the cook the night off," he said.

But Wheeler must have read the truth in his tone. He gazed carefully at Harry. Harry moved his dinner around. "You can do me a favor," the priest said, finally. "I'm going out to Carthage for the evening. I'll be back tomorrow about noon." He wrote down a number and passed it across the table. "Call me if anything changes. Okay?"

"Sure."

They got the check, split it, and walked outside. "How's Julie?" Wheeler asked casually.

Harry was surprised. "I didn't think you'd ever met her."

"She was at one of the Director's brunches a couple of years ago." Wheeler looked toward the west and checked his watch. The moon had begun its drift toward the horizon. "The comet's gone."

Harry grunted something; neither of them was sure what.

"She's a hard woman to forget," Wheeler added.

"Thanks," mumbled Harry. They crunched through the gravel toward Wheeler's car, a late-model beige Saxon. "We're having a little trouble right now."

"I'm sorry to hear it."

Harry shrugged.

Wheeler looked around. "I don't see your car."

"It's at the front gate. I walked over."

"Come on," he said. "I'll take you back."

They pulled out of the parking area, crossed Greenbelt Road, and swung onto the lot at the main entrance beside Harry's Chrysler. "You got a few minutes to listen?" Harry asked.

"If you want to talk," said Wheeler.

He described the dinner with Julie, with its melancholy result and her subsequent departure. He concealed (or attempted to) his indignation, but made no effort to hide his inability to understand her actions. When he'd finished, he folded his arms defensively. "You must have a lot of experience with this sort of thing, Pete. What's the chance that it'll blow over?"

"I'm not sure how experienced I am," said Wheeler. "As a rule, Norbertines don't do much parish work, which is, of course, where you run into domestic problems. I haven't done *any*. But I can recommend a good counselor, if you like. You're not a Catholic, are you, Harry?"

"No."

"Doesn't matter. I can do that, or I can tell you what the consensus is on this sort of problem, how it happens, and the course of action that's usually prescribed."

"Go ahead," said Harry.

"From what you've told me, there's no second man, there's no strain over money, no heavy drinking, and no one's being assaulted regularly. Usually, when there's no obvious cause in a marriage that's been going reasonably well for a number of years, what's happened is that the two people have stopped sharing a single life; each has slipped into an orbit of his own, and the two probably don't converge much, except at meals and bedtime. The people involved may not even be aware of it, but the marriage becomes a bore, for one or both.

"You're near the top of your profession, Harry. How many nights a week do you work?"

"Two or three," said Harry, uncomfortable at the turn things had taken.

"How about weekends?"

"About one a month."

"Only one?"

"Well, actually I work part of almost every weekend." Harry squirmed. "But my job demands it. It's not a nine-to-five kind of thing."

"Chances are," continued the priest, unruffled, "that, when you *are* home, you don't have much time for her either."

Harry thought about it. "No," he said. "I don't think that's true. We go out on a fairly regular basis, to movies and the theater and occasionally to local clubs."

"You'd know better than I," said Wheeler.

"This kind of thing happens often? I mean, between people who've been married awhile? I thought once you got past the first couple of years you were reasonably safe."

"It happens all the time."

"What can I do?" asked Harry. "I don't think she's going to be open to small talk just now."

Wheeler nodded. "Harry, marriages are hard to salvage once they go bad. I'm sorry to tell you that. I only met your wife once, but she struck me as a woman who doesn't act hastily. If that's true, she'll be hard to recover. But I think you can make the effort.

"I'd try to get her away from all the old associations, take her somewhere for a couple of days just to talk things over. Make it as nonthreatening as you can, but get her to a location where there are no distractions and where neither of you has ever been before. And then talk with her. Not about the marriage or your job or your other problems. Just try to take it from the start. You and her."

"It would never work," said Harry quietly. "Not now."

"That's certainly true, if you've decided it's true. Still, you've nothing to lose. I can even offer you the ideal location."

"The Norbertines are in the motel business?" offered Harry.

"As it happens," said Wheeler, "we have a novitiate near Basil Point on Chesapeake Bay. It was donated to us a few years ago, but the truth is that it's of no practical use. It's too big. The property's in a magnificent location, with a lovely view of the bay. I usually make it a point to go out there when I'm in the Washington area. There are only about half a dozen of our people there now. One of them, by the way, is Rene Sunderland, who's probably the best bridge player in the state.

"It has a couple of big houses that we've turned into an abbey and a seminary. But the seminary only has two students. Back in the fifties, the owners added a lodge. We keep it available for visiting dignitaries, but we just don't see many of those. The only ones we ever get are the abbott and the director of the National Confraternity of Christian Doctrine, both of whom like to play bridge with Rene. That means they stay in the main building, and the lodge has been unused for about four years. I'm sure I could have it made available for a good cause."

Harry thought it over. Maybe that was what he should have tried Saturday night instead of the goddam poverty-stricken play in Bellwether. But now it was a bit late. "Thanks, Pete," he said. "I'll keep it in mind."

Usually Wheeler enjoyed the two-hour drive to Carthage. But that evening, he crossed a barren landscape of skeletal trees and long brown grass and flat gray slate—covered hills. There was a sense of decay in the motionless air, as though *this* Route 50 had detoured through time and curved back now on a Virginia grown ancient.

The highway weaved and dipped through bleak furrowed pastures, past abandoned tractors and combines. Clapboard farmhouses stood empty and dark. Occasional junk cars, their engines and carburetors spread on wooden boards or hung from trees, were sunk hubcap-deep in dust and dried mud alongside decaying barns.

Out near Middleburg, he turned on a talk show. He paid no attention to it, but the sound of voices was soothing.

It wasn't Harry's problem that bothered him. There was something else, something deeper, connected not with one more marriage gone to ruin, but with the thing in Hercules. The constellation was invisible at the moment, hidden by a few drifting clouds. Ahead of him, toward Carthage, the sky was heavy and dark, lit by occasional lightning.

It was a familiar, if ominous, cloudscape. In recent years, Wheeler had come to love the familiar and the nearby, to cherish things that one could touch, or know directly, stone and sand and rain and polished mahogany. As the telescopes he used reached ever farther into the night, the things of Earth drew him back, and he wondered whether they wouldn't all be better off if the gathering storm could drown the Hercules signal.

Just past Interstate 81, the windshield began to pick up spray.

It was almost eleven o'clock when he arrived, under a steady drizzle, in Carthage. Saint Catherine's tower, with its big gray cross, rose out of the center of the commercial district. He swung behind the church into a parking lot closed off by an iron fence. A cruising police car paused, watched him get out, and continued on.

The rectory was a two-story flat brick building. A light burned at the rear, over a door slick with rain. As he approached, the door opened, and Jack Peoples hurried outside, bundled against the weather.

Peoples never seemed to change much. He was moderately overweight now, had added a few pounds since the last time Wheeler had seen him. But his hair was still black, and he still seemed capable of enthusiasm, inspired by the right cause. (There had been few enough of those in recent years, given the continuing backward drift of the Church toward the nineteenth century.)

Had things gone differently for him, Wheeler supposed, had Peoples not been born into an old-line Catholic family which had traditionally sent most of its sons into the priesthood (though, from his generation, only Jack had obeyed the call), he might have been a moderately successful accountant or computer technician. He had talent in those directions. "Hello, Pete," he said, taking Wheeler's bag. "Good to see you again." He glanced up past the bell tower. "We're going to get a bad night."

Peoples looked tired. In fact, he always looked tired lately. Jack had been one of those young priests who'd jumped on the Vatican II bandwagon, who'd worn themselves out offering relevance to sex-ridden adolescents, and guitar masses to weary parents. He'd been one of the first to tear out the kneeling benches, but the Community of God had never really arrived. In the end, the parishioners who were to find joy and peace in one another went back to worrying about careers and mortgages in their own hermetically sealed lives, leaving Jack Peoples, and others like him, buried in the wreckage.

They'd met twenty years before in a speech seminar, and had traded visits back and forth ever since. The older priest was a fountain of Church lore and gossip, wryly dispensed with a wit that would have got him in trouble with the Cardinal, had some of the stories got back.

Wheeler's visit had a formal purpose: Peoples had become pastor at Saint Catherine's, effective the previous Sunday. The appointment had been long overdue; Jack had been the only priest there for three years.

Wheeler went up to his room (the same one was always prepared for him when he came to Saint Catherine's), showered, and returned to the pastor's office.

Peoples put down a book and broke out some apple brandy. "How's the program going at Georgetown?" he asked.

"I got a break," Wheeler said. "I don't know whether I told you or not, but the course is a survey of Rimford's work. And Rimford just turned up in town. I think I can get him to come out to the school for an evening."

They whiled much of the night away discussing Church politics. Peoples, who had left the Norbertines early in his career to become a diocesan priest, tended to attach considerable importance to the ecclesiastical decision-making process, as though it had a serious effect on world affairs. For Wheeler, whose perspective had been altered by his visits to the cosmic gulfs, the Church's power structure had acquired a ghostlike ambience.

Abruptly, somewhere around 2:00 A.M., when a second bottle stood empty on an end table, Wheeler realized that he wanted to talk about Hercules. There'd been a lull in the conversation, and Peoples had gone out through glass doors to put some coffee on. Like the adjoining church, the rectory had been built near the end of the nineteenth century. Its delicately carved balusters, hanging lights, and glass-enclosed bookshelves were meticulously maintained. Numerous volumes of standard theological works were packed into the wall behind the pastor's desk, along with books on church finance, several collections of sermons, and a handful of Dickens novels that someone had donated and that Peoples kept prominently on display. "For my retirement," he always told curious visitors.

Wheeler followed Peoples into the kitchen. He was filling a plate with Danish pastries. "Jack," he said, "something's been happening at Goddard. Actually, it's the reason Rimford's in D.C."

He outlined the events of the past week. Peoples, who often served as a sounding board against which Wheeler bounced various speculative, and often farfetched, notions, composed himself to listen. It was a role he'd come to relish, and with it the implied compliment to a parish priest who was thoroughly grounded in Thomas Aquinas and little else. This time, however, the usual array of obscure concepts was missing. The fact of the artificial signal stood out stark and gray in the early morning hours.

Wheeler concluded with his own opinion that they had indeed heard from another species. "Probably dead and gone by now, all of them. But nonetheless, long before we put the first bricks into Babylon, they were out there."

In the silence that followed, the electric clock atop the refrigerator got very loud. Peoples stirred his coffee. "When are they going to announce it? Was it on the news tonight?"

Wheeler tasted the Danish. "They're holding on as long as they can. No one wants to take a chance on the organization looking silly. So there'll be nothing official until there's no question what the signal means."

"Is there a question?"

"In my opinion, no." They gathered the refreshments and wandered back toward Peoples's office.

"I wonder if it'll have much effect outside." The pastor was referring to the world beyond the church doors. "It's hard to guess how people will react to something like that."

"My God, Jack, how can it help but have an effect? It attacks the foundations of the whole Christian position!"

"Oh, I don't think so. The Church has known for a long time that something like this would come. We're prepared."

"Really? In what way?"

"Pete, we've maintained for two thousand years that the universe was created by an infinite God. What does it matter to us that He's made other worlds besides ours?"

Wheeler sat thoughtfully staring at the leather-bound theology books. "For whom did Jesus die?" he asked idly.

Peoples kicked off his shoes. This was the kind of conversation he loved, although he would never have allowed any but a handful of his colleagues to engage him in such a debate, which might conceivably weaken a lesser faith than his. "For the children of Adam," he said cautiously. "Other groups will have to make their own arrangements."

"I wonder if the Altheans retained their innocence."

"You mean that they might never have fallen? No original sin? I doubt it?"

"Why?"

Peoples shook his head. "It just seems unlikely."

"You're suggesting God stacks the cards."

Peoples sighed. "Okay," he said. "It's possible."

"Do you think we'll be segregated? The fallen species from the creatures who retained their preternatural state?"

"It looks to me as if we're already pretty well segregated."

"Jack, to be honest with you, I find this business uncomfortable. I was convinced, I've always believed, that we were alone. There are probably *billions* of terrestrial worlds out there.

Once admit a second creation and where do you stop? Surely, among all those stars, there is a third. And a millionth. Where does it end?"

"So what? God is infinite. Maybe we're about to find out what that really means."

"Maybe," said Wheeler. "But we're also conditioned to think of the Crucifixion as the central event of history. The supreme sacrifice, offered by God Himself in His love for the creature He'd made in His image."

"And—?"

"How can we take seriously the agony of a God who repeats His passion? Who dies again and again, in endless variations, on countless worlds, across a universe that may well itself be infinite?"

After an exhausted Peoples had gone to bed, shortly before dawn, Wheeler roamed through the rectory, examining stained windows, thumbing through books, and, for a while, standing just outside the front door. The wet street glistened in the reflection from a Rexall drugstore.

The church was built in a style that Wheeler thought of as Ohio Gothic—squat, urban, rectangular, brick. Its windows were populated by lambs and doves and kneeling women. The rectory stood at right angles to the larger structure. Between the two buildings lay a fenced-off grass plot. The tomb of an early pastor lay in the center, marked by a rough-hewn stone cross.

The clouds had begun to clear, and a handful of stars floated over the church tower. The sky to the east beyond the warehouses had begun to lighten.

Why is the creation so large? SKYNET looks out almost sixteen billion light-years, to the Red Limit, to the edge of the visible universe. But it is an "edge" only in the sense that there has not been time for light coming from even more remote places to reach Earth. There's every reason to believe than an observer placed at the Red Limit would see much the same sort of sky that bends over Virginia. In a sense, Wheeler thought, Saint Catherine's itself, at this moment, is at the edge of someone's visible universe.

Wheeler turned back inside, locked the door, and wandered through the connecting corridor into the church and through the sacristy, from which he emerged near the pulpit.

The glow of the sanctuary lamp fell across long rows of

pews. Security lights in the rear illuminated holy water fonts and the stations of the cross. He could still see the worn places in the marble floor where the statues had been, back in the days of the Tridentine mass. The old marble altar, of course, had also been long since removed and replaced with the modern butcher block that clashed with decor and architecture in all but the relatively new churches.

He came outside the altar rail, genuflected, and sat down in the front pew.

The air was heavy, filled with the sickly sweet smell of melted wax. High behind the altar, in a circular stained window, Jesus sat serenely by a running brook.

He was remote now, a painted figure, a friend from childhood. As a boy, Wheeler had occasionally, in the exuberant presumption of youth, asked for a sign, not to confirm his faith but as a mark of special favor. But Christ had remained inanimate then, as now. Who, or what, had walked along the Jordan with the Twelve? Too many times, Wheeler thought, I have looked through the telescopes. And I have seen only rock and the light-years.

Ah, Lord, if I doubt You, it is perhaps because You hide Yourself so well.

At about the same time, in the operations center, Linda Barrister was filling in the solutions to a crossword puzzle. She was good at them, and they helped keep her reasonably alert when her body ached for sleep. She was trying to recall the name of a Russian river with seven letters when she was suddenly aware that something had changed. She checked her watch. It was precisely 4:30 A.M.

The auxiliary overhead monitor carrying the TDRSS relay from Hercules X-3 was silent. The signal had stopped.

WHERE IS EVERYONE?

Recently, Edward Gambini of NASA spoke to the annual Astronomical Symposium at the University of Minnesota, supposedly on the subject of the interior mechanics of class K stars. During his remarks, he addressed himself to the question of stable biozones, the probable time periods necessary for the development of a living planet, and finally (or inevitably, if we can accept his logic), the appearance of a technological civilization.

I am somewhat puzzled as to the connection between science fiction and the mechanics of class K stars. It seems, these days, that no matter where Dr. Gambini goes, regardless of his proposed subject matter, he ends up talking about extraterrestrial aliens. Two weeks prior to the Minnesota exercise, he was in New York to speak at a meeting of Scientists Concerned about Nuclear Weapons, presumably to discuss a strategy for peace. What the Concerned Scientists got was a plea that we restrain ourselves so that we can ultimately join the "galactic society" we will one day uncover.

I can think of more pressing reasons to halt the arms race.

The fact is that anyone who invites Dr. Gambini to speak on anything can expect to hear about aliens.

If all this strikes you as a trifle odd, it becomes almost grotesque when you realize that SKYNET, to which Dr. Gambini has access, has looked rather closely at planetary systems within a hundred light-years or so and found nothing that supports the notion that anything may be alive out there.

Many people have argued compellingly that this result implies that we are indeed alone in the universe. It is a position with which any reasonable man would be hard-pressed to argue.

There is an even more telling point to be made. Surely, if civilizations were to develop with any sort of regularity, the Milky Way would, after these last several billion years, be overrun with them. There would be tourists and exporters everywhere!

Even *one* civilization, using relatively unsophisticated vehicles for interstellar travel, the sort of vessel that we should ourselves be able to build in another century or so, would by now have filled every habitable world in the Milky Way and points south. So if they're there, why haven't we seen them?

Where is everybody?

—Michael Pappadopoulis
The Philosophical Review, XXXVII, 6

_5_

HARRY HAD NEVER known a colder October in Washington. The sky turned white, and drizzly knife-edged winds sliced through the bone. Temperatures dropped below freezing on the first of the month, and stayed there. He was, of course, delighted: the assorted pollen that sometimes hung on until nearly Christmas was damped down, and he could count on seven months before the cottonwood and poplar would open another round.

That was also the month Harry conceded his son. He could see no way to provide a home for the boy without Julie. And the fact humiliated him because he knew Tommy expected his father to put up more of a fight.

He was playing in a bantam basketball league with other third and fourth graders. Harry showed up when he could, sitting on the gym floor beside an uncomfortable Julie. The boy played well, and Harry was proud. But there were always tears at the end, and eventually Julie suggested that they work out a schedule to ensure that both parents weren't there at the same time, since things seemed to go better that way.

Harry reluctantly agreed.

At home, the gas heater didn't sound healthy. It banged and hammered and threw loose parts around. He called the service contractor, who cleaned it, charged sixty-five dollars, and went away. After that, the thing stopped working altogether.

Hercules X-3 remained silent, and hope faded that the transmission would be followed swiftly by a second signal. Toward the end of the month, Wheeler's suspicion that the aliens might, indeed, have nothing more to say became common currency. But silence, Gambini argued, is not the natural state of a pulsar.

So they continued to listen.

The second Thursday of November was a bleak, wintry day that clawed the last of the leaves out of the elms behind the Business Operations Section. Rosenbloom showed up unannounced and summoned Harry and Gambini to the Director's suite, which he used on the rare occasions when he was at

Goddard. "I think both your careers," he said, "are about to take off. The President will be making a statement tomorrow afternoon from the White House. He'd like both of you to be there. Three o'clock."

Since Rosenbloom spent so little time at Goddard, the Director's suite smelled of furniture polish rather than cigars. He lit up and slid into a chair beneath a charcoal of Stonehenge. "Ed," he said, "you'll probably be asked to say a few words. The reporters will damn well want to talk to you in any case. You might think about what you're going to say. I suggest you try to come up with some immediate benefits we've gotten out of the Hercules contact or out of the technology we've used. Probably there'll be some peripherals into laser surgery or fiber optics or something. You know, the same way we handled the space program. Look into it." His elation was mixed with a trace of wariness. "Under no circumstances do we want to speculate about another signal. I would like to take the tack that we've intercepted evidence of engineering on a large scale very far away. You cannot overemphasize the distance. We should leave the impression that it's over, and we now know we're not alone. And let it go at that. Tell them anything else is speculation."

"What's the President going to say?" asked Gambini. His mouth was set in an angry line.

"'What hath God wrought?' Same old thing. Even as we speak, I understand he has his people hunting for appropriate biblical remarks."

Gambini laced his fingers across his stomach. "It should be an uplifting show. But if it's all the same to you, Quint, I think I'll pass on this one. For one thing, I'm not exactly proud of the fact that we kept this quiet, what is it now, two months? Some people out there are going to be very unhappy with us, and I'd just as soon not be too visible."

Rosenbloom smothered his first impulse and displayed instead an expression of tolerance. "I understand your feelings, Ed. Nevertheless, it isn't an invitation we're free to decline." He turned to Harry, as though it were settled. "I don't think they'll want you to do any more than take a bow. But you'll have reporters to deal with too, Harry."

"I'm an administrator. They won't expect technical stuff from me."

"Newspaper guys can't read. They'll know you're with the

Agency, and that's all they'll need. Same guidelines as Ed's, okay? No speculation. By the way, I'd just as soon we not bring up this artificial sun business. Let's go for lots of talk about the enormous distance between them and us. Maybe you could come up with one of those illustrations where Earth is an orange, and the aliens are over in Europe somewhere. Or on the moon. Okay?"

"Somebody," said Harry, "is going to wonder why we waited so long to make this public. What's our answer?"

"Tell them the truth. We literally did not believe our instruments. We wanted to be sure before we said anything. Nobody can object to that."

"In that case," said Gambini, *"you* stand out there."

"I intend to."

After they'd left the Director's office, Gambini grumbled loudly about his proposed role in the press conference. "Play it for all it's worth," advised Harry. "You're going to take a lot of heat: you might as well get some benefit out of it. In the meantime, let's hope nobody discovers some sort of musical star that transmits exponentials."

Leslie Davies came in from Philadelphia that afternoon. She seemed more intrigued by events than some of the investigators, and admitted to Harry that she took every excuse she could find to visit the Hercules Project. "Things are going to happen here, Harry," she told him expectantly. "Ed's right: if something weren't on its way, the pulsar would be back to normal."

She invited him to dinner, and Harry gratefully accepted. The only other staff members who regularly ate alone were Wheeler and Gambini. But the priest was back at Princeton, and Gambini showed little inclination for company.

At Harry's suggestion, they skipped the Red Limit and drove instead to the Coachman in College Park, which offered a more exotic atmosphere. "Leslie," he said, after they were settled at a table, "I don't really understand why you're so interested in all this. I wouldn't think a psychologist would care much one way or the other."

"Why not?" she asked, eyebrows rising.

"It's not your field."

She smiled: it was a deep-water response, reserved, noncommittal, amused. "Whose field is it?" When Harry didn't answer, she continued: "I'm not sure that any of these people have the potential for profit I do. For Ed and Pete Wheeler and the rest, the whole project is only of philosophical interest. I shouldn't have said 'only,' I suppose, because I'm as involved philosophically as anyone.

"But I may be the only person here with a professional stake. Listen, if there *are* Altheans, they can be of only academic interest to an astronomer or a mathematician. Their specialties have no direct connection to the issue of thinking beings. That's *my* province, Harry. If there *is* a second transmission, if we get anything at all that we can read, I'll get the first glimpse into a nonhuman psyche. Do you have any idea what that means?"

"No," said Harry. "I haven't a clue."

"Maybe more important than learning about Altheans: we might get a handle on qualities that are characteristic of intelligent beings, as opposed to those that are culturally induced. For example, will the Altheans turn out to be a hunting species? Will they have a code of ethics? Will they organize themselves into large political groups?" She tilted her head slightly. "Well, I guess we've already answered that one. Without political organization, you wouldn't get large-scale engineering projects. In the end, we may not learn a lot about the Altheans, but we stand to learn a lot about ourselves."

Harry had gotten into the noxious habit of comparing with Julie every woman with whom he came in contact. Although Leslie was not unattractive, she lacked the native sensuality of his wife. It was not, he realized, simply a matter of putting an ordinary human being against Julie's classic features. There was also the fact that Leslie was more accessible. Friendlier. And, oddly, that, too, counted against her. What sort of comment was *that* on the perversity of human nature? "Did you know," he asked, "that the White House is going to make an announcement tomorrow?"

"Ed told me. I'm going to plant myself in a bar in Arlington and take notes on the customers' reactions."

"Leslie, if they were going to send another signal, why would they wait so long?"

She shrugged. "Maybe we're only listening to a computer, and the tape reader's burned out. I'll tell you one thing: if we don't get another signal, you're going to have a real problem with Ed." She finished her manhattan. "How about another round of drinks?"

Harry signaled the waiter.

"How well do you know Ed?" she asked.

"I've worked with him a long time."

"He lives in heart attack country. Doesn't he do anything other than look through telescopes?"

Harry shook his head. "I don't think so. Years ago, when I first met him, he used to go to Canada on hunting trips. But he got bored with them after a while. Actually, it's pretty hard to imagine him in a bowling alley or on a golf course."

"It's very sad," she said, her eyes growing distant. "He's so obsessed with trying to analyze the inner machinery of the cosmos that he never sees a sunrise. Rimford's not like that. Nor Pete. I wish he'd learn something from them."

Neither Harry nor Gambini had previously been to the White House on business. (In fact, Gambini freely admitted that, despite having lived a substantial portion of his adult life in Washington, he'd never before been inside the building.) They entered, as instructed, through a connecting tunnel from the Treasury Department and were escorted to an office, where they found Rosenbloom and a self-important, energetic man whom Harry recognized as Abraham Chilton, the administration's press officer.

Chilton had been a highly popular conservative radio and TV commentator before joining the administration. He had a voice like a whip crack and a debater's skill that served him well in his periodic jousts with the press. He looked pointedly at his watch as Gambini and Harry entered. "I'd appreciate it if you gentlemen could get here on time in the future."

"We were told three o'clock," objected Gambini.

"The press conference starts at three. *We* start, or try to, at two." Rosenbloom looked uncomfortable. "Who's Gambini?"

The physicist nodded frostily.

"The President will ask you to say a few words." He reached into a briefcase and withdrew a single sheet of paper. "We'd like it to be along these lines. Try to sound spontaneous." He threw Harry off stride with a sudden laconic grin that suggested no one should take any of this too seriously. But as quickly as Harry defined the sense of the gesture, it was gone.

"The three of you will be seated in the front row when the President enters. He'll make a statement. Then he'll introduce each of you and invite you two to the podium." He indicated Rosenbloom and Gambini. "Dr. Gambini, you'll speak and then go back to your seat. After that the President will take questions. We'll close it out after thirty minutes. When Ed

Young asks his question, that'll be it. Young is a little guy with
blond hair, except that most of it is gone now. He'll be sitting
right behind Dr. Rosenbloom. After the President leaves, you
gentlemen will find yourselves subject to a barrage of questions.
We'd debated getting you right out of here to save you that,
but there's no point: they'll catch up with you wherever you
go, so we might as well get it over with. Anything unclear so
far? Okay. We don't have much time left. Let's go over what
the reporters are likely to ask."

President John W. Hurley strode smiling through the curtains
and took his place behind the lectern that bore his seal. A flip
chart was set to his immediate right. He was of less than average
height, the shortest President in modern memory, and consequently a running target for "short" jokes. Cartoonists loved
to portray him talking things over with Washington, Lincoln,
or Wilson. But he responded in good humor, laughed at the
jokes himself, and even told a few. His lack of stature, usually
a fatal handicap to serious political ambitions, became a symbol
of the man in the street. Hurley was the President everyone
identified with.

Approximately two hundred people were packed into the
small auditorium. Television dollies rolled up and down the
central aisle as the President graciously acknowledged the applause, looked squarely down at Harry in the front row, and
smiled. "Ladies and gentlemen," he said, "I know you've all
seen the numbers on the economy that came out today, and
you expect me to do a little crowing this afternoon. Truth is,
I don't intend to mention the subject." Laughter rippled through
the room. The fact was that, while the President's point of view
generally tended to be well to the right of most of the members
of the press corps, he was nevertheless popular with them.

He looked down at his audience with sudden gravity. One
of the television cameras edged in. "Ladies and gentlemen, I
have an announcement of importance." He paused and looked
directly ahead into the cameras. "On Sunday morning, September seventeenth, shortly before dawn, the United States
intercepted a signal of extraterrestrial origin." Harry, who knew
what was coming, of course, was struck by the sudden absolute
stillness in the crowded room. "The transmission originated
from a small group of stars outside our own galaxy. They are
located in the constellation Hercules and are, I am told, extremely far from Earth, far too distant to permit any possibility

of a two-way conversation. NASA estimates that the signals started on their way toward us a million and a half years ago."

Chairs scraped, but still, except for some startled exclamations, the press corps held its collective breath.

"There was no message: the transmission was simply a mathematical progression that apparently leaves itself open to no other interpretation.

"I should take a moment, by the way, to point out that this achievement would not have been possible without SKYNET.

"We are continuing to monitor the star group, but it has been silent now for several weeks, and we don't expect to hear any more." He paused; when he spoke again, his voice was laden with emotion. "We know nothing, really, about those who have announced their presence to us. We cannot hope ever to talk with them. I have been given to understand that their star group is receding from us at a rate of approximately eighty miles per second.

"It's unfortunate that these . . . beings . . . did not see fit to tell us something about themselves. But they have told us something about the universe in which we live. We now know we are not alone."

Still no one moved. One of the TV technicians, riding on the back of a dolly, briefly lost his balance. "Two of the men responsible for the discovery are here," the President continued. "I'd like them to join me now to help answer any technical questions you may have: Dr. Quinton Rosenbloom, Director of the Space Flight Center at Goddard, and Dr. Ed Gambini, who led the research team." Someone began to clap, and that broke the spell. The room erupted into thunderous applause. Harry, who'd expected to be recognized with the others, was both relieved and disappointed at being overlooked.

Rosenbloom tossed back the first page of the flip chart and delivered a quick course in pulsars, using a series of illustrations assembled that afternoon under Harry's direction. He described the Altheis system, discussed the distances involved, and, somewhat clumsily, compared the incident to ships passing in the night.

Gambini briefly recounted his reaction on the first evening. He stayed within the parameters set for him by the White House, but he was clearly angered. It had been, he said, a near religious experience: to realize that there was someone out there. "The mind that sent the Hercules transmission," he said, "recognized that no habitable world could exist within less than a million light-years. And so it needed a transmitter of incredible power. It used a star."

When he had finished, they took questions.

A political columnist for the *Washington Post*, referring to Beta, asked how an object only a few kilometers in diameter could have such a destructive effect on a star so much larger than the sun. Gambini tried to describe its density, and the President, demonstrating his touch for the picturesque, suggested that the newsmen think of it as an iron sun. "Yes," observed Gambini appreciatively. "Though iron would never do that thing justice. A matchbox full of the stuff would weigh more than North America."

A reporter from the *Wall Street Journal:* "If the signal took a million and a half years to get here, they must all be dead. Anybody want to comment on that?"

Rosenbloom gave it as his opinion that the Altheans, by this time, were undoubtedly gone.

Someone wondered whether it was possible that any of the aliens, in the distant past, might have visited Earth?

"No," said Gambini, who could not conceal the fact that he found the question entertaining. "I think we can say with confidence that they've never been much closer than they are now."

"Then there's no military threat?" That came from the *Chicago Tribune*'s representative.

The President laughed and reassured the world.

"Do we have any idea what they look like?"

"Do they have a name?"

"Where are they going now?" That last was from an ABC correspondent, a young black woman with a dazzling smile. "And isn't Alpha a prime candidate to explode?"

Gambini was impressed. "They're headed toward the globular cluster NGC6341, but it won't be there when they get there." To answer the second part of the question, he began a discussion of H-R diagrams and stellar evolution which the President broke into, gently, explaining that Gambini might want to go into detail for those who were interested after the general meeting broke up.

The President took his last question from Ed Young of PBS: "Sir, do you see any effect on international tensions as a result of this incident?"

Hurley sidestepped adroitly. "Ed," he observed, "there's been a notion around for some years now that technological civilizations self-destruct, that we can expect to blow ourselves

up at some point in the near future, and that nothing can prevent
it. At least we can be reassured that that need not happen. Now
that we know it's possible to survive, maybe we can get serious
about finding a way to do it." He turned, waved at his audience,
wished them good-day, shook a few hands, and was gone.

Harry unlocked the front door, dropped his briefcase on the
floor, threw his coat over the back of the sofa, and turned on
a lamp. He sank into an upholstered chair and reached for the
TV control. The house was filled with noises: an upstairs clock,
the refrigerator, the quiet murmur of power in the walls. A
plastic paperweight, inscribed "SUPERMAN works here," which
Tommy had given him at Christmas, rested atop his desk.

His impression that Gambini had performed well at the press
conference was borne out by the newscasts. The physicist,
displaying dedication and competence, was a gray figure, perhaps, beside the President's colorful showman, but he rose
almost to eloquence on several occasions. And anyone who
knew the project manager would not have missed the wistful-
ness with which he responded to questions about the fifty days
of silence.

Rosenbloom, on the other hand, was at his worst. Harry
got the impression that the Director had stage fright. However
that might have been, the charm he was normally capable of
delivering was utterly missing. He sounded irritated, arrogant,
pompous. Which is to say that his more repellent qualities came
to the fore and held the day.

The network reports themselves were restrained, considering the enormity of the story. Holden Bennett, on CBS, began
with the simple statement, "We are no longer alone." Virtually
the entire thirty-minute newscast was devoted to the press conference, with an announcement of a one-hour special at nine.
There were clips of the Space Center and the Research Projects
Laboratory.

The networks also ran shots of slowed traffic on Greenbelt
Road as people who'd heard the news earlier in the day scrambled to get a look at the Space Center. In fact, with the trees
bare, the lab itself was visible from the highway.

Man-in-the-street interviews revealed mixed interest. Some
people were excited, but many felt that the country was spending too much money on projects of no conceivable benefit to
anybody, at a time when the taxpayers were being asked for
record sums. There was no indication that anyone was nervous.

Reports from Paris, London, Brussels, and other capitals indicated that European reaction was unruffled.

Tass denounced the United States for withholding the information so long, arguing that the event was of supreme importance to all nations. They wondered what else the American government knew that it was keeping to itself.

During the cut from Moscow, the phone rang. "Mr. Carmichael?" The voice was resonant and full and vaguely familiar.

"Yes."

"Eddie Simpson. We'd like to have you on tomorrow's show. . . ."

Harry listened politely, then explained that he was far too busy now, thanks anyway. A second invitation came fifteen minutes later, after which the phone rang continually. At about eight-thirty, a TV news team arrived, headed by Addison McCutcheon, an energetic Baltimore anchorman. Harry, too tired to argue about it anymore, refused to let them in, but allowed himself to be interviewed on his front steps.

"There's nothing more to say," he protested. "You know as much as we do now. Anyway, I'm not an investigator. All I do is make out the paychecks."

"What about the charge," asked McCutcheon pointedly, "leveled this evening by Pappadopoulis that the government kept this quiet hoping to gain a military advantage from it?"

Harry hadn't heard that one before. "Who's Pappadopoulis?"

McCutcheon took on a condescending tone. "He won the Pulitzer a few years ago for a book on Bertrand Russell. He's also the chairman of the philosophy department at Cambridge, and he had some very unkind things to say about you earlier this evening."

"About *me?*"

"Well, not you, per se. But about the manner in which Goddard caved in to the politicians. Would you care to comment?"

Harry was uncomfortably aware of the cameras and lights. He heard a door open across the street and got the impression that a crowd was gathering at the foot of his driveway. "No," he said. "Pappadopoulis is entitled to his opinion. But we never got to a point where we were talking about military considerations." Then, mumbling apologies, he pushed his way inside and closed the door.

The phone was ringing.

It was Phil Cavanaugh, an astronomer who had worked occasionally on contract at Goddard. He was outraged. "I can understand that you might not have wanted to put out any interpretations, Harry," he said, his voice shaking, "but with-holding the fact of the transmission was unconscionable. I know it wouldn't have been your decision, but I wish somebody there—you, Gambini, somebody—had had the guts to tell Hurley what NASA's responsibilities are!"

Later, Gambini phoned. "I'm in a motel," he said. "And judging from how hard it's been to get through to you, I guess you've been having the same sort of problem I have. I think I've been excoriated by every major scientific figure in the country. Even the philosophers and theologians are after me." His snarl dissolved briefly into a chuckle. "I've been referring them all to Rosenbloom.

"Listen, Harry, I wanted to let you know where I am in case anything important comes up. . . ."

At a quarter to nine, Julie phoned. "Harry, I've seen the news." Her voice was tentative, and he understood that this was a difficult call for her to make. "I'm happy for you," she said. "Congratulations."

"Thanks." Harry tried not to sound hostile.

"They'll be making you Director."

"I suppose."

Harry could see more lights in the driveway. "Tommy wants to talk to you," she said.

"Put him on." Somebody knocked at the door.

"Dad." The boy's voice quavered with excitement. "I saw you on television."

Harry laughed and the boy giggled, and Harry felt the strain of it through the phone. They talked about the Altheans and Tommy's basketball team. "We've got a game tomorrow morning," he said.

When she got back on, Julie was subdued. "Things must be very exciting at work," she said.

"Yes." Harry couldn't get the stiffness out of his tone, and he wanted nothing so much as to sound natural. "I've never seen anything like it."

"Well," she said, after another long hesitation, "I just wanted to say hello."

"Okay." The knocking at the door became insistent.

"It sounds like you have visitors."

"It's been bad all night. TV crews and reporters. There's been a small crowd in front of the house most of the evening. Gambini's having trouble, too. He's off hiding in a motel somewhere."

"You should do the same, Harry."

He paused, caught his breath, and felt his pulse begin to quicken. "I don't like motels." He squeezed the words out. "Listen, I have to go: I have to do something about those people outside."

"Why don't you lock up and get out? Seriously, Harry."

He caught an invitation in the words; but he no longer trusted his judgment where she was concerned. "Julie," he said, "I think a celebration's in order. Would you join me for a drink?"

"Harry, I'd like to, I really would—" She sounded doubtful, and he realized she wanted to be asked again. But he by God didn't want to do it!

"No strings," he said finally. He was having trouble breathing. "A lot's been happening, and I need someone I can talk with."

She laughed, the deep burgundy sound that he knew so well from better days. "Okay," she said. "One-night stand. Where will we go?"

"Leave that to me," he said. "I'll pick you up in an hour."

He had trouble getting through to Wheeler, who was obviously also deluged with phone calls that evening. In the end, he had to call a mutual friend in Princeton and send him over to the priest's apartment. When the Norbertine called back, Harry explained what he wanted. "Try to stay off the phone," Wheeler said. "I'll set it up and get back to you. It should only take a few minutes. I'll ring once and call again."

Harry used the time to shower and change. The phone rang several times. But Harry let it go until he heard Wheeler's signal. "It's okay," the priest said. "There are two drainpipes behind the lodge. They'll leave the keys in the one on the south side. You'll need your own towels and stuff. They'll put breakfast in the refrigerator."

"Pete, I owe you."

"Sure. Good luck."

Harry made it a point to be a few minutes late. Ellen opened the door and asked about him in an earnest voice that suggested she, too, had high hopes for the evening.

Julie: she entered from the back of the house, in white and

green. Her heels took her up to about six-three; she'd often joked with people that she'd married Harry principally because there was no one else with whom she could dress properly.

In that moment, crowded with hesitation and regret, she was incredibly lovely. Her lips compressed briefly with confusion, and then she broke into a wide smile. "Hello, Harry," she said.

On the highway, they talked freely. It was as if they were old friends again, facing a common problem. The aura of tension and anger that had infected the weeks since her departure had dissipated. (Though Harry knew it would return when the interlude ended.)

"Living with Ellen's not bad," she said. "But I'd prefer to be on my own."

"I sleep most nights in the office," Harry admitted.

"Some things never change."

Harry bristled. "I didn't sleep over that often."

"Okay," she said. "Let's not get into it tonight."

They traveled the expressway east toward Annapolis. Harry turned south on Route 2 and pulled in at the Anchorage, near Waynesville. They'd been there before, but it had been a long time ago.

The drinks warmed them. "You should be well on your way now, Harry," she said. "You were right there with Hurley."

"I don't think the President's sure who I am. They were supposed to introduce me along with Rosenbloom and Ed. But I guess something happened. Either Hurley forgot my name, or he decided three's too many. Hard to say. But it can't hurt, I suppose. The only thing I worry about now is the possibility that someone'll come up with an alternative explanation for the signal. If that happens, then I get to be one of the people who made the President look dumb."

The Anchorage was a fortunate choice. Besides being located on the road to Basil Point, it turned out to have a moody piano player and bayberry candles in smoky globes.

Ed Gambini had checked in at the Hyattsville Ramada under an assumed name. He hated motels because they never gave you enough pillows and they always looked so distraught when you asked for more. So he lay in bed propped up on two, with the top one folded over, watching the specials on the news conference. All the major networks had run them, and he'd switched back and forth. On the whole, the coverage was intelligent. They'd stressed the proper facts and asked the right questions. And they'd seen through the administration's effort to pretend that the incident was over.

Later he watched an argument (he hesitated to call it a debate) between "Backwoods" Bobby Freeman, television preacher and founder of the American Christian Coalition, and Senator Dorothy Pemmer, Democrat of Pennsylvania, on the Coalition's efforts to require a statement of religious belief from all candidates for federal office.

The phone rang, and Gambini turned down the sound.

It was Majeski. "Ed," he said, "Mel's on the line. Is it okay to give him your number?"

It was the call that Gambini feared. "Yes," he said without hesitation, and hung up.

Mel Jablonski was an astronomer from UNH. More than that, he was a lifelong friend. Gambini had met him at the University of California, when they had both been undergraduates. They'd come a long way since then, but they'd kept in touch. And when Gambini had suffered his breakdown, it had been Mel who'd come forward, held off the wolves who wanted Gambini's job, and offered time and money. "Ed?" The familiar voice sounded tired and far away.

"How are you, Mel?"

"Not bad. You're a hard man to get through to."

"I suppose. It's been a difficult day."

"Yes," Jablonski said. "I would think so."

Gambini searched for something to say.

"Did you really hear that signal back in September?" asked Jablonski.

"Yes."

"Ed," he said, sadly, "you are a son of a bitch."

At about the time Harry and Julie were turning off the expressway onto Route 2, Gambini wandered down to the bar. It was filled to capacity, and it was loud. He took a manhattan out onto one of several adjoining terraces.

The evening was warm, the first decent weather Washington had had in a month. A clear sky curved over the nation's capital. Hercules was on the horizon east of Vega, his war club held aloft in a threatening gesture.

The home of life.

In the west, he could see summer lightning.

A middle-aged couple had followed him out. Silhouetted against the lights of the city, they were discussing in ponderous detail a recalcitrant teenaged son.

Gambini wondered whether there would be a second signal. It was a doubt that he had been careful not to express to anyone. But even if no further communication came, the essential question was answered: we were not alone! Now we knew it had happened elsewhere. And the details of that other event and those other beings, their history, their technology, their experience of the universe, were of enormous interest. But for all that, they were only details and secondary to the central fact of their existence.

Gambini raised his glass in the general direction of the constellation.

The critical moment, for Harry, came when he edged off the Anchorage parking lot and signaled his intentions for the evening by turning *south* onto Route 2. Julie stiffened slightly, but said nothing. He risked a glance at her: she was looking straight ahead. Her hands were folded on her lap, and her face showed no emotion. If he knew her at all, she had a toothbrush in her handbag, but was nevertheless only now making up her mind.

They talked about the Altheans, whether there was any reasonable likelihood that some remnant of them had survived; about Julie's newest assignment, assisting in the design of a circular steel and glass annex of the Corn Exchange; and about how their lives had changed. The latter was a subject both had tried to avoid, but it was there, and maybe it needed talking out. Harry was surprised to learn that his wife was also not very happy, that she was lonely, and that she was not optimistic about her future. Nevertheless, through it all, she gave him no reason to suspect that she regretted having left him. "It'll work out," she told him. "It'll work out for both of us." And then she corrected herself. "All three of us."

Storm clouds were piling up in the west.

Harry almost missed his turn. There was little to mark the road that Wheeler had directed him to watch for. It plunged left at a sharp angle into the trees. He passed an ancient, crumbling stone house and began a long, winding climb uphill.

"Harry," Julie said, "where are we going?" Her voice had the whispery quality of a shallow stream.

This is where I take all my women now, he thought. And

he damned himself for not having the courage to say it. "The property up here belongs to Pete Wheeler's order. It has," he said lamely, "a magnificent view of the Chesapeake."

They came to a pair of gates in a rock wall, on which hung a metal sign announcing that they had arrived at Saint Norbert's Priory. Inside the wall, the road turned to gravel, and the trees fell away. They emerged beneath a pair of manor houses set on the lip of the rise that extended back down to Route 2.

The buildings were similar in mood, possessing an idyllic geometry of stone and stained glass, cupola and portico. One had a widow's walk. Behind them, and far down, lay the waters of the Chesapeake.

"We're not going in there?" she asked. "Harry, for God's sake, this is a monastery." She barely suppressed a giggle.

"Not in there," he said. The road arced out to an overlook, and dipped back into a screen of elms. Just inside the trees, there were lights. "There's where we're going," he said, pointing ahead. Beyond the parking area, the land dipped sharply, so that his headlights swept over the tops of a cluster of trees. He shut them off.

She didn't move, and he felt the silence filling the car. "Wheeler!" she breathed. "Isn't he a Norbertine?"

"I think so," Harry said guiltily.

"He helped you set this up, didn't he?"

He nodded.

"Sex in the seminary. I guess nothing's sacred." She turned serious: "Harry, I'm touched that you've gone to so much trouble, that you'd even *want* me now, after what's happened. I'll stay here with you tonight, and maybe we can make it like it used to be. But only for an evening. That's understood: nothing has changed."

For a glorious, defiant moment, Harry considered laughing at her, packing her back down the road, and taking her home. But he only nodded passively and led her into a firelit front room. Someone had left two wineglasses and a couple of bottles of Bordeaux on a coffee table.

"Very nice," she said, standing on a thick hearth rug, "considering you pulled it off with so little warning." Wheeler had been better than his word: bacon, eggs, potatoes, and orange juice were in the refrigerator; beds were made up; more wine was in the pantry, and some scotch; and, despite Pete's admonition, there were plenty of towels.

They reminisced a bit, and, tentatively, Harry kissed her.

She tasted good, and her breath was warm against his throat. Nevertheless, there was something mechanical in the act. "A long time," said Harry.

Gently, Julie disentangled herself. "It's warm in here. Let's go look at the bay."

The lodge was situated at the peak of a ridge. On the downhill side, away from the manor houses, the slope was rocky and steep and devoid of trees. A footpath ran along the rim out to the clifftop, where it joined a flagstone walk overlooking the Chesapeake. Here, if one wished to turn away from the manor houses, it was necessary to descend the slope by a wooden stairway.

They paused at the intersection of footpath and gravel walk. The lights of the manor houses were bright in the dark waters below. "Wheeler's a genius," she said, as they stood looking down. "He's in the wrong business." A brightly lit freighter was passing slowly south, toward the Atlantic, and its wake widened and broke in long luminous waves across the narrow rocky beach directly below. There were no stars, though Harry was not aware of that until he heard thunder.

They descended the stairway. The long, jagged ridge that marked the western perimeter of the priory grounds appeared to be the result of an ancient cataclysm. Near the cliff, the more gradual slope of the hills had given way to vertical sheets of basalt. The forest reasserted itself and crowded them against the promontory edge.

Harry noticed a small shack in the woods. It was dilapidated, and the windows were dark. As they drew nearer, he discerned something large and round crouching behind the structure. He peered at it, trying to make out what it was, and perhaps, like a child, watching for a sign of movement.

"It's a pump house, I think," said Julie. "Or it was. There should be an old road back in there somewhere. This must all have been part of a single estate at one time." Harry gradually recognized the lines of a storage tank. Two tanks. "They'd have used it back in the twenties to supply water to the main buildings, before they ran the county supply up here."

"Why do you think there's a road?"

"Because the water would have been trucked in."

There was a smell of ozone in the air. Behind them, through the trees and out over the bay, he could see a curtain of falling rain approaching. "Julie," he said, "we should start back."

"In a minute." The walkway took them onto an outcropping,

which supported a stone bench, an iron fence, and an antique lamppost. "How lovely," she said. "That's an oil lamp, I think."

Harry looked out at the vast dark bay. "It must have been visible a long distance."

"I wonder," said Julie, "if anyone out there remembers when there was a light on this point." She pressed her hand against the dark metal. "Harry, where is it? The source of the signal?" She was looking up.

"There," he said, pointing out near the horizon. The constellation didn't look much like a man with a club, but then, Harry had never been able to make out pictures in the sky anyhow. "See the four stars forming a kind of box? That's Hercules's head. The pulsar is on the right side of the box, about halfway between the upper and lower stars."

"Harry," she said, "I'm proud of you."

Lightning flickered overhead, and rain hissed suddenly into the trees. "Come on," said Harry, pulling her back the way they'd come. "We're going to get drenched."

"These are the only clothes I have," she said, breaking into a run. They'd gone a few steps when a downpour rolled over them. Julie stopped momentarily and, overcome by sudden uncontrollable laughter, pulled off her shoes.

"The pump house!" said Harry, striking off toward the old shed.

They ran. The rain hammered into the soil, and its roar blended with the sullen moan of the tide. The lights of the novitiate, which had been high in the trees, disappeared. Harry crashed into a wet branch that knocked him over; but Julie saved him from going down, and they burst moments later into the dry interior of the pump house.

"I don't think," she said breathlessly, surveying her dress, "I've got much left to save." A long strip of it hung from her right shoulder. "Did you arrange this, too?" she asked.

They were standing on some loosely placed boards over a clay floor. A rusting spade leaned against one wall, and a couple of buckets lay in a corner near a pile of burlap. Harry pulled off his wool sweater, which was full of water. "If this is what it would have taken," he said.

"We can't stay here long. Or we'll spend the rest of the weekend in the hospital."

The rain beat savagely on the roof. "It can't keep up long like this," Harry said. "When it lets up, we'll make a run for the lodge. Meantime, you'd better get out of that outfit. It's soaked." He hung his sweater over the handle of the standing spade and tossed her two pieces of burlap.

Her tongue pushed at the inside of her cheek, in the gesture she reserved for inept car salesmen. Then she smiled and unbuckled her belt.

The incoming shift was expected to be no less than fifteen minutes early. Linda Barrister was usually reliable, but she'd had a big night with an old flame in town, had gone to dinner and a movie, and the time had gotten away from her. The other member of her shift, Eliot Camberson, was at his station when she arrived, bleary-eyed and apologetic, more than an hour late.

Camberson was the youngest of the communications specialists. He wasn't much more than a kid, really, tall, freckled, exceedingly serious about his job, inclined to excesses of enthusiasm. On this night, he surprised her.

"Linda," he said, with an amused casualness she found hard to credit later, "it's back."

"What is?" she asked, misled by his tone.

"The signal."

She looked at him, then glanced at the overhead monitor. Camberson flipped a switch, and they got sound: a staccato buzzing like an angry bee. "Jesus," she said. "You're right. How long ago?"

"While you were taking off your coat." He looked down at his console. "But it's not the pulsar."

MONITOR

ATTACK DOG FIRMS INDICTED
Cranking Out "Pussy Cats," State Charges
Demand Continues High

HURRICANE BECKY SLAMS INTO GALVESTON
Damage in Millions; Hurley Declares Emergency

WHITE HOUSE DENIES THERE WAS SECOND SIGNAL

BOMB EXPLODES IN LEBANESE BUS TERMINAL
4 Dead; Christian Alliance Blamed

TWO MORE INDICTED IN PENTAGON SPY CASE
First Test of Peacetime Death Penalty Expected

HOUSING STARTS UP AGAIN
Dow Breaks through 2500 Barrier
Retailers, Technology Stocks Lead Surge

GM UNVEILS SPECTER
Laser Replaces Gasoline Engine

TRENTON PLUMBER BEGINS WALK ACROSS U.S.
"I Love this Country," He Says
Hopes To Arrive in L.A. by Christmas

"LOVE IN THE STARS" HITS
TOP OF CHARTS IN FIRST WEEK

HURLEY REFUSES TO DEAL
WITH TERRORISTS IN NUCLEAR PLANT
Denies Plan to Keep Crisis Secret
Will Not Evacuate South Jersey
But People Are Leaving Anyway

COWBOYS LOSE FIRST

6

At approximately 7:00 A.M., Harry delivered his wife to her cousin's split-level, three-quarters of a mile from home, and accepted a brief kiss from her. It was perhaps the bitterest moment of his life.

When he arrived, late, at his office, the phones were busy with reaction to the press conference. Four student aides had come in to help out. His desk was piled high with telegrams. Calls were coming in from people from whom he hadn't heard in years. Old friends, colleagues with whom he'd worked in Treasury before coming over to NASA, and even a brother-in-law who had apparently not yet heard about his domestic troubles overwhelmed the phones to congratulate him. His mood soared, for the first time, it seemed, in many months; and he was beaming when he got to Ed Gambini's message.

"Please call," it said. "Something's happened."

Harry didn't bother with the phone.

The operations center was bedlam. Extra technicians and investigators were gathered around monitors, laughing and pushing one another. Majeski waved a scroll of printout paper in his direction and shouted something Harry couldn't hear over the noise. In Harry's memory, it was the only time Gambini's assistant had actually looked pleased to see him.

Leslie was in ADP, bent over a computer. When she straightened, he caught an expression on her face of such pure uninhibited joy that she might have been approaching orgasm. (Julie would never have permitted such a display outside a bedroom.)

"What's going on?" he asked a technician. She pointed at the TDRSS monitor. Assorted keyboard characters were flashing across the screen in rapid succession. "About one this morning," she said, her voice pitched high with excitement. "It's been coming in ever since."

"One-oh-nine, to be exact." Gambini pounded Harry on the shoulder. "The little bastards came through, Harry!" His face glowed with pleasure. "We lost the acquisition signal on September 20 at four-thirty A.M. We get the second signal on November 11, at one-oh-nine A.M. Figure in the change to standard time, and they're still operating on multiples of Gamma's orbital period. Eighteen and an eighth this time."

"The pulsar's back?"

"No, not the pulsar. Something else: we're getting a radio wave. It's spread pretty much across the lower bands, but it seems to be centered at sixteen hundred sixty-two megahertz. The first hydroxyl line. Harry, it's an ideal frequency for long-range communication. But their transmitter—my God, our most conservative estimate is that they're putting out a one and a half million megawatt signal. It's hard to conceive of a controlled radio pulse with that kind of power."

"Why would they abandon the pulsar?"

"For better definition. They've got our attention, so they've switched to a more sophisticated system."

Their eyes locked. "Son of a bitch!" said Harry. "It's really happening!"

"Yes," said Gambini. "It really is."

Angela bounced into Harry's arms, pulled his head down, and kissed him. "Welcome to the party," she said.

Her lips were warm and enthusiastic; Harry disengaged himself with reluctance and patted her paternally on the shoulder. "Ed, can we read any of it?"

"It's too soon. But they know what we need to begin translating."

"They're using a binary system," said Angela.

"There're a couple of mathematicians we need to bring in, and it probably wouldn't hurt to get Hakluyt down here as well."

"We'd better notify Rosenbloom."

"It's already done." Gambini smirked. "I'll be interested in hearing what he has to say now."

"Not one word." Rosenbloom glowered at his desktop. "Not one goddam word until I tell you!"

"We can't hide this," said Gambini, his voice trembling. "There are too many people who deserve to know."

Harry nodded. "It makes me uncomfortable, too," he said. "And the government is going to look like hell to the rest of the world."

"No!" Rosenbloom overflowed the chair behind his oak desk. He grunted softly and pushed himself out of it. He wasn't much taller standing than he was sitting. "It probably won't take long, but until we get clearance, I don't want any of this to get out. Do you understand?"

"Quint." Gambini stifled his rage as best he could. "If we do this, if we hold this back, my career, Wheeler's career, the careers of all our people will be finished. Listen: we aren't employees of the government; we're here on contract. But if we participate in this, we can expect to become persona non grata. Everywhere."

"Careers? You're talking to me about careers? There are bigger stakes here than where you'll be working ten years from now. Look, Ed, how can we announce the second transmission unless we're prepared to release the transmission itself? And we can't do that."

"Why not?" demanded Gambini.

"Because the White House says we can't. Hell, Ed, we don't know what might be in there. Maybe the makings for some home-brew plague, or weather control, or God knows what."

"That's ridiculous."

"Is it? When we know that, you can release the goddam thing. But not till then. You'll be interested in knowing, by the way, that the Russians have launched a crash program to put up a SKYNET of their own."

"It'll take them years," said Gambini.

"Yeah." Rosenbloom rubbed his hands together. "Meantime, we have Hercules to ourselves. And the question we have to decide is what we want to recommend to the White House. We seem to have two unpalatable choices. We can suggest they ride things out and say nothing, or admit what they've got and withhold the transmission. Which would you rather do?"

Gambini looked desolate.

"Listen," said Rosenbloom, "I know we're asking a sacrifice. But think about it: suppose we release everything we have and there's information in there that would make a first strike feasible, that would guarantee complete destruction of an enemy with no chance for retaliation. Maybe a technique for negating radar, for example. I can think of all kinds of possibilities. Would you want them loose in the world? Would you?"

"How about," suggested Harry coldly, "if we just shut SKY-

NET down? Stop listening? Wouldn't that simplify things?"

He caught a withering stare from Gambini, but Rosenbloom looked receptive. "I've thought that right from the start."

"Why am I not surprised?" Gambini wore an expression of utter contempt. "I don't deny there's a risk," he said. "But your concerns are farfetched. Has it occurred to you that there's also a risk in allowing the Russians to suspect we have exclusive access to that kind of information? God knows what kind of meetings have been going on in the Kremlin since the press conference yesterday."

"I think," said the Director, "there's already been some consideration given to that. You may've noticed we've begun beefing up security. The White House is sending some people over. I hear, by the way, that Maloney's pushing to get the entire Hercules operation moved out of here and sent to Fort Meade." Maloney was the White House special assistant for national security, a thin, waspish man whom Harry had met on two occasions and had thoroughly disliked.

"That makes no sense!" objected Gambini. "The National Security Agency isn't set up for this kind of operation."

"Why not? There's going to be concern about security. Probably a lot more after the President's had a chance to think about it."

"But all our equipment is here."

"I doubt there's much here that NSA doesn't have a better model of, or that can't be moved."

"There'd probably be some trouble with clearances," said Harry. "They don't let anybody in over there without fairly extensive investigation. It'd take time."

"One or two might not even pass," grumbled Gambini.

"I don't think you need worry about that, Ed," Rosenbloom said. "If this operation goes to NSA, I doubt that anyone except you and Rimford and possibly Wheeler would be invited. Why should they? They have their own mathematicians and codebreakers. In fact, they'd undoubtedly feel they could do the job better than we could anyhow."

"Quint," said Gambini, "has anyone argued this thing with the President? Pointed out to him the advantages of going public? I don't suppose you'd be willing to take a stand?"

"What advantages?" asked Rosenbloom. "And no, it's not in the Agency's interests to push this. If he releases what he's got and it blows up, which it very easily could, there'll be some bodies."

"We've already got some bodies," said Gambini. "Do you have any idea what my standing is right now back home?"

That would be CIT, where Gambini had been a full professor before coming to Goddard on a temporary assignment that had lasted, so far, three years.

"Come on, Ed." Rosenbloom leaned back against his desk, breathing hard. "We're doing what's right for us, and for the President. Try not to make waves. I know how you feel, but the hard truth is that Hurley is right. Maybe, after it's all over, we can get you an award of some kind."

Gambini's eyes hardened. "You talked to Hurley this morning?"

"Yes."

"Suppose I just walked out?"

"I'm not sure," Rosenbloom said patiently, "just what your status would be. You'd undoubtedly be open to prosecution if you went to the newspapers with any of this. Although we both know the Agency would be reluctant to prosecute you. I mean, how would it look?

"But you'd be on the outside. You'd learn only what we felt could safely be revealed. And you'd never be sure what was really happening here. Is that what you want?"

Gambini rose slowly, his mouth a thin line, his cheeks flushed.

"Rosenbloom," said Harry, "you are a bastard."

The Director swiveled in Harry's direction, a look of genuine hurt on his pork-chop features. Then he turned back to the project manager. "Now let's get together. What are we going to do?"

Gambini had taken his jacket off its hanger. He draped it over his arm. "All right," he said. "For now."

Rosenbloom smiled with satisfaction. "And you, Harry? I really hadn't expected a problem from you."

"I don't disapprove of waiting to clear this with higher authority," said Harry. "But I don't think much of the way you treat your people."

Rosenbloom looked curiously at Harry. He was unsettled by his subordinate's reaction. "Okay," he said at length, "I appreciate your honesty." There was another long pause. "Ed, you kept everyone on board this morning?"

"Yes," he said. "No one's gone home."

"You and I should go talk to them."

•   •   •

At 8:00 P.M., the transmission was still coming in.

Harry smuggled a case of French champagne into the Hercules spaces that evening. It was a violation, of course, but the occasion demanded something appropriate. They drank out of paper cups and coffee mugs. Rimford, who'd been called back from the West Coast, arrived with several more bottles. They went through it all, and when another supply appeared mysteriously, Gambini stepped in. "That's enough," he said. "The rest'll be at the Red Limit this evening should anyone wish to claim it."

Harry found a hard copy of the first twelve pages or so of the transmission tacked to a bulletin board. The characters were binary. "How can you begin to make sense out of it?" he asked Majeski, who was watching him with curiosity.

"First," he said, leaning casually against the wall with his arms folded like a young Caesar, "we ask ourselves how *we'd* have encoded the message."

"And how would we?"

"We'd start by giving them a set of instructions. For example, they'd need to know the number of bits in a byte. We use eight." He looked at Harry uncertainly. "A byte," he explained, "is a character. A letter or number, usually, although it doesn't have to be. And it's a result of the arrangement of the individual bits. We use eight. The Altheans use sixteen."

"How can you tell?"

Majeski brought up a sequence on one of the monitors. "This is the beginning of their transmission." It started with sixteen zeroes, then sixteen ones. And it went on like that for several thousand characters.

"That seems simple enough," said Harry.

"That part of it is."

"What would we do next?"

"What we would want to do, but can't as yet, would be to create a self-initiating program. We'd have to assume certain things about the architecture of their computer, but there's reason to believe that the digital approach we use in our computers is the most efficient. If not, it would still be the most basic type, the type a technological civilization would be most likely to possess, or at least to know about. And we would want a program that would run in a fairly unsophisticated model, with limited memory.

"Ideally, the only action needed to get the thing up and running should be for the people on the other end to plug it into a computer and run a search program. In other words, any attempt to analyze the transmission, to look for patterns, triggers the program."

"Nice idea," said Harry. "I assume the Altheans didn't do that?"

Majeski shook his head glumly. "Not as far as we can tell. We've been running it through the most advanced systems we have. And I don't understand that. I really don't. It would be the logical way to proceed." He bit his lower lip. "It makes me wonder if a self-initiating program is really possible."

Harry went back to his office during the late afternoon. He was still feeling immensely pleased, and he found a fresh pile of messages. He read some of the telegrams and started returning calls. One had come from Hausner Diehl, the English department chairman at Yale, whom he had met once at a graduation ceremony.

Diehl answered the phone himself. "Harry," he said, "I wonder if you can explain something to me. Why was it necessary to withhold information on the Hercules discovery for eight weeks?"

Harry sighed.

After Diehl had lodged his complaint and added a warning that a formal protest was likely from Yale, he asked a disquieting question. "A lot of people here," he said, "are not convinced that the truth is out yet. Is there anything we still haven't been told?"

"No," said Harry. "There was nothing else."

And then came the question: "There has been no second signal?"

Harry hesitated. His face warmed. "We described everything we had."

Harry's job did not normally require him to lie; it was not a tactic he was good at, and he was moderately surprised to get away with his reply. But he felt the weight of the deception nonetheless.

It was not a night to eat alone. He called Leslie.

"Yes," she said. "I'd love to."

Harry would have preferred to get away from Goddard altogether for a few hours. The conversation with Diehl had bothered him more than it should have, perhaps. It had, after all, been the only negative note in an extraordinarily successful day. Yet there was something ominous about it, the sense of being on a slippery slope, that depressed him. But Leslie wanted to stay close.

"They're still running the transmission through the computers, and something could happen any time," she said. So they went to the Red Limit.

"They're not going to start reading it tonight?" asked Harry.

"No, of course not. But Ed's worried."

"Why?"

"I think because they expected an immediate breakthrough after they saw the initial setup of the transmission. When I left, he was saying that they'll solve it quickly, or not for years."

"Is it possible," asked Harry, "that it might never be translated?"

"Now, there," she said, raising her eyes from the menu, "is a dark thought."

They ordered fish and a carafe of white wine. Leslie by candlelight was more attractive than he'd expected. "Harry," she asked quietly, after the meal had come, "are things not good at home?"

He hadn't expected the question. "You've been talking to Pete," he said accusingly.

"No. It's easy enough to see. You wear a wedding ring; but you never go home for dinner."

"I guess not," he said. He continued eating, drank some wine, patted his lips with a napkin, and said simply, "It's kaput."

"I'm sorry."

He shrugged.

"I didn't mean to pry."

Her lips caught the light. She wore a sheer white blouse with the top two buttons open. He followed the creamy arc of her left breast down into the lapels. "I don't mind," he said. She smiled, reached across the table, and touched his forearm. "I lost her the night they picked up the signal." He shook his head. "No, I guess it happened long before that."

"Any children?"

"One. A boy."

"That makes it even more difficult."

Harry stared at her again. "Hell with it," he said. He finished his fish, drained the wine, and sat back defiantly, arms crossed.

She said nothing.

"You disapprove?"

"I only disapprove when I'm getting paid, Harry. Then I

disapprove of everything." Her eyes registered regret. "I don't know why that should be. Maybe because the end is always bad."

Harry grinned. "You're a hell of a psychologist," he said. "Is that what you tell everyone?"

"No. I tell patients what they pay me to hear, what's good for them over the short run, because that's all there is, really. To you, I can speak my mind."

"Speak your mind," said Harry.

"You're an interesting male, Harry. In some difficult areas, you're highly adaptive. You've managed, for example, to fit in remarkably well with some of the foremost scientific minds of the age. People like Gambini and Quint Rosenbloom believe damned little of the human race is even worth knowing. But they both respect you. Cord Majeski talks only to mathematicians, cosmologists, and virgins. Rimford talks only to God. Yet they all accept you."

"You don't like Majeski," said Harry.

"Did I say that?"

"I think you did," smiled Harry.

"I guess people like Majeski tend to bring emotions close to the surface, one way or another. But that's neither here nor there." She leaned forward. "What I'm trying to say, Harry, is that I like you. I hate seeing you like this."

"Like what?"

"Harry, any stranger off the street could tell you that you aren't behaving in character."

"How would *you* know?"

"For one thing, you smile easily. But I have yet to see you smile without downcast eyes. Hell, you're doing it now." An edge had crept into her voice.

"I'm sorry," Harry said. "This has been a bad time for me. What do you prescribe?"

She leaned forward. The blouse fell open a bit more. "I don't know. For a start, probably, you should recognize that she's gone."

"You don't know us," he protested. "How can you say that?"

"I've probably said too much already," she agreed. "It's the wine."

"Why do you think there's no hope for a reconciliation?"

"I didn't say there was no hope. You may get a reconciliation. But the woman you remember is gone. Whatever you may have had, and I can see that it was pretty substantial, it gets irrevocably fractured when somebody walks out. It's never the same. A reconciliation is, at best, a holding action."

"You sound like Pete Wheeler."

"I'm sorry, Harry. But if he said that, he was right. What's your wife's name?"

"Julie."

"Well, Julie's a damned fool. She won't replace you very easily. She may or may not be smart enough to realize that quickly. When she does, there's a fair probability she'll be back. If that's what you want, and you play your cards right, your chances are pretty good. But you'll be trapped in a bad situation." She pushed the remains of her dinner away. "Enough for me," she said.

Harry was silent.

"Is that what you want?" she asked.

"I don't know," Harry said. "I know I'd like to have her back."

"I'd like to be twenty-two again." She watched him carefully. "I'm sorry, Harry. I don't mean to be cruel. But we're talking about the same sort of thing."

Majeski was annoyed.

He sat in Gambini's office with his head thrown back, his eyes closed, his cheeks puffed out, and his arms hanging at the sides of the chair. The project manager, perched on the edge of his desk, was explaining something. The mathematician nodded, and nodded again; but his eyes never opened. Looking up, Gambini saw Harry and waved him in.

"Got a question for you," he said, as Harry closed the door.

"Go ahead."

"What would happen if we sent a copy of the transmission over to the National Security Agency and they were able to make some sense of it?"

"They've got a custom-made fifth-generation Cray computer," Majeski interjected. "It might be enough to get us into the instructions. That'd be all we'd need: just enough to get started."

Harry thought it over. He didn't know the NSA people well; they were a community unto themselves, competent, elitist, secretive, scared to death to talk to anyone who might deduce something from their tone of voice. "I don't think NSA has any interest in this project, and I suspect they're busy enough over there that they'd prefer not to get involved anyhow. But there are people around the President, the security people mostly, who'd like to get Hercules out of Goddard and into Fort Meade. If you go to NSA for help, you'll be putting ammunition into their hands. Do that, and it probably won't matter whether they succeed or not."

"So we work on the project at Fort Meade," grumbled Majeski. "What's the difference?"

"The difference," said Harry, "is that *you* won't be working on it, Cord. The project goes over there, it becomes theirs. You work for NASA, not NSA. They'd use you only if they decided you were irreplaceable. Are you?"

"What you're saying is that the computers to solve the transmission may be available, but we can't use them without losing control of the project. That's ridiculous."

Harry shrugged. "Doesn't matter. It's the way the government works."

"This is what we're talking about," said Gambini, anxious to change the subject. He picked up a laserdisc. "It's a complete data set. It's about six minutes long, at a little better than eighty thousand baud." He handed it to Harry. "The Altheans have broken the transmission into distinct sections. We have sixty-three so far. This is number one, and it is very likely a set of instructions."

"But," said Majeski, "we have to get a sufficiently powerful computer."

"And the one ninety-sixes aren't good enough?" asked Harry. "I thought the theory was that the program should work in something basic."

"Who knows what's basic to the Altheans?" Gambini groaned, as if he were literally in pain. "I'm not sure how to handle this, Harry. I hate to waste time with peripheral approaches when it's probably just a matter of finding the right computer. If our assumptions are wrong, and we have to solve this thing by some sort of statistical analysis, none of us may live long enough to see a result."

Harry turned the laserdisc over in his hand. It gleamed in its plastic cover. "Maybe," he said, "you're going at this the wrong way. You've been using the one ninety-six?"

"Of course."

"The biggest we have. And now we want to go bigger yet. But Majeski's logic suggests smaller." Harry's eyes fell on Gambini's personal computer, a portable two fifty-six-K unit.

"I don't know much about computers," he continued, "except that bigger ones are more complicated. More places to store information. More instructions required to make it work."

Gambini's eyes widened. "You mean a smaller computer can do things a bigger one can't?"

"A program not designed to address all the memory in the one ninety-six might not run."

Gambini leaped from his chair and bolted from the office. He returned moments later with an Apple. They cleared off a section of the desk and set it down. Harry plugged it in. "Wait a minute," said Gambini. "Our search programs won't run in this machine. There isn't enough memory."

"Rewrite them," said Harry.

"Jesus," grumbled Gambini. "I hate to think how long that'll take."

"Hold it." Majeski left the office, opened a filing cabinet in the workroom, and came back with a disc. *"Star Trek,"* he said. "This has been around here for years. It doesn't need much memory, and it includes a sequence that allows the *Enterprise* to analyze Klingon tactical positions." He grinned, and shrugged. "What the hell."

He loaded the game, punched in his choice for a mission, and activated the search instructions. Then he turned to Harry. "Go ahead," he said. "It's your idea."

The monitor carried a simulation of the *Enterprise* viewsscreen. It showed a handful of stars, several dozen planets, and a curious disturbance off the beam that might have been something with a cloaking device. Two status boards occupied the lower portion of the screen: ship's systems on the left, combat search and analysis on the right.

Harry added the Hercules disc and keyed it in. The starfield rotated slowly, and the *Enterprise* began to move.

Red lamps over both laserdisc ports blinked on.

"It's reading," said Gambini.

The starship was accelerating rapidly. The disturbance that might have been a cloaked vessel suddenly dropped off the screen. Gradually the stars rolled past the *Enterprise,* much as they had on the old television program, until they thinned out, and then they, too, were gone.

"This doesn't happen in the game," observed Majeski.

The search and analysis board, which carried the legend "No Contacts," went blank.

And a cube appeared.

"Not part of the game!" Majeski squeezed up close to the screen, as if to look deep into it.

The cube rotated at a forty-five-degree angle, stopped, and reversed itself.

Gambini watched hopefully. When he spoke, his voice was tense. "Maybe," he said. "Maybe."

It was a perfectly ordinary cube. And it was going to look goddam silly in the official releases. The Altheans might be good engineers, but they clearly needed some work in public relations. "Why?" asked Harry. "Why the hell do they send us a block?"

"It's not just a block," said Rimford. "It's an essential part of the most significant communication, I would think, in the history of the species."

Harry stared at the older man. "I still don't see why."

"Because they've said hello to us in the simplest way possible. When we discussed the problems related to communication between cultures that had previously been totally isolated, we thought purely in terms of passing instructions. But they've gone a step further: they must have thought we would like some tangible encouragement, so they gave us a picture.

"And they've also set some parameters for the architecture of the computer they expect us to use to get at the balance of the transmission."

Majeski and his technicians had finished making adjustments to the one ninety-six. The mathematician replaced a panel and signaled to Gambini, who loaded one of the standard search programs and then inserted the transmission disc.

They'd tied in several monitors so everyone could see. The working spaces were jammed: representatives from the off-duty shifts had arrived, and a party atmosphere prevailed.

Gambini waved everyone to silence. "I think we're ready," he said. He put the computer into its scan mode, and the laughter died. All eyes turned to the screens.

The red lamps came on.

"It's working," said Angela Dellasandro.

A door closed somewhere in the building, and Harry heard a boiler ignite.

The monitors remained blank.

The lamps went off.

And a black point appeared. It was barely discernible. While

Harry was trying to decide whether it was really there, it expanded and developed a bulge; a line grew out of the bulge, and crossed the width of the screen. Then it turned down at a right angle and described a loop. From the base of the loop, a second line appeared, drew itself out parallel to the first, and at its opposite end formed a second, connecting circle.

It was a cylinder.

Somebody cheered. Harry heard a pop and a fizz.

Rimford stood under a monitor beside Leslie, his face illuminated by pure joy. "So much," he said, "for Brockmann's Thesis."

"Not yet," said Gambini. "It's too early to tell."

A twelve-character byte appeared beneath the cylinder. Rimford's breathing had become audible. "That'll be its name," he said. "The symbol for cylinder. We're getting some vocabulary."

"What's Brockmann's Thesis?" asked Harry.

Leslie glanced questioningly at Rimford, and he nodded. "Harvey Brockmann," she said, "is a Hamburg psychologist who maintains that alien cultures probably would not be able to communicate with one another except on a superficial level. This would happen, he says, because physiology, environment, social conditions, and history are essential to the way in which we interpret experience and, consequently, communicate and understand ideas." Her demeanor grew thoughtful. "Ed is going to argue that he may yet be right, since we're still at an extremely early stage. But I think we've already seen features of Althean approaches to problem solving that are very much like our own. We may get another striking demonstration of that before we're through here tonight."

That caught Rimford's interest. "In what way, Leslie?"

"Think about us," she said. "If we were encoding pictures for another species, what image would we absolutely not fail to send?"

"Our own," said Harry.

"Bingo. Harry, you'd make a hell of a psychologist. Now I tell you what I think we're going to learn; the capability to create a technological civilization imposes essentially similar disciplines of logic and perception that outweigh, and probably heavily outweigh, the factors proposed by Brockmann."

"We'll see," said Gambini. "I hope you're right."

"The cylinder's gone," said Harry.

The point appeared again. This time they got a sphere.

Then a pyramid.

And a trochoid.

"Does Rosenbloom know about this yet?" asked Harry.

"I'm not sure we're exactly ready for a visit by Rosenbloom," said Gambini. "I'll call him a little later, after we're sure what we have. Meantime, we'll want to get these drunks out of here. That was a hell of a precedent you set. Now they all think they can do it."

After a while, the cylinder reappeared, but at right angles to the original figure. A new byte became visible. "It'll be similar to the first one," said Majeski, "and that portion can probably be understood to imply the object itself. The variation between the two should equate to a difference in angle, or some such thing."

They got a third cylinder.

The geometrical figures continued well into the evening. Harry got bored, eventually, and excused himself to call Rosenbloom. It was after midnight by then.

The Director was happy neither at the timing nor at the content of the message. "Keep me informed," he said gruffly.

Harry found a dark office and dozed for about an hour. When he returned to the operations center, he still felt washed out. He found Gambini, told him about the Director's response, and was about to say good night when he noticed that the physicist hadn't really heard anything he'd said. And in fact, the mood of the whole place had changed in a not too subtle manner. "What happened?" he asked.

Various geometrical figures were displayed on different screens. Harry realized that the program was complete, that the investigators were now beginning a more detailed examination. Gambini commandeered a unit. "There's something you should see." He keyed in, and stepped back to allow Harry an unobstructed view.

Leslie walked over. "Hi," she said. "Looks like serious doings tonight. I understand you're responsible, Harry." She beamed at him. "Congratulations."

A sphere took shape and began to rotate. Well off its surface, four points appeared, bulged, and threw out parallel curved lines, which quickly encircled the sphere. The image acquired shading and angle, giving it depth.

"My God," said Harry. "It's Saturn."

"Hardly," responded Gambini. "But I wonder if their home world has rings."

The figure vanished.

Again the familiar black point became visible. This time it lengthened gradually into a tetrahedronlike figure. It was spidery, and its limbs moved in a fashion that Harry found disconcerting.

"We think it's an Althean," said Gambini.

Late Monday afternoon, Gambini retired to his quarters in the VIP section in the northwestern corner of the Goddard facility. He wasn't sure he'd be able to sleep, but the computers were doing the work now, and he wanted to be reasonably alert later.

He fell into bed with considerable satisfaction and sank toward oblivion with the happy thought that he had achieved his life's ambition. To how many men was that inestimable blessing given?

When the phone rang four hours later, he was slow to orient himself. He burrowed deeper into the pillows, listened to the insistent jangling, reached for the instrument, and knocked it over.

The voice on the other end belonged to Charlie Hoffer. "It's finished," he said.

"The signal?"

"Yes. The pulsar's back."

Gambini looked at his watch. "Nine fifty-three."

"One full orbit," said Hoffer.

"They're consistent. What's the length?"

"We haven't done the calculation."

The transmission had been a relatively slow one: 41,279 baud. "Okay," Gambini said. "Thanks. Let me know if anything changes, Charlie."

He punched the numbers into a calculator. It came out to approximately 23.3 million characters.

Partial transcript of interview with Baines Rimford, appearing originally in *Deep Space,* October issue:

Q. Dr. Rimford, you've been quoted as saying that there are a few questions you would especially like to put to God. I wonder if you could tell us what those questions are.

A. For a start, it would be nice to have a workable GUT.

Q. You mean a Grand Unified Theory, tying all of the physical laws together.

A. (Chuckles, suggesting that *Deep Space* is being somewhat general.) We would settle for knowing how the strong and weak nuclear forces, electromagnetism and gravity, interact. Some people argue that they were once, briefly, a single force.

Q. When was that?

A. During the first nanoseconds of the Big Bang. If there was a Big Bang.

Q. Is there any doubt?

A. Well, certainly something happened. But the term "Big Bang" has developed certain connotations; it has come to represent a specific theory of how we all got started. There are alternative possibilities: bubbles, a recycling expansion and contraction, even some variants of the steady state that are beginning to come back into vogue.

Q. I'd like to get back to some of that in a minute. What else would you want explained?

A. I'd like to know why we have order at all. It amazes me that the universe consists of anything other than cold sludge sliding through the dark.

Q. I don't think I understand.

A. Let's start with the Big Bang.

Q. If there was one.

A. Then call it the initiating mechanism, if you like. In any case, something got the universe going in an expansionary phase. And we have immediately an odd coincidence: the rate of expansion is almost perfectly balanced by gravity, which is trying to pull everything back together. The balance is so exact that, after sixteen billion years, we do not yet know whether the universe is open or closed. Let's assume that the initiating mechanism *was* an explosion. Had it been infinitesimally weaker, things would have fallen back into a crunch very quickly. And I mean weaker on the order of an extremely small fraction of a single percent. On the other hand, had it been even a little stronger, the galaxies could not have formed.

Or let's look at the strong force that binds the nucleus together. Again, there is no reason that we can see why it should be precisely what it is. Yet, if it were stronger, we'd have neither hydrogen nor water. If it were weaker, we'd have no yellow suns. There are, in fact, damned near an infinity of such coincidences. They have to do with atomic weights and freezing points and quanta and virtually every sort of physical law you can think of. Change any one of a huge number of such constants, throw an extra proton, say, into the helium atom, and you stand an excellent chance of destabilizing the universe. We seem to live in a place that has been carefully designed, against literally cosmic odds, as a home for intelligent life. I'd like to know why that should be.

—Reprinted in *Systemic Epistemology* XIV

— 7

THE STOCKY, CLEAN-SHAVEN man stood in the doorway of Harry's office and appraised its contents with disdain. "Mr. Carmichael?"

Harry stood up and came around the desk. He wasn't looking forward to this one. "Yes," he said, extending his hand.

The visitor ignored it. "My name is Pappadopoulis," he said, advancing. "I'm the chairman of the philosophy department at Cambridge." He was being pointedly modest; he was actually a figure of international reputation.

Harry detected a faint drumroll. "Please have a seat, Professor Pappadopoulis. What can I do for you?"

He remained standing. "You can assure me that someone here is aware of the significance of the Hercules transmission."

"You need not be concerned," said Harry amiably.

"I'm happy to hear it. Unfortunately, the government's actions don't bear that out. NASA received the Hercules signal in the early morning of September seventeenth and chose, for whatever reasons, to conceal its existence until Friday, November tenth. Does that not seem a bit irresponsible to you, Mr. Carmichael?"

"I think that making a premature statement before we were sure of our facts might have been irresponsible. We used our best judgment."

"I'm sure you did. And it's that judgment that is in question." Pappadopoulis was a heavy man, a proper container, perhaps, for the somber approach to neo-Kantian materialism that had made his reputation in the academic community. His face was set in an attitude of unrelenting hostility, his language was stiff and formal, not unlike the contents of an old book on metaphysics, and his sense of his own worth was stifling. "I'm sadly aware that the same sort of thing is quite likely to happen again should further transmissions be received." He paused and reacted to something in Harry's face. *"Has* something else happened? Are you hiding something now?"

"We've released everything we had," Harry said.

"Please don't try to get by with nonstatements, Mr. Carmichael." He leaned across Harry's desk, reflecting bored irritation and, Harry thought, mild distaste. "Is something happening now that the world should be aware of?"

"No." Damn Rosenbloom. And the President.

"I see. Why do I not believe you, Mr. Carmichael?" He lowered himself into a chair. "To your credit, you are a poor liar." He was breathing heavily from the exertion, and he paused momentarily to gather himself. "Secrecy is a compulsive reflex in this country. It strangles thought, delays scientific progress, and destroys integrity." He drew the last word out before continuing. "I'd assumed that the only reason the information was released at all was that there was no follow-up transmission. *Has* a second signal been received?"

"None of this is getting us anywhere, Professor. I will note your protest and see that the President is made aware of it."

"I'm sure you will." Pappadopoulis gazed at a portrait of Robert H. Goddard on the wall behind Harry's desk. "He'd be embarrassed by all this, you know."

Harry stood up. "Good of you to come by, sir," he said.

Pappadopoulis's eyes bored into him. As a good bureaucrat, Harry thrived on accommodation and compromise. He had little stomach for confrontation that could in no way be productive.

"What has happened has happened," Pappadopoulis observed. "My concern now is with the future. Very likely there will be, or already has been, an additional reception. I had intended to ask what *your* position would be when that occurs. *Your* position, Mr. Carmichael. Not the government's. I am sad to say that I probably already have my answer."

Harry shifted uncomfortably under his visitor's surgical vision.

Pappadopoulis smiled. "I'm happy to see that even a civil servant has a conscience. The people for whom you work, Mr. Carmichael, are interested only in whatever military advantage they can extract from all this. May I suggest that your greater duty is to mankind, and not to a callous employer. Stand up to the bastards!" His voice rose. "You owe it to everyone who's tried to understand the nature of the world in which we live. And you owe it to yourself.

"Years from now, when you and I have long since passed from the scene, you could well be remembered for your courage and your contribution. Sit silent, appease your pathetic masters, and I can assure you that oblivion will be the best for which you may hope." He reached into a vest pocket. "My card, Mr. Carmichael. Don't hesitate to call if I can be of service. And please be assured that, if need be, I would be happy to stand by your side."

"Somebody's got to talk to the President." Gambini stirred his coffee and stared stonily across the cafeteria. "He's only getting one side, the military consideration. He's up there listening to the Joint Chiefs, and all they can see are the dangers. They're so goddam shortsighted. Harry, I do not want to become part of a military exercise. I've waited all my life for this, and the sons of bitches are ruining it. Listen, Hurley has a chance to do some real good here. We won't get world peace out of this, but he has an opportunity to knock down some walls.

"We've never acted as a species. There was a chance at the end of the Second World War and another when we made the moon flight. But this, Harry, this: what more natural way to draw everybody together than the sure and certain knowledge, as Pete likes to say, that there's someone else out there?

"What really frustrates me is that Rosenbloom is perfectly content with the way things're going. And he's right. It could blow up, and people could get burned. But what the hell, Harry, it's been a downhill slide for the last half-century anyhow. Maybe we need a good gambler to change the flow. We've got a mystery, and we'll do a lot better using the planet's resources than trying to solve it without telling anybody what's going on." He looked carefully at Harry. "I think we need to do an end run."

"No," said Harry. "*You* do an end run, if you want. Leave me out. I don't want to wind up in Colorado with Fish and Wildlife."

Gambini straightened his tie and pursed his lips. "Okay. I can't really blame you. But you understand we've become historical characters, Harry. What's been happening here during the last few weeks, and what's going to happen as we get deeper into this thing, is going to be dissected and written about for a long time to come. I want to be sure that, when the summing-up comes, I'm not on the wrong side."

"Funny. That's what Pappadopoulis said to me."

"It'll happen, Harry. This is too big to keep bottled up."

"Why do you need me?" asked Harry.

"Because I can't just walk in the door over at the White House. But *you* can get me in."

"How?"

"They're having the annual National Science Foundation banquet over there Thursday. The President will be passing out awards to some high school kids. It's a big media event, and it would be a good chance to get close to him. But I have to get in first. NASA would have access to some tickets, if we asked." Gambini leaned forward. "How about it, Harry?"

"You don't really care if they put me out in the mountains, do you?" Harry braced his elbows on the tabletop, knitted his fingers together, and rested his chin on them. His marriage was gone, and he'd never liked his job at Goddard that much. Actually, his early days with Treasury, when he'd been surrounded by others much like himself, had not been bad. But he'd been exposed to a lot at Goddard, where men looked into deep space while he arranged their group insurance. Maybe he'd begun to imbibe their contempt for his profession. "It's a little late to get in now, unless we can cut some sort of deal. What's Baines doing Thursday?"

"I can't help but wonder," the President said in his rich baritone, surveying the two dozen young people seated along both sides of his table, "whether we don't have another Francis Crick with us in the room today. Or a Jonas Salk. Or a Baines Rimford." There was a brief stir; and a smattering of applause grew until it swept the room. It continued, and Rimford heard his name echoed from the audience. He rose from his place beside the President and bowed. Hurley smiled and graciously stepped back to allow an unobstructed view of his celebrated guest.

Then he addressed the high school kids. "Perhaps, in a sense," he continued when the reaction had subsided, "it is sufficient for us to reflect on what has brought you here today and on what you now are. I'm sure Dr. Rimford would agree that the future will take care of itself. Take pride in what you have done: it is enough." He shifted his gaze over them, as if looking at some far horizon. "For the moment."

At one of the lower tables, Harry listened with interest. Hurley never used notes, always seemed to speak spontaneously, and it was said of him that he could hold an audience by reading a telephone book. Some who'd been around Washington for a while thought he was the best orator since Kennedy.

Maybe the best ever. But Harry never really thought of the President as an orator, and therein lay his peculiar genius. When one heard Hurley, it was never with a sense of listening to a declamation. Rather, one sat with him in a pair of easy chairs, or in a dimly lit corner of a bar, and talked sense. With style. That was the illusion. Dockworker and economist: Hurley spoke to them all in their own language, and frequently did it at the same time. The gift of tongues, Tom Brokaw had called it.

Harry would have felt guilty about using Rimford to get Gambini into the ceremony, except that the cosmologist was enjoying himself so much. They'd arrived early, at Rimford's insistence, and he'd wandered among the young prizewinners, asking questions, listening to their answers, and shaking their hands.

Gambini sat halfway across the room, gloomily wedged in with two garrulous representatives of the Indianapolis School District, which had a pair of recipients that year, and a young woman from JPL who, discovering his identity, proceeded to object at length to his handling of the Hercules operation, and persisted in glowering at him throughout the banquet.

"Dr. Rimford," continued the President, "I wonder if we can impose on you to make the awards."

"I'd be honored," Baines said, rising and taking his place at Hurley's side, while the audience responded again. One of those tableaux that the press love followed: the President played the role of flunky, calling out the names of award winners, handing their certificates to Rimford, and standing modestly aside while the cosmologist made the presentations. It was, thought Harry, a brilliant performance. No wonder so many loved him, despite all the problems of his administration.

When it was over, the President thanked Rimford, added a few closing remarks, and started for the door. Gambini, surprised by the suddenness of the retreat, jumped to his feet and hurried in his wake. But Gambini had no Secret Service escort, and the press closed over him before he'd gone more than a few steps. Harry watched with growing dismay; Hurley strode past his table, while the harried Gambini tried to break free.

The President paused to speak with Cass Woodbury of CBS. A couple of other reporters crowded in. Woodbury's concern centered on the seizure of the Lakehurst nuclear power plant by a terrorist group. Out on the floor, flashbulbs popped and people laughed. Spectators, trying to get a closer look at the President, pushed against Harry's chair, and someone at his table knocked over a coffee cup. Gambini was no longer visible.

Hurley was winding down his interview with Woodbury, glancing at his watch, obviously within moments of escaping. Chilton, the White House press officer, held open the door that the President would pass through.

Harry got up slowly, more or less hoping that Hurley would leave before he could reach him. But Woodbury continued asking questions. "That's really all I have, Cass," he said, raising his voice to make himself heard over the noise around him. "New Jersey hasn't asked for federal help. But we'll be there if we're needed." He nodded encouragingly into a TV camera, waved to someone in the crowd behind Harry, and signaled to his people to get him out.

Harry was almost at his shoulder now; one of the agents had begun to watch him with growing suspicion.

Another reporter tried to get in a question about the Middle East, and the agent moved to cut her off as Hurley turned away and started for the door. In that moment, Harry crossed his vision. "Mr. President," he said, knowing he was making a terrible mistake.

Hurley required only a moment to place the speaker. "Harry," he said. "I didn't know you were here today."

"Dr. Gambini is also here, sir. We'd like to have a word with you. It's important."

The elation that had marked the President's bearing throughout the presentation did not exactly drain away. But Harry saw sudden lines around his mouth, and the dark eyes behind his steel-rimmed glasses grew wary. "Ten minutes," he said. "In my quarters."

Dostoevski, Tolstoi, Dickens, and Melville lined the walls of the sitting room. The books were leather-bound, and one, *Anna Karenina,* lay open on a coffee table. "These are worn," said Harry, inspecting several of the volumes. "You don't suppose Hurley, of all people, reads Russian novels?"

"If he does, I think he's smart to keep it quiet." Gambini was sitting with his eyes closed, hands pushed into his pockets.

Sunlight streamed into the room. The NSF group was visible through arched windows, spread out across the White House lawn, officials, parents, teachers, and kids, taking pictures, comparing awards, and generally having a good time.

They heard voices in the corridor outside; then the door

opened and Hurley entered. "Hello, Ed," he said, extending his hand. "Good to see you." He turned to Harry. "I wanted to thank you for suggesting Rimford. He was magnificent out there today." The President took a chair opposite Gambini, and solicited his comments on some of the prizewinning projects. Gambini announced himself duly impressed, though Harry could see he was too preoccupied with his own concerns to have paid much attention. "I'm glad you came by," the President said. "I've been meaning to call you. Ed, Hercules has interesting possibilities. I'm intrigued by what you and your people are doing over there. But you know how I get my information? You talk to Rosenbloom, Rosenbloom talks to a couple of other people until it gets to the top of NASA, and then it comes over here to Schneider." That was Fred Schneider, Hurley's meek, eager-to-please science adviser. "By the time it gets to me, I don't know how many distortions it's picked up, what's being shaded, or what's been left out altogether." He pulled a memo pad across the coffee table, wrote a number on it, tore it off, and gave it to Gambini. "That's where you can reach me whenever you need to. If I'm not immediately available, I'll get right back to you. In any case, call every morning at, ah, eight-fifteen. I want to be kept informed about what's going on out there. I especially want to know about any breakthroughs in reading the stuff. I want to know what kind of material we're getting. And I'll be interested in hearing your views on the implications of what we learn."

Somehow Harry wound up with the phone number.

It was a bit warm in the room. "You *are* still making progress?" he continued. "Good. In that case, why don't you tell me why you were so eager to attend the NSF function today."

"Mr. President," Gambini began hesitantly, "we're not being as efficient as we might be."

"Oh? And why not?"

"For one thing, our staff is too limited. We haven't been able to get the people we need."

"Security problems?" asked Hurley. "I'll look into it and try to speed things along a bit. Meantime, Ed, you have to realize the sensitivity of this operation. As a matter of fact, I signed an order this morning assigning code-word classification to the Hercules Text. You'll be getting some assistance with your security measures this afternoon."

Gambini looked pained. "That's just what I'm complaining

about. We can't get things done when we can't communicate with the experts in these various disciplines. Security clearances take time, and we don't always know ahead of time who we're going to need. If we have to wait six months to get someone in here, we might as well not bother."

"I'll see what I can do. Is that all?"

"Mr. President," said Harry, "there's strong feeling among the investigators, and in the scientific and academic communities, that we have no right to keep a discovery of this magnitude to ourselves."

"And how do *you* feel, Harry?"

Harry looked into the President's piercing gray eyes. "I think they're right," he said. "I know there are risks involved here, but somewhere we're going to have to take a chance. Maybe this is the time."

"The academic and scientific communities," Hurley said with studied annoyance, "don't have to deal with the Kremlin. Or the Arabs. Or a hundred and forty tin-pot countries that would like nothing better than to develop a cheap new super-weapon to lob over the back fence at someone they don't like. Or the loonies who're sitting in that power plant in New Jersey. Who knows what might be on those discs?"

"I think," said Gambini, putting everything he had into one roll, "we're being a little paranoid."

"Do you really? That's an easy conclusion for you to draw, Ed. If you're wrong"—he shrugged—"what the hell!" He closed the blinds and shut the sunlight out of the room. "Do you have any idea what it's like to sit on a nuclear stockpile? Tell me, Gambini, have you ever held a loaded gun on anybody? I'm holding a gun on every human being on the planet. No: every human being who will ever walk this world is in my sights right now. You have any idea what that feels like?

"Don't you think I know how this makes us look? The press thinks I'm a fascist, and the American Philosophical Society wrings its hands in anguish. But where the hell will the American Philosophical Society be if we set in motion a chain of events that leads to a catastrophe?" He sneered. It was an expression unlike any he would have allowed himself to use in public. "You can't have the extra people until we're sure we can trust them. If that means an extra few days, or an exfra few years, that's how we'll do it. We keep the transmissions to ourselves. I'll give you this much: you can announce that there's been a new signal, and you can release the pictures, the triangles and whatnot. But the other stuff, what we haven't been able to read yet, until we can tell what it is, it stays under wraps."

An hour later, Majeski greeted them with the latest news. "We've found the Pythagorean Theorem."

MONITOR

ASU BLASTS HURLEY
Science Group Demands Assurances on Hercules

MOVE TO LEGALIZE GAINS STRENGTH
IN CONGRESS
Cocaine, Other Drugs, Will Be Dispensed through Clinics
AMA Announces Support for Measure

DEADLOCK IN GENEVA
U.S. Hints Walkout

OLYMPIAN HOPEFUL HAS LEUKEMIA
Track Star Brad Conroy Collapses during Workout

KIDS DERAIL FREIGHT TRAIN
Iron Bar Upends Diesel; Two Hurt

CURE FOR DIABETES MAY BE CLOSE

DRIVE TO EVICT PUBLIC FROM PETRIFIED FOREST
Permits Only Answer to Vandalism, Says Murray
But Critics Wonder What Will Go Next

TERRORISTS STILL HOLD TWO HOSTAGES
AT LAKEHURST
Nuclear Cloud Could Drift over Philadelphia
Governor Rules Out Use of Force

HOW TO LIVE TO BE A HUNDRED:
"Pa" Decker, on His Birthday,
Recommends Sense of Humor
But It's Getting Harder, He Says

BRITISH SEIZE IRA BOMB
Flying Squad Raids Manchester Pub on Tip

**PENTAGON CHARGES TWO SOVIET MISSILE
PLATFORMS IN ORBIT**

8

HARRY SET UP the press conference for 10:00 A.M. the next day. He brought in an artist to produce some graphics of the Althean star system and spent a sizable chunk of Thursday evening preparing a reluctant Ted Parkinson to deliver a prepared statement, field questions, and release the first data set. Parkinson, who was Goddard's chief of public relations, felt he'd already been damaged by the handling of the Hercules transmissions; he was not entirely happy with management. But they needed his platform skills and his excellent working relationship with the press. Parkinson commented dryly that he hoped it was a relationship that would survive the day.

Rosenbloom was visibly upset.

"The President directed it," Harry said somewhat awkwardly, without getting into details.

The Director huffed. "It's a blunder, Harry. But the damned fool will do what he wants, and nobody can tell him different. us. All right, go with it. But have Ted keep it as short as he can."

The press room would not be adequate for this conference. Harry commandeered every loose chair he could find and grabbed the biggest available space, which was in Building 4. They changed the drapes and hung pictures of whirlpool galaxies, tracking relay stations, and rocket launches. Most of the rear wall was already covered by the Fourth Uhuru Catalog Map, displaying prominent X-ray features throughout the galaxy. Parkinson had several models of boosters and satellites brought over from the Visitor Center.

When they were finished, Harry was satisfied. "We'll try to keep this room available," he told Parkinson as the TV trucks began to arrive. "We're going to need it again."

He retreated to his office and absorbed himself with maintenance reports. A few minutes before ten, he turned on the television. Two NBC newsmen were speculating about the Goddard conference, and, not entirely to Harry's surprise, they immediately guessed that a second signal had come in.

They ran aerial views of the facility and sketched a brief

history of the Space Center, ending with clips from the Presidential press conference of the preceding week. Then, precisely at ten, the cameras cut inside, and Parkinson entered the meeting hall.

The young public relations director projected exactly the sort of image Harry wanted: a youthful, energetic appeal, laced with good humor and a sense of dedication. He did not intend Parkinson to be the sort of press officer so common in the upper tiers of the government, reading a self-serving statement and ducking for cover.

A computer stood beside the podium.

The audience hushed.

"Good morning, ladies and gentlemen," he began. "You will wish to know that, at one-oh-nine A.M. last Saturday, SKYNET detected a second signal from the Hercules group." Deftly, he described the characteristics of the transmission, and then he delivered the bombshell: "I can also tell you that we've been able to read certain small portions of the transmission." The cameras cut to the audience, which, as one, leaned forwardly expectantly.

"What we have so far," he continued after a moment, "is only a beginning: a few mathematical images and some well-known theorems. All of that material is located in the first segment, or data set, of the transmission. The transmission itself now appears to be complete. It has been divided by the Altheans into a hundred and eight data sets. This one"—he held up the silver laserdisc—"appears to be designed primarily as a greeting and instruction manual. Let me take a moment here to say that, despite our progress, we are a long way from actually being able to understand the transmission."

He described the method that had been used to enter the binary code. "We had an assist," he said, "from Kirk and Spock." That got a laugh, and broke the tension. Harry'd had reservations about telling that part of the story, but Parkinson insisted that it was exactly the sort of colorful ingenuity that made good copy and won friends. In the tradition of the Space Center, however, no individual credit was given, and Harry lost his chance at fame.

"Now," he continued, "I'd like to show you the first pictures ever received on earth from another world."

They'd made a videotape. It was about two minutes long, a montage of the cubes and cylinders contained in the instruction manual. While the images ran, Cass Woodbury commented on the contrast between the "mundane figures and their transcendental significance."

The audience applauded the Saturn representation.

And then the computer drew the vaguely spidery figure that *might* have been an Althean.

"What's *that?*" asked a woman from the *Philadelphia Inquirer*. Her voice denoted idle curiosity, nothing more.

"We don't know," said Parkinson. "It could be anything, I suppose. A tree. A wiring diagram. I suspect, before we're finished, we'll find a great deal that we can't explain."

It was a good response; nevertheless, an uneasy feeling crept over Harry. He'd debated leaving that one out, and now wished he had.

Rosenbloom summoned Harry to his office in midafternoon. He arrived expecting to receive a few kind words on the smooth execution of the press conference. The Director never mentioned it.

"Harry," he said, "you know Pat Maloney."

Maloney was a thin, nervous man with a weak mustache, a three-piece suit, and a permanent cringe. He'd begun life as a real estate agent, an occupation at which he'd apparently been successful, had got himself elected to the Jersey City Water and Sewage Board, and had moved on up to his present exalted position as White House special assistant for security.

Harry shook his hand. It was damp.

"And this is Dave Schenken," continued Rosenbloom. "He's a security specialist."

Schenken nodded. He was a tall, wide-shouldered black, with a wedge-shaped face and hard eyes. The amusement with which he regarded Harry did not soften them.

"Dave'll be spending the rest of the afternoon with you," said the Director. "He needs to get an overview on the security system here; and he'll want to make some suggestions."

"Actually," said Schenken offhandedly, "we've already had a pretty good look at your security arrangements." His voice was dry, like paper that had been too long in the sun. "I don't want to be offensive, Carmichael, but it amazes me that nobody's walked off with one of your telescopes."

"We don't have any telescopes," Harry answered curtly, and turned toward Maloney. "Look, maybe we should start by realizing that this isn't a defense installation. We don't keep secrets here."

"In fact, Dr. Carmichael," said Maloney, "you will have to start keeping secrets, or we'll move the Hercules Project someplace where they can."

"I'm not a doctor," said Harry.

"Now, for the record, all the materials related to Hercules are code-word classified. Dave will give you the details. Incidentally, the lower level of the Research Projects Laboratory is being converted now so that you can continue to operate in there."

"Converted?"

"We've restricted access," said Schenken. "And we'll be making some structural changes to the building."

Maloney traced the edge of the Director's heavy desk with his fingertips. It was almost a sexual gesture. "In addition," he said, "we're running security checks on the employees. At the President's direction, we've issued temporary clearances, but it may be that, as a result of our investigations, some of your people will not be able to continue with the program. I mention that to you ahead of time because, with so many involved, I have no doubt there'll be some problems."

Schenken held a bound volume out to Harry. "We'd like you to read this," he said. "Everybody involved with Hercules will get one. It's a description of the procedures for handling classified information and of the responsibilities of the individual employee."

Rosenbloom made no move to intervene. "We *have* a security force," said Harry.

"It's not adequate," said Maloney. "Dave will be running security operations here from now on." He saw Harry's discomfiture. "Try to understand: the nature of the operation is different now. We are no longer talking about issuing a parking ticket or ejecting an unruly drunk from the Visitor Center. We are talking about keeping vital information safe against determined efforts by foreign intelligence forces. You may think what you like, Dr. Carmichael, but it is nevertheless a very serious reality."

Maloney, irritated with Harry, turned his attention to the Director. "The situation is fluid, and as things now stand, Goddard has severe security problems. I would be less than honest with you, Dr. Rosenbloom, if I did not tell you up front that I intend to recommend that the operation here be terminated and moved, probably to Fort Meade. Meantime, we're going to concentrate on the three places where we're vulnerable. We've already talked about the Lab. We will also have to secure NASCOM, where the signal arrives, and the library, where you maintain a duplicate copy of the transmission."

"My God!" thundered Rosenbloom. "You're going to seal off the library?"

"No." Schenken's lips pulled back in a kind of grimace. It was an expression he seemed to use when he believed he was being accommodating. "We're moving the duplicate set into a storage area in the basement, which can be blocked off from the rest of the building. Only the corridor to the storage area will be secured."

"Can they do this?" Harry demanded of Rosenbloom.

"It needs to be done," said the Director. "Just stay out of the way and let them do their job."

Maloney looked bored. "So we understand each other, Carmichael: I don't like this any more than you do. I understand the special problems you have, and we'll try not to create any more trouble than we have to. But we have to maintain control over the transmission, and we will, by God, do just that!"

Harry and Pete Wheeler were having dinner that evening at Rimford's residence in the VIP section behind the Geochemistry Lab. While they grilled steaks and baked potatoes, they drank cold beer and waited for the newscasts.

"Actually, we're not doing badly," said Rimford, when Harry asked about progress with the translation. "We can read the numbers now, and we've assigned working symbols to a lot of the bytes that seem to occur in patterns.

"Some of the symbols are directive in nature—that is, they perform the functions that correlatives or conjunctions would in a grammatical system. Others have a substantive reference, and we're beginning to get some of those. For example, we've isolated terms meaning magnetism, system, gravity, termination, and a few more. Other terms *should* translate, because they're embedded in familiar mathematical equations or formulas, but they don't."

"Concepts," offered Harry, "for which we have no equivalent."

Wheeler grinned. "Maybe." They were sitting in the kitchen. The world outside was dark already, only a bare glow in the west marking the passing of the sun. "How much in advance of us would they have to be," he wondered, "to be able to do the things we know they can do? Are we likely to have anything at all in common?"

"We already know," said Harry, "that we have a common base in math and geometry."

"Of course," snapped Wheeler impatiently. "How could there be any other condition? No, I'm thinking about their philosophy, their ethical standards. I was interested in your account of Hurley's fears regarding the contents of the transmission. He has a valid point." He refilled his mug and drank with a purpose. "But he's worried for the wrong reason. I'm not nearly so afraid of the technical knowledge we may find as I am of the possibilities for poison of other kinds."

"You know," said Rimford, "before the Hercules signal, I'd concluded that we were alone. The argument that a living galaxy would have filled the skies with transmissions seemed very compelling to me. If there were other civilizations, surely there would have been evidence of their existence."

Wheeler started turning the meat.

"And it occurred to me, one night while I was driving through Roanoke, why there might be no evidence." Rimford got up to see if the potatoes were done. "Is there a correlation between intelligence and compassion?"

"Yes," said Harry.

"No," said Wheeler. "Or, if there is, it's a negative one."

"Well," said Rimford, opening his arms to the skies, "that throws out my point."

"Which is what?"

"Any society smart enough to survive its early technological period might discover that even the *knowledge* of its existence could have deleterious effects on an emerging culture. Who's to say what such knowledge might do, for example, to the religious foundations of a society?"

"That's an old idea," said Wheeler. "But you're suggesting we might be listening to the only culture that survived its atomic age without acquiring common sense."

"Or compassion," said Harry. "Baines, you don't really believe that."

He shrugged. "Right now, I'm open to the evidence. But there *is* something else. We know that the Hercules transmitter is a product of extreme sophistication. What happens if we get a million years' worth of technology overnight?" Rimford saw that Harry had finished his beer. He opened two cans, and gave him one. "Toward the end of the nineteenth century," he continued, "some physicists announced that nothing remained to be learned in their discipline. It's an interesting notion. What would happen to us, to all of us, if that indeed were the case? What, then, would be the point of our existence?"

Rimford studied the digital clock atop the refrigerator. It was 6:13. "We may be about to discover the true nature of time. Except that *we* won't discover it. The *Altheans* will tell us. I have to admit that I'm not as ecstatic about the Hercules Text as I used to be."

"Maybe," said Wheeler, "this would be a good night to find something else to think about. How about putting a bridge game together?"

"Thanks," said Rimford, "but I've committed myself to an interview tonight. NBC wants to get several people together to talk about the transmission. They've set up a studio downtown."

"Be careful what you say," observed Wheeler sardonically. "How about you, Harry?"

Harry didn't much like Friday nights anymore. The prospect of getting through one painlessly was appealing. "Can we get two more?"

"I know where we can fill out a table," he said. "There are always a couple of guys at the priory ready for a game."

"Six-twenty," said Rimford. "I suggest we get our steaks and retire to the viewing room to see how the networks have dealt with us."

"There has been a second signal." Holden Bennett's concerned, magisterial demeanor was both somber and soothing. If anything explained his dominance of television news, it was his ability to couple a sense of crisis with the impression that he himself could see beyond its numbing daily impact into the green upland pastures.

NASA's recently adopted logo, a stylized representation of the original Space Telescope, with its energy panels spread like butterfly wings, replaced him on the screen. "In a dramatic press conference this morning at the Goddard Space Center in Greenbelt, Maryland, officials announced that another transmission has been received from the Altheis star system in the Hercules constellation. This time, however, there is an important difference."

The logo faded to an aerial shot of the complex. "The first

transmission was nothing more than a sequence of numbers, which served only to alert us to the presence of a civilization in the stars. But now, they have actually sent us a message. NASA analysts have already made a start at reading the transmission." The Space Center gave way to a brilliant, majestically rotating star system. "Cass Woodbury is at Goddard with the story."

And so it went.

In all, the coverage was restrained and almost understated. The network, however, substituted artists' renderings for the geometrical images. ("The originals wouldn't have much impact on the small screen," said Harry.) They reproduced the cubes and triangles and followed up with a ringed sphere whose identity as a world was no longer in doubt. But the final design: someone had sensed that there was where the story was, and the network allowed the image to take shape precisely as it had on the Goddard monitor.

The effect was chilling, in a way that Harry could not have foreseen. A quick glance at Rimford and Wheeler discounted the thought that it was his imagination. "My God," said Baines. "What did they do to it?"

Harry could see no essential difference. The figure was simply clearer and larger. It looked alive.

The Goddard story overwhelmed the news front for the day. Elsewhere, some Arabs had bombed a hotel in Paris, and another drug scandal was building in pro football.

Addison McCutcheon closed off his Baltimore newscast with a scathing commentary. "At the conclusion of the press conference today, the government distributed two dozen copies of a part of the transmission they call 'Data Set One.' There are one hundred and seven other data sets, of which no mention was made other than that they exist. When he was asked about these, Parkinson said they would be released as they were translated. The translation of *that* particular piece of double-talk is that the administration intends to withhold this historic story until it decides that we can know about it.

"We are once again looking at a government that is in the business of deciding what's good for us."

The network announced additional coverage at ten—nine Central.

When it was over, Wheeler put down his beer can. "That thing," he said. "It *is* one of them."

•   •   •

The Reverend Rene Sunderland, O. Praem., playing against three no trump, startled Harry early in the evening by discarding a good ace of clubs on the opening lead. Moments later, when he got in with a diamond king, Sunderland trapped Harry's queen and ten of clubs against his partner's long suit. Down three.

It was only the beginning.

"They cheated," Harry complained later to Pete Wheeler. "There was no way he could have known. They're signaling each other. He's made half a dozen plays where it just wasn't possible to figure out the lay of the cards."

Wheeler and Harry trailed by more than seven thousand points by then. "If this were a Dominican house," Wheeler replied, "you might have a case. Listen, Harry: Rene is *very* good. And it doesn't matter who his partner is. I've sat opposite him, and he does the same kind of thing. He always plays as if he can see everybody's hand."

"Then how do you explain it? What does *he* say?"

Wheeler smiled. "He claims it's a result of his devotion to the Virgin."

The second half of the evening was no better. Harry watched Sunderland's partner, a creaky brother with vacuous eyes, for indications of furtive signs. But other than a nervous tic that seemed to occur at random, there was nothing.

The community room was empty, save for the bridge players, a middle-aged priest reading a newspaper in front of a TV that was playing to no one else, and somebody bent over a jigsaw puzzle. "Everyone clear out for the weekend?" Harry asked idly.

Sunderland had just completed a small slam. "This is pretty much the entire community," he replied.

Wheeler looked up from the score sheet. "Harry, would you like to buy a nice place by the bay?"

"Is it really up for sale?"

Sunderland nodded.

"What'll happen to *you?*"

"Back to the mills, I guess. Unfortunately, most of us don't have Pete's education."

"Or his talent," said the brother.

"That, too. In any case, this time next year, I expect to be teaching in Philadelphia."

"They should send you to Las Vegas," observed Harry.

"Pete," said Sunderland with sudden gravity, "what's going

on at Greenbelt? Are you involved with these radio signals?"

"Yes," said Wheeler. "We're both with the Hercules Project. But there isn't really much to tell that hasn't been made public."

"There's actually somebody out there, though?"

"Yes." Harry picked up the deck on his left and began to distribute the cards.

"What do they look like?"

"We don't know."

"Do they look like us?"

"We don't know," said Wheeler. "I doubt it."

Toward the end of the evening, Harry and Wheeler rallied somewhat, but it never got respectable.

Afterward, they walked the clifftops, the priest and the bureaucrat, not talking much, but listening to the sea and the wind. It was cold, and they hunched down into their coats. "It'll be a pity to lose all this," said Harry. "Isn't there any way the order can hold on to it?"

The moon was low on the water, and when Harry caught the proper angle it vanished behind Wheeler's tall, spare figure, endowing him with a misty aura. "It's only real estate," he said.

Harry turned away from the bay, letting the wind push at his back. Looming over them, the two manor houses were gloomy and showed only an occasional square of yellow light. The dark forest beyond was in motion, whispering timelessly of other men on other nights. It was a wood that might have stretched to the edge of the planet. "This," he said, "is exactly the sort of place where I'd expect to find the supernatural."

Wheeler laughed. "Rene does that to people," he said. He pulled up his collar. "Well, whatever the spiritual characteristics of this place, we can't justify the expense." He shivered. "Want to start back?"

They walked silently a few minutes, along the flagstone pathway. At its far end, Harry could see the wooden stairs that led to the lower shelf. "I wanted to thank you, by the way, for the invitation to bring Julie up here last weekend."

"It's okay," he said. "Anything we can do to help."

They reached the gravel walk, coming on it from a clutch of elms, and cut across into a rear entrance where the warm air felt good. "We had our problems," he said. "We went walking along the cliff edge and got caught in a cloudburst." He grinned. "We got drenched."

"I'm sorry to hear it."

"We wound up spending half the night in an old pump house."

"Yes," said Wheeler. "I know the place."

Harry's mood lightened. "It's a *good* place. It doesn't look as if anyone's been in there for twenty years."

Wheeler did not reply.

"We used to talk about how it would be to live on an island, away from everything. And there's a lot to that. I think if we could somehow shut out the rest of the world—" Harry looked back over his shoulder, but the woods were dark. "Anyhow, for a few hours, I had my island."

MONITOR

You know, friends, yesterday afternoon I was going home after spending a few hours with some of the good folks at our hospital. And I got down as far as the lobby, where I saw a young man I knew. His name doesn't matter. He's a fine boy; I've known him for many years and his family for many years. As it happens, he had heard I would be there, and something was pressing on him, something he wanted to ask me about.

Several of his friends were with him, but they hovered in the background, as boys will, pretending they were there for other reasons. I could see that the child was upset, that they were all upset. "Jimmy," I said to him, "what's wrong?"

He looked at his friends, and they all turned away. "Reverend Freeman," he said, "we've been watching the reports from Washington, you know, with the big telescope they have there and the voices they're hearing from the skies. A lot of people say they shouldn't be doing that."

"Why not?" I asked him.

And he couldn't tell me. But I knew what he was trying to say. Some people are afraid of what they might find out there. Jimmy isn't the first to ask me that type of question, since those scientists in Washington claimed, a couple of years ago, that they had seen the Creation. You don't hear much about that anymore.

But I will tell you this, brothers and sisters: I encourage their efforts. I applaud the attempt to listen in on this great universe of ours. I believe that any machine that can bring us closer to His handiwork can only fortify the faith that we've protected now for two thousand years. [Applause]

The morning stars sang together, and all the sons of God shouted for joy. [More applause]

I have been asked, "Reverend Freeman, why is the universe so very large?" It *is* big, you know, far bigger than the scientists who profess to know so much could even have guessed fifty or sixty years ago. And why do you suppose that is? If, as the Gospel makes clear, man is the center of creation, why did the

126

Lord construct a world so large that the scientists cannot even *see* its edge, however advanced their telescopes?

When I was a boy, I used to sit out by the barn on summer evenings and watch the stars. And I knew them for what they are: a sign to us of His power and glory. But now I believe I know why He placed them so far apart. He understood the arrogance of those who pretend to seize His secrets and reduce them to numbers and theories. And I say to you that the size of the universe and the huge spaces between the stars and between the galaxies, which are great islands of stars, are a living symbol of His reality and a gentle reminder to us of the distance that exists between us and Him.

There are some now who have begun to say that the voices whispering out of the skies into those government telescopes are devils. I don't know about that. I haven't seen any evidence to support that notion. The skies, after all, belong to God; so I would rather suppose they're angels' voices. [Laughter]

Probably, the creatures we hear will turn out to be very much like ourselves. There is nothing in the Gospel that limits God to a single Creation. So I say to you, brothers and sisters, have no fears for what they might learn in Washington; and do not be concerned with their theories. They are looking at the handiwork of the Almighty, but their vision is limited by their telescopes. We ourselves have perhaps a better instrument.

—Excerpt from a television address by the Reverend Bobby Freeman. (Transcripts are available without charge from the American Christian Coalition.)

9

GEORGE CARDINAL JESPERSON had come to the archdiocese as a conservative in a time of troubles. He'd earned a reputation as a forceful, outspoken champion of the Vatican and the "old" Church. His stand on the nagging issues of priestly celibacy, sexual morality, and the role of women had been brilliantly argued, and had not gone unnoticed in Rome. His great chance had come in the clash with Peter Leesenbarger, the German reform theologian, on the question of the authority of the magisterium. Leesenbarger had argued for the preeminence of individual conscience over the accumulated wisdom of the Church; and his runaway best-seller, *Upon This Rock,* had for a time threatened a second revolution among the American faithful.

While orthodox churchmen argued that the book should be formally condemned, the Pope had wisely (in Cardinal Jesperson's view) satisfied himself by directing that its imprimatur be withheld. And the Cardinal, carefully avoiding any reference to *Upon This Rock,* had contributed to the defense of the papal decision with a brilliant series of closely reasoned essays that were picked up even by those elements of the Catholic press that were traditionally hostile to the Vatican. Leesenbarger had responded in the columns of the *National Catholic Reporter,* which became the arena for an extended series of broadsides by both combatants. In the end, Jesperson had emerged a clear victor to all but the most partisan observers. He was declared the heir apparent to John Henry Newman, with Leesenbarger cast in the role of the unfortunate Kingsley.

Unlike most other American cardinals, who were preoccupied with survival in an age of dwindling revenues and influence, Jesperson recognized early that the way to defend the faith in the United States had nothing to do with long-term loans, retrenchment, or conning the faithful with the guitars and spurious theology of Vatican II. He took the offensive. "We're about Christ," he told his priests' council. "We have the New Testament, we have strong family ties, we have God on our altars. The issues that divide us are not trivial, but they are a question of means rather than ends. . . . " But he had shocked his supporters in Rome by settling back to listen sympathetically to those who disagreed.

And in that way he had, to a remarkable extent, defused the liberal movement within the American Church. To many of its leaders he had seemed, and still seemed, their strongest ally.

But on this Friday evening, while the reports from Goddard continued to reverberate across the land, he faced a new kind of problem. So he gathered his staff, Dupre and Cox and Barnegat, and retired with them into the interior of the chancery. "Gentlemen," he said, sinking into a lush leather chair, "we need to think about what's coming. And we need to prepare our people so they don't get any rude shocks.

"Now, what is coming, I think, is a severe test of the faith. Certainly unlike any other in our time. We should consider, first, what the dangers are; second, how we may expect our people to react; and third, what approach we should take in order to limit the damage."

Philip Dupre was, by a considerable margin, the oldest man in the room. He was the Cardinal's touchstone, the composer of the provocative comment that inevitably changed the angle of light. Generally lacking in creativity, he nevertheless had a good ear for nonsense, whether originating from the Cardinal or elsewhere. "I think you're overstating the case, George," he said. "There's no real connection between the Goddard business and us."

Jack Cox struck a long wooden match and lit his pipe. He was the comptroller, a prudent investor, but a man who, in the Cardinal's view, tended to think of salvation as a series of puts and calls. "Phil's right," he said. "Still, there's ground for awkward questions."

Dupre looked genuinely puzzled. "Like what?"

Lee Barnegat, a middle-aged man whose placid blue eyes concealed administrative and negotiating skills of the first order, removed his collar and placed it on the arm of his chair. "Do aliens have souls?"

Dupre's dour features broke into a slow smile. "Do we care?"

"If we still accept Aquinas," said Cox, "the ability to abstract from matter, to *think*, irrefutably defines an immortal soul."

"What," asked the Cardinal, "is the applicability of Christ's teachings to beings who are not born of Adam?"

"Come on, George," protested Dupre. "We're not tied to Eden anymore. Let the Bible-thumpers worry about that."

"I wish we could," said Jesperson. "But I think we may have a few loose ends of our own." Despite his half-century, the Cardinal still had the youthful good looks of his seminary days. "Did you see the pictures they got from the transmission? One of them is quite different from all the others."

"I know the one you mean," said Barnegat. "It looked like something out of Dali."

The Cardinal nodded. "I agree," he said. "The speculation is that it is a self-portrait. Anyway, I'm glad to see that none of you is shocked. I hope the good people who show up at the cathedral Sunday share your equanimity."

"Why should they not?" asked Dupre.

"Man is made in the image of God. There is cause to doubt that simple truth, perhaps, when one sees what inhabits the streets these days. But it is doctrine, unassailable and eternal. And what are we to say about these creatures, who, as Jack reminds us, themselves . . . possess . . . immortal . . . souls?"

Dupre squirmed uncomfortably. He wore much the same expression he'd adopted at the last meeting when the Cardinal had proposed granting still more latitude to the priests' council. "I hope," he said, "we're not really going to take any of this seriously. I'm certainly not prepared to believe that that odd little stick figure is a picture of a creature with a soul."

"Well, perhaps not," conceded Jesperson. "But I don't think it matters, because, if we can believe our experts, if we have indeed encountered aliens, whatever they look like, it will not be like us."

"But surely," objected Barnegat, "the resemblance referred to in doctrine is of the soul, not of the body."

"Undoubtedly. But even so, we may find many among us who will be sorely tested by the notion of sharing salvation with large insects." The Cardinal's eyes moved among them, resting briefly on each. "What would you say if their transmissions revealed them to be, by our standards, by the standards of the New Testament, utterly godless and amoral? Or worse, what if we are confronted by beings of compassion and apparent wisdom who, after a million years of examining the problem, have concluded that there is no God? Beings, perhaps, who have never even considered His existence?"

Dupre grew thoughtful. "George, I think it may be our own

faith that is failing here. We will not have any revelations that can call into question what we know to be true."

"That sounds like a comfortable position to take," said Barnegat. "Let's go back a little. If these things are as unlike us physically as you suggest, George, I doubt that anyone is going to care much what they think. Phil's probably right in saying that we don't have to worry about it."

"Let me play devil's advocate for a moment," said Cox, "and ask a few questions that may occur to people after they've had a chance to think about things a little. Would every intelligent species in the universe be subject to a test, as Adam was?"

"I would think so," said Dupre.

"And some failed, and some passed."

"Yes," persisted Dupre, but a little more cautiously.

"Then there are undoubtedly numerous species in the universe that do not die."

Dupre coughed. "I fail to follow the logic. Nothing that is physical can be immortal."

"Death was the price of sin. Either we have immortals among the stars or everybody flunked the test. And I submit that, if the latter is the true state of affairs, then we have a spurious test. Or, as many will conclude, a test that never occurred."

They were briefly silent. "If," Barnegat said, "we dismiss the validity of the test—"

"—we have," continued the Cardinal, "dismissed the validity of the Redeemer. I think we are faced with a difficult situation."

Dupre looked uncomfortable. "It's hard to get hold of any of this, George. I think our best course for now is to say nothing, to simply ride it out. Does everybody remember Father Balkonsky? I think we're in danger of emulating his example."

"Who," asked Barnegat, "is Father Balkonsky?"

Jesperson's eyes crinkled with amusement. "He taught apologetics at Saint Michael's. His method was to set up one of the classic objections to the faith—the problem of evil, free will, and God's foreknowledge, whatever. He then proceeded to rebut the arguments, relying more or less on Saint Thomas. The problem was that he seemed much more persuasive with the objections than with the rebuttals. A few seminarians complained. Others suffered through premature doubts about their faith, and a few left Saint Michael's altogether. And, for all I know, the Church."

"Another thing we must be careful of," continued Dupre,

"is taking a theological position that may later become demonstrably false."

"Or worse," added Cox, "ridiculous."

"I agree with Phil," said Barnegat. "Let's restrict ourselves to a general reassurance that nothing can come out of Goddard that is not provided for within the corpus of Church teaching. And let it go at that. Just a brief statement at the masses."

The Cardinal's eyes had closed. The silver cross in his lapel glittered in the soft yellow light from a table lamp. "Jack?"

"I'm not sure I'd want to say anything just now."

"I can't imagine," said Dupre, "a better way to unnerve people than to tell them there's no cause for alarm."

"Okay," said Barnegat. "I can live with that."

Jesperson nodded. "All right, then. We'll draft a letter to the pastors, to be kept in strictest confidence. Phil, you write it. Express our concerns. Instruct them, if questioned, to take the position that the revealed faith is God's message to man and has nothing whatever to do with external agencies. Priests are not to bring the subject up."

For a long time after the others had left, Jesperson sat silently, sunk in his chair. Until recently, the only other worlds he'd ever thought much about had not been of a physical nature. But since the government had begun listening to the stars, he'd taken time to think out the implications. And when, two years earlier, the survey of nearby solar systems had suggested that men were alone in God's creation, he'd been relieved.

But now, this. . . .

When I behold your heavens, the work of your fingers, the moon and the stars which you set in place— What is man that you should be mindful of him, or the son of man that you should care for him?

Dr. Arleigh Packard adjusted his bifocals and spread his prepared address on the lectern. This was his third appearance before the Carolingians. He'd marked previous occasions by revealing the existence of a journal maintained by a servant of Justinian I, covering in detail the emperor's reaction to the Hippodrome revolt; and a document in the hand of Gregory the Great excoriating the Turks and recommending that the crossbow be used against them. He'd let it be known that he had yet another juicy surprise for the society this year.

Consequently, his audience was in a state of considerable anticipation. He was happy to see that Perrault was present, from Temple; DuBuay and Commenes from Princeton; and Aubuchon from La Salle. And it would be understating the facts to fail to notice that Packard himself was excited. The rich Viennese curtains behind him concealed a glass case that held a holograph letter from John Wyclif to a previously unknown adherent, outlining his intention to produce an English translation of the Bible. The letter had been discovered in a London trunk only months before, the property of a dying garment manufacturer who'd never known he owned it.

At the podium, Packard paused briefly, allowing Townsend Harris to step down after his introductory words, using the time to study his text and to allow suspense to build. He was surprised when he raised his eyes to find Allen DuBuay on his feet. "Before we begin, Arleigh," he said in an apologetic tone, "I wonder if we might briefly address another matter of some urgency."

Informality had always been a hallmark of the Carolingians; but they were not inclined to tolerate outright boorishness. Olson, in front, grumbled loudly of Philistines, and a few others turned with obvious irritation toward DuBuay. Packard, maintaining his equanimity despite a barely noticeable tensing of the jaws, bowed slightly and stepped to one side of the lectern.

DuBuay's complexion was curiously tinted, perhaps by the sunlight filtered through the stained-glass window (dominated by Beatrix of Falkenburg), perhaps by some mixture of a more common sort. In any case, he was clearly not himself. His thin hair was disheveled, his tie hung at an awkward angle, and his fists were shoved aggressively into the pockets of his tweed jacket. "I regret interrupting Dr. Packard, and you know I would not do so lightly," he said, moving from his seat near the rear into the center aisle and proceeding briskly toward the front of the chamber.

"Sit down, DuBuay!" roared a voice from the left that everyone recognized as belonging to Harvey Blackman, a paleontologist from the University of Virginia whose interest in the Carolingians was more social than professional. He had developed a passion for another member, a young antiquities collector from Temple.

Art Hassel, a specialist on Frederick Barbarossa, also got to his feet. "This is no time for politics!" he said angrily, by which everyone understood that Hassel had already tried to dissuade DuBuay from his demonstration.

"Ladies and gentlemen," said DuBuay, raising his hands,

palms outward in a placating gesture. "I have spoken with many of you privately. And we share a common anguish at the events of the last few days. The Hercules Text belongs to us all, not to one government. Especially one whose purposes cannot be trusted. Surely, if anyone recognizes the importance of this hour, it should be us—"

"Sit down, DuBuay," said Harris. "You're out of order."

"I would like to move that we issue a statement—"

"DuBuay!"

"—deploring the existing position of the government—"

Someone grabbed his sleeve and tried to pull him into a seat.

Everett Tartakower, on the right, rose majestically, a tall, graying archaeologist from Ohio State. "Just a minute." He crooked one long finger at Townsend Harris. "I don't particularly approve of Dr. DuBuay's methods, Harris. But he has a point."

"Then let him make it with the steering committee!" shot back Harris.

"To be discussed when? Next year?"

Grace McAvoy, curator of the University Museum, wondered aloud whether it would not be wise to get some sense of the content of the Text before continuing the discussion.

That remark was greeted by a chorus of hoots on the left. Radakai Melis, from Bangkok, leaped onto the proscenium and pleaded for order. When he got it (or a semblance of it), he decried the economic policies of the United States and their role in ensuring the continued exploitation of the downtrodden peoples.

Harris dragged Melis off the stage and threw a backward glance at Packard, silently urging him to begin his address. But a woman whom Packard had never seen before had already climbed onto a chair in back. "If matters are left to the goodwill and humanity of *this* government," she urged, "we can be sure we'll never get the whole truth. It's probably already too late! We're going to go on forever asking questions and wondering whether critical pieces of information have not been squirreled away somewhere because some bureaucrat in high office thinks they might be dangerous. I'll tell you what's dangerous at this point: hiding the truth, that's what's dangerous!"

Everyone was out of his chair now, and the shouting became general. A fight boiled out of the seats about eight rows back and swallowed DuBuay.

The only journalist present, a reporter from the *Epistemological Review,* got the story of his life.

Packard, who knew a lost cause when he saw one, watched forlornly for a few minutes, then walked behind the curtain, unlocked the display case, extracted the Wyclif letter, and left the building by a rear entrance.

$$H = .000321y/1t/98733533y$$

Well, thought Rimford, the old son of a bitch is still in the ball game.

It was almost 6:00 A.M. He'd appropriated an office for himself at the west end of the spaces serving the Hercules Project. The days since they'd received the second signal had been embarrassing for him. Despite his reputation, his contribution to the translation effort had been overshadowed by Majeski's single-minded brilliance and remarkable facility with computers. They'd made a reasonable start toward defining some of the syntactical constructions and establishing a vocabulary. But Rimford had been little more than a bystander.

Everyone knew that mathematics was a young man's pastime, but to have it demonstrated to him beyond any doubt, and by an arrogant individual who seemed unaware of Rimford's reputation, had been painful. The numbers no longer came together for him: he sensed no lessening of his ability, yet the intuition of earlier days, when equations rose from a different level of perception than he could now reach, was gone.

But maybe not entirely. Who else would have recognized the significance of the equation in Data Set 41, and consequently, the importance of the entire segment?

The Hercules Project would constitute a sublime climax to his career. When it was done, the essence of the transmission solved and its secrets extracted, when the details could be safely turned over to technicians, he would withdraw gladly to a contemplative existence. And to history.

$$H = .000321y/1t/98733533y$$

Where y equals the distance light travels while Beta completes one orbit of Alpha, and t equals 68 hours, 43 minutes, 34 seconds (the period of Beta's orbit), the resulting figure is suspiciously close to Hubble's Constant: the rate of expansion of the universe.

Magnificent! It was one of the more satisfying hours in a

life resplendent with victories large and small. Rimford settled in to look for other mathematical relationships—the Compton Effect, possibly, or Mach's Principle. Hurley had said it for them all: Who knew what might be buried in these electronic pulses?

But despite his exhilaration, he was tired. And he was violating his lifelong credo: to work at his own pace, to take time out to refuel, and to refuse to recognize pressure. Yet there was much in the numbers and symbols that lay before him that would not allow sleep: suggestions and relationships tantalizingly familiar, their significance just beyond reach. He began easing the symbols of Data Set 41 across the screen: what knowledge might a culture that could manhandle stars not possess? Would they not have measured the length and width of the universe, counted all its planks, and analyzed its cogs and sprockets? Might they not even understand the manner of its creation? And perhaps the reason for its existence?

His eyelids slid shut.

He needed rest. Moreover, the operations center and its offices were not conducive to thought. Or to sleep. So he violated one of the new security regulations: he made a copy of DS 41, slipped it into his jacket, and returned the original to the bank.

His green badge got him through the checkpoint at the top of the staircase without any trouble. There were three guards now, young, brawny individuals who obviously meant business. They were armed, and they had access to a computer. But apparently they were only concerned about outsiders trying to get in, and had not yet adjusted their thinking to include persons on the inside trying to take things out.

The bungalow provided by the Center was spare, but practical. It had a glass-enclosed, heated porch, where Rimford preferred to work. The furniture in the compact living room was comfortable, and Harry had equipped it with a supply of books on Rimford's second love, the theater.

He showered, and tried to slow himself down by making bacon and eggs, even though he was not hungry. But he hurried through his breakfast nonetheless, leaving the toast half eaten. He'd moved his bench and computer back inside after the new security procedures had gone into effect, so that he could work without being seen. Working outside the lab was now prohibited. Notes were not to be taken home, and discussions of Hercules data were severely restricted.

He inserted the laserdisc into his computer, but got no further. Concentration was becoming difficult. He got up, walked three feet to his sofa, and lowered himself onto it.

"We've got a lot of people down here, Harry," said Parkinson. The public information officer was calling from the Visitor Center, just inside the east gate.

"I'm not surprised. We'll probably have big crowds until the story dies down a bit. Can we handle them?"

"Well, they sure as hell aren't going to fit into the regular programs."

"Anybody hostile?"

"Some. Not many. Mostly, they're just like the people we always get here, except now there are so many of them. We got a few carrying signs."

"Like what?"

"'Get out of Honduras.' Stuff like that. There's a banner out there that accuses us of scuttling the school lunch program. And there are some Jesus signs. I think they want us to convert the Altheans. But I'm not so sure. Neither are they."

"Okay," said Harry. "Open up on time. Try to speed things along so we can move as many as possible through the Center and out. I'll notify Security and get some extra units. And I'll be there myself in a few minutes."

Harry notified Schenken. Moments later Sam Fleischner, his administrative assistant, came in. "We're having an interesting morning, Harry," he said.

"I think we're in for an interesting *year*. What's the problem, Sam?"

"The phones are swamped. I brought Donna and Betty in again to help out. That gives us three, plus I've drafted a couple other people. By the way, most of the calls are complimentary. People think we're doing a nice job here."

"Good."

"We're also getting some cranks. One lady down in Greenbelt, for God's sake, claims she has a flying saucer in her garage. Somebody else told us that a bunch of Arabs in pickup trucks were on their way to seize the place." His smile faded. "But some of what we're hearing is eerie. There are rumors around that we're tied in with the devil. People are saying we're doing Satan's work and looking into stuff that God doesn't want known and, well, you know. It's kind of unnerving for a girl to sit there and listen to that."

"We ought to put Pete on TV," said Harry. "That'd really bring them out."

"Listen, there's something else, and I suspect it's tied in with the devil syndrome. That funny-looking picture of the thing with all the arms and legs—it scared a lot of people. They want to know what it is, and it's hard to explain to them how far away the Altheans are."

"What are we telling them?"

"Ted Parkinson told somebody that he thought it might be a battery cable or something. We've been responding along those lines."

"Good. That'll be the position we take until events catch up with us."

"Uh, Harry?" Fleischner's voice suddenly changed.

"Yes?"

"You think that's what the little bastards really look like?"

"Probably. Got anything else?"

"Yeah, we're taking more heat for not releasing everything. I understand they're having trouble at the White House, too. A lot of it over there is apparently coming from Democratic congressmen who are trying to use the issue as a stick to beat the President."

It figured, thought Harry, as he backed his car out of its parking space a few minutes later. Politicians always seemed to be willing to sacrifice the general welfare to win votes. And the fact that there would be a presidential election the following November would magnify every decision made with regard to the Hercules Text. It was curious to think that events that had occurred more than a million years ago could have an impact on a twentieth-century presidential campaign.

One of Dave Schenken's first acts had been to construct a cyclone fence around the Visitor Center, sealing it off from the rest of the facility. Harry parked in the lot outside Building 17 and used an auxiliary gate to get through. Parkinson had not exaggerated: a holiday crowd overflowed the approach road and parking area. They carried balloons and banners, lunch bags and coolers. Greenbelt police had arrived outside, on Conservation Road, and were trying to keep traffic moving on the normally sedate two-lane blacktop.

The visitors had spread out over the grounds and, on the north side, pressed against Schenken's fence. Most showed no interest in trying to get to the Visitor Center; rather, they wandered about in idle conversation, devouring sandwiches and

Cokes. It looked like a good-natured crowd. The few signs evident among them bobbed up and down from strategic positions on hilltops, but no one seemed to be paying much attention.

This, he thought, was the way it should be: a quiet, friendly celebration of an achievement that, in a sense, belonged to them all. He'd intended to enter the Visitor Center through the rear door, avoiding the crowd. Instead, he went around to the front, and walked among them.

They were all ages and both sexes. A lot looked suspiciously like government executives who'd taken the day off. A special day, perhaps; not a day to be passed in the confines of an office, in the manner of a thousand others. They sang and held kids on their shoulders and took pictures. But mostly, they just sat in the warm sunlight and looked at the dish antennas.

The Reverend Robert Freeman, D.D., finished the draft of a fund-raising letter that would go out with the hospital appeal at the end of the week. He read it over, satisfied that it would enlist the sympathies (and money) of his two million followers, and dropped it into the OUT box to be typed.

Freeman was not unlike most of his colleagues, in that he heartily disapproved of other television preachers, but his annoyance was not based on doctrinal differences, or on the natural irritation with a rival who also has his hand in the pot. The simple truth was that Freeman didn't like fakes. He objected in strenuous terms to the flimflammery practiced so brazenly on Sunday TV. "It makes us *all* suspect!" he'd roared at the Reverend Bill Pritchard during the celebrated confrontation between the two leading media preachers at Pritchard's annual revival, which, until then, had been held in Freeman's home state of Arkansas.

Backwoods Bobby was a rarity on the Fundamentalist circuit. He tried never to say anything he didn't truly believe, a policy that was difficult to pursue since he could see there were a few problems with Fundamentalist interpretations. Nevertheless, if there was an error or two buried somewhere in Scripture, he knew it was nothing more than a translator's blunder or a transcriber's oversight. A divine typo, he'd said once. Not to be allowed to invalidate the Gospel simply because we're not sure where the problem might lie. Scripture should be seen as a river. The banks and currents change over the centuries, but the flow is surely toward the Promised Land.

He pushed a button on his intercom. "Send Bill in, please, Barbara," he said.

Bill Lum was his public relations specialist, and Freeman's brother-in-law. Many of his subordinates believed the latter fact to be Bill's sole qualification for his job. But Lum was dedicated to his family and his God. He was handsome, good-humored, undaunted by personal calamity. (His wife—the preacher's sister—had contracted Hodgkin's, and he had a retarded daughter.) Lum projected, in fact, precisely the sort of image that Freeman wished to believe typical of his adherents.

"Bill," said Freeman, after Lum had made himself comfortable with a cigar and a Coca-Cola, "I have an idea."

Lum always dressed in knit open-collar sports shirts. He still looked muscular at an age when most men had begun to slide into their belt buckles. "What's that, Bobby?" he asked. His enthusiasm was never far from the surface.

"There's a lot of attention directed at Goddard these days," the preacher said. "But the real significance of what's happening over there is going to get lost in all the scientific jargon. Someone needs to point out that we've found another branch of the family of God."

Lum took a long pull at the Coke. "You going to do another sermon on it next Sunday, Bob?"

"Yes," said Freeman, "but not next Sunday. I'd like to get an outing together with some of our people in the Washington area. We should go to Goddard. Hold a rally."

Lum looked uncertain. "I'm not sure I wouldn't feel uncomfortable at a place like that," he said. "Why bother? I mean, we covered it last week on the show. And I thought you did a hell of a job, Bobby."

The preacher blinked. "Bill, the story of the age is happening at Goddard. Someone needs to put it into perspective for the nation."

"Do it from the studio."

"There'd be no impact. The ones we need to reach don't watch the *Old Bible Chapel*. No, we need a wider pulpit. And I think the only place we can hope to find it is on the front steps of the Space Center."

"Okay," Lum said. "But I think it's a mistake. You got no control over the crowd, Bob. You remember that mob in Indianapolis last year? There was no talking to them at all."

The preacher looked at his calendar. "The Christmas season would be a good time. Set it up a few days before Christmas.

Four to six buses." He closed his eyes, picturing the Visitor
Center. "Better keep it to four. We don't want to create a crush.
We'll want to get there about midafternoon, okay? I'll lead it
myself."

"Bob, did you want to get a release out on this? If we notify
the White House, they'll clear the way."

Freeman considered it. "No," he said. "If Hurley knew in
advance, he'd tell me to forget it."

When Lum was gone, the preacher conjured up an image
of himself carrying the ages-long battle between science and
religion into the camp of the enemy. It was his opportunity to
take his place among the prophets.

Soviet Foreign Minister Alexander Taimanov had been at
the United Nations when Ted Parkinson announced the reception of the second signal. He'd immediately requested a meeting
with the President, to which the White House acceded. It was
set for 10:00 A.M. Tuesday.

Taimanov was a harsh, uncompromising man in public, an
inveterate foe of the Western world. He came of peasant stock,
had risen to power during the Khrushchev regime, and had
survived. Despite his unrelenting hostility, Taimanov was viewed
by U.S. diplomats as predictable and as a force for stability in
the Soviet Union. "Taimanov understands the missiles," they
said, echoing a remark the foreign minister had made about
Hurley. He could be counted on to resist the encroachments of
the younger commissars (who, unlike him, did not recall the
horrors of the Great Patriotic War) and of the army.

Hurley, himself an ardent nationalist, had found it possible
to deal with Taimanov, and he even developed, reluctantly, an
affection for the man whom the press had dubbed the Little
Bear. He and the foreign minister had cooperated on at least
two occasions to defuse potentially explosive situations. Hurley, summing him up for a political reporter, had observed that,
as long as Taimanov remained in a position of power, relations
with the U.S.S.R. would always be tense, but there would be
no resort to war.

That statement had been made for Soviet consumption rather
than because the President really believed it.

The foreign minister had aged visibly during the last year.
The CIA had been unable to confirm rumors that he'd contracted cancer. But anyone observing his recent public appearances could have had no doubt that something was seriously

wrong. The cold, intelligent eyes peered out from deep wells of despair. His flesh had loosened, and the sense of humor with which he'd parried thrusts by Western newsmen appeared to have deserted him.

"Mr. President," he said, after several minutes of diplomatic small talk, "we have a problem."

Hurley had learned early not to talk to Russians from behind his desk. For reasons he did not entirely understand, they interpreted the act as defensive and invariably became more aggressive. He'd left only one comfortable chair in the room, a wingback placed near the window, to the left of the desk. When Taimanov settled into it, Hurley offered his favorite brand of scotch and then seated himself casually on the desktop, looking down on the foreign minister.

At Taimanov's remark, he leaned forward slightly, but said nothing. They were alone, of course. The meeting without aides or advisers was intended as a symbol of the President's regard for his Soviet guest. Taimanov knew that ordinarily only a head of state could expect such an arrangement.

"Your action in withholding the Hercules transmissions from the general public is quite correct."

"Thank you, Alex," Hurley said. "The editorial writers at Tass don't seem to agree."

"Ah, yes." He shrugged. "They will be spoken to. Sometimes, Mr. President, they tend to act reflexively. And not always responsibly. It is the price we pay for their autonomy under the present leadership. In any case, I'm sure you've already recognized that the current state of affairs creates severe difficulties for both of us."

"How so?"

"You are placing Chairman Roskosky in an untenable position. His situation is already precarious. Neither the military nor the Party is enthusiastic about his efforts to establish better relations with the West. Many perceive him as too willing to accept American guarantees. In all honesty, I must inform you that I concur with that perception." His appearance took on a note of resignation, which said to Hurley, in effect: you and I recognize his naiveté; you have the advantage of us on this one. "His position is not improved by continuing economic difficulties."

"Your economic problems," observed Hurley, "are part and parcel of any Marxist system."

"That is of no moment just now, Mr. President. What you

have to keep in mind is the sensitivity of his situation and the potential for mischief in this business of the radio signals." Uncomfortable in the chair, Taimanov looked around for an escape, but found nothing. "I do not personally believe you will find anything worth concealing—that is, anything of military value. I think we will learn that other intelligent species will be quite like ourselves. They will give away nothing useful."

"What *is* your concern?" asked Hurley.

Taimanov's head wobbled up and down. "Do you play chess, Mr. President?"

"Moderately."

"That fact does not appear in your campaign biography."

"It would not have won any votes."

"I will never understand the United States," Taimanov said. "A land that extols mediocrity and produces engineers of exceptional quality."

"Your concern?" asked the President.

"Ah, yes, the point. The point, Mr. President, as any good chess player or statesman knows, is that the threat is of considerably more use than the execution. It does not matter whether, eventually, you find something of military or diplomatic value in the Hercules Text; it matters only that we fear you might. And the question for you to ponder, sir, is whether that fear is sufficiently deep to provoke actions that neither of us wishes to see." He tilted his glass of scotch, examined it in the light, and finished it with evident satisfaction. The President would have refilled his glass, but Taimanov demurred. "It is all they allow me," he said. "John"—the formality dropped from his tone, and Hurley glimpsed real concern in his eyes—"I urge you to dispel the fears of my government."

"And how can I do that?"

"Provide us with a transcript—we could arrange a suitable forum, perhaps at the Soviet Academy—and let us work together on this project. There would be political advantage for all; and you yourself could negate much of the criticism to which you've been subject. Or, if you prefer, give us the transcript secretly, and we will be discreet."

"You want me to give you material that we've withheld from the American scientific community? Alex, you can't believe I would gain anything by doing that."

"You would gain security, John. The world is dangerously unstable just now. These transmissions, with their terrible unknowns, could cause mischief." While he spoke, he was occasionally afflicted with a spasm of coughing, which seemed to grow worse as the interview lengthened. Hurley got him some water, which at first he ignored. "I think we need to stop playing diplomatic games," he said with difficulty. "This is an extremely serious matter. With a cooperative effort, we could solve the Text much more rapidly. And we could defuse the effort to unseat Chairman Roskosky. I'm sure you know who the probable successor would be, in such an event."

"Alex," said Hurley, "my information is that the new chairman would be you."

Taimanov did not laugh, but his eyes showed an appreciation of the remark. "Consider this matter carefully," he continued. "I understand that I am asking a great deal. But should you reject a conciliatory course, your action could only be interpreted as recalcitrance. It would underscore the failure of the Chairman's policies. And I tell you honestly that, should he be deposed at this time, I fear the consequences for both our countries."

Hurley got down from the desk. He stood, not moving; the fingers of his left hand brushed the back of the chair in which Taimanov sat, and he pushed against it. The leather was soft and pliable. "You know I have the greatest respect for the Chairman," he said. "But we are both aware that he has hardly been conciliatory except where his own best interests dictated. I understand your position, however, and I would like to do what I can to ease the pressure on him. But I have to wonder what you would offer as a quid pro quo."

Taimanov smiled. His teeth were not good. "I did not come prepared to strike a deal, Mr. President. The truth is that I had hoped you would see that everyone's best interests are served by the course of action I have prescribed. However, I'm sure we could work out something that would be satisfactory." Taimanov's breathing was labored. He stopped to sip the water.

"I wish I could say I'll consider it, Alex," Hurley said. "Unfortunately, I can see no way to comply with your request. To be honest with you, I'm sorry we ever received the goddam transmission. And if I had it to do over, I'd dismantle SKYNET, and we could go back to arguing over subs and warheads.

"I *would* be willing, however, to make a gesture for the Chairman. We might, say, pull some missiles out of Western Europe."

"That could do no harm, Mr. President. But I think we have got far beyond that now."

"Yes. Yes, I'm sure we have."

Taimanov nodded slowly, got up, and pulled on his coat. "I will not be returning to Moscow until Wednesday . . . should you wish to speak further."

When he was gone, Hurley hurried to his next appointment, which was a photo session with some union people. His guests found him distracted. His usual ability to push problems aside to concentrate on the matter at hand had deserted him.

MONITOR

U.S. DEMANDS SOVIET REMOVE
BOLIVIAN ADVISERS
Direct Clash with U.S. Troops Possible

MAN IN LEWISTON, MAINE, CHARGED
WITH 81 KILLINGS
New Record for Mass Murderer
Quiet Carpenter "Attended Church Every Sunday"

CONROY WILL NOT QUIT
Track Star Will Try to Qualify Despite Leukemia
Hometown Starts Brad Conroy Fund

SAMARITAN KILLED ON BUS
Came to Woman's Aid During Mugging

"INDIA TEAM" STORMS LAKEHURST PLANT
3 Terrorists, 1 Hostage Killed
Tidal Wave of Criticism
"It Could Have Blown," Says Phila Mayor
Hurley Accepts Responsibility

DEATH PENALTY SOUGHT FOR NUCLEAR
TERRORISM

MISSILE REPORTED FIRED AT TWA FLIGHT
OVER O'HARE
FAA Investigating; 166 on Plane

MERCHANTS EXPECT BANNER CHRISTMAS SEASON
Major Retailers Lead Dow Jones Surge

ANACONDA HAS BEEN MARRIED 2 YEARS
Popular Rock Star Is Insurance Agent's Spouse

GENEVA TALKS STALLED AGAIN;
TAIMANOV BLASTS U.S.
Pope Pleads for Agreement

BRITAIN IS BROKE
Cleary Appeals for Aid to Meet Debts
Bankers Seek Formula
France May Be Next, Warns Goulet

MARYANNE FOUND WEDGED IN WELL
Rescue Workers Digging Second Shaft; Rain Continues

10

THOUGH ED GAMBINI made a few of the daily reports to the White House, the chore gradually became Harry's responsibility. The project manager assigned Majeski to put together a summary each evening, which Harry found on his desk in the morning. He didn't resist the procedure: Gambini was absorbed by events and clearly resented having to take time out to talk to a politician.

Not that Harry actually got to deliver his reports to the President. In the beginning, Hurley himself had responded to the calls, but as the weeks passed and Christmas approached, the President was replaced more and more frequently by young, authoritative men who listened, acknowledged, and hung up.

The reports were, of course, couched in general terms. When, occasionally, a matter rose that Harry thought might be considered sensitive, he took Gambini's memorandum personally to the White House. And of course, like the good bureaucrat he was, he saw to it that Quint Rosenbloom routinely received a copy of everything.

There was a growing sense of exhilaration about it all. Harry enjoyed his access to the topmost levels of government, where he was now known by his first name. It was a heady experience for a minor federal employee. If things went well, if he could avoid blunders and pinpoint the type of information that Hurley needed, he could probably reap an agency directorship. Consequently, he invested a disproportionate amount of his time in the Hercules Project. To his credit, Gambini never grew impatient with his questions. (Although Harry realized that the idealist in Gambini would never have looked for an ulterior motive.) And Harry found himself swept up in the excitement of the hunt for the elusive nature of the Altheans.

The work of establishing the "language" of the transmissions was proceeding slowly and with moderate success. That it was proceeding at all, Rimford told Harry, considering the enormous complexity of the problems involved, was a tribute to Cord Majeski and his team of mathematicians.

Harry brought his son out to Goddard on his visiting day. There'd been a delay at home because the insulin supply had run low and Harry had to take the boy to the People's drugstore. That was always a depressing experience, rendered even more so by Tommy's good-natured resignation to his disease.

The boy loved to ride around at the Space Center, looking at dish antennas and communications equipment and satellite models. But in the end, he'd been most interested in the duck pond. There were still seven or eight mallards floating around on the cold water. Harry wondered when they would leave.

Tommy was tall for his age, with his mother's elegant features and Harry's oversized feet. ("That'll change as he gets older," Julie had reassured him.) The ducks knew about kids, and they crowded around him before he had a chance to get his bag of popcorn open. They were quite tame, of course, and when Tommy proved a little too slow, they tried to snatch the food from his hand. Tommy giggled and retreated.

Harry, watching from a distance, recalled all the evenings he'd worked late, the weekends given to one project or another. The government had recognized his efforts with scrolls and cash awards, and last year he'd been inducted into the Senior Executive Service. Not bad, on the whole. But a tally of some sort was mounting, with his scrolls and cash on one side. And on the other?

Tommy among the ducks.

And Julie in the pump house.

Later, they had dinner and went to a movie. It was a bland science-fiction film with a group of astronaut-archaeologists trapped in an ancient ruin on another world by a killer alien. The effects were good, but the dialogue was wooden and the characters unbelievable. And anyhow, Harry was near the end of his tolerance with aliens.

Julie had moved into a condo in Silver Spring. When Harry returned Tommy Sunday evening, she took a few minutes to show him through the unit. It looked expensive, with hardwood appointments and central vacuuming and a scattering of antiques.

But she seemed dispirited, and his tour was, at best, a mechanical display of rooms and knickknacks.

"What's wrong?" he asked, when they stood finally alone on her patio, looking north on Georgia Avenue from the fourth floor. It was cold.

"They've increased Tommy's dosage," she said. "His circulation hasn't been so good. That's why he needed more this morning."

"He didn't say anything to me," said Harry.

"He doesn't like to talk about it. It scares him."

"I'm sorry."

"Oh, Harry, we're *all* sorry." She closed her eyes, but tears ran down her cheeks. "He's taking *two* shots now." She'd thrown a white woolen sweater over her shoulders. Below, a police car approached Spring Street, its siren loud and insistent. They watched it angle through a jammed intersection and pick up speed until it turned into Buckley. They could hear it a long time after that.

Gambini's morning memorandum was strange: "We have the Witch of Agnesi."

Harry put it aside, went through the rest of the IN basket, and disposed of the more pressing business. He was looking at a new set of management analysis guidelines when his buzzer sounded. "Dr. Kmoch would like to see you, Mr. Carmichael."

Harry frowned. He had no idea what that could be about. Adrian Kmoch was a high-energy physicist on loan to the Space Center. He was working with the Core advisory group that functioned as technical consultants for the High Energy Astronomy Observatory elements of SKYNET.

He did not look happy.

Harry pointed him to a chair, but made no attempt at diplomatic niceties. "What's wrong, Adrian?"

"Harry, we wish to hold a meeting." His German accent was barely noticeable, but he spoke with the precise diction that invariably marked the European foreigner. "I've reserved the Giacconi Room for one o'clock this afternoon. And I thought you might wish to attend."

"What's it about?"

"It is becoming very difficult to continue working here. There are serious ethical problems."

"I see. I assume we're talking about the Hercules Project?"

"Of course," he said. "We cannot, in conscience, support a policy which withholds scientific information of this nature."

"Who is *we?*"

"A substantial portion of the investigators currently working at Goddard. Mr. Carmichael, please understand that this has nothing to do with you personally. But what the government is doing here is terribly wrong. In addition, its actions are putting extreme pressure on those of us who seem to our colleagues to acquiesce. Carroll, for example, has been informed by his university that if he fails to speak out against the government's position on Hercules, his tenure will be reviewed."

"What's the purpose of the meeting, Adrian?"

"I think you know." Kmoch's eyes fastened on Harry. His limbs were long, and he walked with a perculiarly stiff gait that, in Harry's view, was rather like the way his mind worked. Kmoch was a subscriber to ideals and ethical systems, a man who took principles very seriously, no matter who got hurt. In all, there was much of the wooden plank in Kmoch's thinking. "I am going to urge that we walk out."

"Strike? You can't strike. It would be a violation of your contract." Harry got out of his chair and came around the desk.

"I'm aware of the contract, Harry." Oddly, his tone grew more threatening with the use of the administrator's first name. "And please don't try to intimidate me. Many of us have careers at stake. What will the government do for us when we cannot continue to earn our livelihood? Will you guarantee me employment within my specialty?"

Harry glared back. "You know I can't do that. But you have a commitment here."

"And you have an obligation to us. Please keep it in mind." Kmoch turned and stalked out of the room. Harry stared after him, considering his options. He could deny the use of meeting space, he could warn of sanctions, or he could attend the meeting himself and use it as an opportunity to present the government's point of view.

Harry knew there'd been some friction. Several of Gambini's people had spoken of a growing coolness among their colleagues. He wondered whether he should alert Security. The unit was no longer his to direct, and he didn't trust Schenken. The presence of uniforms or of the hard-eyed young men in snap-brim hats could well provoke the sort of trouble he hoped to avoid.

He turned to the dictionary, looked up "Witch of Agnesi," and smiled. It was a geometrical term, describing a plane curve that is visualized as symmetrical about the y-axis and asymptotic to the x-axis. Harry wasn't sure what "asymptotic" meant, and after he consulted *Webster's* again, he was still not sure. He understood that it was somehow tied to infinity.

Harry added the Witch to the other principles the aliens were known to possess: Faraday's Law of Electromagnetic Induction, the Cauchy Theorem, assorted variations of the Gauss Hypergeometric Equation, assorted Bessel functions, and so on. When, he wondered, are they going to tell us something we don't know?

It was obvious also that the White House was getting impatient. The reaction against the government was spreading. At home, few newspapers supported the President's position; and three of the four networks had attacked him in editorials. The so-called Carolingian Movement, named for the unruly historians who had broken up the conference at Penn, now had chapters on most major campuses. They'd been writing angry letters to editors and applying pressure to legislators.

American embassies were being stoned on a fairly regular basis; the State Department had protests from virtually everyone (among the Western alliance, only West Germany, Britain, and Sweden had refrained); and the government was pilloried daily at the United Nations. Japan threatened to cut off its exports to the United States, and there was talk of an oil embargo. And for all this, the President had little to show: a few well-known mathematical exercises, now augmented by the Witch of Agnesi.

Harry had come to hate the daily report. There'd been a couple of calls from Hurley in which the President had tried to conceal his growing exasperation. Gambini also had received at least one. But he was unconcerned. "Serve the dumb bastard right. Maybe after a while he'll figure out what he should do."

It had crossed Harry's mind that Hurley had allowed himself to be placed at Gambini's mercy. Obviously, he trusted the project manager, as did Harry, really. Still, Gambini would understand that a discovery of military significance would increase the chances of the project's being taken from him and would certainly eliminate any lingering possibility that the government would do what he wanted: release the transcripts. Consequently, Gambini would be tempted to withhold any such discovery.

Harry knew, and the President should have guessed, that Gambini remained under terrible pressure from his colleagues, most of whom would not welcome him back when his usefulness to the government had ended. A week never passed when some major figure did not use the press to assail Edward Gambini and urge him to refuse to cooperate with the "paranoid" policies of his government. Gambini never defended himself and never, in public, criticized the President.

His secretary buzzed. "Mr. Carmichael, Ted Parkinson is on the line."

Harry punched the call in. "Yes, Ted?"

"Harry, I think we ought to close the Visitor Center for a while."

"Why?"

"Some of the people out here are turning ugly. There are more demonstrators now and college kids carrying Carolingian signs. We've had a couple of incidents today."

"Anybody hurt?"

"Not yet. But it's just a matter of time. A lot of the kids are bringing alcohol in with them. There's no easy way to stop it. The security people have been tossing them out whenever they see it, but that just tends to make things worse."

"I'd like to avoid shutting it down, Ted. That would look as if we're going into a state of siege, and it'd probably just produce more demonstrators."

"It may be about to get worse, Harry. I got a call a few minutes ago from Cass Woodbury. She said that Backwoods Bobby and several busloads of his supporters are going to be here this afternoon."

"You're kidding."

"You ready for the kicker?"

"Go ahead."

"He's on *our* side this time."

"Yeah," Harry said. "He would be. There's no way he'd want the Soviets to get their hands on anything we have. Anyhow, he's supported this President all along. They think alike. Hurley's just a bit more sophisticated is all."

"I've let Security know."

"They may have their hands full out there this afternoon. What time is Freeman coming?"

"About three."

"That gets the evening news. Freeman's no dummy. He loves to see the investigators at one another's throats; this gives him a chance to get in on the fun and grab some national publicity. I think we can count on him to do what he can to keep things stirred up." Harry looked at his watch. "Okay, Ted. I'll be over later. Freeman's not likely to be interested in talking to us, but if he is, be careful what you say. He has a talent for twisting things."

"By the way," said Parkinson, "I heard there's trouble at Fermi. They're meeting right now to decide what they want to do. The word I'm getting is that a strike is a foregone conclusion and that the only thing in doubt is how tough they'll get with the government."

"Hell, they're cutting off their own noses," said Harry. "Who cares whether an accelerator lab in Illinois closes down? Certainly not the public. And consequently not the President."

It was 8:45. Harry had just time to go over and talk to Gambini. Maybe, at least, he could come up with something to break the long streak of negative reports to the White House.

Cord Majeski could not have said just when he realized the strings of numbers constituted a schematic. He recognized the basic design of a set of solenoids and a transducer; there appeared to be heating and cooling elements and a timer. "And the rest of the stuff," he told Gambini, "I can't make out at all." He'd drawn a rough diagram, but it didn't look like anything Gambini was familiar with.

"Can we build a working model?"

Majeski blinked and pinched the bridge of his nose. "Maybe," he said.

"What's wrong?"

"I can't find any power specifications, Ed. What do you figure it will take to make it work?"

Gambini grinned. "Start with house current. See if you can put it together, Cord. But give it a low priority. I'd like to get the translations completed first."

Majeski's disappointment was plain. "You could be talking years, Ed. We've got a lot of material."

"Well, we won't wait that long. Just put the thing aside for now. We'll get to it."

He found Leslie nibbling thoughtfully at a tuna sandwich. She didn't see him until he slid into a seat beside her. "Harry," she said. "How are you doing?"

"Okay. I didn't know you were back in town."

"I got in last night. Just in time, apparently. I hear Bobby Freeman will be paying a visit today."

"Yes," said Harry. "They're expecting him at the Visitor Center this afternoon." He couldn't make out whether she was serious or not. "Why would you be interested in Freeman?"

"Harry," she said, "he is a one-man study in mob psychology. He never says a word that makes sense, and yet two million Americans think he walks on water."

"Backwoods Bobby is living proof that you don't have to have a brain to acquire power in this country. You can't be ugly, but it sure as hell doesn't matter if you're stupid."

"That's a little harsh," she said, amused. "By what standard is he stupid? If you can get him off religion, he seems to be reasonable enough. In fact, given the parameters within which he works, he's remarkably consistent. If the Bible *were* to turn out to be divinely inspired, I think he'd have a leg up on the rest of us."

"You're talking nonsense," said Harry.

"Of course I am," she said with a wink. "I guess you know they had a breakthrough of sorts yesterday."

"We're not supposed to talk about any of that stuff in here," Harry said acidly. "Secrecy is the order of the day. What happened?"

"I guess we're all prisoners of the age," she said. "I can understand why they worry. I really don't know what I'd do if I were in Hurley's place."

"He's looking for a weapon," Harry said.

"And Ed, I suspect, would like to find a congenial mind. Rimford wants to discover whether the Rimford Model will survive. And you, Harry? What would you wish for?"

"An end to it," said Harry.

"Really?" She shook her head. "I'm disappointed in you. You're on the ultimate adventure."

"I suppose. But all I seem to get out of it is a lot of bitching. The latest is a meeting this afternoon called by some of the contract investigators. They're threatening to walk out."

"Anyhow," she said, as though the possibility of a strike were of no consequence, "we're beginning to get some sense of the structure of the language. But there's something very odd about it."

"Hell, Les, there's going to be a lot of odd stuff before we get finished."

"No, I don't mean *unusual* odd; I mean *irrational* odd. It's clumsy, Harry. It's *so* clumsy that I hesitate to call it a language."

"Clumsy?"

"Awkward. Comparative degrees, for example, are expressed by numerical values, both positive and negative. It's as if you talked about *good* on a scale of one to ten, without ever introducing *better* or *best.*"

"That seems reasonably precise."

"Oh, it's precise. My God, is it precise. Adjectives are the same way. Nothing, for example, is ever dark. They establish a quantification standard for illumination and then give you a benchmark on the standard. It's maddening. But what really fascinates me is that if you translate it into English, freely substituting general terms, you get some very striking poetry. Except that it isn't poetry, I don't think, but I don't know what else to call it." She shook her head in bewilderment. "One thing I'll tell you, Harry: in this form, the way they transmit it, it is *not* a natural language. It's too mathematical."

"You think it's something they devised purely for the transmission?"

"Probably. And if that's true, we'll lose a major source of information about them. There's a direct link between language and the character of its speakers. Harry, we really need to be able to send this stuff out. I know all sorts of people who should be getting a look at it. There are too many areas where I just don't have the expertise. Sitting here bottled up with it, it's frustrating."

"I know," said Harry. "Maybe things'll change now. Some clearances have come through, and we can start bringing in a few more people."

"It's a code, Harry. That's all it is: a code. And you know what's strangest of all about it? *We* could have done better. In any case, what counts is that we're starting to read it. It's slow going, because there's still a lot to do." She discovered her sandwich, almost untouched, and took a bite. "I think Hurley's going to be disappointed."

"Why?"

"The bulk of the material that we've been able to break into so far reads like philosophy. Although we can't even be sure of that because we don't understand most of the terms, and maybe we never will. I'm not even sure we aren't being subjected to some sort of interstellar gospel."

Images drifted through his mind of the President and Bobby Freeman reacting to that. "It's the best thing that could happen to us," he said.

"Harry," she replied, "I'm glad you think it's funny, because there's an awful lot of it. Listen: they divided their transmission into a hundred and eight sections. We've gotten into twenty-three of them so far, of which sixteen, and parts of several others, seem to have this general philosophical character."

"Is there any history? Do they tell us anything about themselves?"

"Not that we've been able to find. We're getting commentaries, but they're abstract, and we can't really make out what they relate to. There are long mathematical sections as well. We think we found a description of their solar system. If we're reading it correctly, they have six planets, and the home world *does* have rings. They *are* circling the yellow sun, by the way.

"But this other stuff. They paint with broad strokes, Harry. From what I've seen, they're not much interested in the sorts of things you build weapons from. You know what I really think the transmission is? Basically?"

Harry had no idea.

"A series of expanded essays on the good, the true, and the beautiful."

"You're kidding."

"We know they're interested in cosmology. They have enough knowledge of physics to baffle Gambini. They've supplied mathematical descriptions for all sorts of processes, including a lot of stuff we haven't begun to identify. We're probably going to learn what really holds atoms together and why water freezes at thirty-two degrees and how galaxies form. But there's a sense in the text that all that is"—she searched for a word—"incidental. Trivial. The way they establish their credentials, perhaps. What they really seem interested in, where it seems to me their energy is, is in their speculative sections."

"It figures," said Harry. "What else would we expect from an advanced race?"

"They may have given us their entire store of knowledge. Everything they consider significant."

Harry was realizing that he enjoyed spending time with her. Her laughter cheered him, and when he needed to talk, she listened. Her ability to leave Philadelphia at every whim suggested that she had no strong emotional attachment there. Furthermore, she embodied a fierce independence that implied she was on her own. He did not, of course, ask her point-blank, since that would have conveyed the wrong impression. Leslie was far too prosaic a woman to engage his interest.

Still, unaccountably, he felt comfortable with his conclusion that there was probably no man.

They walked together toward the lab, Harry carefully keeping a proper distance, but warmly aware, perhaps for the first time, of her physical presence. She needed almost two strides to each of his. But she stayed with him, apparently lost in thought, although if he'd been watching carefully he might have noted that her eyes strayed occasionally in his direction and then looked quickly away.

They walked across a bleak landscape under a gray-white December sky, threatening snow. When they arrived at the lab, Leslie hurried into the rear office that she'd taken over, and Harry wandered over to talk to Pete Wheeler.

The priest was seated at a computer, painstakingly punching in numbers from a set of notes. He looked relieved to have a chance to get away from it. "Are you going to Kmoch's meeting this afternoon?" he asked.

"I haven't decided yet."

"It'll be an unfriendly audience. There's a lot of hostility right now. Did you know that even Baines is beginning to get some pressure? The Academy wants him to refuse to cooperate further with the project. And to take a public stand."

"How the hell can *anyone* pressure Baines?"

"Directly, they can't. But you know how he is. He hates to have anyone think ill of him. Especially all those people he's worked with for a lifetime. To make matters worse, of course, he thinks they're right."

"How about you?"

"I guess some people have complained to the abbott. He says the Vatican isn't worried, but there's been some pressure from the American Church. But I don't think there'll be anything overt. They're extremely sensitive right now about being seen as a roadblock to progress."

"The Galileo syndrome," said Harry.

"Sure."

"You look worried."

"I keep thinking how all this must look to Hurley. He's in a no-win situation, and he'll be damned no matter which way things go. You really want my opinion, Harry?" He rubbed the back of his neck. "Historically, governments are not good at keeping secrets. Especially about technology. The only one I can even think of that retained control of an advanced weapon for a long time was Constantinople."

"Greek fire," said Harry.

"Greek fire. And that's probably it for the whole course of human history. Whatever we learn here, Harry, whatever's in the Text, will soon be common property." His dark eyes were troubled. "If Hurley's right and we discover the makings of a new bomb or a new bug, it'll be only a matter of time before the Russians have it, or the IRA, or the other assorted loonies of the planet.

"I don't think that's the real danger, though God knows it's serious enough. But at least it's a danger everyone recognizes. Harry, we're about to be inundated by an alien culture. This time we are the South Sea islanders." He shut off his monitor. "Do you remember a couple of years ago when Gambini and Rimford and Breakers used to get into those long arguments about the number of advanced civilizations in the Milky Way? And Breakers always said that if there were others, we'd be able to hear some of them. They'd be transmitting to us." Wheeler extracted the disc he'd been working with, and returned it to the master file. "I've got to get out of here for a while," he said. "Want to come along?"

"I just came in," said Harry. But he followed the priest outside, thinking about Breakers. He'd been a cynical old son of a bitch from Harvard who hadn't lived quite long enough to hear the great question answered.

"Baines published an article recently," continued Wheeler, "titled 'The Captain Cook Syndrome,' in which he says a wise culture might recognize that contact with a more primitive society, however well intentioned, could do nothing but create problems for the weaker group. Maybe, he said, they're silent out of compassion.

"But our aliens chatter. They tell us everything. Why would they be different? Ed thinks they bungled the transmission code, made it more difficult than necessary. Could they be slow-witted? Could they possibly be incompetent?"

"That's hard to buy," said Harry. "After they manipulated that pulsar. No, I can't believe they're dullards. Maybe their solitude has something to do with it."

"Maybe. But that doesn't help us. Harry, we are about to be invaded as surely as if the little critters arrived in saucers and began rumbling around the terrain in tripods. The transmission, which we are now beginning to be able to read, is going to change us beyond recognition. Not just what we know, but how we think. And undoubtedly it'll affect our values. It's a prospect I can't say I relish."

"Pete, if you feel that way, why are you helping?"

"For the same reason everybody else is: I want to find out

what they are. What they've got to say. And maybe what the implications are for us. It's all I care about anymore, Harry. And it's the same with everyone. Everything else in my life right now seems trivial. And that brings us back to Kmoch's meeting, Harry. If I were standing outside looking in, I'd be pretty damned mad, too."

"Kmoch's talking about a strike."

"He's not the only one. But if you go in there today, you'll be lucky if you don't get assaulted. I mean, people are *mad*."

There were a few flakes in a stiff, cold wind coming out of the northwest. Just beyond the perimeter fence, three men crouched on the roof of a two-story frame, repairing shingles. In the adjoining back yard, two teenagers were unloading firewood from a pickup.

Wheeler wore an ugly oversized green cap. "It belonged to a student I had a few years ago at Princeton in a cosmology class. I admired it pretty openly, I guess, and at the end of the semester he gave it to me." It jutted far out over his eyes.

"It looks like something you took from a mugger," Harry said.

They stopped at an intersection and waited for a mail truck to pass. "I've got something to tell you," said the priest.

Harry waited.

"I found some equations in the text that describe planetary magnetic fields: why they develop, how they work. Some of it we know already, some of it we don't. They go into a lot of detail, and it isn't really my specialty. But I think I can see a way to tap the earth's magnetic field for energy. Lots of energy."

"Can we *get* at the magnetic field to use it?" asked Harry.

"Yes," replied Wheeler. "Easily. All that's necessary is to put a few satellites up, convert the energy to, say, a laser, and beam it to a series of receivers on the ground. It'd probably solve our energy needs for the indefinite future."

"How certain are you?"

"Reasonably. I'm going to tell Gambini about it this afternoon."

"You sound hesitant."

"I am, Harry. And I don't really know why. Solving the power problem and getting away from fossil fuels sounds like a pretty good idea. But I wish I had a better notion how something like this, sprung all at once, might shake things up. Maybe we need an economist out here, too."

"You worry too much," said Harry. "This is the kind of

useful information we need. The good, the true, and the beautiful may make for interesting talk at lunch, but taxpayers would be more interested in doing something about their electric bills."

Harry called his White House number. "Please tell him we might have something," he said.

The voice on the other end belonged to a young woman. "Come in this evening. Seven o'clock."

The stars are silent.

Voyager among dark harbors, I listen, but the midnight wind carries only the sound of trees and water lapping against the gunwale and the solitary cry of the night swallow.

There is no dawn. No searing sun rises in east or west. The rocks over Calumal do not silver, and the great round world slides through the void.

> —Stanza 32 from DS 87
> Freely translated by Leslie Davies
> (Unclassified)

11

A BUBBLE UNIVERSE drifting over a cosmic stream: Rimford's features widened into a broad grin. He pushed the mound of paper off the coffee table onto the floor and, in a sudden surge of pleasure, lobbed a ball-point pen the length of the room and into the kitchen.

He went out to the refrigerator, came back with a beer under one arm, and dialed Gambini's office. While he waited for the physicist to answer, he pulled the tab and took a long swallow.

"Research Projects," said a female voice.

"Dr. Gambini, please. This is Rimford."

"He's tied up at the moment, Doctor," she said. "Can I have him call you?"

"How about Pete Wheeler? Is he there?"

"He went out a few minutes ago with Mr. Carmichael. I don't know when he'll be back. Dr. Majeski's here."

"Okay," said Rimford, disappointed. "Thanks. I'll try again later." He hung up, finished the beer, walked around the pile of paper on the floor, and sat down again.

One of the great moments of the twentieth century and there was no one with whom to share it.

A quantum universe. Starobinskii and the others might have been right all along.

He didn't understand all the mathematics of it yet, but he would; he was well on the way. By Christmas, he thought, he would have the mechanism of creation.

Much of it was clear already. The universe was a quantum event, a pinprick of space-time. It had been called into being in the same way that apparently causeless events continue to occur in the subatomic world. But it had been a bubble, not a bang! And once in existence, the bubble had expanded with exponential force. There'd been no light barrier during those early nanoseconds, because the governing principles had not yet formed. Consequently, its dimensions had, within fractions of an instant, exceeded those of the solar system, and indeed those of the Milky Way. There had been no matter at first, but only the slippery fabric of existence itself erupting in a cosmic explosion. Somehow an iron stability had taken hold, expansion dropped below light speed, and substantial portions of the enormous energy of the first moments were converted into hydrogen and helium.

Not for the first time in his life, Rimford wondered about the "cause" of causeless effects. Perhaps he would find also the secret of the unaccountable: the de Sitter superspace from which the universal bubble had formed. Perhaps, somewhere in the transmission, the Altheans would address that question. But Rimford understood that, no matter how advanced a civilization might be, it was necessarily tied to this universe. There was no way to look past its boundaries or beyond its earliest moments. One could only speculate, regardless of the size of the telescope or the capability of the intellect. But the implications were clear.

He paced the small living room, far too excited to sit still. There were any number of people with whom he would have liked to talk, men and women who had dedicated their lives to this or that aspect of the puzzles to which he now held partial solutions, but security regulations stood in the way. Parker, for example, at Wisconsin, had invested twenty years trying to explain why the velocity of universal expansion and the gravity needed to reverse the outward flight of the galaxies were very nearly identical. So balanced, in fact, that even after the computations that included nonluminous matter in the equation, the question of an open or closed universe remained unanswered. Why should that be? Rimford's eyes narrowed. They had long suspected that the perfect symmetry of the two was somehow dictated by natural law. Yet that was an unacceptable condition, because absolute cosmic equilibrium would have precluded the formation of the galaxies.

But now he had the math, and he saw how symmetry between expansion and contraction was generated, how it was in fact two sides of a coin, how it could have been no other way. Yet, fortunately for the human race, the tendency toward equilibrium was offset by an unexpected factor: gravity was not a constant. The variable was slight, but it existed, and it induced the required lag. That would also explain, he was sure, recently found disparities between deep space observations and relativity theory.

What would Parker not give for five minutes tonight with Rimford!

Unable to sit still, Baines left the cottage, drove out to

Greenbelt Road, and turned east under slate skies.

He'd been on the highway about half an hour when rain began to fall, fat icy drops that splashed like wet clay against the windshield. Most of the traffic disappeared into a gray haze, headlights came on, the rain stopped, the sky cleared, and Rimford sailed happily down country roads until he came to a likely looking inn on Good Luck Road. He stopped, went in, collected a scotch, and ordered a prime steak.

His old notion of the initial microseconds of the expansion, which had included the simultaneous creation of matter with space-time, brought about by the innate instability of the void, seemed to be wrong on all counts. He wondered whether some of his other ideas were also headed for extinction. In the mirror across the room, he looked oddly pleased. The scotch was smooth, accenting his mood. Assuring himself that no one was watching, he raised a toast, downed the rest of the drink, and asked for another.

He was surprised at his own reaction. His life work had blown up. Yet he felt no regrets. It would have been good to be right. But now he *knew!*

He had never had a better steak. Midway through the meal, he scribbled an equation on a cloth napkin, and propped it up where he could see it. It was a description of the properties and structure of space. If any single mathematical formula could be said to constitute the secret of the universe, that was it!

Good God, now that he had it in his hands, it all seemed so logical. How could they not have known?

The Altheans did indeed manipulate stars, in Gambini's phrase, but in the wider meaning of the verb. In fact, they manipulated space in the sense that they could alter its degree of curvature. Or they could flatten it altogether!

And so could he!

My God! His hands trembled as, for the first time, he considered the practical applications.

A shadow passed across the room. It was only the waitress, with the coffee. She was an attractive young lady, bright and smiling, as waitresses in country inns invariably are. But Rimford did not smile back, and she must have wondered about the plain little man in the corner who'd looked so frightened at her approach.

Later, when he'd gone, she picked up the napkin with the string of numbers written on it. By six o'clock, she had tossed it into the laundry.

• • •

The meeting in the Giacconi Room was not openly hostile, but Harry felt a distinct chill. About fifty people were present: some seemed angry, but most, apparently surprised to see him, looked embarrassed. Kmoch tried to rouse them, and Harry could see that they were unhappy with the course of events. Two others took their turns, but they also were not very articulate. That might have been a result of frustration, but he doubted it. In Harry's experience, physical scientists did not usually excel as speakers.

Forty minutes or so into the meeting, they invited Harry to defend himself. He got up, looked around, and thanked everyone for being present.

"I know this is a problem for you," he said. "It's been one for me, too, but I realize that some of you are in trouble over the Hercules secrecy. And I realize something else: that each of you has dedicated your life to understanding what makes things work. And one of the biggest of those things is now being kept from you, from everyone, by a government that must seem terribly insensitive. Some have even said its actions are criminal."

In a conversational tone, he outlined the President's dilemma, described the fears that, he said, kept them all up at night, and inquired whether they really wanted to heap blame on a man whose only concern was that Hercules might bring a plague of technical knowledge into an unprepared world.

When Harry finished, there was a general discussion, in which almost everyone wished to get a protest on record. The strongest statement came from Gideon Barlow, of NASCOM Support and the University of Rhode Island, who warned Harry that their patience was not without limit.

Kmoch prudently failed to ask for a strike vote. Instead, he proposed a committee be elected to compose a letter voicing the group's reservations. The move passed with a nearly unanimous show of hands.

At the door, Louisa White of MIT told Harry that next time management wouldn't get off so easy.

Harry said he understood, and came away quite pleased with his performance.

Bobby Freeman arrived in a caravan of four old school buses. They'd been scrubbed down for the occasion, and black hand-painted letters on their sides proclaimed them the property of the Trinity Bible Church. A cheer went up from a portion of the crowd. The buses rolled in past heavy automobile traffic, past demonstrators carrying banners that demanded Hurley be impeached and that the Hercules Text be released, took their directions from base police, and swung into assigned parking areas, while television cameras followed their progress.

Freeman descended from the lead vehicle, smiling broadly to liberal cheers. He was hatless, wrapped in a threadbare coat and a long, loose scarf. The crowd surged forward; security men, Freeman's own, mixed freely with them, restraining them, trying to control access to the great man. The preacher embraced a group of children, the ends of his long scarf flying. His supporters were middle-class types, mostly white, kids and their mothers and older couples. They were thoroughly combed, and the kids had shining faces and wore colorful school jackets, and everyone carried a Bible. It was cold, but nobody seemed to notice.

He lifted a young boy in his arms, and said something that Harry couldn't hear. The crowd cheered again. People reached out to touch his sleeve. An old man climbed into a tree and almost fell when Freeman waved in his direction.

The wind played with his gray hair. His cheeks were full, his nose broad and flat, and he appeared irritatingly content. But his manner was not the vacuous sort of complacency one usually finds in the professional television preacher; rather, the impression was of a man who had come to grips with the great dilemmas of human existence and who believed he had found a solution.

"He's sincere," Leslie whispered.

"He's a fake," said Harry, who was unsure, but who felt a reflexive duty to attack TV preachers.

"We're going to get a sermon, I believe," she said.

Freeman's men had cleared a small circle for him. Harry picked up a couple of security men and pushed through the crowd to the preacher's side. "Reverend Freeman," he said, "we have a VIP door open for you." Harry indicated the general direction.

"Thank you," said the preacher, launching his words into the gusting wind. "I'll wait my turn. And go in with my friends." He joined the long line, while the few people in the immediate area who had heard the exchange cheered.

"That misfired," said Leslie, amused.

"You want to try your luck?"

She shook her head. "It's a losing game," she said. "The crowd and the cameras are out *here*."

Harry punched Parkinson's number on his hand radio. "How are you doing, Ted?"

"We've cut things down as much as we can, Harry."

"I want it faster. Set up a special demonstration in one of the conference rooms if you have to. Move some people out of there. I want to get at least a hundred more inside as quickly as we can."

Parkinson growled. "Why don't we just claim we're having a power failure and shut down for the day?"

Back near the buses, which were still discharging passengers, signs waved. And a scuffle began. Dave Schenken, who had appeared at Harry's side, spoke into a radio.

A young man in a coat and tie, obviously one of Freeman's people, leaped onto the hood of a bus. "Bobby!" he cried, above the murmur of the crowd. "Bobby, are you in there?"

A few amens rolled back at him.

"This is a setup," said Leslie.

"I'm over here," came the preacher's cheerful baritone.

"Bobby," said the man on the bus, "I can't see you."

Someone must have produced a portable pulpit or a wooden box. Freeman rose suddenly head, shoulders, and waist out of the crowd. "Can you see me now, Jim? Can *you* see me, friends?"

The crowd cheered. But when the noise subsided, Harry heard a few catcalls.

"Why are we here, Bobby?" asked the man on the bus.

"This is not a good situation, Harry," said Leslie.

"We're here to bear witness, friends," said Freeman in the deep, round tones that seemed so much bigger than he did. There was more applause, and again it was followed by an echo of boos. "There must be some Philadelphia baseball fans here," joked the preacher, and the crowd laughed. "We are standing in a place where people have not always been friendly to the Word, but where they are being touched by the Word all the same."

The laughter stopped. The outer perimeter of the crowd stirred uneasily. Someone in back threw something. It landed close to Harry with a sound like soft ice. "Jimmy wants to know," continued the preacher, not noticing, "why we have come here today. I can tell you: we are here because God is using this place, this scientific installation"—he pronounced the words the way somebody else might have said "whorehouse"—"for His own purposes. God is at work here this afternoon, using the devices of these men of stricken faith to confound them.

"But that is not important. God can confound the unbelieving any time He wishes." He pronounced "God" in a singsong manner and gave the name two syllables. "What *is* important is that the message from the skies, whatever it may be, has been delivered, like the message from Sinai, to a God-fearing nation." Cameras were clicking now, and the news-pool van was getting it all. "There are some among us who would give this message to the atheists in the Kremlin. *Give* it to them, not knowing what it says, because we cannot yet read it. Not knowing what knowledge might be hidden within it. Not knowing, and not caring, what use the masters of enslaved Russia might make of such knowledge. Well, *we* know, don't we, brothers and sisters?"

"We know," replied a chorus of voices.

"Sit down, buddy," came an angry voice. "You're holding up the line." That got some cheers, too. In spite of himself, Harry smiled.

"I'm not sure why you're laughing," said Leslie. "You've got a dangerous situation here."

A substantial space had opened between Freeman and the Visitor Center.

"That man has a point," said Freeman good-humoredly. He disappeared into the crowd, which surged forward, and then he rose again, closer to the building. "Are you still there, Jim?"

The man on the bus waved. "I'm here, Bobby."

"Can you see the antennas?" He held both arms out toward the twin units mounted atop Building 23, visible over a cluster of trees. "We've come a long way from Moses, friends. Or we like to *think* we have."

"Why don't you go home?" someone bellowed. "Nobody here wants to listen to that."

"And take your loonies with you," added another voice.

The crowd surged suddenly, and a few people fell forward onto the grass apron that surrounded the Visitor Center. There were screams of fear and rage, and Harry could see someone with a Jesus sign whacking away with it at persons unknown until the sign disintegrated.

Several fights erupted back near the buses. A wave of people broke loose and ran for their cars.

Uniformed officers moved in.

Meanwhile, Freeman was still talking. The trouble had developed so quickly it had caught him in midsentence, and he was not a man to leave anything unsaid. But he was lurching violently, and Harry suspected someone had hold of an ankle or a leg and was trying to pull him to the ground.

"Leslie," he shouted over the noise, "things are getting a little uncertain out here. Maybe you'd better wait inside."

She glanced at the crush of people now in the doorway, some trying to get clear of the commotion out front, others turning to watch. "I can't get inside now, and I couldn't see if I did."

"Friends," Freeman said, raising both his palms and his voice, "why are you so easily angered?"

Leslie cupped her mouth and put it next to Harry's ear. "That's a mistake. He isn't used to this kind of audience."

"He's going to get hit in the head if he's not careful," said Harry.

Abruptly, the preacher vanished.

"That's it," Schenken said to his radio. "Shut it down."

"It may be a little late," muttered Harry.

The cluster of space near Freeman closed up, and a series of pushing matches deteriorated almost immediately into a general scuffle. The fights in back spilled into one another, a few beer bottles flew, and the line into the Visitor Center broke and ran. People rolled back and forth, like heavy seas, some scattering toward the relative safety of the parking lot and the surrounding high ground, others cheering combatants, threatening security men, and, for the most part, enjoying themselves immensely.

The Visitor Center was constructed largely of glass. Harry watched a rock arc gracefully out of the parking area, sail overhead, and shatter one of the doors.

The security forces hauled a few adolescents out of the struggling mob, and it appeared briefly as if things were under control. Then someone fired a shot.

Whatever holiday mood might have remained dissipated. A sound like the wind at night rose from the crowd. There was an uneasy hesitation, and a second wave began to run away. One or two here, a few there, and rapidly the retreat became general. People spilled across flagstones and out over lawns toward any visible open space. One of Schenken's security men appeared, holding his hands over his head, blood spurting between his fingers.

A group of screaming schoolchildren, shepherded by a couple of panicked teachers, was overtaken and run down. Harry, chilled, looked for help, but saw none. He pushed into the surging mob, which immediately swept him off his feet with a flurry of elbows and kicks and punches. He gasped and allowed himself to be carried along until he caught his breath, and then he tried to plant his feet. He didn't see Leslie anymore, and the one or two security people nearby seemed caught up in the general surge, just as he was.

His throat swelled, and he was having problems breathing. Blood dripped out of his sleeve. But he kept his eyes on the spot where the kids had been. As things cleared out, he was sickened by what he saw: some were down, not moving, their limbs bent, others writhed on grass and concrete; a few huddled with sympathetic adults. One of the security people had got in among them, and was trying to help when more shots sounded behind him. They turned the stampede back on itself, and Harry watched people getting trampled. The little mound of injured children was once again in the track of the beast.

In perhaps the finest moment of his life, Harry placed himself in front of the mob. They hammered into him, driving him back. Individual screams became general and merged into a single deafening roar. He recovered, dug in, absorbed the surge, and was still standing when it passed.

Several people wandered in shock across the battleground. Off to one side he could see Leslie, fragile in a light cashmere jacket, trying to get to him until, in a sickening moment that he would carry with him forever, she, too, was engulfed.

His first impulse was to go after her, but he held on instead where he was, barring the approach to the injured children.

A news helicopter looped in and drifted over the scene. The Center's ambulance, its red lights blinking, came through the utility gate on the west side and rode across the lawn. Moments later, the Greenbelt medivan also arrived.

One of the Trinity Bible Church buses was trying to get away from the melee with barely half a dozen people on board. Harry swayed. One bloodied boy, a year or two younger than Tommy, lay immediately behind him. A medic hurried over, put a stethoscope to his chest, and signaled quickly for a stretcher. But Harry knew. Anyone who looked into the medic's face would have known.

Leslie was beside him, holding his arm. He didn't know how long she'd been there.

Later they would say there had been only one death.

Schenken came over to complain about the large numbers of people who were allowed into the Visitor Center. "You see what happens," he said. "I suggest we put a checkpoint on the outer gate, like the one at the main gate, and stop letting just anyone come in here."

"You mean keep the visitors out of the Visitor Center?"

"Look," said Schenken. "I got three guys in the hospital as a result of this; and we have had a riot on the premises. That isn't going to do my career any good, so I'm already not very happy. Don't get smart with me, okay?" He started to walk off, but spun around and jabbed a finger at Harry. "If I had my way, there wouldn't *be* a goddam Visitor Center. What purpose does it serve, anyhow?"

"It's the reason we're here," said Harry, smoldering. "It's the point of the organization. And by the way, if you wave that finger in my face again, I'm going to break it off and shove it down your throat." Schenken appraised him, decided he meant it, and backed off. It was the first time in living memory that Harry had physically threatened another adult. After all the carnage, it felt good. "What was the shooting about?" he asked.

"One of the Reverend's people was an off-duty cop. Fired a warning shot. You believe that?" Schenken sighed loudly at the depths of human stupidity. "Waving a gun around in a mob like that. Goddam loony. We haven't accounted for the second series of shots."

"What happened to Freeman?"

"We got him out of here first thing. He's over at the dispensary now. He's limping a little." He smiled maliciously.

The grounds were covered with the rubble of battle: beer bottles, placards, sticks, paper, even a few articles of clothing. In the driveway immediately in front of the entrance to the Visitor Center, the TV pool van lay on its side. A few of the Space Center's employees, in blue coveralls, were beginning the cleanup. Maybe two dozen cars remained in the general parking lot. Either they were too wrecked to move or their owners had been hauled off to hospitals or jail. Parkinson had sent a young woman out to record plate numbers so they could begin the task of locating owners.

Harry drove to the dispensary, where he found Freeman lying on a couch. His right arm was in a sling; his jaw and the bridge of his nose were taped. "How do you feel?" he asked.

The preacher looked genuinely repentant. "Dumb," he said. He was slow to focus on his visitor. "Wasn't it you," he asked, "who wanted me to use the side door?"

Harry nodded. "It was."

"I should have done it." He offered his hand. "I'm Bobby Freeman," he said.

"I know." Harry ignored the gesture.

"Yes. Of course you do."

"My name's Carmichael. I'm an administrator here. I wanted to be sure you were all right. And I was also curious why you did that."

"Did what?"

Son of a bitch. "Started a riot," rasped Harry.

Freeman nodded in agreement. "I guess I did. I'm sorry. I came here to help. I don't understand how it happened. I mean, there weren't that many people out there, other than mine. But I know why they didn't want to hear what I had to say. It's a hard thing to look the truth square in the eyes."

"Reverend Freeman, you want the truth? It was cold out there today, and you were holding up the line!"

The President looked grave. His features, which were in no way striking in ordinary light, had taken on a hard, flinty appearance in the glow cast by the table lamp. "Harry, I was sorry to hear about the trouble today."

Harry cleared his throat. They were alone in the Oval Office. "I'm not sure yet how it happened," he said. "But Freeman didn't help."

"So I heard. Why did you give him the opportunity to speak?" There was a tired sort of bitterness in his voice. "Schenken, anyway, should have known better." He peered at Harry, and his assessment was visibly unfavorable. "Never mind," he said. "It's not your fault. Did you know we had a fatality?"

"The little boy?"

"A third grader visiting here from Macon." Hurley picked up a pack of cigarettes from his desktop, offered them to Harry, and lit one. "Judging by the tapes, I suspect we're lucky we didn't have a full-scale catastrophe out there. I understand Freeman is planning a memorial service tomorrow. I'd ask him not to, but he's already aware that it'll embarrass me. If there's one thing he can't resist, it's a chance to appear on national television. He'll take advantage of TV tomorrow to berate the godless elements in this country that are responsible for the tragedy, by which he usually means the universities, and sometimes the Democrats. But we're the ones who'll look foolish. Now, I hope what you're bringing me tonight is worth the price we're paying."

Harry was seated under a rarity: a portrait of Theodore Roosevelt in a thoughtful mood. Teddy had always seemed to be the most remote of Presidents. Unlike, say, Jefferson and McKinley, who belonged to distant epochs, the Roughrider embodied an age that had never really existed. Who stood for reality today? John W. Hurley? Or Ed Gambini? "Pete Wheeler thinks he's found a way to extract energy from the magnetic belts around the earth."

"Oh?" The President's expression did not change. The tip of his cigarette glowed and then faded. "How much energy?" He leaned toward Harry. "How complicated a process?"

"Pete thinks it will provide global supplies. The source is damned near limitless. We don't have the practical details yet. That's going to take some time, but Wheeler says the mechanics won't be difficult."

"By God!" Hurley erupted from his seat, clenching both fists over his head in a triumphant gesture recognizable from his campaigns. "Harry, if it's true, *if* it's true." His eyes locked on Harry. "When will I have something on paper?"

"By the end of the week."

"Make it tomorrow. By noon. Give me what you have. I don't care if it's handwritten. I don't care about theory. I want to know how much power is available and what it will take to get the system operational. You got that, Harry?"

"Mr. President, I don't think we can put together anything useful in so short a time."

"Just do what I ask. Okay?"

Harry nodded.

The President stood beside his desk. "Your jaw is swollen. Is that from this afternoon?"

"Yes, Mr. President."

"Be more careful, Harry. I need you. Gambini and the others over there, they're good men, but they don't have any responsibilities, really, except to themselves. I understand that. They live in a world where men are reasonable and where there are no enemies but ignorance.

"I need your good judgment, Harry." Hurley gazed with immense satisfaction at his visitor. "If I were to ask Gambini what to do about the arms race, he would advise me to stop making arms. A beautifully logical response, and yet utterly wrongheaded, of course, since it ignores the fact that the arms race has long since taken on a life of its own. No single nation can stop it. I'm no longer even certain that we and the Soviets working in collusion could stop it.

"But maybe Father Wheeler has provided an answer. Is there anything else you wanted to tell me?"

"No, sir," said Harry, rising. He felt, somehow, as if he had gained weight during the interview.

Baines Rimford did not drive back to his quarters after leaving the inn on Good Luck Road. Instead, he wandered for hours along bleak highways, between walls of dark forest. The rain that had cleared off in midafternoon had begun again. It was beginning to freeze on his windshield.

God help him, he did not know what to do.

He soared over the crest of a hill, descended too swiftly down its far side, and entered a long curve that took him across a bridge. He could not see whether there was water below, or railroad tracks, or only a gully; but it was, in a sense, a bridge across time: Oppenheimer waited on the other side. And Fermi and Bohr. And the others who had unleashed the cosmic fire.

There must have come a moment, he thought, at Los Alamos, or Oak Ridge, or the University of Chicago, during which they grasped, really understood, the consequences of their work. Had they ever met and talked it over? Had there been a conscious decision, after it became clear during the winter of 1943– 44 that the Nazis were *not* close to building a bomb, to go ahead anyway? Or had they simply been caught up in momentum? In the exhilaration of penetrating the secret of the sun?

Rimford had spoken once with Eric Christopher, the only one of the Manhattan Project physicists he'd ever met. Christopher was an old man at the time of the meeting, and Rimford had mercilessly put the question to him. It was the only occasion he could recall on which he had been deliberately cruel. And Christopher had said, yes, it's easy enough for you, fifty years later, to know what we should have done. But there were Nazis in our world. And a brutal Pacific war and projections of a million American dead if we could not make the bomb work.

But there must have been an hour, an instant, when they doubted themselves, when they could have acted for the future, when history might have been turned into a different channel. The choice had existed, for however short a time: they could have refused.

The Manhattan Option.

Rimford hurried through the night, pursued over the dark country roads by something he could not name. And he wondered fiercely whether the world would not be safer if he died out here tonight.

Leslie had picked up a swollen eye at the Visitor Center. It was beginning to discolor, and she she'd also acquired some bruised ribs. "Stay clear of revivals," she said, measuring the extent of the swelling with her fingertips.

"You look like a lady boxer," said Harry.

"And not a very competent one. What did Freeman have to say for himself?"

They were in an Italian restaurant on Massachusetts Avenue, just off Dupont Circle. "He accepted responsibility. I was surprised."

"It must have been difficult for him. I don't think he's seen much adversity in his life. At least not the kind that he has to share the guilt for. He knows a child died, and he knows it wouldn't have happened if he'd stayed away. And I suspect that'll be hard on him. Freeman is much better at being the victim."

"I asked him why he did it," said Harry. "I knew the answer: it was an easy opportunity to make the evening news."

"That's true," she said. "But it doesn't go far enough. I don't think he does it for exclusively selfish reasons. Other than the inner satisfaction he gets from being the Lord's right-hand man, of course. Freeman is no hypocrite, Harry. He's a believer. And when he talks about a world ringed by the Jordan, and directed by a Deity who cares about His creatures, when he quotes Psalms that are so lovely one wonders whether they did indeed come out of a human brain, it is very easy to want things to be that way. I mean, it's a better arrangement than you folks have. Gambini tried to explain to me once why the universe has no real edge, despite the fact that it began in an eruption of some sort, and I didn't have the vaguest idea what he was talking about. Your world is cold and dark and very big. Freeman's is—or was—a garden. The truth is, Harry, that I find God more comprehensible than a fourth spatial dimension."

Her luminous eyes had grown distant again, as they had been on the first night he'd seen her. "Gambini wouldn't want to live in a garden," he said.

"No, I don't suppose he would. His telescopes would be useless in Eden. Still, all these years he's been a driven man, Harry. And what is it that's driving him? He wants the answers to the big questions. I think, in his own way, Ed Gambini is a kind of twentieth-century Augustine. It's probably no coincidence that there's a priest among his closest colleagues." She touched a handkerchief gently to the injured eye and winced. "I won't be able to see out of it tomorrow," she said. "How do *you* feel?"

Everything ached. "Not real good," he confessed.

They were silent after that. Their dinners came, spaghetti for Harry and linguine for Leslie. "You miss them quite   lot, don't you?" she asked suddenly.

Harry's expression didn't change. "They've been a big chunk of my life. Julie said in effect that I didn't really care whether they lived or died. And I know she meant it, believed it. But it isn't true. It was never true. I'm going through the most exciting period of my career now. God knows where all this will lead. But the truth is that I get no pleasure out of it. I'd trade it all." Harry pushed at his food with a piece of bread. "I'm sorry. This is what you do for a living, isn't it? Listen to people talk about how they've made a mess of their lives."

She reached across the table and took his hand. "I'm not your doctor, Harry. I'm a friend. I know this is a difficult time for you. And I know it must seem as if you'll never really come out of it. You're at bottom right now. But you're not alone, and things will get better."

"Thanks," he said. And, after a moment: "She's hard to replace." He smiled at her. "For a moment, I thought you were going to say you'd been through something like this yourself."

Leslie in the flickering candlelight: she grew thoughtful. Her rich eyes got lost somewhere, and there were shadows in the soft hollows of her cheeks. It struck Harry, quite suddenly, that she was achingly lovely. How had that simple fact eluded him until tonight? "You're right," she said, "in recognizing she's unique. You won't find another to her measurements. But that doesn't mean you won't find a better set of measurements."

She did not smile, but something mischievous watched him from her eyes. "And no," she continued, "I was not going to tell you I've been through a similar experience. I'm one of the lucky ones who've never been touched by a great passion. I can say, perhaps to my shame, that I've never known a man who wasn't easy to give up."

"You don't sound as if you think very highly of us," said Harry, not as aloof as he tried to sound.

"I *love* men," she said, squeezing Harry's palm. "They just ... well, why don't we let it go at that?"

They went to the Red Limit for a nightcap. It was late, and they didn't talk much at first. Leslie sat stirring a drink, staring down into it, until Harry asked her if she was still playing the riot over in her mind.

"No," she said, "nothing like that." Their eyes met, and she shrugged. "I've been spending most of my time translating. And I've been getting an impression from the text that's, well, shaken me a bit."

"What do you mean?"

Her breathing had changed. She opened her purse, groped momentarily until she found a wrinkled envelope bearing the logo of a Philadelphia bank, and began to write. Upside down, it looked to Harry like verse. "This is a liberal translation," she said. "But I think it captures the spirit of the thing." She slid it across to him.

> I speak with the generations
> Of those whose bones are in the barrow.
> We are restless, they and I.

Harry read it several times. "It doesn't mean anything to me," he said. "What's wrong?"

She wrote again on the envelope:

> Having passed through the force that drives
> the world flower,
> I know the pulse of the galaxies.

"I'm sorry," said Harry, frowning. "I'm lost."

"It's out of context," she said. "But the 'world flower' is, I believe, evolution; and the mechanism that drives it is death!"

She looked sufficiently unnerved that Harry ordered another round of drinks. "The material I have is filled with things like that, suggesting a very casual acquaintance with mortality. There are also references to a Designer. God."

"We got a world full of Presbyterians?" Harry said.

"Funny." She closed her eyes and began to quote the Hercules Text:

> I have touched the living chain.
> Have known the storm within
>   the proton.
> I speak with the dead.
> Almost, I know the Designer.

"They're only poems," said Harry.

"Yes," she said. "I know. But I don't understand any of it. Harry, the composers of these verses tell us time and again, in a variety of ways, that they have died, that theirs is a community of the living and the dead." She crumpled a napkin and flipped it across the table. "Oh, I don't know. It's not simply a few odd quatrains. There's a sense throughout the material of a race that somehow transcends mortality."

"I'd like to read some of it," Harry said.

"I wish you would," she replied. "I'd feel better."

Harry reached for her; her hand was cold.

After Carmichael had gone, John Hurley stood a long time near the curtains, watching the traffic on Executive Avenue. He'd come to the White House three years before, convinced that accommodation with the Soviets was possible, that in the end common sense could prevail. That happy notion had become the undisclosed cornerstone of his presidency. And the measure of his failure.

He suspected that other men, on other nights, had stood brooding beside these windows: other men in the shadow of the nuclear hammer, Kennedy and Nixon and Reagan and Sedgwick. They, too, would have yearned for the easier times of a Cleveland or a Coolidge. They, too, must have wished desperately for a world free of nuclear weapons, and in the end they must have grown to hate their antagonists in Moscow.

The frightened, angry men of the Kremlin had never responded to reason. During his own administration, he'd watched his chances and, when the moment seemed right, had made his offers. The Soviets had reacted by increasing pressure in Central America and the Philippines. Reagan had been right, of course: the Soviet rulers were bastards, but it was no longer politic to point that out in public. Certainly if there was a way of dealing with them, he had not yet found it. And the Hurley strategy had become one with the American position since 1945: wait for the leavening effect of time to soften the Soviet posture. And so the waves of weapons mounted, year after dreary year, generation after generation, until hardly anyone now lived who could remember when it was not so. And, perhaps most disquieting of all, the walk along the precipice had come to seem like the natural order of things.

The terrible truth was that a tiger was loose in the world. And the real danger from the tiger, perhaps, was not that it might, in some irrational spasm, launch an attack: rather, its disruptive policies encouraged nations to play one superpower off against the other. With the result that the planet bled constantly.

Harry Carmichael's news might have changed all that.

At a stroke, particle-beam weapons would become feasible. The technology was there, had been there, for a decade. But the enormous power needed to operate the projectors had never been available. Hurley had in his hands the key to realizing Reagan's dream of a planetary shield against nuclear war. Possibly the United States would be able to guarantee everyone, even the goddam silly Soviets, a safer existence.

It occurred to the President that Carmichael had brought him immortality.

Goddard's library was located in a specially constructed facility just west of Building 5, the Experimental Engineering and Fabrication Shop. Rimford had stopped home first to get his green ID badge. Now, the badge dangling from a chain around his neck, he mounted the library steps and entered the building.

He descended to the lower level and identified himself to a guard. Had the guard concentrated less on the photo on the plastic card and looked more closely at the subject's eyes, he might have hesitated. As it was, he only entered a routine query into the computer, which came back negative. Rimford signed in on the log and proceeded into the secure area. Halfway down a polished hall, still within sight of the guard, he stopped before an unmarked door and inserted his ID

The total Hercules transmission consisted of approximately 23.3 million characters divided into 108 data sets, recorded on 178 laserdiscs. Only two complete sets existed: one in the operations center in the laboratory building, and the other here.

The discs themselves occupied a small corner of the middle

shelf at the back wall. They were stored in individual plastic sleeves, labeled, and maintained in slots in a cabinet designed originally for the library's word-processing records. Briefly, the text had also been stored in Goddard's central computer system, but Schenken had raised security considerations and it had been erased.

Two computer stations had been placed along the south wall of the storage room. The only other pieces of furniture were a couple of chairs, an old conference table, and, at the far end, a battered credenza. Rimford was so preoccupied with his own thoughts that he was at first unaware that he was not alone.

"Can't decide which one you want, Dr. Rimford?"

Gordie Hopkins, one of the technicians, was seated before a console.

"Hello, Gordie," Rimford said, selecting the two discs that constituted DS 41, the cosmology section. He took his place beside Hopkins without turning the other computer on. Instead, he thumbed through his notebook, pausing occasionally to give the impression he was contemplating its contents. But his attention was riveted on Hopkins.

Rimford had heard that some of Gambini's people had got into the habit of working in the library, where it was quieter. But it was unfortunate running into someone just now. He glanced at his watch: almost ten. The library would close at midnight, and he estimated he'd need at least an hour.

"I don't think I understand why you'd want me involved in this project." Cyrus Hakluyt folded his hands carefully in his lap and watched an old, battered station wagon pass the gray government car in a storm of slush and dirty water.

"We have in our possession," said Gambini, "a complete physiological description of an extraterrestrial life form. Are you interested?"

"Jesus," Hakluyt said in a fragile monotone. If there was a single characteristic one might use to describe the micro-biologist, it was the contrast between his feathery voice and the conviction with which he customarily spoke. His smile was weak and perfunctory; and his long spindly trunk ended in a set of narrow shoulders. He blinked behind heavy bifocals. Gambini knew that his visitor was only in his early thirties, and yet one would not have guessed. "Gambini, you are not joking?"

"No, I'm not. Some of the material in the Hercules Text appears to be an attempt to describe genetic structure and broader biological functions. We think they may have tried to give us a comprehensive account of the biosystem of their world." Gambini paused. "Unfortunately, we have no one here with serious qualifications."

"Where are we going now?" Hakluyt asked.

"Goddard. We have a VIP apartment set up for you."

The tip of Hakluyt's tongue touched his delicate lips. "That can wait. I want to see what you have first."

Gambini smiled in the dark. Hakluyt was a bit on the prissy side, but he was going to be good to work with.

Hopkins had all but finished his research for the evening. But Rimford could see that he was looking for an opportunity to open a conversation. Casual acquaintances almost routinely tried to steal his time. It had been a problem throughout his career, growing worse as his reputation increased.

He'd learned to turn away, to explain that he was busy, to say no. But tonight he felt paralyzed. Perhaps he did not really want Hopkins to leave.

As the technician busied himself cleaning up his work station, he remarked offhandedly that it was an exciting time.

"Yes," replied Rimford.

"Dr. Rimford," Hopkins said suddenly, "I should tell you that I'm proud to be working with someone like you."

"Thank you," Rimford said. "Soon you will discover that the personalities of all of us will be submerged by the event. But thank you all the same." Rimford continued to mask his impatience. He allowed himself to be drawn into an extended discussion of Hopkins's project, a statistical analysis of alpha-numeric characters in the first six data sets. But he resented the young technician's intrusive presence. And he was annoyed with himself. Hopkins didn't even have a sense of humor. The poor bastard'll never go anywhere, he thought.

It was almost eleven when Hopkins announced that he had a few things to attend to at the lab and that his shift would be over at midnight.

Uncertainly, Rimford watched him leave. When the door closed with the loud final snap of the electronic lock, he turned on the computer and instructed it to unlock the files. An amber lamp glowed and went out. Rimford removed DS 41A from its plastic jacket and inserted it into the port. Then he called up the operating menu. It was cold in the little room; there was only one heat duct, and it was inadequate. Nevertheless, he felt perspiration sliding down his arms, and a large drop formed on the tip of his nose.

The computer memory, of course, was empty. I am doing the right thing, he told himself. No other course is open. And he loaded the empty memory onto the disc as a file replacement. In that instant, the data contained on DS 41A vanished. He repeated the procedure for DS 41B.

That was the data set he knew to be deadly. But he dared not stop there. And one by one, he removed each disc from its transparent plastic jacket and wiped it clean. He grew numb during the process and tears welled in his eyes.

At a few minutes after midnight he emerged from the storage room and checked out with the guard, who had waited patiently. It was hard to believe that the man could be unaware that some terrible thing had happened in the security area. Rimford had no doubt that his face had lost its color and that the conflicting emotions which tore at him were fully displayed across his broad features. But the guard barely looked up.

Now the lab had the only copy of the Text. He left the library and walked, not wishing to drive on this night, toward it. And if his conscience had begun to weigh on him, he cheered himself by contemplating Oppenheimer, who had done nothing.

But he was glad there was no moon.

MONITOR

HOUSING BIAS CHARGED IN SEATTLE
City, 8 Suburbs Probed by U.S.

GODDARD RIOT VICTIMS SUE U.S.
Class Action Expected; 2nd Child Dies
Schenken Fired as Security Director

SOVIET SUB REPORTED TRAPPED IN CHESAPEAKE
(Associated Press)—Informed sources revealed today that U.S.
Coast Guard and Navy vessels had tracked a Soviet L-Class
submarine into the mouth of Chesapeake Bay . . .

BEAR KILLS CAMPER AT YELLOWSTONE
Boy Tried to Save Lunch, Says Girl Friend

CONGRESS APPROVES SPECIAL FUND FOR CITIES
Police, Education, Jobs Programs to Get Help

BOLIVIAN GUERRILLAS OVERRUN PERUVIAN
POLICE POSTS
Army Routs Rebels in Heavy Fighting near Titicaca

LAKEHURST TERRORIST SUES GOVERNMENT
Skull Fractured during Counterstrike
Family of Dead Gunman Also Contemplating Action

NORTH DAKOTA CURBS MEDICAL COSTS
Under New Bill, State to Set Fees
AMA Warns Quality of Medicine Will Decline

PAKISTAN GETS U.S. MISSILES
Pentagon Retains Control of Warheads

PRAGUE DEFIES ARMY ULTIMATUM
Workers Riot; Armored Corps Rebels
Soviets Promise Aid

NUCLEAR WAR "PROBABLE" IN THIS DECADE
Club of Rome Resets Clock at Two Minutes to Twelve
Pope Calls for Disarmament

12

At approximately 3:00 a.m., Ed Gambini's phone began to ring. He surfaced slowly through the insistent jangling, rolled over, snapped on the lamp, and looked at his clock. "Hello?"

"Ed? This is Majeski. We have a problem. I think you ought to get over here right away."

He swung his legs over the side of the bed and rubbed his eyes. "What's wrong?"

"Baines wants to talk with you," he said.

"Baines? What the hell's he doing down there at this hour? Put him on."

Majeski's voice took on a plaintive tone. "I don't think he'll talk on the phone. You'd better come over."

Gambini growled, banged the instrument down, and stumbled into the bathroom. Forty minutes later, still seething, he stalked into the operations center. Majeski met him and pointed toward Gambini's office. Rimford was asleep behind the project manager's desk.

"What's going on, Cord?"

"I don't care who he is," whispered Majeski loudly. "The dumb son of a bitch has gone crazy!"

"Baines?"

"Yes, Baines!"

"What did he do?"

Majeski held up two laserdiscs, so that Gambini could read the labels. They were parts A and B of DS 41, the cosmology segment that Rimford had been working on. "What about them?"

"They've been wiped. So have the library duplicates. The whole data set is gone, Ed." Majeski's voice tightened. "The goddam text is gone!" He twisted the back of a wooden chair. "He's got no right to do that, Ed. I don't care what he says!"

"Baines did it?" Gambini was incredulous. "Why? What'd he say?"

"Ask him. He doesn't want to talk to *me*."

Rimford was awake now, and Gambini was suddenly aware of his eyes through the glass partition. They were round and accusing and very large, and they drove Majeski's angry whine into the perimeter somewhere. "What?" asked Gambini, as though he could be heard through the glass. "What is it?" He opened the office door, stepped inside, and closed it softly behind him.

Rimford was crumpled and tired. "Ed," he said, "destroy the Text. Destroy all of it."

Outside, Majeski and the six other people on duty were watching. Gambini remained standing. "Why?" he asked. "Why should we do that? What did you find?" He sat down, prepared to be reassuring. Actually, despite the loss of Data Set 41, he felt a curious frustrated satisfaction at having become a father-figure to Baines Rimford.

The blue eyes blazed. "What's the last thing you'd want to find?"

"I don't know," Gambini replied desperately. "Plague. A bomb." His lungs were laboring. "How bad can it be?"

"When I came in here this morning, Ed, when I walked through that door, I intended to destroy everything. I did destroy the library copies."

"I know."

"You should finish the job."

Gambini felt cold. "Why didn't you do it when you had the chance? Weren't you sure?"

"Yes!" he said, striking the desktop. Pens, clips, and paper flew. "I was sure, but I couldn't take that kind of decision on my own shoulders. Maybe that's what happened before. At Los Alamos. I don't know."

Gambini looked out at the circle of witnesses. He waved them impatiently back to their terminals. They went reluctantly, but still they watched. "Data Set forty-one is only cosmological in nature. What could you possibly find in it?"

"A cheap way to end the world, Ed. You could do it with the resources of virtually any Middle Eastern nation. Even a well-financed terrorist group could pull it off. By any reasonable measure, I am now the most dangerous man on the planet.

"Among other things, I know the specifics of spatial curvature. There are, under normal circumstances, in the area of fifty-seven million light-years to a degree of arc. That number varies considerably, of course, depending on local conditions. And if that seems too small a number, it's because the universe is not the hyperbolic sphere I predicted and we all assumed.

It's a twisted cylinder, Ed. There is much of the four-dimensional Möbius in it. If you could travel around it and return from the opposite direction, you'd be lefthanded when you got back!"

"And you destroyed all this?" A chill formed at the base of Gambini's spine and expanded slowly.

"You're not thinking. Space can be bent. Within a finite area, the degree of curvature can be increased, eliminated, or inverted. It doesn't require much power. What it *does* require is technique. Ed, we're talking about *gravity!* I could arrange to have, say, New York City fall into the sky. I could turn the state of Maryland into a black hole!"

Rimford got wearily to his feet. "God knows what else is in those discs, Ed. Get rid of them!"

"No." Gambini shook his head. "You know we can't do that! Baines, the Text is a source of knowledge beyond anything we'd dreamed. We can't just throw it away!"

"Why not? What can we possibly learn from it that exceeds, in any substantive way, what we already know? Hurley, for God's sake, understood that. They've shown us we're not alone, he said, before we really knew they'd speak again. That's what matters. The rest of it is detail."

Gambini's face hardened. "If you wanted the Text destroyed, really wanted it, you'd have done it yourself."

Rimford was on his feet, headed for the door. "Maybe you're right," he said. He put on his coat. "I've got an afternoon flight, Ed. If you *do* erase the damn thing, you can tell them I advised it."

He walked out past Majeski and the others, nodding briefly as he went. Majeski stared after him.

When he was gone, Gambini called Harry and, in cryptic language, explained what had happened.

"We'll have to replace the library set right away," Harry said. "If Maloney hears about this, it'll be another piece of ammunition he can use against us. Can you recover the DS forty-one discs?"

"No. We're not permitted to keep copies anymore. Any duplicates we make have to be wiped." Gambini ground his teeth. "Damned fools! They're getting just what they deserve!"

"Forget that for now," said Harry. "Have someone make up duplicates of everything. Of the entire transmission. You know how they were labeled? Put identical labels on. Make sure there's a number forty-one set, too—just leave it blank; that's all you can do. Don't let any of the people on the day shift use the library. I'll have a classified messenger at the security desk in your spaces at eight. Have the duplicates ready to go. Does anyone else know?"

"Just the midnight shift."

"Okay. Let's try to keep it in the family."

"Eventually we'll have to admit we don't have it, Harry."

"We can have an accident later. This isn't a good time. We should bring Pete in on it. If you have no objection, I'll call him. Can we meet this morning?"

Wheeler was the last to arrive. He strode into Miranda's, on Muirkirk Road, and joined Harry and Gambini in a booth. "Baines is right," he said. "We should wipe the thing. I'm sorry he didn't do it last night."

"Until now," said Harry, "we've had no solid evidence that there would be anything dangerous in the Text."

Wheeler looked dismayed. "It amazes me that you'd *need* evidence. How could we for a moment think of turning a million-year-old technology loose on this world? We haven't learned to handle gunpowder safely!"

"This is the first time you've said anything," rasped Gambini. "Why haven't you taken a stand before this?"

"I'm a priest." Wheeler managed a smile. "Any action *I* take tends to reflect on the Church. And it's difficult in a matter like this: we're still trying to explain ourselves about Galileo. I've sat passively by; I certainly could not have acted as Baines did. But I can tell you that, whatever their motives, the Altheans have done us no favor."

"Why?" demanded Gambini. "Because Rimford could see a way to misuse some of the information? Hell, there are risks, but they're damned slight, considering the potential for benefit. We need to just take it easy and not panic. I suggest we simply alert the investigators to our concerns and have them report anything that could create a problem. Then, if something develops, we'll deal with it in a rational manner."

"I'm not so sure that we're talking about things that can be identified all that easily," said Wheeler.

"Goddammit, Pete, there's no way I can argue against that kind of statement. But I think we have to be reasonable about this. Has it occurred to you that our best hope for survival as a species may depend on what we can learn from the Altheans? If we get technological breakthroughs, maybe there'll also be some ethical ones, some new perspectives. Harry, would you want to take the responsibility for destroying a source of such knowledge? Even Rimford, after what he found, couldn't bring himself to do it."

"We need a political solution," said Harry. "Which is to say, we have to temporize. We won't know the real nature of the problem until we find out what we've got."

"I agree," said Gambini. "But I think we need to know a couple of other things right now. Pete, are you going to stay with the project?"

"Yes," said the priest, his voice hardly a whisper.

"Do I need to worry about the safety of the Text?"

"No. Not from me."

"All right. Good. I'm glad we got that settled. Now, is anyone else having morality problems about this?"

"I don't think so," said Harry. "Though I think we'd better start being alert to the possibility. Listen, we've got something else to talk about. You'll be happy to hear this, Ed."

"Good news for a change."

"Yes. The White House is still getting a lot of pressure, so they've decided to set up an office to review what we're doing here. They're saying that they'll release whatever they can."

"Well, that's good to hear," said Gambini. But after he'd had a moment to think about it, he asked archly, "Who's going to decide what's safe?"

Harry kept a straight face. "Oscar DeSandre," he said.

"*Who?*"

Even Wheeler grinned.

"Oscar DeSandre," Harry repeated. "They tell me he's a top man in military high tech. And I guess he's got a staff of experts, and they can always talk to us if they're in doubt about anything." They all looked skeptical. "I'd like to get a package out to him this afternoon, if we can. And then they'd like something once a week. We'll set up a schedule of some sort."

"Okay," said Gambini.

"I think we'd be wise to police ourselves," said Wheeler, "and not automatically ship everything out."

"I agree," said Harry. "Ed, I'll get you DeSandre's phone number. I'd like you to call him today, try to give him some idea of the sorts of things he should be looking for. Meantime, we need to set up a mechanism to make sure that somebody we trust reads everything. And we need to get Cord, Leslie, and Hakluyt involved. Tell them what's at stake, and ask them to red-flag anything that might create problems."

"It seems to me," said Wheeler, "we've got three categories of information: material for DeSandre, stuff that can go only to Hurley, and stuff that shouldn't get out of here at all."

Their breakfast came, and they ate in relative silence. "I'm not sure," Gambini said, well into his meal, "but I think we're talking treason. Harry, what the hell kind of bureaucrat are you?"

"What do you think Rimford's legal status would be if word of last night's episode got out?" Wheeler asked.

Harry smiled. "Most they could get him for is destroying government property." He looked at his watch. "I've got to get over to the library before the messenger arrives."

"What are you going to do?"

"Switch discs. I'll replace the old ones with the new set, and, except for number forty-one, it'll be like nothing ever happened." He shrugged. "Simple. Meantime, you two think things over."

"Harry," said Gambini, "I'll never agree to their destruction."

"I know."

Harry got to the library minutes before his messenger arrived, cleared through with his green card, and signed a receipt for the package. Inside the Hercules storage room, he removed from their plastic sleeves the discs that Rimford had erased and locked them in the credenza. Then he unwrapped his parcel. Gambini had done a good job. The replacements were virtually identical to the ones he'd just hidden away, even to the lower-case identification labels.

When he'd finished, he signed out, returned to his office, and found some paperwork on his desk. Rimford had checked out and gone home.

Though Oscar DeSandre thought of himself as a White House staffer, he was physically based in the Executive Office Building. He was not happy: he had only one assistant and a part-time aide available to help with the Hercules Project. And the aide was of limited value, since she had not yet received her clearance.

Gambini's first package had arrived just moments after he walked in the door. DeSandre's responsibility was to read through the transcript, assure himself that it contained nothing that would adversely affect the national interest, and release it to the press. That seemed simple enough, but he realized there were terrible bear traps hidden in this type of job. It was a position with negative potential; he could do well only by staying out of trouble. If he missed something, his whole career could very easily go up in one magnificent blast. Moreover, his time was horribly constricted just now. Hell, it was *always* horribly constricted. The new flap over lie detector tests routinely used in some high-level security clearance procedures would take most of his efforts for a while. And he had problems at Fort Meade as well. So DeSandre leafed quickly through the ninety-five-page document that Goddard had sent over, to get the flavor of it. Then he called in his assistant. She brought several telephone memos with her, calls to be returned. He glanced quickly through them and put them aside. "Look for technical stuff," he told her. "Most of it reads like chunks of a philosophical tract. There's no problem with any of that. But we don't want anything going out that could conceivably have military implications. Okay?"

The assistant nodded.

And that was how the existence of a series of alien philosophical precepts came to make the news next evening. It did so in a relatively modest way, taking second billing to a congressional vote that had defeated an administration-backed attempt to remove price supports from the electronics industry.

The precepts did not have the sort of effect they might have had, because the version released to DeSandre was literal and bore little resemblance to Leslie's more poetic translations. Furthermore, ethical and aesthetic similarities with human values were apparent, and the media concerned themselves with that facet of the story. It was a full two days later that NBC produced a set of translations into modern English prose, which created a mild sensation. Cass Woodbury, in her studied, resonant voice, gave some of the lines pointed meaning:

> I am alone. I make life, handle the atom, and speak
> with the dead. And God knows me not.

There was a great deal more, along similar lines. At home, watching the telecast, Harry shivered.

So did the Cardinal.

His phone began ringing at about nine-fifteen, and he called in his staff at ten. Barnegat couldn't be reached; he was in

Chicago. Cox and Dupre arrived within a few minutes of each other and were already in a heated argument when Jesperson arrived with Joe March, who was archdiocesan head of the Society for the Propagation of the Faith. March was not part of the Cardinal's inner circle; but it had long been his custom to introduce persons to these meetings who he felt could make a contribution. Dupre, who had seen the program, was indignant. "Communication with the dead! It's absurd! I keep hoping," he continued, "that the press will one day develop a sense of responsibility. They've put the most sensational reading on all this that they can. But the transcripts released by Goddard don't justify any such interpretation."

"I'm damned if I can see what all the fuss is about," Cox said. "These things happened a million years ago. But if there's a possibility that people will be misled by these stories, then we have a responsibility to act."

Dupre's heavy eyebrows came together. "I can't see that anyone will take any of this seriously unless *we* take it seriously. Will the Vatican issue a statement?" he asked.

"In due time. They don't want to look as if they're being stampeded." Jesperson allowed himself a smile. "They must have got His Holiness up in the middle of the night. There was a meeting of some sort. I talked with Acciari this morning. He thinks the whole thing is a plot by the Western powers in retaliation for the See's refusal to cooperate in the Philippines."

Cox looked bored. "Do you have any idea what the official line is going to be?"

"They haven't decided yet. But Acciari believes His Holiness will question the validity of the interpretation and throw in a few choice remarks about the direction modern society is taking."

"In other words," said Cox, "they're just going to tell everyone to ignore it."

"A sensible position," said Dupre. "We should do the same."

"Come on, Phil," objected Cox. "What better way could you find to call attention to the fact that we're a little jittery about it all?" He squinted at Dupre as if he were examining a balance sheet. "They can probably get away with that in Italy. But not here."

"Jack," Dupre said with rising heat, "I'm not suggesting we tell people to look the other way. But I think we need to be very careful about getting everyone stirred up. I think we'll be all right if we don't create problems for ourselves. But if we make an issue of this, people are going to demand answers. And I don't think we have any, because there're really no questions."

"The whole thing is ridiculous," said March, a man utterly secure in his black cassock. "People talking to the dead. God wouldn't allow any such thing."

Dupre was drawing small circles on a notepad. "I suspect we would be wise," he said without looking up, "to avoid declaring what God will or will not allow."

"Phil." In times of stress, the Cardinal's eyes seemed to take on a scarlet glow that matched the color of his office. He radiated that vaguely infernal light now. "What is the theological status of communication with the dead? Is it prohibited?"

"No," said Dupre, drawing the word out while he considered how to continue. "Many of the miracles are, after all, no more than such events. Fatima. Lourdes. Postmortem appearances by many of the saints have been officially accepted into the record. And Jesus himself talked with Moses and Elias in the presence of witnesses. What, after all, is prayer but an attempt to communicate with the next world?"

"Except in this case," said Cox, "the next world answers."

"Yes." Dupre touched his lips with his index finger. "As uncomfortable as that may be, such notions are not new, and I think we'd do well to suggest that we're not at all upset. If, that is, we suggest anything. I would still recommend we just ride it out."

"Nonsense!" March said with a chuckle. "It smells too much of fortune tellers and spiritualism. The Vatican is right: we should denounce the entire business. God only knows what they'll be claiming to hear next!"

"It occurs to me," said Cox, "that the ability to communicate with the Church Triumphant may have been one of the preternatural gifts lost by Adam's sin. We talked about this before— but I wonder whether we are not seeing a culture whose founder was wiser than ours." The remark was followed by an uncomfortable scraping of chairs: Cox seldom strayed into the spiritual uplands.

Jesperson turned toward him. "Jack, do you consider that a possibility?"

Cox seemed surprised at the effect his remark had induced. "Of course not. But it *is* theologically tenable."

March sat straighter in his chair but said nothing. Though

the Cardinal seldom looked directly at him, he nevertheless observed the elderly priest carefully, as though gauging his reactions. March remained skeptical and unblinking throughout. Anyone who had been watching Jesperson closely might have noted that he seemed visibly relieved by what he saw.

"All we have," continued Cox, "is a rumor. And we don't know how things are going to go. I agree with Phil that we don't want to get caught looking foolish. On the other hand, I think we need to recognize that some people may have trouble with these events. Consequently, we should be reassuring. Surely we'll be safe in pointing out that whatever happens on Mars, or wherever this place is, is of no concern to us. We've seen nothing that should disturb any good Catholic."

Jesperson listened until the arguments began to repeat themselves. Then he intervened. "I'd be less than honest with you," he said, "if I did not confess a certain amount of anxiety over this business. We may be entering a new age. And new ages are traditionally uncomfortable for those doing the steering.

"It strikes me as an odd paradox that the princes of the Church have traditionally resisted scientific advance. We, who should always have been in the forefront of the search for truth, have historically dragged our feet. Let's not get caught at it again. At least not in this archdiocese. We should take Jack Cox's position that we have nothing to fear from the truth, that we are as interested as anyone else in new revelations of the majesty of God's work."

"I didn't say that," objected Cox.

"Odd," said the Cardinal. "I thought you had. We will not suggest, directly or otherwise, that the people at Goddard are twisting the facts or that they are misinformed. We will allow this thing to play itself out. And perhaps, if we put ourselves in the hands of the Lord, we may even enjoy the experience.

"We won't address the matter officially at all, because we consider the Goddard project none of our business."

"George," said Dupre, "if the Vatican puts out a statement—"

"I know," said the Cardinal, smiling. "But no one listens to the Pope anymore. Why should they start now?"

Harry, who might not have been as interested in Althean philosophy as he'd allowed Leslie to believe, settled in for the evening with the bulky binder she'd given him. He read for three hours, but it was difficult going. Some terms were not yet solved; syntactical relationships were not always clear, and Harry sensed that even a perfect translation in simple English would have been baffling. It reminded him of a cross between Plato and haiku; but there was no escaping the overall sense of gloomy intelligence or, paradoxically, the suggestion of a wry wit that was just beyond his grasp.

The Altheans were concerned with many of the problems that obsessed his own species, but there were subtle differences. For example, a discussion of morality explicated in considerable detail the responsibilities an intelligent being has toward other life forms and even to inanimate objects; but his obligations to others of his own species were ignored. Then, too, a philosophical treatise on the nature of evil examined only the catastrophes caused by natural forces, overlooking those that result from human (or inhuman) malice.

Gamma must have been a world of oceans. Again and again, there appeared the metaphor of the seas, of the wandering ship, of the questing mariner. But the waters are calm. Nowhere do squalls rise; nor does one feel the surge of heavy tides. There are neither rocks nor shoals, and the coasts glide peacefully by.

Too peacefully, perhaps.

"The great islands in the gulf are uniformly cold. And the shores are dark."

Sec. 102(a) The Congress hereby declares that it is the policy of the United States that activities in space should be devoted to peaceful purposes for the benefit of all mankind.

(b) ... Such activities shall be the responsibility of, and shall be directed by, a civilian agency ... except that activities peculiar to or primarily associated with the development of weapons systems, military operations, or the defense of the United States ... shall be the responsibility of, and shall be directed by, the Department of Defense. ...

(c) The aeronautical and space activities of the United States shall be conducted so as to contribute materially to ...

(1) the expansion of human knowledge of phenomena in the atmosphere and space. ...

—National Aeronautics and Space Act of 1958

IF THERE WAS anything particularly irritating about Cyrus Hakluyt, it was difficult to put a finger on. Yet people were inevitably uncomfortable in his presence. It might have been his eyes, which were unnaturally close together; it was easy to imagine them focusing on one through the barrel of a microscope. His speech was guarded, and he showed no real interest in the people he was working with. Harry suspected that he was somehow limited by the dimensions of the things he studied. Nevertheless, in his first report, given at Gambini's daily staff meeting on Christmas Eve, he displayed an unexpected sense of the dramatic. "I can tell you," he said, "what they look like."

That got everyone's attention. Gambini laid aside his glasses, which he had been polishing; Wheeler stiffened slightly; Majeski's dreamy eyes focused. And Leslie glanced sharply at Harry.

"I isolated their DNA several days ago," Hakluyt continued. "There's still a great deal to be done, but I have a preliminary report. There's a fair amount of guesswork involved, because I can't be certain of some of the construction materials. To begin with, the Altheans are most certainly not human. I'm not quite sure how to categorize them, and it would probably be best if I didn't try. I *can* tell you that these creatures could live quite comfortably in Greenbelt." The thin smile drifted across his lips.

"Nevertheless they are unlike anything in terrestrial biology. The Althean appears to combine both plant and animal characteristics. For example, it is able to photosynthesize." He looked directly at Leslie.

"Then they were never a hunting society," she said. "That might mean no wars, or even a concept of war."

"And consequently," added Majeski, "no thought given to weapons potential."

"Very good," said Hakluyt approvingly. "My thoughts exactly. The Althean also appears to have no vascular system, no lungs, and no heart. It has teeth, however. Big ones."

"Wait a minute," said Wheeler. "How can that be? They have no stomach, have they?"

"Defense, Father Wheeler. I would guess they had some predators to deal with at one time. They do have nervous systems and controlling organs that have to be brains. Their reproductive systems are asexual. And, although I can't be sure, I believe the creatures would be slightly larger than we are. Certainly on earth they would be. They have exoskeletons, probably constructed from chitinous material, and, of course, they have sense organs. I don't think they hear quite as well as we do." He leaned back smugly in his chair. "The eyes are especially curious: there are four of them, and two do not seem to be receptive to light."

Hakluyt's brow creased, and his voice was less pedantic when he continued. "There's no lens, so I can't see how it could function as a receptor for any kind of radiation. Moreover, the nerve that connects it to the brain doesn't appear to be capable of an optic function. No, I think the organ collects something, or maybe projects something, for all I know, but not any kind of radiation *I'm* familiar with."

"I'm not sure what that leaves," said Majeski.

"Nor am I." Hakluyt examined the tabletop. "I would estimate their life span at approximately a hundred fifty years. On a side note, we can be sure they're capable of genetic manipulation."

"How?" asked Harry.

"Because we can do it ourselves on a modest scale. I'm learning a lot from them, Carmichael. I don't know what their limits are, but I have a good idea about their minimum capabilities. And that's another curious thing: their life span, by any reasonable measure, is exceedingly short."

"Short?" said Gambini. "You said it's a hundred and fifty years!"

"That's not much for a species that can dictate the architecture of its DNA."

"Maybe it tacks on the extra years," said Harry, *"after* birth rather than before."

"No," said Majeski. "That would be the hard way to do things."

"Correct." Hakluyt smiled. "Why perform adjustments for millions of individuals when you can do it once? I don't understand it: they seem to have consciously chosen to wear out early."

"I have a thought," said Leslie. "Maybe we have a species that voluntarily accepts an unnecessarily early death. And if we read them right, *they talk to their dead*. That can't be a coincidence. Cy, is there anything peculiar in their physical makeup that suggests a life cycle incorporating a second existence of some kind? A chrysalis effect?"

Hakluyt shook his head. "Not that I can see. But at this stage, I'm not sure how much that means. Unless there's an unknown factor, and there easily could be, the creature that would develop from the DNA plan they sent us would meet an organic death in the same way that any terrestrial life form would. It would be dead. Period."

Wheeler nodded and scratched out something he'd written on his notepad. "I'm surprised," he said, "that they and we both use DNA to control genetic characteristics. Aren't there other possibilities?"

"Yes." Hakluyt bit off the word and let it hang in the still air. "Diacetylenes might work. Or crystals. But these alternatives are not as flexible or as effective as the nucleic acid group. Actually, the options open to nature in this matter are surprisingly limited."

"Dr. Hakluyt," said Harry, "you say they have the means to prolong life. Do you now grasp some of these means?"

"Carmichael, you look to be about, uh, fifty?"

"A little younger," Harry said. "I've had a hard life."

Hakluyt's smile did not change. "You can expect maybe thirty more years. By then you will have whitened, your blood will be sluggish, and I suspect the memory of youth will be quite painful." His eyes fell on Leslie. "And what will *you* be in thirty years, Dr. Davies?" he asked cruelly. "And why do you suppose that is? Why does the mechanism you inhabit fall apart in so short a time? Gambini, how long a period is eighty years?"

Gambini's gaze never left his notepad.

"Ask a cosmologist," said Hakluyt, "and you're asking someone who really understands about time. Well, I'll tell you why you break down so quickly: because your DNA *shuts you down*."

"Please explain," said Wheeler.

"It's simple." Harry felt as if Hakluyt would at any moment announce a quiz. "We used to think that aging was really just an accumulation of wear and tear, diseases, damage, and misuse, until the body's ability to repair itself was simply overwhelmed. But that's not what happens. The DNA we carry controls evolution. Some people are inclined to think of it as a kind of external being that seeks its own development and uses other living creatures as"—he looked around the walls, seeking a term—"bottles. Houses. In any case, one of its functions is to ensure that we are safely out of the way of our progeny. So it kills us."

"In what way?" asked Majeski.

"It shuts off the repair mechanism. I would guess that's happening in you, Cord, right about now." Hakluyt adjusted himself more comfortably, adjusted his glasses, and adjusted his expression, which now faded to a more somber glow, like a coal in a dying fire. "If you want to avoid aging, all that's necessary is to tinker with the instructions your DNA puts out. The Altheans seem to know quite a lot about the technique for doing just that."

"How much," asked Wheeler, repeating Harry's question, "do *you* know about it?"

"You mean how much have I learned from the Text? Some. Not a lot, but some. There hasn't been time yet, and there's still too much material we can't read. But I'll tell you this: it's in there. And so is a lot more."

Near the end of the meeting, the door opened and Rosenbloom put his head in. "Gentlemen," he said, "And Dr. Davies, I know you're busy, but I wonder if we could have a few minutes outside."

The people in the operations center had been gathered together, and Patrick Maloney stood at their head. A gold clasp anchored a gray-black tie, and his black pointed shoes were polished to a mirrorlike shine. He was, Harry thought, a man of glossy qualities.

"Ladies and gentlemen," said Rosenbloom, "I think most of you know Pat Maloney, from the White House. Pat, this is the Hercules team." Harry caught the pride in Rosenbloom's voice. It was a good moment.

Maloney, however, had possibly presided at too many public occasions. Despite the nature of his responsibilities, he projected the image of a public man, a failed politician, possibly, a man too honest for the calling and not subtle enough to hide his handicap. He spoke and acted in a manner that seemed almost reflexive. "I think I've met most of you at one point or another," he said, "and I know how busy you are. So I won't take much of your time." He rose slightly on his toes and sank again. "You've been under a lot of pressure, and we know it hasn't been easy for you. But we wanted you to be aware how important your contribution is.

"Let me begin by telling you that Hercules has already paid an enormous dividend: we may now have the means to defend our cities against nuclear attack."

Maloney paused for effect. He received polite applause, hardly what the occasion seemed to demand; it was a sober reflection of the scientists' resentment of the government's policies, of which he had become a symbol. Toward the rear of the room, a mathematician from American University showed his disdain by walking out.

"Over the last few weeks," Maloney continued, choosing not to notice, "the President has been under considerable pressure because he would not release the Hercules Text. We know that has made your job more difficult and that it has created personal problems for many of you. But we can now see the wisdom of that position. Some of you may not yet know that Dr. Wheeler has learned how to extract enormous amounts of energy from the magnetic belts that circle the earth.

"Dr. Wheeler, would you come forward, please?"

The priest stood uncertainly near the rear. His associates parted for him, and he approached Maloney with the enthusiasm of a man getting on close terms with a scaffold.

"We are now in a position to launch ORION." Maloney rose again on his toes and settled slowly. "By this time next year, the arms race will be over. The long night of mutual terror will have ended, and the United States will have restored a measure of sanity to international relations." He extended an arm to the reluctant Wheeler and drew him into an open circle. "This will have been made possible by Dr. Wheeler's contribution.

"To show his appreciation, the President has directed that the Hercules unit be granted the Jefferson Medal for Distinguished Achievement in the Arts and Sciences." He unsnapped a black case, revealing a gold medallion on a striped green and white ribbon. "Unfortunately," he added, "as is customary in awards of this nature, the discovery and the medal are both classified. There will be no mention of it outside the Hercules spaces. The medal itself will be displayed in an appropriate location here in the operations center.

"In addition, the President has expressed his wish that Dr.

Wheeler be awarded the Oppenheimer Certificate for Outstanding Service." The two dozen or so people present applauded, and Maloney held up a framed, beribboned parchment for their inspection, and then handed it gracefully to Wheeler. A flashbulb popped: the photographer was Rosenbloom.

"You have every reason to be proud, Pete," continued Maloney. "You may well have made the decisive contribution to the cause of peace in this age." Wheeler mumbled his thanks and smiled weakly at his colleagues. "The certificate," Maloney added, "will be placed alongside the Jefferson Medal."

After the ceremony, Wheeler lingered a moment with Harry. "The award is aptly named," he said.

"What do you mean?" asked Harry.

"I keep thinking about Baines's comment: Oppenheimer is the guy who should have said no."

Harry had a long afternoon among the late shoppers. He wandered the downtown streets of the capital, hoping to lose himself in the crowds, loading up on game programs and books for Tommy and wondering about the etiquette of Christmas presents for an ex-wife. Eventually he bought a plant, a gift that seemed sufficiently neutral.

He arrived at seven. Julie always took Christmas very seriously: a bright, jeweled tree dominated the living room, wreaths were hung in all the windows, and colored lights were stretched in a bright sprinkle across the balcony. The scent of evergreen was on everything, and the woman herself seemed quite happy to see him. In the spirit of the season, she would have been reminiscing over past holidays. But Harry looked in vain for any real sign of regret.

She was properly grateful for the plant. After setting it near a window, she kissed him chastely and gave him his present. It was a gold pen. "Every rising executive should have one," she said.

Tommy's HO model train was on a platform in the living room. Julie had tried to add a set of switches to the familiar figure-eight layout, but she hadn't tied the track down securely enough to allow them to work. Harry finished the job and sat for an hour with his son, while the little freight looped endlessly through a mountain tunnel, past a couple of farms, and down the main street of a peaceful snow-covered town with glowing street lamps.

She poured sherry for Harry and herself, and they drank a

silent toast: Harry, to what might have been; Julie, to the future. Then, without touching her, he said good night. It was, they both knew, the last time they would meet as other than strangers.

If Jack Peoples had expected any visible change in church attendance as a result of the Goddard revelations, he was disappointed. The number of the faithful neither lessened nor increased.

He took his usual station just outside the doors after the nine o'clock mass, which was being celebrated by a young priest from the District who helped out on Sundays. It was cold, and Peoples had wrapped himself in his black overcoat. Across the street from the church, some adolescents were burning Christmas trees.

The Offertory bell rang, its bright silvery cadence floating in the still morning air. He thought of Pete Wheeler and his hopeless quest: Indeed, if man has a response at all to the gulfs beyond the earth, it is in the fragile sound of that bell on Sunday morning.

Then they were singing, and he could hear people moving toward the altar rail for communion. Their formal obligation completed, a few people emerged, and hurried past Peoples in embarrassed silence. The pastor was always sorely tried not to judge these parishioners, the same ones each week, who lived so close to the edge of their faith.

The second wave rolled out after the distribution of the Holy Sacrament, and then came the general exodus, to the energetic accompaniment of Sister Anne's choir singing "O Little Town of Bethlehem." Peoples smiled and shook hands and exchanged idle talk. His parishioners seemed unchanged, untouched by the grotesque stories that now seemed to be proliferating on TV. With one exception, there was no sense that anything extraordinary had happened.

The exception was a child, a nine-year-old girl whom Peoples knew by name. She was intelligent, well-mannered, a credit to her family and her Church. And she wanted to know about the Altheans and their dead.

Phil Dupre's prescribed response might have worked with a committed adult: "It has nothing to do with us."

But the child, what could he tell her?

Of such are the kingdom.

MONITOR

SUBLIMINAL ALIENS

Blue Delta, Inc., a distributor of electronic novelties, announced today that it will begin next month to market a subliminal tape composed of selections from the Hercules Text. According to a press release, "Much of what the Altheans have to say about nature and courage is remarkably like the best in ourselves. However, they have a mode of expression that, once one gets beyond the difficulties of translation..."

COLLIE DOVER JOINS CONCERT GAMMA

Westend Productions, Inc., announced today that internationally acclaimed film and stage star Collie Dover will join an all-star cast set to open in Hollywood with Concert Gamma, a tribute to the Altheans. Ticket sales have been brisk....

STARSONG EXHIBIT TOMORROW AT NATIONAL

Everett Lansing's collection of astronomical photographs, more than a hundred of which have been produced by the optical capabilities of SKYNET, will be on display tomorrow at the National Art Gallery. The collection includes "Views of Centaurus," a series of stunning color portraits of the sun's closest neighbor, which won the Kastner Award last year in the field of scientific photography.

LONGSTREET'S ANNOUNCES ALIEN CUISINE

... Diners with more exotic tastes might wish to visit Avery Longstreet's Inn at either of its two locations, in the Loop or in Schaumburg. Instead of simply embellishing old favorites with new sauces, Longstreet's has actually produced a few dishes, mostly (but not exclusively) meat-based, which do indeed seem to be completely novel. We particularly recommend...

WHITE LINES SCHEDULES INTERGALACTIC CRUISE

The view of the Hercules group is particularly lovely from the sea, according to White Lines Tours, which expects overflow booking for its Sea Star cruises. In addition to the view from the deck, passengers on the four-day voyage will be able to look through the giant reflector at Hobson Observatory in Arizona by TV hookup. Cast off for the stars by contacting your travel agent or White Lines . . .

CASS COUNTY TOYS WILL MARKET ALTHEAN FIGURES

Cass County, a small Nebraska toy and game manufacturer, will be first on the market with a wide range of movable Althean figures. Lydia Klaussen, announcing the coup to the company's shareholders, said that the aliens will "somewhat" resemble the image thought to be a self-portrait. She did not elaborate.

14

MAJESKI GOT OUT of the oversize bed, padded across the wooden floor, and stood for a time near the window. The Adirondacks were lovely in the approaching dawn. Behind him, Lisa stirred. Her black hair was spread across the pillow, framing her face and a shoulder.

He was glad to get away for the weekend. Lately, Ed had become exasperating to work with. The political pressure never let up, and Gambini always took a beating no matter what he did. His health had never been very good; now it was deteriorating visibly. If Majeski were in Gambini's shoes, he'd tell Carmichael and the White House to go to hell. And then he'd walk out!

He looked back into the room, at the Rensselaer portable generator set on a rubber mat on his coffee table. And at the rickety chest of drawers he'd bought at a garage sale over in Corinth years ago. He stared at it a long time: it was an unremarkable piece of furniture, scratched and chewed and discolored. And its bottom drawer stuck.

Who would have believed that it held, in that same bottom drawer among his socks and underwear, an alien device, a machine conceived on a world unimaginably far away?

Except that the alien device didn't do anything.

He turned on a lamp, tilting the shade to keep the light off Lisa, and opened the drawer. The thing looked like a carburetor with coils, loops, and a circuit board. It had taken him almost two months to assemble, and he didn't know yet whether he had it right. Or whether he could ever get it right.

He removed it, carried it over to the coffee table, and tied it in to the Rensselaer. The portable allowed him to control the flow of power in a crude sort of way. But that didn't seem to help much. He made some changes in the circuit board, proceeding in a methodical fashion so that he always knew where he'd been, and switched it on. He was still trying to get a response an hour later when he felt a prickling along his right arm, near the device. At about the same time, before he had a chance to think about the unusual sensation, Lisa gasped, threw off a quilt, cried out, and leaped from the bed, all in a single fluid motion. She cowered in a corner of the room, staring at the mattress and the rumpled blankets. Then her eyes found Majeski. They were full of fear.

"What happened?" he asked, glancing nervously behind him at the window. "What's the matter?" And in that moment he noticed that, whether from shock or from some less obvious cause, the hairs on his right arm were erect.

It was a few moments before she found her voice. "I don't know," she said at last. "Something cold touched me!"

In another age, Corwin Stiles would have been picketing restaurants along Route 40 or lobbing bags of blood at draft offices. He thought of himself as an idealist, but Wheeler suspected that he simply enjoyed exposing other people's defects. During the second Reagan administration, he had taken a master's in communications from MIT and, after five uneventful years in commercial television, had won a post with Sentry Electronics, which supplied technical personnel for NASA operations. When Pete Wheeler began unraveling the possibilities inherent in planetary magnetic fields, Stiles had been with him. And if the priest was shaken by the fact that his discovery was being appropriated exclusively for military use, Stiles was incensed.

Through the late winter and into the early spring, he urged Wheeler, and anyone else who would listen, to mount a formal protest. "We should all show up outside the main gate," he told Gambini one morning, "and shake our fists in the general direction of the Oval Office. Let the press know we're going to be there, and tell them everything."

Gambini never took the young technician seriously. He was accustomed to hearing preposterous proposals from the Hercules personnel. But Stiles learned to resent, also, the mindless inertia of his fellow workers. Even Wheeler, who understood the enormity of what was happening, refused to act.

Stiles gradually recognized that, if the truth was to get out at all, it would have to be his responsibility. But he was restrained by the habits of a lifetime, which had thrown up few opportunities to break rules for good causes. And now he would have to risk jail.

The catalyst came during the first week of March. An elderly husband and wife were found frozen in their farmhouse outside

Altoona, Pennsylvania, after a local utility turned off their electricity for nonpayment of bills. The utility explained that it mistakenly believed the farmhouse to be abandoned because its occupants did not respond to correspondence and couldn't be reached by telephone. An investigation was promised. But Stiles wondered how many more elderly couples were huddled in cold buildings against the bleak winer.

And where, he demanded of Wheeler, was there any sign that the administration was interested in tapping the colossal reserves of energy that had been made available to it?

On the following Sunday, Corwin Stiles met one of Cass Woodbury's associates in a small restaurant in a remote town on the edge of the Blue Ridge.

A man is entitled to only one great passion in a lifetime. Whether it's music or a profession or a woman, everything else pales in its afterglow. The searing shock so changes one's chemistry that if the object is lost, the experience can never be repeated. Only anticlimax remains.

Cyrus Hakluyt, molecular surgeon, articulate observer of the natural order, and former third baseman, had, during adolescence, pursued a seventeen-year-old cheerleader named Pat Whitney. Her absence had, for many years, been the central reality of Hakluyt's existence. Now, a decade and a half later, he was pleased to think that she, too, was advancing in age, that her DNA had shut down her repair mechanisms, and that no one was forever.

It was some consolation.

Hakluyt had grown up in Westminster, Maryland, a leafy college town west of Baltimore. Although he'd lived relatively nearby, he had not returned to it since his father's death fifteen years before, during his first semester at Johns Hopkins. The girl, he knew, had married and moved on. His old friends were gone, too, and the town seemed desperately empty.

On the same Sunday that Corwin Stiles was having lunch in the shadow of the Blue Ridge, Hakluyt put aside his work and drove into western Maryland. He could not have said why, except that his research into Althean genetics had made him acutely conscious of the passage of time.

Hakluyt, in fact, had always been sensitive to the fleeing years. His thirtieth birthday had been traumatic, and he'd watched the premature retreat of his hairline with gnawing fear. Now, while he grew daily more hopeful of the possibilities that the Hercules Text might promise, the green rolling hills around Westminster seemed less threatening, and the lost days of his youth were no longer quite so remote.

Westminster was bigger than he remembered: a couple of office buildings had been erected on the outskirts, and a shopping mall had sprung into existence. Western Maryland College had expanded, too, and he passed several new housing developments on the south side as he drove into town.

The house in which he'd grown up was gone, swept away to make room for a parking lot. Most of the rest of his neighborhood had disappeared along with it. Gunderson's Pharmacy had survived, and the C&I Lumberyard. But not much else.

They'd added a new wing to the high school, a glass and plastic monstrosity that threatened to overwhelm the old brick building. Bells sounded inside as he passed: just as in the old days, the bells rang seven days a week and were shut off only during the summer. It was good to know there was some stability in the world.

The athletic field had a new backstop. Despite poor vision, Hakluyt had been a fair infielder once, at a time when they'd all expected to play forever. But after leaving Westminster, he'd never put on a uniform again.

The hamburger spot where he used to take Pat Whitney was still there. He smiled as he drove by, surprised that, after all these years, he could still feel the familiar pulse in his throat that only she had ever induced. Where was she now? And for the first time, perhaps, since the terrible night when she'd sent him into the dark, he could think of her without anger.

Ruley Milo arrived at his executive suite in the state of disarray with which he customarily greeted Monday morning. But this had been an extraordinary weekend. He'd managed a Saturday evening dinner with the head of the City Council, planting the seeds for solving licensing problems with some commercial real estate held by one of Burns & Hoffman's clients. And on Sunday he'd finally succeeded in bedding the black bitch who'd been running him all over Kansas City.

Two of his account executives, Abel Walker and Carolyn Donatelli, tried unsuccessfully to intercept him on his way in. Both were wearing anxious frowns, but Walker fretted about everything, and Donatelli, of course, was a woman. An attractive one, but still only a woman. He'd fondled her with his eyes any number of times, but he prudently kept his hands off.

Never fool with the office staff: it was Milo's most basic moral principle.

His head hurt, and, of course, he hadn't had enough sleep. He got some orange juice out of his office refrigerator, decided against adding vodka, and slid down onto the leather sofa.

The intercom buzzed. When he didn't answer, his secretary pushed the door ajar. "Mr. Milo," she said. "Al and Carol would both like to speak with you." While he considered his response, she added, "The market opened down twenty."

Milo grunted, climbed to his feet, and turned on the computer. "It's more than thirty now," said Walker, pushing past the secretary.

Donatelli filed in behind him. "Pennsylvania Gas and Electric is off six," she said.

"What the hell happened?" asked Milo. PG&E was still on the firm's buy list for conservative investors who wanted good income with security.

"Did you have your television on this morning?" asked Donatelli. Milo shook his head. "There's a rumor that the people at Greenbelt, the ones who've been working on that message from outer space, have found a way to produce cheap power. A lot of it."

"Goddammit, Al, nobody's going to believe that."

"Maybe," said Donatelli, "but some of the money market managers must have expected the news to drive the market down. And they sure as hell don't want to stand around and take a beating. They've sold everything, and they're probably looking to pick the stuff back up this afternoon or tomorrow at a substantial discount."

"Vermont Gas is down five and a quarter," said Walker. His voice was squeaking. "The utilities are hardest hit, but we're taking a beating right across the board."

Milo punched up some averages. The major oils were already off by more than 10 percent. Heavy equipment firms, especially those that served the utilities, had tumbled. Banks were down sharply; so were a number of service companies. Christ, even the high-tech firms were losing ground despite good news last week.

Only the automobile manufacturers were bucking the trend. GM, Ford, and Chrysler had all spurted. Naturally, if the rumor was well founded, oil prices would collapse, gasoline would become even cheaper, and more people would return to big cars.

"Have we begun calling our clients?" asked Milo.

"They've been calling us," said Walker. "And they're upset. Especially the smaller accounts. Ruley, I've had a couple of people today talk to me about suicide. They're getting wiped out. Lifetime savings going up in smoke. Okay? These aren't people trying to make a killing in the market: these are our electric company accounts!"

"Keep calm," said Milo. "These things happen. What do we tell everybody who opens an account with us? Don't invest anything in the stock market that you can't afford to lose. It's right in the brochure. But you're right, of course. We don't want it happening under our auspices. Make sure when you talk to these people that you point out who's at fault. But tell them we expect to see a rally. The unfortunate thing is that utilities tend to be slow to recover from things like this. What about our major customers?"

"They've been calling us, too," said Walker.

"Of course they have. What are we telling them?"

"We don't know what to tell them," said Donatelli. "I called Adam at the Exchange and he says the sell orders aren't coming in as fast now but that they're still heavily backlogged."

"Which means we'll lose another thirty points by noon. Okay, we couldn't get any sales in before then anyway. Let's just ride it out. We'll probably get a rally this afternoon and recover maybe thirty percent of the initial losses. What happens after that will depend on what the government has to say." He shut his eyes tight. "Christ, sometimes I hate this business."

"All right, start calling the list. Reassure them. Tell them we're watching developments. Anybody wants to sell, let them sell. Personally, I think this might be a good time to buy. And you can tell them that."

When he was alone, Milo got on the phone to Washington.

Rudy McCollumb was a railroad man. He was retired now, but that didn't change his essential nature. Rudy had ridden the old steam-driven eighteen-wheelers across the prairies, hauling lumber to Grand Forks and potash to Kansas City. He'd started in the dispatch office in Noyes, Minnesota, during the Second World War. But he had no love for things that didn't move, so he applied for every brakeman's job that came open until they gave him a freight that ran down to the Twin Cities.

After that, he was a conductor with the Great Central for forty years and could have been station master in Boulder once, but that didn't suit him, so Rudy kept riding until his hair whitened and the wind carved his features to resemble the scored slabs on the Rocky Mountain run.

At the end they gave him a thousand dollars and a watch.

He settled in Boulder, in a small apartment off the main line. He added the thousand to his savings, which were substantial, and invested it all in the Great Central. For four years, he collected generous dividends, and the value of the stock went up a few points.

But the railroad's primary source of revenue was coal. The endless strings of hoppers carried it from the western mines to the eastern power companies; and when the big board crashed on Monday, March 11, the Great Central and Rudy's money went with it.

On Tuesday evening, after a day-long drinking bout across the street from the Boulder yards, he threw a brick into the plate glass window of Harmon & McKissick, Inc., Brokers.

It was the first time in his life that he'd consciously broken the law.

Marian Courtney knew immediately something was wrong: the blue Plymouth was straddling two lanes as it approached from the west on Greenbelt Road. It slowed near the main gate and made a sudden left directly into oncoming traffic. Horns blared; it sideswiped a Citation and spun it sideways against the center strip. But the Plymouth kept coming.

She stepped out of the inspection booth onto the small hook of paving that divided the roadway. Reflexively, her right hand brushed the .38 on her hip, but she did not unclip the safety strap that held the weapon in its holster.

The car slowed; Marian had a glimpse of the driver as he straightened after the turn. He looked, she realized with a chill, like Lee Oswald, a creature of black moods and arrogant pretensions. He was smiling at her when she saw the .45.

The window behind her exploded.

Something tugged at her belly, she dived back inside the booth and lay on the floor while he methodically blew out the rest of the glass. Then he drove casually out onto Road 1 and poured automatic gunfire into a group of pedestrians. They scattered screaming; several went down, and two or three lay still after he passed.

Security forces were slow to respond. The Plymouth was on Road 2, almost out of sight, before a pursuit vehicle left the main gate. Marian's radio came alive. She brushed the glass shakily out of her hair. Her supervisor was sprinting toward her from the gatehouse, his eyes wide, his hands held out to her.

It was the last thing she saw.

The driver of the Plymouth killed three more in a wild chase across lawns and through parking areas before they cornered him behind the house that Baines Rimford had occupied, and blew him in half. All together, seven were dead. Of the critically injured, three, including the gate guard, died that night.

The assailant turned out to be a welfare father from Baltimore, who was under a peace bond for threatening low-ranking employees of Eastern Maryland Power & Gas.

Senator Parkman Randall, Republican from Nebraska, had no idea what the Oval Office meeting would be about, but he hoped the President had something he could take home to his constituents. Farm policies during this administration had been a disaster. Randall had played the loyal soldier, supporting what he could and opposing what he had to, knowing always that the President understood. The stock market collapse that had begun on Monday wasn't helping matters. And he had other problems: abortion, the gun issue, prayer in the schools. Each was a politician's nightmare, an issue that allowed no easy compromise. And on each, he had eventually been forced to take a position and to vote. Randall knew, as every good politician knows, that votes on sensitive issues never win friends, but invariably lose voters.

He was up for re-election in November.

The members of the Senate Defense Committee gathered in their caucus room and rode the underground jitney to the White House. Chilton was waiting for them when they debarked, and he escorted them to the Oval Office.

The President stood as they entered and advanced to shake their hands. He was smiling, and Randall knew his man well enough to understand immediately that the news, whatever it was, would be good. He was grateful for that, at least.

"Ladies and gentlemen," he said, after everyone had settled into place, "I have an announcement of some importance." He paused, enjoying the moment. "We've lived under a nuclear sword now for almost half a century. There has never been a day in our lives that we haven't been aware of the possibility, at any moment, of an armed attack that could destroy the United

States and probably every hope for a human future as well. There has never been an hour that we have not been at the mercy of Soviet self-interest. And we have waited for the miscalculation, for the accident, for the madman. Or for the technological breakthrough that would set us free.

"I am in a position to tell you today that the waiting is nearly ended."

The men and women who sat around the perimeter of the office had, collectively, spent almost two centuries in politics; they were not easily impressed by talk. But they sensed something different tonight. The eloquence was gone; instead of the measured rhythmic tones and sparkling phrases, they heard only his elation. "The United States is about to activate ORION."

Through the window, Randall watched the inevitable demonstrators, protesting South American policy today, environmental issues tomorrow. They walked in tireless circles outside the gate. They never went away, they criticized everything, and they had no solutions. .The people in the office began to applaud, and Randall joined them.

"ORION is a particle-beam weapon," the President continued. "It attacks guidance and other electronic systems on board enemy missiles, rendering them useless. That is, the missiles will not go where they are aimed. And even if they could, they would not detonate when they arrived."

"Mr. President," asked Randall, "how long will it take?"

"Our best guess," said the President, "is thirty days. The shuttles have already begun ferrying the hardware into orbit."

Chilton was passing among them with a tray on which rested thirteen glasses. Each of the seven men and five women took one. The President took the last. John Hurley retrieved an ice bucket from behind his desk, lifted a bottle of champagne from it, and removed the cork. When Ed Wrenside of New Hampshire hurried forward to help, the President waved him back with a smile and filled their glasses one by one.

"Ladies and gentlemen," he said, "I give you the United States."

MONITOR

WHITE HOUSE DENIES NEW ENERGY SOURCE
"I Wish It Were True," Says President
DJIA Off 740 Points in Week

ALTHEAN RUNAWAY BEST-SELLER
Michael Pappadopoulis's *Translations from the Althean* surged to the top of the *New York Times* best-seller list during its first week of release. Despite critical charges that the volume contains more of Pappadopoulis than the Altheans, bookstores reported mounting sales.

AYADI DENIES HAVING BOMB
"I would have no use for one," the Ayadi Ztana Mendolian told a crowded gathering of Iraqis and Jordanians yesterday. "The Almighty does not need my help to destroy Israel." Later he attended a soccer game.

MARKET SLIDE BLAMED ON SPECULATORS
Short sales by insiders probably triggered the market collapse this week. "The averages were too high, and we were ripe for something like this," said Val Koestler, electronics specialist for Killebrew & Denkle. "There were other factors that contributed, of course: the steady climb in interest rates over recent weeks, increased tension in the Middle East, the latest unemployment figures. People were jittery..."

SOVIETS WALK OUT OF GENEVA
Declare U.S. "Frivolous"
Hurley Seeks Clear-Cut Military Advantage, Says Tass
Taimanov Returns to Moscow

MAN WIELDING PICKAX SLAUGHTERS SIX IN PEORIA BAR
Claims Extraterrestrials Talk to Him on Channel 9

CHINESE REINSTATE BIRTH RESTRICTIONS
Human Rights Groups Denounce Action

TALIOFSKY WINS CHESS TITLE AND DEFECTS
Moscow Charges Champ Lured by Sex and Drugs

HARRY WAS WORKING late in his office when the fire engines went by, headed north toward Venture Park, the VIP housing area. His angle of vision was bad, but he could make out a fiery glare in the sky.

It was a quarter to eleven.

He pulled on his coat, walked swiftly to the north end of the building, and hurried out onto the lawn. Flames and moving lights were visible through a screen of trees. They seemed to be centered on Cord Majeski's house.

From the direction of the main gate, he heard more sirens.

Harry broke into a run, knowing somehow with the fatalism that recent weeks had induced that the fire would be connected with the Hercules Project. Always now, things were connected. There was no rest.

Majeski's house: it had been a two-story frame, painted light and dark brown, with a small deck on the west side and a storm door and a single concrete step in front. Emergency vehicles cluttered the street in front. Lights blinked, and people stood in small puzzled groups, staring at what remained. It was the damnedest thing Harry'd ever seen.

The kitchen, the rear bedrooms, and part of the dining room were gutted. A few blackened timbers hung precariously together, hissing and sputtering under white streams of water. The air reeked of charred wood.

The front of the house stood untouched, glowing frostily in the bright night, a lovely thing of blue crystal and cold fire. It reflected the revolving lights of the emergency vehicles and the steady glow of the street lamps. A silver arc centered on the house spread out across the lawn almost to the sidewalk. Two elms and some azaleas, caught within the arc, were laced with hoarfrost.

"What *is* it?" someone asked as Harry walked up.

Leslie stood off to one side. She'd thrown a coat over her nightclothes and, holding it tightly around her, stared disconsolately at the wreckage. She did not see him as he approached.

"Where's Cord?" he asked gently, placing his hand on her shoulder.

She filled the space between them and pressed against him. It was her only answer.

Harry heard an order to cut the water, and the hoses went limp. Some of the firemen started poking at the rubble. More sparks flew up.

"Why is it so cold?" she asked.

Harry's face was already numb. "There's a wave of it coming from somewhere," he said, looking around curiously. "I think it's the front of the house!" He held his palms out in that direction. "Jesus!" he said, "it *is*. What the hell's going on?"

Medical technicians and security officers were still arriving. Pete Wheeler's car bounced across some grass fields, dropped into the street, and stopped half a block away. He got out and stared.

The security people were cordoning off the area. Others were closing in on the house. "The front of the place looks as if it's encased in a layer of ice," Harry said.

There was a momentary stir among the firemen. They'd gathered in the rubble where the kitchen had been, and they were looking down at the debris. Then they signaled, and someone came forward with a stretcher. They lifted a blackened human form, placed it on the stretcher, and drew a blanket over it.

Leslie trembled in his arms.

Wheeler hurried up; his eyes had gone wide at sight of the house. It was the first time Harry had seen Pete Wheeler lose his equanimity. Harry murmured a greeting, but the priest's attention was fastened on the front of the dwelling.

They carried the stretcher toward one of the emergency vehicles. "He's a Catholic," said Harry.

Wheeler shook his head impatiently. "Later. Why is everything frozen up there?"

"Damned if I know," said Harry. The security people had been holding back the few bystanders who'd appeared, but now they themselves were looking curiously at the glazed siding and concrete and shingles.

"Even the ground," remarked Wheeler, "has acquired a sheet of ice." He knelt just outside the edge of the whitened arc, keeping his hands in his pockets. HIs breath hung before him. Harry had no feeling in his nose and ears. The rocks and pebbles and concrete within the circle glittered. Harry reached for one, but Wheeler pushed him away with a shout. "Supercold," he explained. "I doubt you'd get your hand back. Keep everybody off it, Harry. I'm not sure that shoes would be much protection."

Harry relayed the warning. "What is it?" he asked.

"It'll thaw out in a few days, I suppose," said Wheeler. He walked toward the rear of the house. Goddard's emergency coordinator, Hal Addison, was poking in the wreckage with two of his assistants.

Wheeler asked if he could look around, and Addison, wearing a baffled frown, readily assented. He inspected the thin border between the section that had burned and the area that had apparently frozen, walking back and forth, kicking at timbers and brick dust and charred wood.

"What are you looking for, Pete?" asked Leslie, joining them.

"I don't know," he said. "But there'll be something here somewhere. Right in the middle." And with that, he gave a cry of satisfaction and pointed beneath a blackened beam. Harry helped Addison's men move it.

In the debris was a blob of melted metal.

"This is where we found the body," said Addison.

"Pete," asked Harry, "do you know what happened?"

"Inferno at one end," said Wheeler. "Supercold at the other. I'll tell you what it reminds me of: Maxwell's Demon."

Leslie Davies was angry. Harry could see it in her eyes, and he wondered how she managed to conceal her emotions from her patients. She stood at her front door, with her hand on the knob, under bitter late winter stars, in a bathrobe, a nightgown, and a pair of slippers. And her mind was elsewhere. "We need some controls," she said finally, pushing the door open, but still not moving from the concrete step. "Baines was out working on his own, too. You or Gambini or somebody is going to have to set up some procedures to stop the free-lancing. Did you see that hunk of slag that Pete pulled out of the debris? How's anybody going to make sense of that? It just means someone else gets to blow himself up later." Her eyes had fastened on him. They were round and weary and wet.

"I'm sorry about Cord," Harry said. He'd never liked Majeski and suspected that Leslie hadn't either. But that didn't seem to matter now.

They went inside. "Harry," she said, "Cord's not the only victim. Everyone associated with the Hercules Project—Ed,

Pete Wheeler, Baines, you, maybe even me—we should be at the peak of our professional careers, but somehow the project generates only disasters."

Harry didn't know what to say; everything he could think of sounded frivolous, so he only watched her. Her voice shook; her nostrils had widened, and her breathing was uneven. The long stem of her throat disappeared into the bulky folds of her robe, a bland, shapeless garment that completely concealed the body beneath. She started out of the room.

"Maybe Pete's right," Harry said. "Maybe we *should* destroy the discs."

That stopped her. She turned and looked at him. "No," she said softly, "that's no solution."

"Baines called it the Manhattan Option. Get rid of it while there's still time."

"I'll make coffee," she said. "Pete doesn't have an open mind." She disappeared into the kitchen. The refrigerator door opened and closed, water ran into a pot, and then she was back at the doorway.

"Sometimes I think," Harry said, "he's concerned that there may be a threat to the Church."

"No. It's more complicated than that. Wheeler's a strange man; I don't understand how he could have become a priest. Or maybe it would be more accurate to say that I wonder how he could have remained one. He doesn't believe, you know. Not in the Church. Certainly not in God. Although I suspect he'd like to."

"That's absurd. I've known Wheeler for fifteen years. He wouldn't stay with the order if he didn't believe."

"Maybe," she said. "But he may not be aware of his true feelings. We all keep secrets from ourselves. I've known people, for example, who don't know they hate their jobs. Or their spouses. Or even their kids."

"And you?" asked Harry, impulsively. "I wonder what secrets you have."

She nodded thoughtfully. "Coffee's ready."

"Pete is the sort of man," she said later, "who never stops changing. He couldn't hold a credo for a lifetime. And anyhow his training is all in the other direction. He's a skeptic by profession: he makes his living by dismantling other people's theories." The fire engines were beginning to pull away. "Does that make sense? Compared to what he is today, he was a child when he took orders. The Norbertines saw to his education, and he remains with them out of a sense of loyalty."

"I don't believe it," said Harry. "I know him too well." She had been standing by the window. Now she seated herself beside him on the sofa. It was a standard GSA issue with sliding square vinyl cushions. She'd thrown an afghan over it, but it didn't help much; it was still lumpy and treacherous. "Why," he asked, "would he feel threatened if he has no faith to lose?"

"Oh, he has a faith to lose. Harry, he has probably, almost certainly, not admitted to himself that he no longer believes in the Christian God. But he's nevertheless convinced that the orthodox position is a sham: Pete Wheeler no more seriously thinks that he'll one day walk with the saints than you and I believe in ghosts." She kicked off her shoes, pulled her knees up under her, and sipped her coffee. "He's denied God in his heart, Harry. For him, that's the final sin. But there can be no sin where there is no God. And *that* is the faith that the Altheans threaten with their talk of a Designer."

She was silent for a time. "And you?" asked Harry. "What threatens *you?*"

Her eyes dimmed. Shadows moved across her jaw and throat. "I'm not sure. I'm beginning to feel that I know the Altheans pretty well. At least the one who sent the transmission. And what I get is a terrible sense of solitude. We've assumed that the communication is from one species to another. But I get the distinct sense that there's only one of them, sitting in a tower somewhere, utterly alone." There was something in her eyes that Harry had never seen before. "You know what it makes me think of, with all this talk of Wheeler? An isolated God, lost and drifting in the gulfs."

Harry put his hand over both of hers. She was lovely in the half-light.

"The data sets," she continued, "are full of vitality, compassion, a sense of wonder. There's something almost childlike about them. And it's hard to believe that the senders are a million years dead." She wiped at her eyes. "And I'm not sure anymore what I'm trying to say."

He watched her breast rise and fall. She turned her face toward his. Harry studied the warm geometry of softly curving lip and high cheekbone.

"I'm never going to be the same, Harry. You know what? I think it was a mistake to bring the translations back here and read them alone at night."

"You're not supposed to do that." Harry smiled. "Does anybody around here obey the regulations?"

"In this case, at least, I should have. I'm beginning to see things in the night, and hear voices in the dark." Her head fell back, and a sound like laughter rose in her throat. He caught her eyes and became aware of his own heartbeat.

His arm circled her shoulder, and he drew her forward. Their eyes joined, and she folded herself against him. Harry was acutely conscious of the body under the robe. It had been a long time since an honest female passion had been directed, without reservation, at him. He savored it, holding her, tracing the line of her jaw and throat with his fingertips. Her cheek was warm against his. After a time she whispered his name, and turned herself, turned him, so that she could reach his mouth. She fitted her lips gently to it.

They were warm and full, and her breath was sweet. He explored her teeth and her tongue, and sensed the long well of her throat.

Slowly, he loosened the robe and drew it down over her shoulders. Beneath the filmy texture of the nightgown, her nipples were erect.

Senator Randall knew why they were there before either said a word, had known since they called the day before to announce they'd be flying in. Teresa Burgess carried the same heavy black bag she'd carried through half a dozen campaigns in Nebraska. Like its owner, it was somber and inflexible, constructed of stiff leather, and frayed around all the moving parts.

In her, as in most people with a fiercely competitive nature, competence and ruthlessness had erased the gentler qualities from her expression, if not from her character. She represented the banking interests in Kansas City and Wichita, where she'd supported Randall for twenty years as faithfully as her father had supported the first Senator Randall.

Her associate was Wendell Whitlock, the ex-officio party boss in the state. Whitlock had been an auto salesman at Rolley Chrysler-Plymouth ("Deal with Your Friends") when Randall was trying to win a place on the Kansas City School Board. Later he sold dealerships, and eventually he sold influence.

Randall broke out the Jack Daniels, and they laughed and talked about old times; but his visitors were restrained and not entirely at ease. "I guess you don't think we can make it in November," he said finally, looking from one to the other.

Whitlock put up a hand as though he were going to protest

that no such consideration was abroad. But the gesture dissolved. "These haven't been good times, Randy," he admitted. "It's not your fault, God knows it isn't, but you know how people are. The goddam combines control the prices, interest rates are high, and your constituents aren't very prosperous. They got to blame somebody. So they're going to take it out on the President, and you."

"I've done what I could," protested Randall. "Some of the votes that upset people, the second farm bill, the milling regulations, the rest of it, that was compromise stuff. If I hadn't gone along, Lincoln wouldn't have got the school appropriation, the defense contracts that went to Random and McKittridge in North Platte—out in your country, Teresa—would have gone to those bastards in Massachusetts."

"Randy," said Burgess, "you don't have to tell us any of that. We know. But that isn't the point."

"What is the point?" Randall asked angrily. These goddam people owed him a lot. Burgess's Wheat Exchange would still be a tin-pot operation in Broken Bow if it hadn't been for him. And Whitlock owed his first decent job with the party to the senator's intervention. He wondered what had happened to loyalty.

"The point," said Burgess, "is that there's a lot of money at stake here. The people who've backed you stand to lose their asses if they do it again and you don't win."

"Hell, Teresa, I'll win. You know that."

"I don't know it. The party is going for a ride. Hurley is going to lose, no matter who the Democrats run, and the people associated with him are going to take the pipe. People may like him personally, but they're not going to stand for his policies anymore. And nobody in the Senate is more closely linked to him than you are. Randy, the truth is, you probably won't even be able to get the party's nomination. Perlmutter is popular downstate. And he looks strong in Omaha and Lincoln."

"Perlmutter's a kid. What could he do for the state?"

"Randy." Whitlock didn't sound so soothing now. He'd grown a mustache since Randall had last seen him. It was hard to understand why: he looked devious enough without it. "This isn't like before. There isn't a farmer in the state who'll vote for you. My God, more than half of those people out there are calling themselves Democrats now. You ever hear of Democrat farmers before?"

"Farmers always bitch," said Randall. "They forget their gripes when they get in the voting booth and they're looking at a choice between one of their own and some goddam liberal who wants to give their money away."

Burgess's chin rose. "Randy, the farmers have no money. Not anymore. And so you don't get the wrong idea, they're not alone in this. Now, I'm not saying that my people would leave the party, Jesus no, but I *am* saying that, for the sake of the party, they're going to be pushing for a fresh candidate. And they like Perlmutter."

"You two," Randall said accusingly, "could change all that."

"We could keep most of the money in line," Whitlock admitted. "We could probably even cut Perlmutter out. But he'd take his people with him, which would split us at a time when we need everybody." He took a deep breath. "Randy, if you step down now, the governor will find a decent situation for you—they're talking about Commerce—and you get spared the embarrassment of November."

"Whit." Randall sought his eyes, but they were, as always, elusive. "Hurley isn't going to lose."

"I wish that were true." Whitlock smiled.

Burgess, who was perhaps more observant, leaned forward. "Why not?" she asked.

"It's a defense matter." He hesitated. "I'm not free to discuss it."

The banker shrugged. "I'm not free to commit anyone on idle rumor, Randy."

No one moved.

"We're probably going to be able to do something about the Soviets."

On the night that Cord Majeski died, Cyrus Hakluyt was at home in Catonsville. Unlike most of his colleagues, he had no inclination to allow the project to swallow his personal life. He did not put in the overtime that Gambini seemed to expect of everyone, working seven days a week into the early morning hours and then retreating to the bland frame houses that Harry Carmichael had provided in Venture Park.

Hakluyt had spent the evening with friends, some of whom might have noticed in the usually somber microbiologist an uncharacteristic exuberance. Cy was in a good mood. No one present, even Oscar Kazmaier, who'd known him from Westminster days, had ever before seen him drink too much. But they had to take him home in the early morning hours.

Actually, Hakluyt could recall two earlier bouts with the bottle. They had occurred on the evening he'd lost Pat and the afternoon that Houghton Mifflin had bought *The Place without Roads*. His Nobel, which had been awarded for his work with nucleic acids, had prompted no such eruption.

He was a little late getting to the lab in the morning, where, of course, everyone was talking about Cord Majeski's death. A memo was tacked to the bulletin board giving the name and address of Majeski's father and sister.

"He was building a device he'd found in the Text," said Gambini. "We don't know what it was supposed to be, but Pete thinks it had something to do with statistical manipulation of gases inside magnetic bottles. But it must have gotten away from him."

"I guess," said Hakluyt. "Was anyone else hurt?"

"No. He was alone in the house."

"Do we know why the experiment blew up?"

"It didn't. Exactly." Gambini frowned. "Listen, Cy, he might have achieved statistical control of the first law of thermodynamics."

Hakluyt didn't laugh, but it took all his restraint. "If I follow what you're saying, it's not possible."

"The first law isn't absolute," said Gambini. "It doesn't *have* to be that heat passes from a warm gas to a cool one. It's only highly probable, because of the molecular exchange. But some of the molecules in the warm gas move more slowly than some of the more active molecules in the cool gas. And vice versa. Cord's device may have acted as a monitor, creating a Maxwell's Demon."

Hakluyt sat down. "What's that?" he asked.

"James Maxwell was a nineteenth-century physicist who proposed that, if a demon could sit between two compartments, one filled with a hot gas and the other with a cool gas, he could create an interesting effect by allowing only the fastest molecules from the cool side to enter the hot chamber, and letting only the slowest molecules from the hot side to pass into the cool chamber."

"What would happen," finished Hakluyt, "is that the hot gas would get hotter, and the cold gas would become colder! And you think," he said skeptically, "something like that happened to Majeski? It's absurd."

"Have you seen the house? Go down and take a look. Then

come back and we'll talk about absurdities."

Hakluyt stared into Gambini's eyes. His spectacles had slid forward on the bridge of his nose and he persisted throughout the conversation in peering over them. "Okay," he said. "Maybe it's time we asked ourselves what we're dealing with on the other end of this transmission. Has it occurred to anyone that the bastards are vindictive? I mean, why else would they send us directions for something that would blow up in our faces?"

"No!" snapped Gambini. "We're just not being careful enough. Nobody's going to go to all the trouble they did to play a goddam joke! Park of the problem here might have been that we simply didn't understand the specifications. Maybe we're not as bright as they think we should be! We couldn't even work out the power specs."

"Maybe they don't use electricity."

"Well, then, magnetism. Or gasoline. Or somebody turning a crank. Whatever it is, there should be some indication of how much to use."

"Unless it's something you *don't* measure." It was a remark that Gambini repeated later to Harry, and Harry, for reasons he did not understand at the time, immediately thought of Father Rene Sunderland. "How about some *good* news?" continued Hakluyt, suggesting they retire into Gambini's office.

"Majeski wasn't very likable," said Gambini. "But I'll miss him."

"He was all right," Hakluyt said. "He did his job, and he didn't make trouble for anybody. In the end, you probably can't ask much more than that."

"What's your good news?"

Hakluyt removed his glasses and placed them on Gambini's desk. The lenses were thick, mounted in steel frames. Hakluyt was physically so slight that he seemed somehow less substantial without the spectacles. "I've worn them all my life," he said. "I'm nearsighted, and I had an astigmatism. My family has a long line of eye problems. They're all myopic." He smiled delicately, picked up a *Webster's,* and held it over the glasses. "I got my first bifocals when I was eight." He let the book drop. It smashed the spectacles flat.

Gambini watched, mystified. "Cy," he said, "what the hell are you doing?"

Hakluyt swept the pieces casually into a wastebasket. "I don't need them anymore." He looked triumphantly at Gambini. "You know why we had all those vision problems?"

"Genetic," said Gambini.

"Of course," snapped Hakluyt. "But why? The repair mechanisms aren't properly directed, that's why. The equipment to put my eyes in decent order was always there. But the coding was incorrect. Ed, rewrite the coding and you wind up with 20-20 vision."

"Son of a bitch," said Gambini, beginning to glow. "You've been able to do that?"

"Yes! I can do some of it. I can do it for *you*, Ed, if you want. I can make your eyes twenty-one years old." He took a deep breath. "I never knew what it was to see well. Even the glasses didn't help much, really. I always felt as if I were looking at the world through smeared windows.

"This morning, from my car, I watched a cardinal sitting on a branch out near the main gate. A few weeks ago, I'd have had trouble seeing the tree."

"And you can do the same for anyone?"

"Yes," he said. "For you. For anybody. All it takes is a little chemistry. And I'd need a blood sample."

Gambini sat down. "Are you sure?"

"Of course not. I don't know enough yet. But, Ed, I think this is only the beginning. You know how I did it? I sent bogus instructions to several billion cells. The sort of instructions my DNA shoud put out if it really cared about my welfare. I've still got a lot to learn, but I don't think there's anything we won't be able to do—stop cancer, strengthen the heart, you name it."

"You mean, stop deterioration generally?"

"Yes!" Hakluyt's voice literally rang. It was the first time Gambini had seen him actually appear happy. "Ed, I'm not sure yet where all this will lead. But we're going to come away with the means to cure epilepsy, Hodgkin's, cataracts, you name it. It's all there."

Gambini removed his glasses. He only used them for reading. He needed new ones, had for years, but he suspected that stronger lenses would weaken his eyes still more, and consequently he refused to return to an optometrist. It *would* be good to be rid of them. To be rid of the back that ached on damp mornings and the loose flesh around his waist and under his jaw. To be rid of the dark fear that came occasionally in the night when he woke suddenly aware of the beating of his heart.

My God, what would such a thing not be worth? To be young again . . . "Does anyone else know?"

"Not yet."

"Cy, what would happen to a man who stopped aging?"

Hakluyt took a while to answer. "That's a good question," he said. "If we intervene in the scheduled breakdown of the body, other factors will probably come into play. There certainly would be psychological considerations. But as far as your physical welfare goes, if you don't get betrayed by your DNA, and if you stay off the wrong airplane, it's hard to see why you should die."

Gambini picked up a large paper clip and turned it over and over in his fingers. "Probably we should say nothing about this to anyone, Cy."

"Why?" asked Hakluyt, immediately suspicious.

"Because we would have a very hard time if people stopped dying."

"Well, of course we'd need to establish controls and eventually make some adjustments."

"How do you think the White House would react if I reported this to them? You've seen the problems we've had because we released some Althean philosophical tracts. And the goddam energy story caused a stock market crash. What would *this* do?"

"We should suggest the White House turn it over to the National Council for the Advancement of Science."

"Or the Boy Scouts of America." Gambini laughed. "They'll turn it over to nobody. It's too dangerous. If people find out that something like this is around, God knows what would happen. I'll tell you this much: if we give this to Hurley, we'll wind up with a bunch of immortal politicians, and nobody'll ever hear of the technique again."

"Then we should submit it ourselves to the NCAS and let them decide how to handle it."

"Cy, I don't think we're communicating. Rimford thought he'd found something so dangerous in the transmission that he destroyed both copies of one of the data sets."

"What did he find?"

"A way to manufacture black holes." Gambini let that sink in. "But that's not in the same league at all with what you have. My God, Cy, imagine a world in which people stopped dying. Even for a little while. If they stop dying from natural causes, they'll start dying from something else. Famine, probably. Or bullet holes."

"But the NCAS—"

"No one can handle something like this. We've got to deal with it the same way Rimford dealt with his problem."

"No!" It was almost a cry of pain. "You can't throw this away. Who the hell do you think you are to make that kind of decision?"

Gambini's forehead was damp. "I'm the only person in a position to do it. If it goes beyond this office, we'll never contain it." He stared for long moments at the wall. "We'll talk about it," he promised. "But in the meantime, no one's to know." He took a ledger out of his desk and consulted it. "You've been working with DS one-oh-one."

"Yes."

"Bring it here. Along with your notes and any other records you have on this."

Hakluyt's eyes went very wide, and the blood drained from his face. He looked near tears. "You can't do this," he said.

"I'm not doing anything right now except ensuring that nothing happens until I want it to."

Waves of pain and rage rolled through Hakluyt's eyes. "You're a madman," he said. "You know, all I have to do is tell Rosenbloom or Carmichael what you're doing and you'll find yourself in a jail somewhere."

"I'm sure you're right," said Gambini. "But I wish you'd stop a moment to consider the consequences. In any case, if I have to, I'll destroy DS one-oh-one." He held out his hand. "I'll also need your library ID."

Hakluyt produced the plastic card, dropped it on the desk, and started for the door. "If anything happens to those discs," he said, "I'll kill you."

Gambini waited a few minutes, then went out to Hakluyt's station, retrieved the laserdisc, gathered the microbiologist's papers, and locked them in his filing cabinet.

An hour later, he let himself into the storeroom at the library and signed out the duplicate DS101. With an armed guard at his side, he brought it back to the Hercules spaces and put it, too, in the cabinet. Then he resisted the temptation to destroy both and be done with it.

MONITOR

PRESIDENT WARNS SOVIETS OVER SOUTH AFRICA
Rebels Strike Johannesburg
Constellation Reported En Route

MASSACHUSETTS FIRM HITS BIG TIME WITH
ALTHEAN T-SHIRTS

BASEBALL SEASON DELAYED BY STRIKE
First Test of NOBF
Fans' Organization Threatens Boycott

PROGRESS IN WAR ON CANCER
Early Detection Remains Key

"SIGNALS" OPENS IN WASHINGTON
New Musical Salutes Altheans

MATHEMATICIAN KILLED AT GODDARD
Cord Majeski Dies in Gas Line Explosion

WHITE HOUSE PREDICTS MARKET RECOVERY BY
END OF YEAR
President Points to Strong Housing Starts, Employment
Figures

KANSAS CITY STAR SAYS MISSILE SHIELD IMMINENT
Pentagon Denies Reports

AYADI ATTACKS HERCULES PROGRAM
"Trafficking with Satan"
Baghdad (AP)—In a statement issued today from his headquarters at Government House, the Ayadi Itana Mendolian
branded the U.S. Hercules Project as either "a pack of lies" or
a communication with Satan. In either case, he said, "a just

231

God will surely reward the avengers." This was widely seen as a call for action by terrorist groups known to be operating in Western Europe and the United States.

BAINES RIMFORD ANNOUNCES RETIREMENT

16

Harry's allergies were growing worse. He went to the dispensary to see if he could get a stronger prescription, and a strange thing happened. While he waited, Emma Watkins, the attractive young receptionist who brightened the otherwise sterile sitting room, mentioned casually that she'd mailed off the copy of his medical record just an hour before. "To whom?" asked Harry, feeling as if he'd come in during the middle of the conversation.

She hesitated, trying to remember, and pulled his file. "Dr. Wallis," she said.

"Who?"

"Dr. Adam Wallis." She showed him a formal request, with Harry's signature on an accompanying release. But it wasn't his handwriting.

"Who's Adam Wallis?" he asked.

"Don't *you* know, Mr. Carmichael?" Her manner suggested that Harry was one of those high-ranking people who have a hard time keeping their minds on practical matters. "His stationery says he's a GP." She disappeared into the back of the room and returned with the *Physicians' Directory*. "He's not listed," she said, after a few moments of page-turning.

"Why would anyone be interested in my medical history?" asked Harry. He wondered whether it might be somehow connected with Julie. But how?

The address on the stationery was in Langley Park. He drove over in the evening and found a two-story frame house in a new subdivision. Lights were on, and children were visible through the windows. The name on the mailbox was Shoemaker.

"I never heard of him," said the man who answered the door. He told Harry he'd been living there for eight years. "I don't think there's any doctors in the subdivision. The local ones are all over at the Medical Building."

Harry stood on the doorstep, puzzled. "You'll probably get a package for him tomorrow, from Goddard." Harry took out the Xerox copy of Wallis's letter and compared the addresses again. He was at the right place. "I'd appreciate it if you'd just turn it around and send it back."

"Sure," he said.

Two days later, Harry's medical record was back, marked "Return to Sender."

Leslie went back to her office in Philadelphia for three days each week. But routine work with patients who were having problems with kids or suffering from sexual dysfunction—those two complaints constituted about ninety percent of her practice—had become tiresome. Her attitude toward that aspect of her life's work had, in fact, been deteriorating for two years. She'd been preparing to dissolve her practice before the call from Goddard had come the previous September. She knew now that she would never go back to full-time consulting with individual patients.

But she had no idea what she *would* do. What would be left for her after Hercules? She'd been planning to conduct a study on the addictive effects of TV on various segments of the population. That such data would be enormously important she had no doubt. But how tiresome the gathering of it would be! How tiresome the rest of her life would be!

One of her patients for some years had been Carl Wieczaki, a former Phillies infielder who had made the All-Star team at twenty-two in his second season, had gone to Portland two years later, and was out of baseball at twenty-six. He was a potbellied bartender when he came to Leslie, and she'd seen how terrible it is to achieve the peak of one's life so young!

The Wieczaki syndrome.

She was susceptible to it herself.

When the last appointment for the day cancelled, she decided to walk home. The weather had turned summery, and since she didn't plan to go out that evening, leaving her car in the lot would be no inconvenience.

She cut across the Villanova University campus, stopped at the bookstore to pick up a novel, and enjoyed an early dinner on City Line Avenue.

There was a ball game at Mulhern Park, and she lingered to watch the last few innings.

A couple of hundred people had turned out for the contest between two high school teams. It was, she learned, opening day, and the crowd was being treated to good pitching and defense on both sides. Leslie was particularly struck by the visitors' center fielder, a tall, lean boy of exquisite grace. Although Leslie had played basketball in college, she'd never taken much interest in watching organized sports. They seemed to her a scandalous waste of valuable time. But on that warm evening, hobbled by the uncertainties in her life, she was anxious to lose herself for an hour or so in something harmless.

It was hard to take her eyes off the center fielder. He pulled down several long drives, cut off an extra-base hit that should have rolled all the way to the cyclone fence bordering the field, and threw out a runner who tried to advance on an overthrow of second. She watched, after each inning, as he came in from his position. His eyes were blue and intelligent; he had a good smile; and once, when he looked up and saw her, he grinned and, just perceptibly, nodded.

He was a lovely child, and she wished him a good life.

He came to bat late in the game with two out and the score tied and lined the first pitch into the alley in left center. The hundred or so fans on the visitors' side rose in unison, and the boy was off like a young leopard.

With two outfielders in pursuit, the ball hit the base of the fence on the fly, and caromed high into the air. The shortstop hurried out to take the relay, while the runner rounded second and sprinted toward third. The fence was deep, and everyone realized he had a chance to go all the way. The left fielder caught up with the ball as the runner approached third. The coach was frantically waving him home.

He cut the corner at the bag and raced down the final ninety feet.

"Go, Jack!" the fans called.

The execution by the defense was flawless. The outfielder fired a strike to the shortstop, who allowed it to go through. It bounced once and arrived, Leslie thought, simultaneously with the runner. But the catcher blocked off the plate and swept the tag across a leg as both players sprawled into the clay. The umpire's right fist jerked up!

In the bottom half of the inning, the home team scored on a pair of hits wrapped around an infield out, and the game was over.

The center fielder helped his team collect bats and gloves. But when they headed for their bus, he lingered near the bench. At first Leslie thought he'd misunderstood her interest in him, but he never looked up at her. Rather, he stood quietly in the shadows, and she could see that final sprint around the infield replaying itself in his mind.

She wished there were something in her own life that she wanted so badly.

The Soviet Reconnaissance Satellite XK4415L, of the Chernev series, floated in geosynchronous orbit above the Mojave Desert, where it could observe two U.S. Air Force bases and a missile tracking range.

On the thirtieth of April, during the late morning, its infrared cameras picked up a series of six plumes, long streaks of white mist soaring toward the summit of the eastern sky. The satellite's instruments identified them as MXs and tracked them out of the atmosphere. An array of electronic eyes and ears fed data into onboard computers, which compared performance against known capabilities. But well before the missiles arrived at their apexes, they went awry. All six wobbled off in unexpected directions, turned over, and fell back toward the surface.

Several hours later, a second series of eight ICBMs staggered across the sensitive registers of the satellite. At a few minutes before midnight Moscow time, Colonel Mikos Zubaroff entered one of the numerous briefing rooms on the west side of the Kremlin, threw his bulging briefcase onto a flat wooden lectern, handed a filmstrip to an aide, and removed eight copies of the reconnaissance analysis from the briefcase. Each was in a red folder stamped with a supersensitive classification.

Marshall Konig arrived moments later; he walked quickly to the front of the room and scrutinized Zubaroff. "It is true?" he asked.

"Yes."

"They destroyed all fourteen?"

"Yes."

He was silent. One by one the others entered, Yemelenko and Ivanovsky and Arkiemenov and the rest, grim men who understood the nature of the threat from the West and who were tonight, perhaps for the first time in their military careers, pessimistic about the nation's future.

Zubaroff waited until they were all seated around the green baize–covered table, and then he briefly recounted what the Chernev had observed. His aide projected slides taken a few seconds apart, which chillingly revealed the simultaneous loss of control in both flights of missiles.

"Do they not," asked Konig smoothly, "have the capability to blind the Chernev?"

"Yes," said Zubaroff. "We have no doubt they can do so."

"Yet they chose *not* to do so. Perhaps they are trying to mislead us?"

"Perhaps. But we don't really know that their failure to act was a deliberate choice. A test of a weapon of this nature," the colonel said, "would be very closely guarded, even within their own organization. They may have failed to inform the people who would have neutralized the Chernev." He might have added that they all knew from experience that such oversights happened even among the people's forces.

They heard Taimanov's voice in the hall. A moment later the foreign minister entered and took a place at the far end of the table.

"But," persisted Konig, "it might nevertheless be an elaborate hoax. The missiles could have self-destructed."

"That is possible. But the Chernev detected microwaves from a higher orbit. We suspect that it is peripheral radiation of some sort."

"And the device emitting the radiation?"

"—Is not in my field of expertise. Rudnetsky believes it could be the particle-beam weapon."

With those words, the atmosphere became funereal. "The American press," Taimanov said, "has been reporting rumors of such a thing. If in fact they have it, I do not like to think what the bastards will try to do with it."

Harry's allergies got so bad that he took a day off and went to bed. His eyes swelled, his throat began to hurt, and he could not stop sneezing. The next morning, he went back to the dispensary, where a medic gave him another injection. It dried out his sinuses, but left him sleepy. When he showed up at the Hercules staff meeting during the latter part of the morning, he looked distinctly unwell.

Gambini reported some progress in translating Althean descriptions of electromagnetic phenomena, and Majeski's replacement, Carol Hedge, had uncovered enough on statistical relationships to suggest that Wheeler was probably correct in ascribing the accident to Maxwell's Demon. Her presentation woke Harry up.

Hedge was an attractive black from Harvard-Smithsonian. Harry watched her appreciatively and once caught Leslie smiling at his reaction to her. When she'd finished, Gambini asked for comments, noted one or two expressions of concern for safety in future experiments, and turned the meeting over to Wheeler.

"I think I've got another bomb," said the priest. "We're finding detailed and exceedingly fundamental descriptions of electromagnetic radiation, harmonics, particle theory, you name it. At the moment, I have answers to all kinds of classic questions. For example, I think I know why the velocity of light is set where it is. And how a photon is constructed, although that's the wrong verb. And I have a few insights to offer into the nature of time." But Wheeler's comments, which should have elicited a celebratory mood, were delivered in a somber voice.

"You're not going to tell us," Leslie asked, "that we can build a time machine, I hope?"

"No. Fortunately, time machines are probably prohibited. The nature of the universe won't permit their construction. But I wonder whether you'd care to settle for an exceedingly efficient death ray? We're going to have a whole new technology for creating articulated light—concentrated radiation that could be used for a variety of constructive purposes, but which will also have one hell of a military application as a long range weapon. It would possess significant advantages over bombs, by the way. For one thing, it'd kill people without blowing holes in the real estate, thereby making war profitable again. And the beams travel at light speed, so there'd be no chance of defense or retaliation. It's ideal; the military would love it."

"I think," Hakluyt said evenly, "that we have another data set to destroy."

"There's more," continued Wheeler. "Unfortunately, a good deal more. Harmonic manipulation, for example."

"What can you do with harmonics?" asked Harry.

"At a guess, we could probably disrupt climate, induce earthquakes, bring down skyscrapers. Who knows? I don't think I want to find out. Harry, what's so funny?"

"Nothing, really, I guess. But it occurred to me that Hurley is trying to make the world safe from a weapons system that has just become obsolete."

It was an uncomfortable moment.

"I don't suppose," said Wheeler, "there's any way that a detailed description of physical reality—an advanced description—could help having this sort of effect. I'm putting it all into a report, which you'll have before you go home this evening. I think we've reached a Rubicon, and we're going to have to decide what we want to do."

"How many data sets are involved?" asked Hakluyt.

"Almost every one I've looked at. About a dozen, so far."

Gambini slumped back in his chair. "There's something else you might as well know," the project manager said. "Cy, tell them about the DNA."

Hakluyt smiled wickedly. He looked different without his glasses. But it was more than that. He appeared healthier somehow. Harry had trouble, at first, understanding why his impression of the man had changed. "I've discovered," he began, "some techniques for restoring the repair functions of the body. We should be able to rewire DNA so as to do away with most genetic disorders and those normally associated with aging."

"Wait a minute," said Leslie. "What precisely do you have, Cy?"

"At the moment, not very much. Dr. Gambini found it necessary to lock up the data set from which I was working."

Gambini colored slightly, but said nothing.

"What were you working *on?*" pursued Leslie.

"A way to stop cancer. To prevent physical deterioration. To ensure there are no more crib deaths, and to clear out the hospitals! We can eliminate birth defects and mental retardation. We can change the entire flow of human existence.

"You people talk about weapons and war. Maybe, if we showed a little courage, we could remove some of the causes of war. Give everyone a decent life! With the things we're learning here, we can create prosperity around the globe. There'd be no point anymore in maintaining standing armies."

"You really believe that?" asked Wheeler.

"I think we need to *try.* But we have to get the information out. Make it available."

"What you are going to make available," said Gambini wearily, "is more misery. When there are too many people, you get famine."

"God knows," said Wheeler, "the Church has been saddled with that reality for a long time now, and they don't want to look at it either. But I'm not so sure we'd be correct in withholding something like this."

Good for you, Pete, thought Harry, noting Hakluyt's relieved expression. He'd expected no help from that corner.

"It's obvious," Leslie said, "that we need to make a very

basic decision. We've talked about withholding things from the White House, but until now we haven't had to do it. But I think we have to think about that, and we have to think about what's going to happen down the road. What are we going to do with the material we *can't* release to anyone?"

"If we start holding stuff back," said Harry, "and we get caught at it, everything will unravel. The project will be taken away from us and given to people the government can trust."

"No." Gambini's index finger was pressed against his lips. "They'd have done that already if they could. Their problem is that there's no one they can trust who'd be any real help to them. They've got codebreakers and engineers, but for this stuff they need physicists. That's why they've been so patient with us."

"Cy," asked Wheeler, "I take it you'd vote to turn everything over to NCAS?"

"Yes. It's not a move I'm comfortable with, but it's the best of several bad alternatives."

"What move would you be comfortable with?" asked Leslie.

Hakluyt fiddled with the top button of his shirt. "None," he said. "Maybe there is no reasonable way."

"How about you, Harry?" asked Gambini. "What would you recommend?"

It was a bad moment, and Harry hadn't yet sorted everything out. If they withheld information and got caught at it (and you could not rely on these guys to be discreet), his job would go, his pension, everything he'd worked for all his life. Worse, it might even open them up to charges of treason.

But what alternative was there? If they released this stuff to the White House, advanced weapons and DNA reprogramming and whatever the hell else was in there, what would the world be like in five years?

"I don't know," he said. "I really don't know. I guess we have to sit on some of this stuff. Even Cy's material. I keep thinking about what would happen if people stopped dying."

Gambini's eyebrows rose in surprise, and Harry thought he detected, after that, a new respect in the project manager's bearing toward him.

"Pete?"

"The DNA material should be released. We have no right to withhold it. As for the rest of it, we really have no choice but to keep it to ourselves. *I* certainly won't be party to turning it over to the government. *Any* government."

"Okay," said Gambini. "I'm inclined to agree—"

"I haven't finished yet," said Wheeler. "There's no way we can retain control over this information indefinitely. Leslie's right when she says we need to think about the long term. Eventually, if we continue to collect it, it'll get out. We have in this building the knowledge that would provide almost anyone with the means to obliterate an enemy so quickly and completely that retaliation need not be taken into account. *That*, so that we are all clear, is what we are talking about. And when the disaster comes, it is we who will be responsible. The Text is a Pandora's box. For the time being, the information is contained. Some of it's out, but most of it is unknown, even to us. I suggest we shut the lid. Forever."

"No!" Leslie was on her feet. "Pete, we can't just destroy the discs! Do that and we lose everything. I know there's a terrible risk here, but the potential for gain is enormous. Hercules may eventually prove to be our salvation. God knows we're not making it on our own."

"Okay." Gambini shook his head. "We seem to have some disagreement here. I think Wheeler's right, except for his suggestion that we release Cy's DNA material. I'm sorry about that, Cyrus, but it's how I feel. I don't know how long we can simply bide our time. The longer we hang on, the more difficult the letting go is going to be."

"You're both wrong," said Leslie. "Pete, you're a dealer in ultimate causes and final purposes. What practical reason have we for existence other than to learn things? To know what lies beyond our senses? If we destroy the Hercules recordings, it seems to me we do a terrible disservice not only to ourselves but to the people who conquered a pulsar to let us know they were there."

"We know they're there," said Wheeler, his voice sharp and resonant. "That's enough!"

"It is *not* enough," said Leslie. "It is never enough. Somehow we must find a middle ground. I don't ask anyone to believe we can keep this under control indefinitely. Certainly in the long term we can't. But right now we can. If we keep our mouths shut and watch what we give our assistants to do and consult with one another, we should be all right. For a while, at least."

"Listen to the lady," said Hakluyt. "She makes sense. If you destroy the Text, your act will be irrevocable. There'll be no going back, and I can assure you it is an act you will regret all your lives. And the rest of us with you.

"In any case, whatever we do here, the things that are in those recordings will come anyhow, and at the rate science is moving today they will be upon us very soon. So I submit to you that technical knowledge is *not* what we stand to lose. What we will lose is our contact with another species. Destroy those discs, and we will never know any more than we know right now. And it is more than possible that, during the life of our species, we will never meet another. And you would throw that away because we lack the courage to do what needs to be done?"

Harry's voice, when he spoke, was barely a whisper. "How about a holding action? We could hide the Text somewhere. For a few years. Maybe indefinitely. Until the world is a little more ready for it."

"And where would you hide it?" asked Hakluyt. "Whom do you think you could trust with it? Not me, certainly. Not Ed. Not, I think, anyone in this room. We've dedicated our lives to finding out how the world works. You'd be asking the mice to guard the cheese."

Harry sighed. He'd been in government too long not to recognize that approach. Hakluyt, of course, was wrong. If most of the persons in the conference room were dedicated to research, Harry, at least, was dedicated to survival.

Gambini refilled his coffee cup. "We'll try to keep things to ourselves for the time being. We're all going to need to decide what gets passed on and what doesn't. Anybody comes up with anything else that we have to worry about, I want to know about it right away. Pete, I understand your concerns. We'll try to be careful. But I can't bring myself to destroy all this."

"No," said Wheeler. "Not now or ever."

The meeting broke up in gloom and disarray. "I suggest," Leslie said, "that we need a new perspective. The Arena sent us some tickets for *Signals*. Anybody care to come?"

"Isn't that the show about us?" asked Gambini.

"Yes. Or at least it's about a radio contact. It's a musical."

"That," said Wheeler, "seems appropriate."

The U.S.S. *Feldmann* plowed through the white waters of the Barents Sea approximately three hundred miles west northwest of Murmansk. The ship had been steaming patiently back and forth for a week on a course roughly parallel to the Russian coast.

Feldmann was a converted Spruance Class destroyer. Her helicopters, missile launchers, gun mounts, ASROC, and torpedo tubes had all been removed. In their place, the navy had packed an assortment of electronic surveillance equipment, which allowed the vessel to monitor naval and merchant marine activity at the far northern ports. *Feldmann*'s special interest was Soviet submarine operations.

Lieutenant (j.g.) Rick Fine, one of four operational intelligence officers on board, took his job seriously. He realized that the survival of his country, should hostilities begin with the Soviet Union, would depend on the American ability to take out the Russian submarine force in the opening minutes of the war.

During the final years of the twentieth century, while ICBMs grew increasingly accurate and destructive, and while manned bombers receded into history, the submarine assumed a dominant position in the opposing triads by virtue of its ability to hide in the vast oceans. In an effort to counteract the threat from the enemy's ever growing fleet of subs, the United States began development during the 1970s of a vast network of supersensitive underwater listening posts. Eventually code-named ARGOS, the system went operational in piecemeal fashion; but, by the end of the second Reagan administration, the navy was in a position to track everything that moved in the world's strategic oceans. And this capability, combined with that of ORION, had the potential to render the United States invulnerable to nuclear attack.

While *Feldmann* patrolled the frigid waters off the northern coast of the U.S.S.R., the navy was fitting, or having fitted, a fleet of destroyers and cruisers with particle-beam projectors. Stationed at all times between Soviet missile subs and their targets, the navy's ships would be able to take out the missiles as effectively as the satellites would destroy the ICBMs. The nuclear stalemate, although Fine had no way of knowing it, was almost at an end.

Feldmann was a supplement to ARGOS. Its primary mission was to monitor short-range, high-speed transmissions among the subs and their bases. But she was a flexible ship, prepared to take advantage of any target of opportunity.

All this was accomplished from a reasonably safe distance by purely electronic means. *Feldmann* was listed as a naval weather research vessel, and the crew did some of that, too. The Soviets knew about the ship, of course, just as the Pentagon knew about the Soviet trawlers off the American coasts.

Fine was due to relieve the watch at midnight, and as usual when he was on the graveyard shift, he was unable to sleep. He gave up eventually, knowing that he'd be more tired from staring at the overhead than he would from reading or writing a few letters.

Fine was short and heavyset. His reserve commission had come from OCS in Newport, Rhode Island, where he'd nearly flunked out. Two-thirds of his class had failed, and it had been a near thing with him. A liberal arts graduate, Fine had found the technical material in the engineering and weapons courses very nearly beyond him. In the end, he'd made it by teaching himself trigonometry on Sundays, the only free time the candidates had. And he'd done one other thing. They'd received officer-type uniforms during the sixth week. Fine, then on the edge of oblivion, had purchased the insignia of an officer, the eagle and crossed anchors. He'd put it on a spare hat, and though he was not authorized to wear it, he'd placed the hat above the row of textbooks on his desk each evening as he sat down to work.

He left his cabin, watched a movie in the crew's quarters, and then went out on deck.

The nights off Murmansk, even in May, were brutally cold. A bright yellow moon limned the calm, polished surface. The stars were brilliant through a white trailing mist. Fine had sailed in most of the world's oceans, and it seemed to him that nowhere did the stars seem nearer than inside the Arctic Circle.

He wouldn't stay out long, not in these temperatures. He hunched over the rail, watching the boiling wake. Above him, eight or nine antennas rotated at varying rates, and the steel deck plates trembled slightly with the steady throb of the engines.

A few men in parkas moved quietly past him. Fine had majored in history, and he tended to think of himself now as the modern brother of the Romans who had once patrolled the outposts of Western civilization. "Fine!" One of the men in parkas had doubled back. "Is that you?" It was Brad Westbrook, *Feldmann*'s communications officer.

Fine nodded easily, playing the role of the old veteran. Westbrook was on his first cruise and was not part of the intelligence-gathering unit.

"We've got our sub back again," Westbrook said. "What are you guys doing anyhow?"

In fact, the submarine Westbrook referred to had been shadowing them since their arrival on station. The sub was the *Novgorod*, one of the older Tango diesels. The Soviets routinely followed intelligence research vessels and, in fact, could be expected to stay with them all the way back to Liverpool. But only the intelligence people knew the details of that; the division between the surveillance team and the shiphandling people was absolute. Even the ship's captain had limited knowledge of the exact nature of *Feldmann*'s mission, though, of course, he could guess most of it.

"What's new about that?" asked Fine. "You've seen the sub before."

"I feel like I'm getting to know them personally." He nodded across the other beam. In the bright moonlight, a couple of thousand yards out, the gray shark fin of a conning tower sliced through the calm water. It was turning in toward them while he watched, describing a wide arc.

Feldmann's bow lifted slightly, and Fine felt the surge of power in the bulkheads as the ship's four GE turbines gathered steam. They began a sharp turn to port, away from the sub. Forward, he saw the captain emerge from his quarters and hurry up the ladder to the bridge.

"Cat and mouse," said Fine. "It happens sometimes."

The conning tower slid below the surface, leaving only a ripple.

Fine went below. The spaces occupied by the intelligence group were located immediately behind the Combat Information Center. He punched the code into the serial lock, pushed the door open, and walked into a surprise.

Usually, at the end of a watch, the atmosphere tended to become casual, but the half-dozen enlisted men in the listening post were hard at work over monitors and on-line secure circuits. The lieutenant whom Fine would relieve was conferring with his traffic analyst. "Rick," he asked, looking round, "what's going on up there?"

"Tag with the *Novgorod*. The real question is what's going on down here?"

"The Soviets are putting everything they have into the water. Even the two Victors that've been in dock for the last month. Jesus, Rick, I've never seen anything like this."

They were his last words.

The men on deck never saw the torpedo.

At the Arena, the million-light-year-long radio signal was represented by a coterie of glowing winged dancers who floated across the theater's center stage beneath a ringed world and a distant galaxy. In this version, the Althean signal was picked up on an old Zenith console receiver in a gas station in Tennessee. At first, of course, no one believed the broadcast. The sender spoke English in a sultry female voice, replied to questions, and made witty asides to the audience.

"She has," observed Leslie, "a more lively personality than *our* alien."

Things turned out satisfactorily, as they tend to in musicals.

Harry was now reading regularly from the Althean binder, which Leslie kept supplied with fresh translations. She was getting better, but Harry still found most of it incomprehensible. On the evening they saw *Signals*, he came across a disquisition on the nature of aesthetics. But the only classes of objects considered were natural: sunsets and misted seas and flying beasts of undetermined type. (Yes, always the seas.) There was never a hint that the Altheans found any beauty in their own kind, either in their appearance or in the works of the mind.

He wondered whether the authors of the Text would have attributed any such quality to their own effort.

And if there was a single overriding image from the binder that he could not drive from his mind, it was that of the dark shores slipping silently past.

MONITOR

SOVIETS CLAIM SPY SHIP INSIDE TERRITORIAL WATERS
Refused to Heed Warning? Hurley Blasts "Piracy"

COAST GUARD SEIZES RUSSIAN TRAWLER OFF HATTERAS
Deny Retaliation for *Feldmann* Attack

SIX ALABAMA RESIDENTS ON *FELDMANN*
Freeman Conducts Memorial Service in Chattanooga

ANGRY MOB SURROUNDS TAIMANOV IN NEW YORK
Soviets Charge Police Slow to Respond;
8 Injured Outside U.N.

THEATER ROUNDTABLE
by
Everett Greenly

THE SIGNALS ARE MIXED. *Signals*, which opened last week at the Arena, has a lot of good music, some energetic dance routines, a fine cast, and good direction. Unfortunately, it's not enough to save a script that gets mired almost immediately in sacrificing substance for cheap laughs. We've come to expect more from Adele Roberts, who, last season . . .

CANCER CLAIMS 17-YEAR-OLD ATHLETE
Mesa (Tribune News Service)—Brad Conroy, the young track star who, six months ago, seemed headed for the Olympics, died this morning of a rare and virulent form of leukemia. . . .

800 DEAD IN MISSILE ATTACK ON PASSENGER JET
Arab Terrorists Demand Massive Prisoner Release "Or Ground-to-Air Assaults Will Continue"

WSG&E MAY GO CHAPTER 11

. . . The giant utility, whose stock lost 70 percent of its value during the March slide, is still in deep trouble. A projected new issue offering, which was to have helped meet long-term obligations due this month, had to be canceled. WSG&E is now seeking extensions from several worried creditors. . . .

RANDALL DENOUNCES RUSSIANS IN SENATE
Arms Appropriations Bill Gets New Life

ADMIRAL JACOB MELROSE had gotten himself into a mortgage
he couldn't handle. He'd bought a modest estate in Fairfax
County, using his life's savings and the proceeds from some
shrewd investments in a midwestern paper company to produce
a substantial down payment. But it wasn't working out, and
he was going to have to sell. Tonight, knowing what was
happening in the Atlantic, all he could think was that it probably
didn't really matter.

He was in the White House Situation Room with eighteen
very quiet men and women. The President was the last to enter.
He closed the door behind him, exchanged worried glances
with Max Gold, the secretary of state, and nodded to Melrose.
The admiral pursed his lips, looked down at his boss, Rob
Dailey, chief of naval operations, and took his position at the
lectern.

"Mr. President," he said, "ladies and gentlemen. You're
aware of the sinking of the *Feldmann* on Tuesday night. You
should also be aware that the ship was attacked during a general
deployment of Soviet missile subs. Damned near everything
the U.S.S.R. has is now at sea, headed toward precisely the
stations we would expect if they were planning to initiate hostilities. Refitting and extensive maintenance programs for their
combat aircraft have been curtailed. The number of Blackjacks
they now have in the shop is a little more than a quarter the
total we would expect to find. Missile launching sites have
gone to an advanced state of readiness, and the Soviet army
has been trying to move unobtrusively into forward positions
along the West German frontier." Melrose stepped away from
the lectern and stared down at men and women whose features
were familiar to the vast majority of Americans. Rich, powerful, and, for the most part, talented. They watched him now,
fearful, hoping for the reassurance he was usually able to offer.
But not tonight, he thought. And maybe never again. "I have
to tell you," he continued, "that all indications suggest the

Soviet Union is about to launch a full-scale attack on the United States."

The President had known in general terms what was coming. The others had arrived only with the knowledge that Melrose appeared exclusively in times of perceived crisis. Harbison from Defense whitened so sharply that the admiral thought he was becoming ill. Mrs. Klinefelder from NSC drove a fingernail through her palm. There was also some profanity; but for the most part the President's people waited patiently for the details.

"Maybe it's an exercise," offered Al Snyder, the special assistant for foreign affairs.

"Diplomatic traffic is heavy," said Melrose. "Their merchant ships are being called home. Tactical aircraft are being moved to forward bases—"

"For God's sake!" Clive Melbourn, the President's chief of staff, was hunched into a tight knot. "I thought we could read most of their diplomatic codes. Don't we know what they're saying?"

"Yes," replied the admiral. "We understand most low-level diplomatic and army systems. They give us information about personnel changes, maintenance requirements, that sort of thing. But they don't have much to say about policy."

"Mel." Patrick Maloney had been studiously jotting notes. "What else might they be doing? I mean, what other possibilities are there that might explain their actions?"

Melrose studied the small group of men and women and concluded that most of them were genuinely frightened. That was good. "Mr. Maloney," he said, "if you were on a dark street, and someone with a club was coming your way, I'm not sure there'd be a constructive purpose in looking for more than one explanation."

"When?" asked the President. "When will they attack?" His voice was hoarse.

"They'll be watching us for some indication that we know what's going on. They undoubtedly believe we do. But they don't know for sure. I would guess that if they see any move on our part to upgrade readiness, they would be severely tempted to launch immediately."

The air was still and tight. Gold lit a cigarette. Santanna from the CIA leaned back comfortably and crossed his legs. (Nothing ever flustered the director.)

Hurley got to his feet. He'd had time, a couple of hours, to get ready for this, but he was still having trouble controlling his voice. "If things continue as they are," he asked, "when will they reach their point of maximum advantage?"

"The subs will be on station in about seventy-two hours. After that . . ." He shrugged.

The President turned to Armand Sachs, the Chairman of the Joint Chiefs. "How high can we go without alerting the Soviets?" he asked.

"That's hard to say, Mr. President—"

"It's *easy* to say!" Melrose broke in. "Any step you take will be seen in Moscow. Their communications intelligence and their satellites are too good for us to have any realistic chance of deceiving them."

Sachs glared at the admiral. "I don't think it matters," he said. "In fact, the worst thing we could do is to hide our knowledge of what's going on. If we go to Yellow, they will sure as hell not try anything. They have no chance whatever of surviving unless they can achieve complete surprise. And the bastards know it!"

"Mel," Hurley asked, "why did they attack the *Feldmann?*"

"I haven't got a clue, Mr. President. I know the secretary of state spoke with the Soviet ambassador yesterday. If I may ask, what was his story this time?"

Gold never lifted his eyes from the table. "The Russians claim the *Feldmann* was spying, and that it intruded into their coastal waters."

"That's a goddam lie," said Melrose. "They were a good fifty miles outside the limit. Matter of fact, the equipment's not as effective if we get in too close."

"In any case," said Gold, "that's their story. But I don't think I understand the President's question. They sank the *Feldmann* to conceal their deployment, didn't they? Am I missing something?"

The admiral walked to the lectern at one end of the long room and pushed a button. A wall map of the Soviet Union lit up. "*Calloway* is posted off Vlad, and *Huntington* is down here at Camranh Bay. Neither ship was approached. But there were major sorties from those two sites as well. There's no point in attacking only one ship."

"Moreover," added the President, "they allowed *Feldmann* almost three hours of observation time before attacking her.

They had to know it was too late."

"Yet they blasted the ship," said Maloney. "Maybe frustration?"

"I've had a lot of experience with the Soviets," Gold said in his somewhat bloated manner. "It's not hard to visualize a local commander taking advantage of a chance to ingratiate himself with his superiors."

Melrose weighed the suggestions. "Possibly a knee-jerk reaction," he said. "That could be. But we know the commander at Murmansk pretty well. He would be unlikely to show initiative or to risk getting into trouble. I don't know. Maybe we're playing mind games. Or maybe we *did* get the sub commander mad. But that's hard to buy, too. Soviet officers just don't behave that way. That is, they do not act without specific orders."

"What," asked the President, "has been the effect of the attack?"

Patrick Maloney scratched himself and examined his knuckles. "Nothing." he said. "It's a pure blunder. All it really accomplishes is to warn us."

"Yes," said Hurley. "It serves as an effective punctuation mark. I don't think they were at all interested in trying to hide what they were doing. I wonder whether they weren't trying to be sure they had our attention."

"Why?" asked Melrose.

"I have an appointment this evening with Taimanov," said Hurley. "Maybe we'll get some answers then."

Harry was surprised to find Hakluyt waiting in his office when he returned from a late afternoon seminar on motivation. "I need help," he said, after Harry'd hung up his jacket and dropped wearily into a chair. "I want to break into one of Gambini's filing cabinets."

"The one with the DNA stuff? Cy, I can't do that for you."

"Why not? Harry, Ed Gambini's a fanatic. He's got solutions locked up in there that researchers have been trying to find for sixty, seventy years. Listen, the crazy bastard told me he'd destroy everything if I made any effort to get it away from him. Does that sound rational to you?"

Harry blew his nose, then put a eucalyptus lozenge in his mouth to try to get rid of a tickle in his throat.

"What would you think of me, Carmichael, if I had a cure for your hay fever, and refused to give it to you?"

Harry blew his nose again and smiled weakly.

"And that's only a runny nose, Harry. For God's sake, suppose you had cancer!"

"What do you want me to do?"

"Show some guts." Hakluyt hadn't used that word in twenty years. "You're the administrator of this place. You can get your hands on the key. Do it, and we'll go over tonight, late, and get the stuff out."

Deep in Harry's stomach, something ached. Was he getting an ulcer? Christ, why was it always up to him? These people around him—Gambini, Hakluyt, Wheeler, Leslie, Rimford— always seemed to know what was right. He'd seen no evidence of hesitation in any of them, save perhaps with Baines's reluctance to destroy the Text. "No," he said softly. "I can't do that."

"Harry, please. It's a security cabinet. I can't get into it without your help." Hakluyt extracted a black leather case from his pocket and held it out. "I can *pay,* Harry. I can pay with something you could never buy."

Harry looked suspiciously at Hakluyt, then at the case. Inside it, two vials, a bottle of alcohol, and a hypodermic needle lay on a red felt lining. "What is it?" he asked.

"A young man's eyes. I'm not sure what more."

Harry took a deep breath. "There are people whose eyes are much worse than mine. Give it to them."

"It wouldn't work for them. It's designed for you, Harry. You might as well use it; it's no good to anyone else."

"How could that be?" Harry looked narrowly at the microbiologist. "You're Adam Wallis!" he said. "The phony doctor."

"I needed a recent urinalysis, a blood analysis, a few other things. I apologize for that, but I wasn't sure how you'd react." He produced a cotton swab and saturated it with alcohol. "Roll up your sleeve, Harry," he said.

"You're asking quite a lot in exchange for my being able to read the *Post* without my glasses. Cy, I think Ed Gambini is right! I think we're talking about a time bomb, and I don't want to be any part of turning it loose."

Hakluyt nodded. "Your sleeve, Harry. No obligation. I just want you to have a sense of what's locked in that cabinet. You have a son, don't you?"

"Yes." Harry's defenses went up.

"His name's Thomas."

"Yes." Reluctantly, Harry bared his arm and felt the needle

slide beneath the skin. "You'll need a booster. Since I'm not licensed for this sort of work, I can't arrange for anyone else to do it. I'll come by your office Thursday afternoon."

"Why did you bring up Tommy?" Harry, sensing what was coming, had begun to perspire.

"I understand the boy has diabetes."

"Yes."

"Harry, I can't make any promises. Not at this stage. I know a little, but not enough. If I can get the disc away from Gambini, I *might* be able to do something." The microbiologist rose from his chair like an avenging deity. "Get the cabinet open, Harry. For God's sake, *do it!*"

Taimanov refused the offer of a drink. "Mr. President," he said, "I have been meeting with you and your predecessors for almost thirteen years. I must confess to a personal affinity for you: you are an honest man, insofar as persons in our profession are permitted to be honest. And I would like to believe that there is a bond of friendship between us."

Hurley, concealing his anger, acknowledged the compliment.

"I must also say that, although many of these meetings have taken place under difficult circumstances, this is the first time I have spoken with a man in this office"—he paused and leveled a knife-edged gaze directly at the President—"under the imminent threat of war."

"Why?" asked Hurley. "Why are you doing this?"

"Did I say you were honest?" asked Taimanov. "You are not being honest now. Tell me about your timetable for OR-ION."

"Six months to a year," Hurley lied smoothly.

"Mr. President, our sources indicate that it is quite close to going operational. Another shuttle flight, possibly two. And after that? We would be at your mercy, would we not?"

"It's a defensive weapon."

"So it is. And what would you say to us when you hold the gun to our heads and we are disarmed?"

It was a question they'd anticipated, and the secretary of state had suggested that Hurley fall back on his personal relationship with the foreign minister. "He knows you would not threaten them with the bomb," the secretary had said. But the argument sounded empty now, devoid of either persuasion or good sense. Hurley peered deep into Taimanov's icy eyes.

What *would* he do when ORION was in place? What would his responsibility be to the nation that, for half a century, had wrestled with Soviet ambition and ruthlessness? It would be the Americans' opportunity, perhaps never to come again, to end it! To establish a true Pax Americana and to get on, unhindered, with the business of disarming the world's lunatics.

The President saw himself increasingly as the man who would be remembered for having brought peace to this brutal period, for having set the tone for an entry into the sunlit meadows of the twenty-first century. The Hurley Age.

Prosperity would follow, an era of good feeling, at first enforced by the total military domination of the world by a benevolent United States. But eventually there would develop a global order unlike anything men had seen before. It could be had; it was within reach. And the terrible irony of it was that the Soviet Union, the nation that was prepared to risk everything to stop him, would be a prime beneficiary. "You know me, Alex," he said after a long hesitation. "You know I would never launch an attack."

"You'd have no need," the foreign minister said reasonably. "We would stand before you quite naked, would we not? All of this difficulty might have been avoided had you been able to see your way clear to grant us access to the Hercules Text. Now the complications are endless, and the dangers terrible." He looked up at the Teddy Roosevelt portrait. "You have expressed your admiration for the first President Roosevelt many times. If he were in your place and given the capability to act with impunity, what could we expect?"

"I'm not Teddy Roosevelt," Hurley said.

"Then shall I tell you what *we* would do?" Taimanov was not an old cossack like the two generations of Soviet leaders who had preceded him. His family had been prominent in St. Petersburg during the time of the Romanovs. They'd survived the Revolution more or less intact, maintained their influence and traditions, and continued to send their sons abroad to school. Taimanov had been at Oxford when the Wehrmacht had begun its autumn stroll through the European countryside.

"What would you do?" asked Hurley.

"Contrary to popular opinion in the West, we would not wish to see a world in which there was no United States. But we would like to see an American nation that is less suspicious and perhaps less smug. To use favorite adjectives of your press, Mr. President, your country is paranoid and arrogant—an evil combination. There is, after all, no real conflict of interest between us and you. There has never been a war between the Soviet Union and the United States for that very reason. Our interests do not collide.

"Only in this postwar world, where our fear of each other has taken on a life of its own, is there danger. We would like to remove that danger and retain the United States as a friendly associate. If we had no longer to fear an attack by you, you would see how quickly our attitude would change. But that happy condition, apparently, can be accomplished only by force or by the threat of force. In a word, we would ensure your friendship. As you would doubtless endeavor to ensure ours.

"Mr. President, fortunately there is a solution, but it will require courage."

"And what do you suggest?"

"If your concern is truly for peace and not domination, you will share with us the secrets of the Hercules Text."

"I see."

"I understand that this is not an easy request for you to consider favorably. Before you answer, however, you must understand that my government views its current position as untenable. No one believes that the United States would not use its advantage to destroy the political power of the Soviet Union. I, for one, am sure that you would not go so far as to employ nuclear weapons even if we defied you. Unfortunately, that is not a widely held view. Incidentally, to be candid with you, I'm not even persuaded that ORION will work. But we would not wish to be forced to put it to the test, and so we must assume that it will do what your people think it will do.

"My government will not allow you to utilize your advantage."

The room felt cold.

"As you are aware, Mr. President, the Soviet Union is now in an advanced state of military readiness. I am instructed to inform you, first, that any shuttle flight, from this moment, will be considered an act of war. Should such a flight occur, we will react immediately and with all the forces at our disposal.

"Second, we freely admit we cannot maintain our present condition for an extended period. You must understand, Mr. President, that we believe we are in a state of mortal danger. We will allow you six days from midnight tonight, your time, to find a way to share ORION with us. If you refuse, we will consider ourselves driven to take whatever defensive measures seem appropriate."

"Alex, you're asking the impossible. I can't give ORION away."

"Why not? As you say, it is a defensive weapon. If your interest is truly global safety and not military expansion, then I must ask you why not?" For the first time during all their dealings, Taimanov seemed to have lost his sense of cool diplomacy. He was angry. "This is your chance, John. Don't let it slip away or we will all slide into the abyss!"

Hurley did not consciously note that the Russian had used his first name. "It's not whether I want to or not, Alex. This is a question of capability. I *can't* do it! If I gave ORION to you, they'd impeach me!"

The foreign minister did not smile. "President Reagan said years ago that he would do it."

"Reagan didn't have the device in his hands. Talk is cheap."

"Yes." Taimanov got up. "It is." He offered his hand, but the President only stared silently at him.

Hurley allowed the foreign minister to get to the door, and then he, too, rose. "Alex?" he said.

Taimanov paused.

"It means disaster."

"Yes, Mr. President. I believe it does."

MONITOR

Since its creation in the fog and blood of the 1917 Revolution, the U.S.S.R. has relied on force, and the threat of force, to achieve state objectives. With the consolidation of the Soviet state under Joseph Stalin during the 1930s, and the unexpectedly dominant position it was able to assume after the Great Patriotic War of 1941–45 in a Europe devastated by the struggle, these objectives became unrelentingly expansionist and continue to point to national ambitions that accept no limit.

In the modern world, Soviet military forces are armed, trained, and equipped for conventional and nuclear warfare around the globe. The threat to the security of the West has never been greater, and in the light of recent developments in missile and submarine technology, NATO can expect no lessening in the Soviet drive to achieve hegemony during the coming decades.

The willingness of the Soviet government to employ threat or direct military action, where feasible, is documented by fifty years of efforts to destabilize uncooperative governments, assassinations, unconventional warfare, intimidation, and outright invasion. Throughout the bleak history of the second half of the twentieth century, which, in a sense, may be said to have begun with the Soviet Union's treacherous nonaggression pact with Hitler, and its subsequent invasion of Poland when that nation was trying to defend itself against the Nazis, the record shows instance after instance of oppressive and often murderous national behavior.

After its brutalizations in Poland, the U.S.S.R. attacked Finland and, during the course of World War II, seized most of the nations of eastern Europe. In 1950, it instigated, and supplied, the invasion of South Korea. The East German regime maintained its existence against a popular uprising only with Soviet help. Nikita Khrushchev threatened to use force against Poland in October 1956. Weeks later, Soviet tanks overran Budapest when the Hungarians attempted to gain their freedom. Soviet armor was also needed to hold the Czechs in line in

1968. In 1979, the U.S.S.R. invaded Afghanistan. During the early 1980s, when Polish labor unions showed signs of gaining popular support, the Kremlin's influence, wielded indirectly this time, was again used to maintain the Communist regime.

In recent years, Soviet resources have fueled revolutions in Bolivia, Peru, the Philippines, and several African nations.

—Abstract from *Soviet Military Power*, 1995
Issued by the U.S. Department of Defense

18

"IT'S A BLUFF," said Gold.

Santanna knocked his pipe against an ashtray. "I agree," he said, "up to a point. Roskosky has had his hand forced by the military. There's no doubt in my mind that he will back off if we stand up to him. But we don't know the extent of the army's influence just now, although it's clearly considerable."

"What would give the Soviets the idea they could attack us and survive?" asked Melbourn.

"Twenty-five years of military neglect in this country," said Sachs. "Except during the terms of Reagan and the present Executive, the Pentagon has been a whipping boy for a long line of politicians. It's a tradition in this country."

"Mr. President," asked Klinefelder, "have you tried to speak with him?"

"Roskosky? Yes. They say he's not well."

"We don't think he's in charge any longer," said Arnold Olewine, the national security director. "There's been a reshuffling of deputies in the Supreme Soviet over the last month. Roskosky's people have been getting the less influential jobs, and in some cases they've been left out altogether. Things have changed at the top, but we're not sure exactly how or to what degree."

"What's the worst case scenario?" asked the President.

"There are a couple of extremely discomforting possibilities," said Santanna. The Soviet hierarchy was his specialty. "The army may simply have taken direct control. They've been trying to do that now for almost twenty years, and they have two people ideally placed in the event that Roskosky falters.

"Or Andrey Daimurov may have engineered a coup. Daimurov is First Party secretary, and a man with a messianic complex. He's a psychotic who believes that the only way to save Soviet civilization from being overrun is to take out the United States. He's been described by CIA psychoanalysts as a kind of mystical Communist, in that he believes in historical necessity and has concluded that he's the foreordained agent of history who will carry Soviet society to supremacy. *Ipso facto*, there is no real danger to the Soviet Union from his actions. He believes that a war can be successfully waged against us, so long as *he* wages it."

"Is there any evidence," asked the secretary of defense, "that Daimurov is, in fact, in charge?"

"No direct evidence, though his friends seem to be prospering, and he's been seen publicly with most of the power brokers. I will say this: we feel that, if a void were to occur at the top today, Daimurov would be the most likely successor."

"Kathleen." The President looked down the table at the director of NASA. "The timetable calls for the final two shuttle launches in the ORION series to take place within the next three weeks. Can they be moved up?"

Kathleen Westover considered the problems. She did not yet have lines in her face, but it was possible, in moments of stress, to see where they would form, around her eyes and mouth, and curving across her pale, broad forehead. "It's possible. But we'd have to sacrifice some of our safety procedures. We could give you, um, a few days."

"Armand." The President addressed Sachs. "From the moment the shuttles go up, what's the shortest possible time before we can hope to have ORION operational?"

Sachs shook his head. "We'd have to get together with NASA people to answer that, Mr. President."

"How long do you think? What's the best we can hope for?"

"If everything went perfectly?" Sachs glanced at Kathleen Westover. "And we dispensed with all the tests . . . maybe forty-eight hours."

Westover nodded her agreement.

"It's too long," said Pat Maloney. "Isn't there any other way? Could we manage a launch, say, from Australia? Would it be possible?"

"No," said Westover. "We'd have to build facilities. Even with unlimited time, we couldn't keep it secret."

"Why did the Soviets set the deadline at six days?" asked Gold. "They want a lot from us. Why give us only six days?"

"Their assault forces," said Sachs, "are now operating at a readiness condition one level below red alert. That's a terrible strain on them, and they can't maintain it very long. Matter of fact, if we were inclined to give them the war they seem to be looking for, the way to do it would be to hold them at that status for the entire six days, give in to their demands at the last minute, and hit them immediately after they downgrade."

The conference was unlike any Hurley had attended before in a public career stretching across thirty-five years. Each statement seemed to be made in a vacuum; each was followed by a long silence, broken usually not by a comment but by the movement of a chair or the flare of a cigarette lighter.

"What happens," asked Westover, "if we give in to their demands?"

"We can't do that," said Sachs. "Once they knew we were open to that sort of blackmail, there'd be no end to it. This isn't the first time they've threatened war. Suppose Truman had caved in over Berlin? Or Kennedy during the Cuban blockade?"

"There's another even more compelling reason," said Hurley. "We still don't know the extent of what's in the transmission. If they were only demanding the power source for ORION, it might be an option. But they want the entire package. That's out of the question."

Gold pushed his fingers through his thick white hair. He was a big man with grainy features like a photograph that hadn't quite printed right. "I agree that we have no choice but to assume that they're bluffing and to determine the manner best suited to turning the situation to our advantage." His hands trembled.

General Sachs shook his head, dumbfounded at the stupidity of the men who sat in the President's council. "That course, Mr. Gold, is suicide! The only possible stance we can take is to assume the worst and get ready to blow the bastards out of the water the minute they try it."

So they considered their alternatives, and at a little after 2:00 A.M., they filed out of the conference room. Sachs remained behind, who was bundling briefing papers into his leather case, Hurley invited the general upstairs for a drink. But the President had little to say. He walked to the window, trying to imagine what it would be like, the missiles curving in over the Canadian wilderness, long silvery lances riding the lightning.

"John." Sachs's voice was cool, remote, distant from decision. Only Hurley's name would survive, if anything did, and it would be synonymous with catastrophe. "John, there is very little time."

The ulcerous thing in Hurley's stomach clawed at him.

Ten days before, he'd strolled through the sunlit gardens of his family home on the Virginia coast, while Anna, his grand-daughter, ran laughing among the pines. They'd been good hours, laced with salt air and bourbon and a sense of impending history. He'd felt like Alexander then.

"John," came Sachs's voice, more insistent, "they are *not* bluffing. Unless the intelligence people are wrong, and Ros-kosky is still in charge, we have to assume they are not bluffing."

"And you would have us attack first."

"There is no other rational strategy. If we give them the first strike, we'll retain enough to annihilate them, but we cannot hope to survive."

"I know," said Hurley. "We can take their subs out in the first wave."

"And that means we'll make it, John. We'll take a lot of casualties, but we'll make it!"

"Yes." The President was too weary to argue the point.

Anna had round black eyes and short stubby legs. She was his son's first child and, like all nine-year-olds, a fountain of petulance and laughter. They had taken an afternoon together to fish, he and the girl, to the delight of the TV people.

Where could he hide the child?

There was a thought that came to him often: if the talk fails, and the deterrent fails, and the missiles come, swift as daggers at midnight, what would be the point of retaliation? Hardly a day went by that the question didn't surface at odd moments, that he didn't poke at it, turn it over, and try to thrust it away. He wanted now to tell it to Sachs, but he said nothing. The burden could not be shared.

The white telephone, which was his direct line to SAC headquarters at Offutt Air Force Base in Nebraska, was little more than a silhouette in the half-light. It had no dial, an appropriate reflection of the condition that would exist after he'd used it.

A cold moon floated over the Washington Monument.

The general liked scotch. He finished his drink and remained silent in the background. Hurley knew he wanted to take ad-vantage of this opportunity to talk sense to his Commander-in-Chief. But Sachs assessed the situation correctly. He too did not speak.

Only one man on the planet shared the President's emotions this night, and he was across the Atlantic, probably also staring bleakly from a window. The thought suddenly struck Hurley that Roskosky might not even be alive.

• • •

Someone was knocking at the front door. Harry picked up his watch—it was a quarter after five—and pulled on his robe.

A black government car was idling in his driveway, and a tall man in a three-piece suit waited impatiently. "Secret Service," he said, flashing a plastic card at Harry. "They would like to see you at the White House, sir."

"When?"

"Breakfast, Mr. Carmichael. They expect you at six-thirty."

"What's it about?" he asked.

"I have no idea."

"Okay," said Harry. "I'll be there."

"Good," said the agent. "You can ride with us."

"That won't be necessary," said Harry.

"It will, Mr. Carmichael. Please hurry."

Harry's first thought was that Hakluyt had made good on his threat and gone to the President. But no, he wouldn't have done that. He knew the dangers, and he was scared to death that, after the spadework was done, the politicians would move in.

He rode uneasily downtown. A second vehicle, preceding them around Executive Avenue, carried Hakluyt and Gambini. Leslie and Wheeler were waiting inside the White House.

They seated themselves at a table laden with pastries and coffee. Chilton came in to inform them that the President was on his way, but he was barely out of the room when Hurley entered. He had a surprise: Baines Rimford was with him.

The serving staff passed among them with bacon, eggs, and fried potatoes, and then withdrew. Hurley wasted no time. "Dr. Davies," he said, "gentlemen, we have a problem." He recounted the sinking of the *Feldmann* and the ultimatum by Taimanov in terms sufficiently stark as to leave no doubt of his fears. "None of our choices," he summed up, "is very palatable."

"Don't the Soviets understand what an attack on us will do to the atmosphere?" roared Gambini. "Even if we didn't respond, they can't live! How in hell can they be so dumb?"

"The Soviet military does not officially subscribe to the nuclear winter theory, Ed. Neither, I'm sorry to say, does ours."

Harry watched Pete Wheeler slowly collapsing, the head sagging, the shoulders dwindling, until he seemed little more than a ragged puppet set against the table. Who was responsible, if Pete Wheeler wasn't?

"Give them what they want," said Gambini. "If you really believe they're bent on war if you refuse, you have no choice."

"No," said Rimford. "That's no solution. Deal with them for the particle-beam weapon. Get some concessions, if you can, and then let them have it."

"That's not what they're asking for," said Hurley.

"At least," said Harry, "they've been smart enough not to make their demands publicly."

The President nodded. "It's taken them a long time, but they've finally learned something about how the American political system works."

"Why have you asked us here?" rasped Wheeler.

"Because you gave us ORION. As you can see, we need something else." He looked at each of them in turn. "Is there anything more, in theory or in fact, that could be used to get us out of this situation?"

"ORION," said Leslie, "hardly turned out to be a blessing."

"It would have been," said Hurley, "if Parkman Randall had kept his mouth shut. That dumb son of a bitch caused a lot of this so that he could get his seat back in November. And by God, if we're still here in November, I can tell you where that son of a bitch is going to be." The President inhaled and threw up his hands. "Well, anyhow, I don't want you to think this is your fault, Pete. It isn't. The weapon you gave us can change everything if we can get it operating."

"Mr. President," said Rimford, "I accepted your invitation to come here this morning because I think you need to know that the members of the Hercules team do not want to be thought of as weapons developers. Nevertheless, that is how we can expect to be remembered! I left the project for that reason. And if you want the truth, yes, the Text contains concepts that could be converted into weapons of unimaginable power."

"For God's sake, Rimford, the survival of the country's at stake. What do you have?"

"No, Mr. President," said Rimford. "I have nothing to give you. And I urge my old friends to give you nothing."

"Come on, Baines," Hurley said angrily. "Christ, they're at our throats."

"So they are. And you'll have to solve the problem. Talk to them. Deal. Work things out. You can do it. It's always possible to work something out."

Hurley choked down his anger and turned to Gambini. "Ed, we need to concentrate on the materials Baines was working on."

"I destroyed them," said Rimford.

The President flared at Harry. "And *you* didn't see fit to report it?"

Harry looked up at the President of the United States, whose eyes had filled, not with rage, but with disapproval.

"I take it," Hurley said, "that you are all in agreement with Baines?"

"Yes," said Harry. "I think we are."

"Did it occur to you that you were betraying a trust? And the defenses of your country? I can understand your concerns, and I can even sympathize with your refusal to contribute to the development of weapons. But for God's sake, you had an obligation to say so, to be honest with me."

"We could not!" interjected Gambini. "The nature of what we had did not permit our turning it over to you, or to anyone. You may be assured—"

"Doctor, I'm not assured of anything right now other than that we have a very serious problem and you are not being much help. It is, unfortunately, desperately late, and I'm not sure whether, if we survive this, I won't have you all hanged."

"That's it," said Harry, when they'd reconvened at the lab. "We'll be out of business by tomorrow. Or Friday at the latest. Depends on how long it takes Hurley to get his people together. Either way, the Hercules Project will be moved to Fort Meade."

Gambini sat wrapped in gloom. "He must know he can't get results out of a bunch of codebreakers and party physicists."

"He knows he can't get results out of *us,*" said Leslie. "What do we do now?"

"Make everything public," said Hakluyt. "Turn it all loose. That'll change the equation."

"It sure as hell will," Wheeler said frostily. "What about the new weapons?"

"We've already got doomsday weapons, Pete," said Hakluyt. "Don't you think a hydrogen bomb can be transported by suitcase? There's nothing in the Text that can make things any more dangerous than they already are. The human race has shown a remarkable restraint over the last half-century. The stuff in the text may be what's needed to force us, finally, to confront the issues and do what needs to be done."

"And if it doesn't?" asked the priest.

"Then we're no worse off. Listen, Rimford was excited because he'd found the Grand Unified Theories in there somewhere; but he'd already been working on that. In fact, in one of his books, he predicted that we'd have it ourselves by the end of the century. The same thing is probably true of most of the technical material; it's certainly true of the genetic data. All we're doing is moving the timetable up a few years. Well, what the hell, let's do it! Let's make the most of what we've got!"

"I think," said Wheeler, "that we need to disengage our personal involvement with the project and stop being investigators for a few moments. We tend to assume that knowledge, in and of itself, is good. That the truth will somehow make us free. But the fact may well be that the truth is too terrible to behold. It seems to me there is only one consideration before us this morning, and that is the welfare of the species. What are we really talking about here? I'll tell you what it is: we're trying to balance Cy Hakluyt's curiosity about the structure of the double helix with human survival."

Wheeler looked from one to the other, much as the President had done earlier at the emotional height of the breakfast conference, but the priest's eyes were much more disturbing. And Harry realized why: Hurley had supreme confidence in his ultimate ability, however desperate the situation had become, to stave off the crisis; but Wheeler feared that events had already gotten beyond control.

"I vote with Baines," Harry said. "Destroy the goddam thing. If we can save the DNA disc, do it. Otherwise, destroy everything. And hope that none of it ever comes our way again."

"No." Leslie was near tears. "You can't do that. God help me, I don't have an answer to this, but I know that just chucking everything and hiding under a rock isn't the way to go."

"I agree," said Gambini. "Destroying the transmission would be criminal."

"The survivors, if there are any, may be deciding what's criminal," Wheeler said bitterly. "Whatever you decide to do, you'd better be quick about it. I think Harry's right; we won't have control of the project much longer."

"I'm damned if I can see who they could turn the project over to," continued Gambini. "Everyone *I* can think of has been alienated. Even some of the government investigators have walked off in a huff. Who's Hurley got?"

"He'll find someone," said Harry.

Through the long morning, they covered the ground again and again. Harry, the administrator, knew that Wheeler was right, that the Hercules Text was far too dangerous to release. And while the increasingly angry conversation swirled around him, he thought about the Altheans under their starless skies: a species with no literature, no history (did time, somehow, stand still under Altheis Gamma?), no art; with devices that seemingly lacked a power source. Their dead were somehow not really dead. They transmitted principles that could be used to make terrifying weapons. And they indulged in Platonic philosophy.

The man in the tower, Leslie had said. Not unlike Father Sunderland rattling around in the priory overlooking Chesapeake Bay, playing preternatural bridge.

What had Leslie said of the linguistic system employed in the transmission? Not a natural language. Awkward. *We* could have done better. How could that be?

The meeting broke up, as all the others had, in indecision and rancor. And when they were filing out, while Harry was still thinking of Father Sunderland, Cyrus Hakluyt whispered to him that he might not have another chance to save his son. "Do it, Harry," he said. "For God's sake, do it!"

Later, Pete Wheeler sat down at his table for lunch. The priest wore a haunted expression. "I need help, Harry," he said. They were in a corner of the cafeteria, away from anyone who might hear.

"You want to get rid of it?"

"Yes, but we have to do it tonight."

Harry was shocked at the suddenness with which events had come to a head. He had known all along, of course, that a moment of decision was inevitable. But somehow he had managed not to think about it, had pushed it aside. "I'm still not sure it's the right thing to do."

"There is no 'right' thing anymore, Harry. All we've got is a least of evils."

"How do you suggest we go about it?" Harry's stomach was fluttering.

"The cleanest way," he said, "is to set up a magnetic field. It would scramble the data sufficiently to make further translation impossible."

Harry had stopped eating. "How do we arrange that?"

"A battery-powered electromagnet would do nicely," Wheeler said. "I already have one. In fact, I bought it the day after they gave me the Oppenheimer Certificate. It fits into my briefcase.

"I've come close a couple of times to using it," he went on, "but there was always a chance of getting caught. All I had to do was walk the magnet within a few feet of the discs. But the problem was that the effect would be immediate. And the guy with the briefcase would be awfully visible. But tomorrow, if they descend on us and start moving the project to Fort Meade, the computers will be down—"

"Yes," said Harry, "there'll be a hell of a lot of confusion."

"If we set it up right, we should be able to wipe both sets of discs and not get caught."

"No." Harry sounded like a man in pain. "Pete, we can't just *erase* the text. There must be a better way."

"Find it," said Wheeler. "I'll be interested in your solution."

An hour later, Harry received a phone call from a friend in the General Services Administration. "NSA has ordered three vans sent to your place, Harry," she said. "Did you know about it?"

"No," said Harry. "When?"

"Tomorrow morning, nine o'clock. What's going on?"

"We're moving," said Harry. "I guess."

MONITOR

YEAST-MADE VACCINE SHOWS POSITIVE RESULTS
AGAINST LEUKEMIA
Early Detection Still Vital

WARS MAY BE CAUSED BY GROUP SOCIAL
DISORDERS
Social Phobics Show Taste, and Talent, for Power
Look Out for the Man Who Eats Alone

POLES SEIZE NUCLEAR BOMB IN WARSAW
Solidarity Denies Involvement

MOBS SMASH FOREIGN CARS IN TOLEDO
1 Dead, 14 Injured in Outbreak
Victims Claim Cops Stood Aside

DAMASCUS RIOTING IN FOURTH DAY
Saudis Urge Truce
Alam in Hiding

RUSSIAN PILOTS REPORTED OVER BOLIVIA
Pentagon Denies U.S. Ground Troops Will Be Used

EARTHQUAKE KILLS SIX IN MONTANA
Tremors Continue; More Shocks Expected

SUPPORT GROWS FOR FILM CENSORSHIP
New Studies Lend Support to Anti-Violence Group

LATEST KREMLIN SHAKE-UP KEEPS EXPERTS
GUESSING

ICELAND, BRITAIN ARGUE OVER FISHING RIGHTS
Castleman Says the Navy is Ready

HARBISON DENIES *ORION* RUMORS
Says Anti-Nuclear Shield Not Yet Feasible

SOUTH AFRICA TESTS FIRST BOMB
Ninth Nation Joins Nuclear Club

19

DURING THE AFTERNOON, Harry conducted the second meeting of a three-day management seminar on methods of igniting creativity in subordinates. The attendees were from a wide range of government agencies, and after his experiences with Hakluyt, Wheeler, and the rest they constituted a refreshingly prosaic group. But while they talked earnestly of free-rein techniques and abolishing parameters, it occurred to Harry that the Hercules strategy had, from the beginning, been in the hands of investigators; and therein, perhaps, lay the problem. Their one manager had stood passively aside.

Maybe, he thought, the hour of the bureaucrat had come.

He took his son to the Smithsonian that evening. They wandered among dinosaurs and spaceships in the bright galleries, but there was, as always now, a shadow between them. Tommy's manner, when with his father, became almost mournful. And they seemed most at home in the archaeological sections, walking among water-stained stone blocks from excavated temples whose towers had once gleamed in the sun.

In the Hall of Technology, beside a model of the Champollion facility, Tommy asked, as he did whenever they went out together, whether things had changed, whether he and his mother might be coming home. He always put it that way: it was Harry and the house on Bolingbrook Road that represented his center of gravity.

Harry shook his head. Julie had begun to recede in recent weeks. The life they'd had together seemed remote now, and its individual parts were fossils, so many horned skulls in glass cases.

Only Tommy retained life.

Harry watched him tracking mesons through an electrical field, quick yellow streaks across a green screen, liberated by a process described in detail on a metal plate. The boy had gotten interested in subatomic physics after a conversation with Ed Gambini, during which the physicist had described particles so small that they had no mass whatever. "That's *small!*" Tommy had said, trying to visualize what such a condition meant.

And Harry had stood by, fingering the packet of sugar cubes he always carried as insurance against hypoglycemia.

Harry'd been present when his son was learning to administer the insulin. The doctors had explained to Tommy, and to his parents, that it was important to rotate the injection site to prevent skin damage. They'd made a chart; and the shots had gone into the arms and the legs and the abdomen. The boy had accepted the situation more easily than his parents had—probably because Harry and Julie understood the long-term effects of diabetes.

And the cure lay, perhaps, in Gambini's file cabinet.

Perhaps.

Harry had to put on his glasses to read the plate on meson liberation. He could detect no improvement in his eyesight.

The President would have been active during the day preparing to secure the Hercules machinery. At this time tomorrow evening, Gambini almost certainly would no longer be in charge. They'd probably offer him a consultancy, and maybe Wheeler as well. And the project itself? Harry had no doubt that it would not survive in any recognizable form at Fort Meade.

They stayed until closing time. Later, they walked through the warm evening along Constitution Avenue, talking about pterodactyls and computer games. Behind them, at the Smithsonian, they were turning out the lights.

After taking Tommy home, Harry went back to his office. He phoned Wheeler, but as he expected, no one answered. A second call, to the security station at the library, revealed that two people were logged into the Hercules record room. Neither of them was Wheeler. If the priest hoped to erase both sets of discs, he'd have to begin the way Rimford had begun: arrive at the library somewhat before the midnight closing time and wait for everyone to leave. Then he'd be free to do as he wished. His only constraint was that, once he destroyed the library set, he would have to finish the job before the damage was found. That would give him until 8:00 A.M.

There was no way he could fail, but there was also no way he could conceal his part in it. In the operations center, everything would be disrupted as he walked through with his electromagnet!

It was almost eleven when Harry left his office, fearful that he might have delayed too long making up his mind. He went to the library. The two people the guard had mentioned were astronomers who worked in Wheeler's group. Harry explained to them that the room was going to be used to brief some visiting NASA officials who were between flights. "If it's not inconvenient," he said, "we need to be alone."

After they left, Harry unlocked the credenza in which he'd concealed the discs that Rimford had erased. If Wheeler kept the schedule he expected, he had about twenty minutes.

He was seated at one of the terminals when Wheeler walked in at ten minutes to twelve.

"I didn't expect to find you here," said the priest. He was carrying a thick briefcase.

"They'll ask you to show them what you have in there when you leave," Harry said.

"The guard's already seen it. He wasn't impressed."

"Pete, you're going to get caught."

"I know."

"What about the assurances you gave Ed? You led him to believe you wouldn't do anything like this."

"Gambini isn't in charge anymore." He shook his head. "All bets are off, Harry."

"You were worried about scandal before. Don't you care about that anymore?"

"There might have been no likelihood of scandal if you'd been willing to help," he said accusingly. "Anyway, the stakes are too high now. It would be scandalous *not* to act."

"I'll help," said Harry. "I can find a pretext to shut the library down in the morning—power failure, maybe; we've had them before—so nobody would find out for at least another twenty-four hours."

"That would give us time," said Wheeler, "to get the other set at our leisure, after operations have been terminated for the move."

"Yes." Wheeler bent over Harry's shoulder and looked at the monitor. Binary characters filled the screen. "It's Data Set forty-two," said Harry. "The end of the world. It doesn't mean a thing to me."

"There are seven discs in that series," said Wheeler, "starting with forty-one, the one that upset Baines. And yes, it is indeed the end of the world, in many colors and quite a few different shapes."

Harry removed the silver disc and shut off the computer. "Here," he said.

The priest set the briefcase down on the table beside the master file. "Put it back," he said. "With the rest of them."

Harry nodded and inserted it into its slot.

Wheeler released the snaps on his briefcase and opened it, revealing the electromagnet. To Harry's surprise, it looked like an ordinary electric motor that one might pick up in a hobby shop. It was attached to a pair of lantern batteries.

The discs gleamed, clean and bright and full of promise for the future. Wheeler's thumb rested on a toggle switch.

"Go ahead," said Harry.

"There's something terribly symbolic about this," said Wheeler.

"The priest on the destruct button? Maybe there's another way."

"No. There *is* no other way." He pushed the toggle, and Harry heard the whine of the electromagnet.

At 6:00 A.M., when he could be sure that Gambini was not there, Harry stopped by the lab. An hour later he closed down the library for a surprise inspection of the physical plant. He arranged to send two inspectors over from Logistics to make it look good, and then he answered a summons to Rosenbloom's office, where he was asked to wait until Gambini arrived. Then the Director made it official. "What the hell were you guys thinking of?" he demanded. "All our careers are in the toilet now. Dumb sons of bitches."

"Is that really what you're worried about?" asked Gambini. "Your career?"

"It's my own fault," he said. "I should have kept on top of this thing." He turned angrily to Harry. "I trusted you, Carmichael. I really thought I could depend on you."

Harry shifted uncomfortably under the unrelenting gaze. Rosenbloom looked genuinely hurt. Why the hell was everyone always laying the blame at *his* feet? Harry wondered. He was paid to keep the power on, maintain personnel records, and see that the checks arrived on time. Where in his job description did it say that he had to accept responsibility for decisions of national and global significance? "I did what needed to be done," he said.

"Yeah," said Rosenbloom. "Whatever. When this is over, Harry, I'm going to *break* you. Understand?" He tugged at his belt. "Anyhow, the NSA people will be here in two hours. They'll want both sets of discs, all notes, and anything else associated with the project, special computer configurations, everything you have." His eyes locked with Gambini's. "If it helps, Ed," he said, "there was no way to win with this. That's what I tried to tell you in the beginning. I'm sorry I didn't follow my first impulse, and turn it all over to NSA right away."

"I assume," asked Gambini, "they want *us* to help them pack?"

"Do what you can. I understand they're going to want to keep you on. You and a few others. I've got a list here somewhere." He searched around on his desk, found a piece of paper, and held it out. "Technicians mostly. They don't seem to think much of your team. I'm planning a move into private industry myself."

Harry was relieved that there was no talk yet about federal prisons.

Maloney was with them when they came. He rode in the front car, gazing stolidly ahead, as de Gaulle must have done going into Paris. Two other men with expensive suits and granite expressions rode with him. It was difficult to tell who was in charge. The three GSA vans trailed behind.

They circled the lab and came at it from behind, backing the vehicles in close the rear entrance. The doors of the vans popped open, and half a dozen men in coveralls climbed down onto the asphalt. Each had his name and picture on a plastic badge. The driver of the car talked briefly with Maloney, and then left in the direction of the library.

Harry couldn't resist a smile as he parked his own car and followed the NSA team inside. Their bearing was a mix of military and Ivy League, drill-squad precision and casual talk of quantum mechanics. And, Harry realized, these were the men who, after collecting the Hercules data, would continue the project.

Gambini was deep in conversation with Leslie Davies when the NSA team entered the operations center. He appeared unaware of their presence until Maloney planted himself in front of him. The others were spreading out. A few investigators and technicians stopped work to look up at the interlopers.

"Ed," Maloney said uncomfortably, "I thought you'd have been prepared for us."

"I guess we assumed that Hurley would come to his senses," Gambini said.

"I'm sorry about this. We still want you to head up the operation."

"Under whose control?" asked Harry.

"It'd be no different from what it was here. Project guidelines would be set by the Director, of course. Otherwise, you'll be on your own, Ed. Now, would you ask your people to help with the move?"

Gambini turned away without a word, walked into his office, picked up a sweater, retrieved a gold pen he'd left on his desk, and came back out. "Good-bye, Harry," he said, offering his hand. "You've done a hell of a job." The operations center had grown quiet behind him; Leslie and Wheeler, Hedge and Hakluyt, and the systems analysts and communicators and linguists had stopped what they were doing and were watching him. Some eyes were wet. "You've all done a hell of a job," he said. "I'm proud to have worked with you on this. Some of you have been invited to continue with this project. I know how much it means to you, and I want to tell you that it would be no disgrace to do so. I'll understand. I think we'll all understand."

Then he was gone, and there was an awkward silence, filled finally by Maloney, who cleared his throat and asked for attention. "I wish I could extend to everyone," he said, "an opportunity to continue with the Hercules project. Unfortunately, our requirements are limited. In any case, Mr. Carmichael informs me that Goddard has need of most of you. We've asked specifically for some, and a list has been distributed. We urge those whose names are on the list to stay with the project. Please inform Mr. Carmichael of your decision by the end of the week." He looked at Harry, who was staring angrily back.

They started with the computers. Some had been especially configured to work with the Text; so they removed the discs they found, carefully recording where they'd been found, carried the units out, and placed them in the vans. Systematically, Maloney led a search through desks and filing cabinets that produced a mountain of notes and formal documents. Harry was surprised that, even in the computer age, the project had generated so much paper.

They labeled everything according to location: "Gambini's desk, 2nd left-hand drawer," and so on. "It's the way archaeologists do a dig," said Wheeler. "I don't think Maloney expects us to be much help."

Hakluyt looked as though he had a thundering headache. He approached Harry at his earliest opportunity. "It's our last chance. You've got to get them out now," he said, referring to the data set Gambini had locked away, the discs on which the DNA-altering information was stored. "If these bastards get their hands on it, we'll never see it again."

"Don't worry," said Harry. "I'll take care of it."

Hakluyt wiped the sweat off his face. He was drenched. *"When?"* he asked, trying to keep his voice down. "They'll get to the cabinet anytime! It may already be too late."

"Cy, I said I'll take care of it. Try not to worry." He turned away.

The NSA people were returning discs to the master storage file and the various supplementary files maintained by each department. One of the men who'd ridden with Maloney, a wrinkled individual with splotched skin and flaxen hair, approached Harry. "We're missing one," he said.

"It's in Gambini's office." Harry, feeling Hakluyt's eyes on his back, unlocked the filing cabinet and stood aside. Gambini was not organized and had a tendency to use file drawers the way other people use cardboard boxes. The wrinkled man worked his way gradually to the bottom and came out with two gleaming laserdiscs, both labeled DS101. "One of them," Harry explained, "is from the library set."

He turned guiltily. Hakluyt was contemplating him with pure malevolence. Then the microbiologist was gone, fleeing through the door and down the bleak gray-walled corridors.

Wheeler had gone to his cubicle. He came back with the leather case that contained the electromagnet.

"Is it on?" asked Harry.

"Yes."

Harry gently took it from him. "My turn," he said.

Wheeler smiled, relieved. "You sure?"

"There's no question it'll work?"

"As long as you get within a few feet."

Harry carried the bag out into the corridor and stationed himself near a water cooler directly in the line of traffic. He leaned the briefcase against the wall, took a long, slow drink, and walked away from it.

He retreated past the doorway to the operations center, to a point where he could watch, but be out of the way.

The cartons were moving quickly now. Leslie and Gordie

Hopkins and Linda Barrister and Carol Hedge and all the others who'd worked so hard on the project during the previous eight months stood in angry silence while the brown boxes bobbed along the corridor, past the water fountain, up one flight of stairs, and out into the sunlight.

By one o'clock everything was out of the building. The NSA car, of course, was long since back from the library, and the driver was careful not to leave it. Standard procedure, of course, with top secret material. The trunk would be full of discs. Maloney presented Harry with a signed inventory of what they'd taken. "The National Security Agency," he said curtly, "will reimburse you."

And then, under a brilliant sun, the four-vehicle convoy set off toward the main gate.

"It's going to take them several hours to discover that their discs are worthless," said Wheeler, as they passed out of sight. "Maybe several days. If we're lucky, they'll never figure out how it happened. Maybe we can get someone eventually to suggest a theory involving high-tension lines or something."

"This is what you've wanted all along, isn't it, Pete?"

"Yes, I suppose so."

"You don't look very happy."

"It was a matter of survival, Harry. But we've paid a high price." He squinted in the bright afternoon light. "No, I don't feel very happy. I've violated everything I'm supposed to stand for."

The air was very still. About a dozen of Gambini's people had joined them in the parking lot. They all looked lost.

"I'd better get the briefcase," said Wheeler.

"Destroy it," said Harry. "The briefcase *and* the magnet. Eventually, there'll be questions asked."

Wheeler clasped Harry's hand. "Thanks," he said. "It would have been a lot harder to do alone."

The guard's station outside the library storage room was abandoned. Carrying a briefcase, a black one this time, Harry walked past it, inserted his card into the lock (which had not yet been removed), and opened the door. Hardly glancing at the empty space that the duplicate Hercules Text had occupied, he went directly to the credenza and knelt down before it. It was a battered old piece of furniture, its legs chipped and its veneer scored. Rings from coffee cups intersected across the finish, and one metal pull was missing.

It had come over from GSA six years ago, part of a large shipment retrieved when the Defense Department closed down a major portion of Maguire Air Force Base. No one had wanted the credenza, so Logistics had pushed it into a storage room in the lower level of the library. Where it was the hope of the world.

Harry took a small brass key from his pocket, unlocked the doors, and pulled them open. Silver discs gleamed inside. One by one, he removed them, placed them in individual sleeves he'd brought with him, and put them in the briefcase.

Most of the Hercules team gathered that evening at the Red Limit for a farewell dinner. They were not literally scattering: most of the technicians would be staying on at Goddard in various projects. Among the investigators, Carol Hedge and Pete Wheeler would be asked to assist in ongoing operations, although neither yet knew it. Harry did not expect that Pete would stay.

No one had yet opted for the NSA offer. That surprised Harry until he had a chance to think about it. And he wondered how it happened that a man as astute as Hurley could surround himself with people like Maloney.

Cyrus Hakluyt had checked out without a word to anyone.

And Leslie was going back to Philadelphia. "Then maybe to an island in the South Seas," she said. "I've had enough for a while."

There were no speeches, but several expressed themselves emotionally on how they felt. "It was," said one of the systems analysts, "a little like being in combat together." Harry thanked them for their loyalty and predicted that, when John W. Hurley had long been forgotten, the Hercules team would be legend. "They may not remember our names, but they'll know we've been here."

They applauded that, and, for the few hours they remained under the familiar beams and arches of the Red Limit, they believed it. And for Harry the comment marked yet another milestone: it was the first time he'd been disloyal in public to a man for whom he worked.

Farewell parties always impose a kind of funereal atmosphere he thought, occasioned by the symbolic close of an era. Every handshake, every brief meeting of the eyes, takes on special significance. But the relatively subdued affair staged by the Hercules team was especially intense in its emotions, perhaps because the thing that would not come again was unique in human history, and the forty-some men and women gathered in the modest restaurant off Greenbelt Road represented all who had ever looked at a star and wanted some answers. Well, they had by God found some answers, and maybe no one could really ask for much more.

Harry stayed till the end, until they'd broken up into small groups and begun to drift apart. Angela Dellasandro took a moment, around eleven, to tell Harry that he was inordinately good-looking. (She had, by then, put away several manhattans.) And she also said she was worried about Ed Gambini. Harry reassured her, and she drifted off.

"She's right," Leslie said. "He's safer away from the project, but there'll be a dangerous period until he makes the adjustment."

"No," said Harry. "He found his aliens. I think he's satisfied now. He'll be okay."

They stood facing each other on this last of nights. "When are you leaving?" he asked.

"Tomorrow."

"I'll miss you, Leslie." He found himself suddenly staring at the ice cubes in his empty glass. "I'd be happy if you stayed," he said.

She squeezed his arm. "You're not sure, Harry." She smiled at him self-consciously. "Call me if you get to Philadelphia. We've got a lot to talk about."

"I *am* sure," he said. "I've just been married too long. Everything comes out sounding wrong because I still feel as if I shouldn't be saying it."

She buried her face in his shoulder, and he could feel her laughter. But when she looked up, he did not see amusement. "I love you, Harry," she said.

Just before midnight, they came for Gambini. They walked up the stairs to the second floor, their footsteps muffled by the sullen roar of the Atlantic, and they knocked at his door. When he opened up, his eyes full of sleep, they showed him IDs, pushed into his living room, and stood aside to make room for an enraged Pat Maloney.

"What's wrong?" Gambini asked.

CYRUS HAKLUYT REPLIES TO A CRITIC

Dr. Idlemann's assertion that death is an integral part of nature's plan for the ongoing renewal of the species assumes that there is, in fact, a design of some sort. One is hard-pressed to find anything that could be described as conscious intent in the harsh system into which we are born and which, in the end, kills us and our children. The only intelligence evident is our own. And one can only wonder at the sort of reasoning that regards blind evolution as benevolent and somehow wiser than we.

The truth is, we owe nothing to the future. We are alive now, and we are all there is. To paraphrase Henry Thoreau, we stand on the dividing line between two vast infinities, the dead and the unborn. Let us save ourselves, if we can. When we have done that, when we have ceased to hand to our children a legacy of cancer and aging and loss, *then* we can begin sensibly planning for the sort of existence that an intelligent species should have.

—Cyrus Hakluyt

Extract from *Harper's* letter column, CXXXII, number 6, author's response to a communication from Max Idlemann, M.D., an obstetrician in Fargo, North Dakota, who objected on numerous grounds to an article by Cyrus Hakluyt in the May issue. Dr. Idlemann seemed particularly incensed that Hakluyt had failed to recognize the long-range damage that would occur from any major breakthrough in prolonging the human life span.

20

HARRY TOOK LESLIE home, to the house on Bolingbrook Road and, by the light of the street lamp, in Julie's bedroom, undressed her. One by one, he dropped her clothes in the middle of the carpet. When he'd finished, she turned slightly, on some whim, perhaps, or from reserve, and her navel and the single nipple that had been visible passed into shadow. But her eyes stayed with him, and her hair was a pale radiance in the light that came through the curtains. "You're lovely," he said.

She opened her arms to him, and he felt the soft press of her small breasts through his shirt. Her lips were wet and warm, and he tangled one hand in her hair. They rocked gently, while the box elders rubbed the side of the house and Harry's manual alarm clock ticked loudly on the bureau. The flesh at the nape of her neck, just below the hairline, was firm and almost muscular.

He lifted her; she burrowed into him, and he could feel her heartbeat. On the queen-size bed, she fumbled with his shirt, laughed when one button stuck, and jerked it loose. "I'll fix it for you," she whispered, sliding the garment down off his shoulders. She flipped it casually into the dark and pressed one palm against his belly, just down inside his belt buckle.

Harry bent over her, fitted his mouth to hers, and, in good time, took her.

They talked, and slept, and made love, and talked again.

They talked about themselves mostly, and how they enjoyed each other. And they talked about the Altheans, from whom they expected to learn nothing more. "I wonder why," she said, while they lay lazily entangled with each other, "they never told us about their past. There was no history that I could find. And no psychology, by the way. In fact, nothing of the social sciences. It's over now, and the illusion of the lone alien in the tower is stronger than ever. I really don't understand it."

"What will *we* be like in a million years?" asked Harry. And, without waiting for an answer, he went on: "There's a priest in Pete's order who plays bridge like nothing I've ever seen. You get the feeling when you play with him that the cards are all face up on the table. I mean he did things that were just not possible unless he could see all the hands. And I wonder whether, in some sense, he could?"

"I don't know," said Leslie. She traced the line of his shoulder with a fingertip. "What has he to do with the Altheans?"

"If telepathy can happen, or whatever it is that Rene Sunderland seems to be able to do, what's the end product after, say, a million years of evolution?"

She closed her eyes and lay back. Her head sank into the pillow. "If ESP is possible, and if we developed it, I would think that in time we'd lose our individual identities."

"And our languages! What use would a race of telepaths have for language?" They looked at each other; both had the same thought: *We could have done better.*

"It fits," she said. "For that kind of community, I suspect history, at least as we use the term, would cease to exist. There'd be no more politics, probably no conflict, at least among members of the species. And I have another thought for you: in a community being, there'd be no real death. The individual cells, units, members would die, but not the central intelligence."

"In fact," said Harry, "it might be that only the bodies would die; once you've become part of the central mind, you may have achieved a kind of immortality."

She stirred against him, and Harry stroked her cheek lightly and her hair. For the time, the Altheans fled into the night. But later, half waking and half asleep, he thought of them again. Or he may have dreamed of them. When the telephone rang, just before dawn, he woke knowing *why* the Altheans had sent their signal. And he was both sad and frightened.

He lay unmoving, his legs entwined with Leslie's, listening to the insistent jangle, recalling that this was how it had begun on the night Charlie Hoffer had called to tell him that Beta Altheis was doing something strange. But then it had been a different woman and a different fear. Oddly, in a way he could not understand, this was more personal.

"Aren't you going to answer it?" Leslie asked, her voice startling in the dark.

He picked it up. "Hello?"

"Harry!" It was Wheeler. "I just got a call from one of our

priests over at Saint Luke's. They brought Ed in tonight. He had a heart attack!"

Harry sat bolt upright. "My God," he said. "How bad is it?"

"I don't know yet. He's still alive. I'm going over; I'll call you when I find out."

"What's wrong?" whispered Leslie.

Harry covered the phone. "Ed had a heart attack tonight. He's at Saint Luke's."

Wheeler's voice had taken on a harsh timbre. "Harry, Gambini probably knows the Hercules Text has been lost. Some of Maloney's men brought him in."

"How could that have happened?" asked Harry. Leslie was out of bed now, getting into her clothes.

"I think they were a little smarter at NSA than we expected and checked the discs right away. It's the only thing I can figure. They must have assumed Gambini had a hand in scrambling the Text, so they went after him right away."

And *we* did it, thought Harry. "Thanks for letting me know, Pete," he said.

"What's the rest of it?" asked Leslie as she slid her watch over her wrist and picked up a shoe.

"The Text is gone," said Harry. "Scrambled. Both sets."

She stopped to stare at him. "Both sets?" Her voice trembled.

He nodded. "It must have happened somewhere between Goddard and Fort Meade."

"Oh, Harry," she said, "those damn fools." She threw the shoe at the floor. "Are they sure? How in hell could they lose both sets?"

"I don't know."

"I assume Hurley will conduct an investigation."

"I'm sure he will," said Harry.

"Damn," she said. She stood frozen in the cold gray light. "I'm going over to see how Ed's doing. Want to come?"

"Not now," said Harry, struggling with his conscience and with prudence. "Leslie," he said hesitantly.

She was at the window, looking down into the street. "Yes?"

"I have a copy."

She turned slowly, not sure what he meant. "Of what?"

"The Text."

Leslie didn't come away from the window, but he could see

the energy flow back into her frame. "How could that be?" she asked suspiciously.

"Long story," he said, wondering what tale he could concoct. "I'll explain later."

"Where is it?"

"In the trunk of my car."

"In the trunk of your *car?* Harry, what kind of place is *that* to hide anything?"

"I was going to do better tonight, but you kind of got in the way."

"Well, you'd better get to it, because someone's sitting out there in a van."

Harry saw no one. A gray van, stenciled "Jiffy Delivery Service," was parked halfway down the street. But the driver's compartment was empty. "They're in back," she said.

"How do you know?"

"I saw the flare of a match."

Harry tried to think. Could they know? Could they possibly *know?* Pete's phone call: they might have tapped the lines. What had Wheeler said exactly? Harry had been careful, because Leslie was in the room, but had Pete said anything that might have given them away? "You go see how Ed's doing. I'll hide the discs."

"Where?"

"I haven't decided yet," he lied. Her eyes pierced him for that, and he wondered whether, in that moment, he'd lost her. "Wait until I'm gone," he said. "Then call a cab."

Harry went down into the attached garage and opened the trunk of his Chrysler to assure himself that the Text was still there. He had placed the discs in individual plastic sleeves and packed the sleeves in a lunch cooler. He took time now to seal the cooler with masking tape. Satisfied, he added a spade and a crowbar, closed the lid, and went back into the house to see if anything had changed out front.

The van was still there, but he could see no other cars. While he watched, Hal Esterhazy emerged from his house across the street, walked to the end of his driveway, and picked up his *Post*. Leslie was behind Harry when he turned around. "You pulled a switch on them, didn't you, Harry?"

"Yes," he said.

"My God, they'll put you away for the rest of your life if they catch you. Harry, how could you *do* that?" But she did not look entirely displeased. They went into the garage, she embraced him again in an impulsive act that somehow contained within it all the passion of the night. Then Harry keyed the garage door opener, started the car, and backed quickly out, leaving Leslie behind.

The van did not move.

Harry drove somewhat more quickly than usual along Bolingbrook Road and turned north on the pike. It was still early morning, and traffic was light.

He wandered through the Maryland landscape, seeking out narrow country roads. A gray sky began to build and, when he stopped at a gas station outside Glenview to call in sick, rain was falling. It slanted into the trees and the tomato fields and turned the clay driveway of the gas station outside the phone booth into a quagmire. He dialed Rosenbloom's office.

"He's not in yet, Mr. Carmichael," said the Director's secretary.

Harry never took his eyes from the road up which he'd come. Engulfed now in swirling rain, it was satisfactorily empty. "Tell him I'm having problems with allergies," he said. "I'll be in tomorrow." The truth was that this was the time of year when his allergies were usually at their worst. And he felt fine!

Maybe it was the rainstorm.

He hurried through the downpour to his car and bounced back out onto the two-lane road.

He was no longer sure where he was. The road was long and straight, running alongside railroad tracks. There was no traffic to speak of. Now and then he passed a pickup, and once a long black Continental closed in behind him. But he slowed, and it pulled out and roared by, sluicing water across his windshield.

He wondered about the van. Maloney's men—or the FBI, for all he knew—could not be aware of his part in the incident, because they'd gone directly to Gambini to ask questions. Depending on the circumstances, Gambini's coronary might have looked like the result of a guilty conscience. In no case, however, could they know precisely what had happened. Ed was probably in no position to tell them anything. As long as he and Wheeler kept their heads, they were in no danger. Eventually, with luck, NSA would come to accept the notion that a freak accident of some sort had occurred. Were they now checking the route between Goddard and Fort Meade, seeking an explanation? And watching the principal suspects for some indication of guilt? Like jumping into a car and driving all over the Maryland countryside? Well, there was no help for it. He had to get the discs to a safe place.

Anyway, he thought, Leslie was probably wrong about the van.

The rain stopped and started again. Harry filled his tank at a two-pump Amoco with a cafe attached. He got a *Post* out of the machine, went inside, sat down at the counter, and ordered coffee and doughnuts. The headline did nothing for his state of mind:

SOVIETS RECALL AMBASSADOR
Kremlin Rejects Demand for *Feldmann* Restitution

Through a streaked, dingy window, Harry watched the afternoon darken. Distant thunder rumbled. The rain quickened: it drummed ominously on the roof and ran down the cracked panes. The highway withdrew into the cloudburst, and even the gas pumps grew indistinct. Harry's sense of security increased accordingly.

He finished his snack, waited a few minutes for the storm to lessen, gave up, and made a mad dash for the car. As he was pulling out of the station, a gray Chevrolet stopped beside the pumps. There were two men in it, and Harry had a bad feeling about them. One got out and (he thought) took great pains not to look at the departing Chrysler.

He kept his speed down, trying to look casual, and watched through his rearview mirror until he couldn't see the gas station anymore. Once out of sight, he pushed the pedal down as far as he dared. He held the wheel tightly now. The drenched landscape rolled past, and his tires plowed through the water. At the first intersection, he turned left and then, a few miles down the road, right again. Still the highway stretched empty behind him.

More than once, he wondered whether the most prudent course might not be simply to lose the discs, weight them, perhaps, and lob them into one of the muddy streams wandering across the landscape, and be done with them.

He turned southeast, toward the Chesapeake.

The rain slackened finally. And the farms became a less prominent feature, replaced by villas and expansive brick ranches and small towns with clock towers and McDonald's and main street shopping districts. In Norton, he went left at a minor intersection, swung into a theater parking lot, and waited to see if anyone was behind him. In Eddington, he left the car on a side street, rented a Dodge, and transferred to its trunk the cooler full of discs, the spade, and the crowbar.

Near Carrie's Point, he thought he saw the gray Chevrolet from the gas station again. But it was turning away from him, into a bank drive-in, so he couldn't be sure. He kept going. At Newmarket, he connected with Route 2 and followed it south, through tumbled rocks and rolling hills.

The Norbertine priory couldn't be seen from the highway under the best of conditions. In the fog and rain, even the top of the ridge was invisible.

Harry made his left turn, passed the old stone house, and started up the hill. In late spring and summer, the vegetation tended to close over the winding road, creating a tunnel effect. Large flat-bladed fronds sucked at the car, and water continued to pour through the branches. The rock wall and the gates were overgrown with hedge and shrub, almost invisible to a motorist entering the Norbertine grounds. The trees opened up, but it didn't matter much: fog lay heavy on the grass, and the big manor houses were insubstantial shadows.

He looped carefully past them toward the west. The elms that screened the lodge huddled against the blast of the storm. Harry eased past the building about twenty yards and turned off onto the grass. It was as far as he could go: the road ended, and beyond this point the ground dipped sharply.

He got the spade and crowbar out of the trunk, leaving the discs until he was ready for them, and stumbled and slid downhill through the rain. He entered the forest, following a footpath that went in the right general direction, and kept walking until he found the pump house. Inside, everything was as it had been when he and Julie were here. The spade he'd seen before was still on its nail, but he'd prudently brought his own. Even the burlap pile that he'd laid over the half-built wooden floor on that memorable night was undisturbed. The place was dry, and the earth beneath the boards showed no sign of the deluge that had been falling all morning.

He selected a likely place, in a corner away from the door and away from the single window. He pried up some of the floorboards, using care not to damage them and, shivering in his damp clothes, began to dig.

The storm subsided somewhat, but a brisk wind rose off the Chesapeake. It hammered against the dilapidated building and it scattered the fog so that the manor houses suddenly appeared sharp and clear through the trees.

Eventually, Harry reasoned, when it was over and forgotten, he'd come back here and retrieve the Text. By then, he'd know how to store it permanently, put it away somewhere until the world had changed sufficiently to use the Hercules data safely. Or, perhaps, until a group had sprung up that could be trusted with the power in the discs. Harry had considered the possibility of founding such an organization himself, handing down perhaps from generation to generation the secrets from the stars. Sort of like the Rosicrucians, he thought with a grim smile. The Carmichael Society.

He kept digging.

And he realized that he still wasn't sneezing.

Despite the long ride through farm country, he felt no allergic reactions. Now that he thought of it, he'd had no problems the day before either. In any other year, this kind of experience would have put him in bed for a week. Well, by God, maybe things were going to turn around for him at last.

He was about two feet down by then and so preoccupied that he failed to hear the approach of a car. He looked up when the engine died, but he hadn't really heard it, at least not consciously, so he just shrugged and kept on with his work.

The only sounds were the crunch of the spade, and his breathing, and the storm.

He didn't allow himself a break; he wasn't going to feel safe until the discs were in the ground, the boards were back in place, and he was on the road home. But his shoulders and back were beginning to ache, and he was contemplating taking a few minutes off—he was almost deep enough now, and he would have liked to finish it and get out of there—when he heard a hinge creak.

The pump house door swung open, and Harry looked into the bored eyes of the two men he'd seen in the Chevrolet.

They were quiet, efficient men, clean-shaven, in hunters' clothes. The taller of the two might have been a lawyer: he was long and lean, with unkempt sandy hair and an easy smile. His companion, who was older, stepped forward and asked casually whether his name was Carmichael.

Harry measured his chances against them. But a lifetime of respect for law officers rendered him indecisive. "Yes," he said. "What do you want?"

The man who'd spoken produced an ID. "FBI," he said. "Read him his rights, Al."

"What the hell's going on?" demanded Harry in as indignant a tone as he could muster.

"We want to ask you some questions." He read Harry the Miranda warning off a plastic card. "Do you understand your rights?" he asked.

"Yes," said Harry.

"Okay. Mr. Carmichael, what were you going to put in the hole?"

The van remained.

Leslie watched it through the curtains while Harry drove away. Then she considered how she should leave. The house had a rear door, and the back yards in the vicinity were not fenced. She could keep the house between herself and the van, cut through adjoining property, and probably come out on the next street unseen. But the grass was wet, it was early morning, and she was in the middle of a housing development with no transportation.

On the other hand, why should she allow herself to get caught up in this and behave like a fugitive? She had, after all, done nothing wrong. But the van waited, and she was reasonably certain that whoever had struck the match was still inside.

Leslie picked up the phone and called a cab. It came about twenty minutes later, pulling into the driveway. She locked the front door and strolled to the waiting vehicle in full view, probably, of surveillance cameras. Well, she thought, there goes my reputation. The driver's eyes lingered on her as he opened the door. "Goddard" she said.

She wondered whether they would go inside to search the house now that she was gone. Had they known all along she was there? But why were they interested in Harry? Somehow they must be aware he had the Text.

She was impressed. She had no doubt that Harry had ruined his life and placed her own career in jeopardy. But she was glad he'd done it.

Harry would wind up in jail. Probably for a long time. She sat contemplating that melancholy prospect all the way to the Space Center, and her eyes were red when she emerged from the taxi outside her quarters at Venture Park.

She retrieved her car and, forty minutes later, pulled into the parking lot at St. Luke's.

An officious middle-aged woman with pinched features was alone at the reception desk. She squinted through thick bifocals at Leslie. "Can I help you?"

"I'm Dr. Davies," she said. "An associate of mine, Dr. Edward Gambini, was brought in during the night. Cardiac problem. I'd like to see him or talk to someone familiar with his condition."

"Is he a patient of yours, Doctor?" the receptionist asked, her eyes raised conspicuously to the clock. It was twenty-five after seven.

"Yes," she said, tossing her professional ethics overboard more casually than she would have thought possible.

The woman consulted her computer. "He's in room four-sixteen. But Dr. Hartland is in charge, and he won't be in until about ten. The patient can have visitors," she said reassuringly, "but hours start at nine. Would you like to speak with someone at the nurses' station?"

"Please."

Dr. Gambini, the nurse reported, was awake. "But the chaplain is with him just now. Are you his personal physician?"

"Yes. How serious is he?" The mention of the chaplain was alarming.

"Father just came by," the nurse said, hesitantly. "I'm sure Dr. Hartland would have no objection if you wanted to see Dr. Gambini."

"Thanks," she said. "I'll come up."

The blinds were drawn, and Gambini lay white and pale on the bed. His eyes were shut. A television screen glimmered fitfully in the corner over his head. It was set so the patient opposite could watch, but he seemed to be asleep with the headset over his ears. The "chaplain" turned out to be Pete Wheeler, in clerical black. "Nurses always make that assumption," he remarked innocently.

"I'm an M.D. today, myself," she admitted, leaning over the still figure on the bed. "Ed?"

His eyes opened, and she was glad to see they were lucid. "Hello," he said.

"How are you doing?"

"Not so good." His voice was a hollow rasp. "The dumb sons of bitches lost everything, Leslie. Can you believe that?"

He looked back at Wheeler. "Tell her, Pete."

"It's true," the priest said. "Both sets of discs have been scrambled."

"Everything's gone," moaned Gambini. "It wouldn't have happened except that the goddam security restrictions prevented us from making more copies." His voice gave way, and he coughed heavily for a minute or two.

"Don't talk," said Leslie.

But he shook his head from side to side, and tears filled his eyes. "They think it was a heart attack," he said. "Do you know when it happened? Right in front of Maloney. Christ, I was so embarrassed I could have died!" His deep sunk eyes lingered on Leslie, and he realized what he'd said and snickered.

She smiled and brushed his hair back from his forehead. "Apparently you're going to be okay," she said.

"He's in good shape," said Wheeler. "They want to run some tests, but his doctor says he has nothing to worry about."

"Pete," he said, "they need some help over at NSA. Round up a few of our people. You know who. Talk to Harry; he can arrange it. Maybe they can save something. Get yourself over there, too. I think they'll be a little more accommodating now.

"I just can't believe it," he continued, wiping his eyes. He lost interest in his visitors and clamped his teeth tight together. His fingers were clenched.

"What kind of sedative do they have him on?" Leslie asked Wheeler.

He had no idea.

"Whatever it is," she said, "it isn't enough to calm him down. I think, for a start, you and I ought to get out of here and let him rest. But first, I believe I can do something for him." She took his left arm and stroked it gently until he looked up at her. "Ed," she said, "Harry has the Text. It *isn't* lost."

Gambini's expression was slow to change; but the priest looked as if he'd been struck a heavy blow. "Harry has a copy?" Pete asked incredulously.

Leslie realized immediately she'd made a mistake. But there was nothing for it but to tell the truth. "He's out now hiding it. For the duration."

"Good old Harry," said Gambini. "The son of a bitch is all right." A broad grin was spreading across his face.

"Who else knows?" asked Wheeler.

"Apparently Maloney. Someone had Harry's house staked out this morning."

"And Harry's trying to hide it. Do you know where?"

Gambini tried to sit up, but Leslie restrained him. "No," she said. And if I did, I don't think I'd tell you. "I have no idea."

Wheeler sat thoughtfully for a few moments. "I think *I* do." He got up and started for the door.

"I'll go along, Pete," said Leslie.

"That's really not necessary. Why don't you stay here with Ed?"

"I'm too worried to sit this out. I'd like to go."

"All right, then," Wheeler said, seeing no easy way out of it. "But I want to stop by my apartment first."

Usually, when he was in Washington, Wheeler stayed at Georgetown University. But the Space Center had also provided a house, and the priest had, during recent months, been dividing time between the two temporary residences.

He'd left the briefcase containing the electromagnet in the visiting faculty dayroom at Georgetown where he felt it would be reasonably safe until he had time to dispose of it. He recovered it now and carried it out to the car in which Leslie waited. "Let's go," he said.

"Okay." She pulled out onto Wisconsin Avenue. "Which way?"

"Chesapeake Bay. Cut over to the Beltway."

Wheeler was a thoughtful, morose, taciturn man in the best of times. But on the long ride out to Saint Norbert's Priory, he seemed locked in depression. Leslie knew him, as they all did, well enough to understand that he would have preferred that the Text stay dead. But his disappointment appeared to be deeper than that, and it seemed to include an element of bitterness.

"Where are we headed?" she asked.

"There's a place along the bay," he said as they passed through Billingsgate. "Harry told me once that it would be a good place to hide from the world. He had something else in mind then, but he might be thinking of that place now, too. We'll see."

At Carsonville, they were held up by a collision between a tractor-trailer and a motorcycle. The truck had been carrying newsprint; rolls of paper were scattered for a mile. After an hour or so, the police got things somewhat cleaned up, and they proceeded in a single lane. Rain continued to fall heavily. Wheeler rode with his arms folded, staring gloomily at the slick highway.

By late morning they were approaching Basil Point under skies that had begun to clear. She made the turn from Route 2 a little too sharply, dropped the right wheels off the shoulder into mud and wet leaves, spun slightly, and regained the road.

"Take it easy," the priest said. "No point getting us killed."

They climbed the ridge, and rounded the long loop past the manor houses. Ahead, under a screen of trees, she saw a lodge. Just beyond it, overlooking a steep descent, two cars were parked side by side.

"Stop here," said Wheeler.

They were in the middle of a field. "Why?"

"Here!" he repeated, with sudden exasperation. And then, after she had complied: "Harry's car isn't here, and those two don't belong to the Norbertines."

"Maybe he rented one."

They got out and hurried across the wet grass. "We're too late," Wheeler groaned.

One vehicle had a CB radio; a large red tubular signal light was pushed under the front seat. "It's a portable blinker," said Leslie. She circled the second car, saw nothing to draw her attention, looked down the side of the hill at the trees near its base, and turned toward the lodge.

"No," Wheeler said, "not that way." He remained standing in front of the cars, staring out over the treetops. The downside of the hill was steep, carpeted by long grass. At bottom, about fifty yards down, the trees started again.

The wind carried voices to them. In the stillness, they seemed to come from all directions.

"They caught him with the discs," the priest said in a curt whisper. "Les, we've got to rescue them."

"Them? We've got to rescue them? I came to help Harry, Pete. As far as I'm concerned, they can have the discs."

"Of course," said Wheeler. "That's what I meant."

An odd look passed between them. He began to breathe more easily. "Get down the hill," he said. "Please. I'm going to create a diversion. Do what you can—"

She was gone before he could finish.

The grass was slippery underfoot, but she negotiated it quickly, and slid and plunged into the trees at bottom. Although the voices had stopped, she could hear people walking. Above her, Wheeler was gone, and she could see only the lodge and the bumpers and grills of the two cars.

Sunlight began to filter through the branches, and something buzzed around her head.

"This way!" a voice cried. "It's dry over here!"

And she saw them, two men in overshoes walking single file with an obviously unhappy Harry between them. The taller of the two, who brought up the rear, watched the prisoner (she thought) almost sympathetically. The man leading the way stomped through the bushes and high grass with evident irritation. Everything about them suggested they were police officers: they systematically surveyed the surrounding trees, and they walked with the resigned manner one sees in lawmen who've just landed a miscreant.

Fortunately, the miscreant wasn't handcuffed.

She moved closer and crouched behind an oak. They passed her, Harry so close that she could have poked him with a short branch. He looked briefly in her direction, but she dared not show herself.

Leslie was behind them when they came out of the woods and started up the hill.

She waited anxiously, wondering what Wheeler could possibly do to distract the agents long enough for her to snatch Harry away. Her whole world was about to end. She, the priest, Harry—all of them would show up on the late news, being escorted by marshals into a federal courtroom somewhere. She'd be shielding her face with a newspaper, and they'd give her eight years.

If she got the opportunity, she promised herself she would slug both Harry *and* Wheeler. But how could she be angry with Harry, who even now appeared to be looking for a chance to escape? The agent in front, watching him, said something. But Harry, towering over both men, maintained an expression of open defiance that seemed utterly out of character.

The taller agent stopped and looked directly at her. Leslie had moved from the oak, and now hid behind a leafy screen that seemed suddenly transparent. He continued to stare until Harry's attention was also drawn in her direction. And finally the agent turned away. She stood up immediately in full view!

To his everlasting credit, Harry did not react.

They'd gone about four more steps when the agents' car, the Chevrolet, edged forward, and began, slowly at first, to roll down the hill. The lawmen reacted quickly: one stayed with Harry while the other, the sandy-haired man, scrambled to get alongside the vehicle, which was gathering speed.

Leslie bolted up the incline. Harry watched her coming, and the agent with him saw something in his prisoner's eyes. He half-turned toward her, reflexively going down on one knee, but Harry planted a foot against his buttocks and sent him sprawling into space, past the charging woman. "Top of the hill," Leslie shouted, never slowing her pace.

Unaware of what had happened, the sandy-haired man ran alongside the Chevrolet, wrenched the door open, but couldn't get in. He grabbed for the steering wheel just as the car bounced off a rock and veered suddenly away from him. He was yanked from his feet and dragged.

Wheeler waited by Harry's rented car. "Where are the discs?" he asked.

Harry looked uncomfortably at the priest. "In the trunk," he said.

The two men at the bottom of the hill had recovered themselves and were starting toward them. Their car was wedged between two trees. One was shouting something. "Let's go," said Wheeler, climbing into the back seat of the rented vehicle. "Leslie, you should get your car out of here. They'll trace it."

Harry had started the engine. She hesitated, then jumped in beside him. "Hell with it," she said. "They know who we are."

As they backed out, showering gravel in several directions, Harry got a glimpse of Wheeler's briefcase, which he'd laid on the back seat. His heart sank.

Max Gold lit a cigarette. "What are you going to do?" he asked.

The President pushed his chair away from the desk and crossed his legs. His jacket lay on the settee where he'd dropped it casually a few moments before. His sleeves were rolled halfway up his forearms, and his tie was jerked loose. But he looked mysteriously pleased. "What would *you* do, Max?"

"Our first priority is to recover the Hercules Text," he said.

"Yes, it would seem so."

"And we need to keep the incident from the Soviets."

"The KGB already knows part of the story."

Gold's cigarette flared. "Which part?"

"That the discs were scrambled when they got to NSA."

"How the hell could they have learned that?" the secretary exploded. "Christ, John, when you find out who gave *that* away, hang the son of a bitch." He stared in hot fury at the President. "Would you explain something to me, please? How can you sit there grinning at all this?"

"Max," said Hurley, "I believe *I* am the son of a bitch you want to hang."

"You?" Gold's jaw sagged.

"We gave the information to Colonel Bridge."

The secretary of state was appalled. Bridge was a Soviet agent in the Pentagon, the highest known penetration the KGB had made. The American counterintelligence community had known about him for years. But he'd been left in place and even given occasional worthless (and sometimes not so worthless) secrets to keep his credibility high with his masters and to keep him available as a conduit for misinformation that the United States wanted passed to the Kremlin. "Why?" he demanded. "In the name of God, John, why would you give *that* away?"

"Because it'll help take the pressure off the people in Moscow who've got themselves, and us, into this corner. If there is no more Text, we can't very well give it to them."

"What about ORION?"

"The particle beam? I don't mind their having that. It's just the method of getting it to them that makes me uncomfortable. Maybe we could funnel that through Bridge, too." His amusement deepened. "Afterward we could probably catch Bridge and have a big trial, public scandal and all that. The Soviets would be left with no doubt that everything they got from him was authentic, including the fact that the discs are lost. That's the bottom line."

Gold felt the weight on his own shoulders lessening. "I never believed," he said, "that the Soviets would have really attacked anyhow."

"Maybe. It's a question we can each address, I hope, in our memoirs."

"So now it's simply a matter of getting the duplicate discs back from Carmichael, and it will be clear sailing."

"Max, Max." The President broke out a bottle of brandy and two snifters. "We're rid of them," he said, pulling out the cork and pouring some into each glass. "Why would I want them back?"

"But you're not rid of them," said Gold. "The KGB isn't going to simply buy all this without looking at it a little more closely. The discs could end up in their hands."

"Yes," said Hurley. "That's possible. But it isn't Harry Carmichael we have to contend with here; it's Pete Wheeler."

"The priest?"

"Yes. Carmichael would not have done this on his own. We've been going over his life very carefully, Max. Harry's a dull man who has a lot of respect for authority. No, it's the priest who wanted the discs destroyed. And it's the priest who would have known how to do it. Carmichael would never have known.

"But I don't think Harry could bring himself to destroy it. So he made a copy somehow and got it out of the facility."

"And you think he can keep it safe? From the KGB?"

"You worry too much, Max. The KGB thinks it's gone. No reason for them to think otherwise. And if I know Wheeler, by now it *is* gone."

Gold began to laugh. "Then it's over," he said. "It's really over."

"I think so."

"What will you do about Carmichael?"

Hurley sighed. "I like Harry. Despite everything, I like him. The Soviets will expect us to try to keep the entire business quiet. That means no arrest and no trial. I've already called the bloodhounds off.

"To maintain the illusion, we'll have to punish Harry administratively and quietly. His career, of course, goes no further. Maybe he'll resign. If not, we may have to give him some sort of job on the northern border. Maybe working for Immigration."

They fled west across southern Maryland toward the Potomac. "There's a ferry at Hay's Landing," said Wheeler.

The rain had begun again. It washed down out of a cold sky into drowned forests. "We need to stop somewhere and get Harry some dry clothes," said Leslie.

"How do we get to the ferry?" asked Harry.

"I don't know. I'm not sure where we are."

"I'm not sure why we're running away," said Leslie. "There isn't really anyplace to go."

Harry was watching telegraph poles. They were almost hypnotic somehow, rooted symbols of a vanishing world, orderly,

solid, uncomplicated. Wheeler had said little since they'd left
the priory. The tension between the two men was palpable, and
Leslie was beginning to realize there was something she didn't
know.

Harry was frustrated: he had used his best judgment throughout, had done the right things, and yet he still felt guilty. "I
couldn't just let you destroy them, Pete," he said finally. And
Leslie understood at last.

The priest nodded. "I'm going to finish what we started,
Harry." They were approaching a crossroad. An abandoned gas
station stood on one corner, its rusted Texaco standard rising
and sinking in the storm. The pumps were gone, a few old
tires were stacked at the side of the building, and an ancient
Ford had been left in one of the bays.

For the second time, Harry heard the sharp snaps of the
catches on Wheeler's briefcase. "Pete," he said, turning off the
road into the station and jolting to a stop. "You don't want to
do this."

"You're right, Harry. I don't, but I have no choice."

"You've got a second chance, Pete. This time, there'll be
no going back."

Leslie turned in her seat and saw the electromagnet. "Is that
how you did it?"

"How'd you manage the switch?" asked Wheeler. "I thought
we were reasonably thorough."

"This is the library set," Harry explained. "You erased the
same set of discs that Baines got earlier."

Wheeler smiled grimly. He kept a tight grip on the case and
held his finger against the switch. Harry closed his eyes as
though expecting a bullet.

The priest's demeanor might have been that of a confessor,
sunk in thought at the iniquities and stupidities of the human
race. "So it comes down to me after all," he said.

"Pete, listen. Wait. There's more to this than you know."
He sensed Leslie tensing beside him and wondered whether
she was getting ready to climb over the seat and jump the
priest. But there was no way. He laid a restraining hand on her
forearm. "We don't need to give the Text to anyone. We can
hide it somewhere, until the world is ready for it. Bury it in a
desert, put it in a bank vault. I don't care. But we don't *have*
to destroy it."

"It'd take centuries," said Wheeler. "In the meantime, someone would find it. Or the people you entrust with the secret

would betray it. No. The risks are too high."

"The *benefits* are high, Pete. And there's something else you don't know. It's not just us, *this* world, who will pay the price if you pull the switch."

Uncertainty flickered in Wheeler's dark eyes. "What don't I know?"

"The nature of the sender. Pete, no one could ever understand what they were doing out in the gulf, how the Althean system could have escaped its parent galaxy, or why no such galaxy seemed to exist. We insisted on perceiving them as a species like ourselves. But I think what we really have is a creature who is looking for something else alive and thinking in an empty universe. You remember the lesson of the early days of SKYNET? All those sterile worlds. Literally thousands of terrestrial planets, all embalmed in carbon dioxide or riddled with craters.

"It must be like that everywhere. And maybe, after we've advanced a little beyond where we are now, that emptiness will get to all of us, the way it's already gotten to Gambini. The way it might have gotten to the Altheans. So they took their planetary system and went looking, not through the stars, because the odds against finding life there were too great, but through the galaxies. And they used the most practical search technique they could think of."

"The Text," breathed Wheeler.

"Yes. How long have they been out there? You agreed that Alpha and Gamma are artificial suns. The pulsar system is unstable, so either they have to have a way to stabilize it or they create a new system every few million years. Pete, they're looking for *us!* Throw that switch, obliterate the Text, and we may never be able to reply. Because we'll never succeed in convincing anyone of the truth! And who's going to spend money on a project to send a radio signal that won't arrive at its destination for two million years!"

"Harry," said the priest, "with or without the discs, no one would bother. What's the difference?"

"We'd be a hell of a lot more persuasive if we had a record of the transmission, Pete." Harry relaxed a little. He was winning. "There's something more," he said. "Leslie has said all along that she had a sense that we were listening to a lone man in a tower somewhere, not to a species. Pete, there's a fair amount of evidence that the Altheans are a group creature of some kind, a single intellectual entity." Harry had twisted around in his seat so that he was face to face with Wheeler. "There's only *one* Althean. It's damned near timeless. Immortal. And it's alone."

The rain beat against the cars.

Wheeler closed the briefcase. "This is probably a mistake," he said.

Harry was breathing again. Leslie squeezed his hand, then reached back and squeezed Wheeler's. "Next order of business," said Harry, "is to get another car. One they won't be looking for."

"Maybe we should steal one," said Leslie.

Harry grinned. "We might have to."

"What do we do with the Text?" asked Wheeler.

"How about a bus terminal locker for the time being?" suggested Leslie. "The sooner we get it off our hands, the better."

"You've been watching too much TV," said Harry.

They crossed the Potomac on the hovercraft ferry at Hay's Landing and rented another car at Triangle, using Leslie's name in an effort to confuse pursuers. Harry finally collected some dry clothes, changed in a men's room in a downtown hotel, and got a map.

They drove northwest toward Manassas.

It had cleared finally, although there was still no sun. "I have an idea," said Wheeler. "I think I know where the discs would be safe. For a long time."

"Where?" asked Harry skeptically.

"Give them to someone with experience in these matters— the Church. Now wait a minute: before you say anything, we earned a reputation transmitting the essential elements of classical civilization to Renaissance Europe. Compared to that, this is a small job. Harry, Les, there's a parish in Carthage. It's a small community. A mill town. The pastor up there is an old friend of mine."

"You want to hide the Text in a church?"

"In the altar stone, Harry. In the altar stone!" He leaned forward with frenetic energy. "There's no safer place."

Leslie nodded.

"If we can get it there," Harry said.

"Keep to the country roads," Leslie advised.

Harry nodded. "Pete, there's one more thing. I want to pull out Hakluyt's disc and give it to him."

"I have no problem with that," said Wheeler.

Harry looked at the woman. "Les?"

"Do it," she said.

"In due time, I think he'll be able to cure my son."

"I have my doubts about all that," Wheeler said.

And maybe he was right: when Harry pulled over to look at the map, he still had to put on his reading glasses. The serum apparently hadn't worked.

He took a deep breath, sucking damp air and pollen into lungs long ravaged by an assortment of allergies. And the air tasted sweet and clean.

There's a scene in Milton, in the eighth book of *Paradise Lost*, I believe, which may describe the situation. God and Adam were talking, and Adam was bitching about the landscaping and his economic status and one thing and another. And he complained about being alone. "All I have to talk to," he said, "are animals."

And God promised He'd look into it. And then I guess He must have thought about it some more. "Adam," he said, "who is more alone than I, that know nothing like myself in all the wide world?"

And that, ladies and gentlemen, is precisely the unhappy dilemma of the marvelous being who recently took time to draw our attention.

Closing remarks on the nature of the Altheans by the Reverend Peter Wheeler, O. Praem., at the annual gathering of the American Philosophical Association in Atlantic City in November.

EPILOGUE

RIMFORD HAD GONE out for some eggnog. But he drove onto the desert. Sirius and Procyon, the bright pair, lingered on the horizon. Guarding their secrets, he used to think when he looked on them a few years ago. But they lay exposed now, under Ed Gambini's eyes. They had fourteen known worlds between them, indexed and catalogued by mass and composition. All were sterile.

The mesas moved ponderously against the desert sky.

The Althean had done a remarkable thing. He'd examined a pair of quasars, widely separated in the viewing hemisphere, each approximately eighteen billion light years distant, one a little more, the other a little less. *And he had determined they were the same object, seen from different perspectives! That could only mean that his telescopes had penetrated completely around the vault of the cosmos!* Moreover, since the quasars were not precisely on opposite sides of the sky, it was clear that the universe was not spherical.

The desert looked unfamiliar. Years before, when he and Agnes were newly married, and he was stationed at Kitt Peak, they'd driven across this same stretch of wilderness on another Christmas Eve. That seemed a long time ago now. In those days the sky was filled with mysteries. But tonight he held the universe in his hands, understood everything except, perhaps, the secrets of his own existence.

A few details remained unclear, but they were trivial: points about light and wave theory, that sort of thing.

He knew the size and shape, the essential architecture of the universe. And he understood why the cylinder was twisted, the only reason it *could* be twisted: it was wrapped around something else. And what could that something else be but a second universe? Or, more correctly, the anti-matter aspect of this one.

Beneath the desert stars, he tried to summon his old powers, to visualize the two systems locked in each other's embrace, a cosmic double helix.

And he understood a great deal more. For him, the great question had never been the shape of the universe, but the subtle mysteries of its working parts. How had the laws come to be that decreed light speed or packed enormous stores of energy into the atom or designed the proton? That the universe was habitable, indeed that it existed at all in a structured form, required a set of coincidences of incredible proportions. He recalled the old analogy of the monkeys with the typewriter. How long would it take the chimp to produce, by pure accident, the Bible?

The odds on the monkey were considerably better than the odds that *this* universe could happen by accident. Which was to say, it was utterly impossible for a Baines Rimford to drive a car across a desert on a December evening.

There were theories, of course. There were always theories. Some argued for an infinite number of bubble universes drifting through a superspace void. Others believed that the universe happened an infinite number of times until, *by accident*, nature got everything right.

They were hardly satisfactory notions. But Rimford had an idea: if the universe existed as two disconnected entities, tied together somehow but eternally separate, then expansion and contraction would necessarily occur in both systems on a similar timetable. But under no imaginable circumstances could the timetable be exact. That is, at the beginning of each cycle, there would be two fiery eruptions into material existence, but never at precisely the same instant.

The problem with the old idea of universal oscillation is that there is no way to transmit information from one phase to the next. Everything is wiped out in the cosmic crunch and subsequent explosion that heralds each new epoch. But the Althean believed that coded data could be passed back and forth between the matter and antimatter universes: this works, and that does not. So that, eventually, over incredible gulfs of time, you get an evolved cosmos.

You get the starry skies over Pasadena.

But it was the next step that was unsettling.

If the universe was indeed evolving, what was it evolving toward?

There was evidence that the ultimate goal was to create an ideal refuge for intelligence. And how could that be unless someone had written into the cosmic programming a directive that such an end be sought?

Rimford was not inclined toward religion. The notion of a supreme being raised more questions in his mind than it answered. As did a suggestion offered some years ago that, if indeed the bubble universe concept was correct, then the superspace in which it was adrift might be home to a race of designers.

For where would they have come from?

There was another possibility. He wondered whether the universe itself might not be holistic in some sense: a pattern that strove reflexively for order in its early incarnations. And, having eventually, after countless tries, learned how to make hydrogen, and consequently stars, it went on, seeking consciousness and, eventually, intelligence.

It would need *us!*

The red and white running lights of four jets lifted from the desert on his left, and he abruptly realized he'd gone all the way out to Edwards. He watched the planes climb into the jeweled dark. Immediately ahead of them, the moon lay partly hidden in a tangle of cumulus. Yes: however it had happened, it was a magnificent universe.

He continued up to the intersection with Route 58 and called Agnes from a restaurant. "I missed my stop," he said.

"Okay, Baines," she replied. This wasn't the first time he'd wandered off, but he could hear the relief in her voice. "Where are you?"

"Four Corners," he said. It was a pedestrian answer.